PRAISE FOR THE WORKS
OF MICHAEL McGARRITY

Backlands

"McGarrity writes about the landscape of the American Southwest with loving detail and rough-hewn eloquence, but he is equally good here with the human stories and the historical backdrop. . . . Through it all, though, the story of a hard-bitten father and a son forced into adulthood before his time—of loves lost, droughts endured, obstacles overcome—claims our emotions much in the manner of Ivan Doig's similarly heartfelt historical fiction." —*Booklist*

"McGarrity's well-researched details about life in New Mexico during the Great Depression will appeal to historical fiction fans, and his details about life on the ranch will appeal to readers of fiction set in the West." —*Library Journal*

"McGarrity knows New Mexico, and it shows with his authentic descriptions from transcendent beauty to parched ugliness. The Roaring Twenties, the dust bowl years, the Great Depression, and the years of World War II are conveyed with truth. The precariousness of ranch life is eloquently detailed in a way that makes the reader care." —Genrefluent

"[An] enthralling saga." —Historical Novel Society

Hard Country

"*Hard Country* joins the ranks of superior historical novels . . . worthy of the great writer of Westerns Eugene Manlove Rhodes. And happily, Rhodes is a character in the book." —Robin Martin, *The Santa Fe New Mexican Pasatiempo*

"Michael McGarrity really gets—and loves—the Southwest: its colors, its rhythms, its blessings, its cussedness. Here McGarrity . . . gives us something most unusual these days: an expansive, lyrical period Western in the tradition of A. B. Guthrie Jr. and Larry McMurtry. Savor this one—they don't make cowboy epics like this anymore." —Hampton Sides, bestselling author of *Hellhound on His Trail*

continued . . .

"It's a pleasure to go the long haul with McGarrity. The lives of this cast of characters feel real, as if we might have lived these lives."
—*Alamogordo Daily News*

"The evocation of real people in a real land. McGarrity is an accomplished storyteller, and he writes with clarity, perception, and authenticity. Those who read this novel will find it engaging, and they will come away with a deeper understanding and appreciation of the Old West and of the part it played in forging the American imagination."
—N. Scott Momaday, Pulitzer Prize–winning author of *House Made of Dawn*

"A 'Western' in the sense that *Lonesome Dove* was a Western. It transcends the genre, a great and true American novel of the West with immense power, beauty, and sweep. It is an unforgettable book. I loved it."   —Douglas Preston, coauthor of *Gideon's Corpse*

"A stunning saga of the Old West—a tale rich in both heartbreak and the uplifting spirit of the brave men and women who settled the territory against all odds. It's the great storytelling of Michael McGarrity, one of my favorite writers, that brings the past alive with such superb authenticity. Saddle up with McGarrity and let him take you back—I loved going to the wild New Mexico territory with him."
—Linda Fairstein, *New York Times* bestselling author of *Terminal City*

"A compelling and richly imagined epic told by a master storyteller. Michael McGarrity has his finger on the pulse of the Old West and a knack for drawing the reader in. He also has a marvelous way of illuminating the human heart in characters tough and determined enough to stake a claim on a wild and hard country. I didn't want the story to end. It is just that good."
—Margaret Coel, author of *Buffalo Bill's Dead Now*

"An epic Western . . . awesome in its scope. There hasn't been anything like it in quite a while. I was taken back to sagas such as A. B. Guthrie Jr.'s *The Big Sky* and *The Way West* as well as Vardis Fisher's *Mountain Man* and Larry McMurtry's *Lonesome Dove*. This is a big story with big characters in a big land."
—David Morrell, *New York Times* bestselling author of *The Brotherhood of the Rose*

ALSO BY MICHAEL McGARRITY

Tularosa

Mexican Hat

Serpent Gate

Hermit's Peak

The Judas Judge

Under the Color of Law

The Big Gamble

Everyone Dies

Slow Kill

Nothing but Trouble

Death Song

Dead or Alive

Hard Country

BACKLANDS

A Novel of the American West

MICHAEL McGARRITY

NEW AMERICAN LIBRARY

New American Library
Published by the Penguin Group
Penguin Group (USA) LLC, 375 Hudson Street,
New York, New York 10014

USA | Canada | UK | Ireland | Australia | New Zealand | India | South Africa | China
penguin.com
A Penguin Random House Company

Published by New American Library, a division of Penguin Group (USA) LLC. Previously published in a Dutton edition.

First New American Library Printing, May 2015

 REGISTERED TRADEMARK—MARCA REGISTRADA

NEW AMERICAN LIBRARY TRADE PAPERBACK ISBN: 978-0-451-47166-6

THE LIBRARY OF CONGRESS HAS CATALOGUED THE HARDCOVER EDITION AS FOLLOWS:

McGarrity, Michael
Backlands: a novel of the American west/ Michael McGarrity.
p. cm.
ISBN 978-0-525-95324-1 (hardcover)
1. Ranch life—New Mexico—Fiction. 2 Family life—New Mexico—Fiction.
3. Depression—1929—New Mexico—Fiction. 4. New Mexico—History—20th century—Fiction.
5. Western stories. 6. Historical fiction. I. Title.
PS3563.C36359B35 2002
813'.54—dc23 2014004445

Printed in the United States of America
1 3 5 7 9 10 8 6 4 2

Set in ITC Baskerville Std
Designed by Leonard Telesca

For the ghosts of family past:
Joseph, Ruth, Joanne, Timothy, Marjorie, Eleanor, and Crockett

For the love of family present:
Emily, Sean, Meghan, Flynn, and Darby

Write what should not be forgotten.

—Isabel Allende

Backland

The word commonly refers to an area remote from centers of population. . . . In farming regions backland is the acreage far from the road or farmhouse. . . . The distinction is almost always with land lying farther away, beyond.

—Robert Morgan, *Home Ground: Language for an American Landscape*

ACKNOWLEDGMENTS

With my deepest gratitude to Hilary Hinzmann, who got me started and has been with me all the way. Thanks, amigo.

The American Southwest, 1930

PAINTED DESERT

Flagstaff

US 66

ATCHISON, TOPEKA, AND SANTA FE RAILWAY

MOGOLLON RIM

HUALAPAI MOUNTAINS

Prescott

ARIZONA

MAZATZAL MOUNTAINS

Colorado River

US 80

Phoenix

SAN FRANCISCO PLATEAU

Gila River

GALIURO MOUNTAINS

Yuma

MOHAWK RANGE

DRAGOON MOUNTAINS

Willcox

Lordsbu

SOUTHERN PACIFIC RAILROAD

Tucson

FLYING W RANCH

Tombstone

MEXICO

Gulf of California

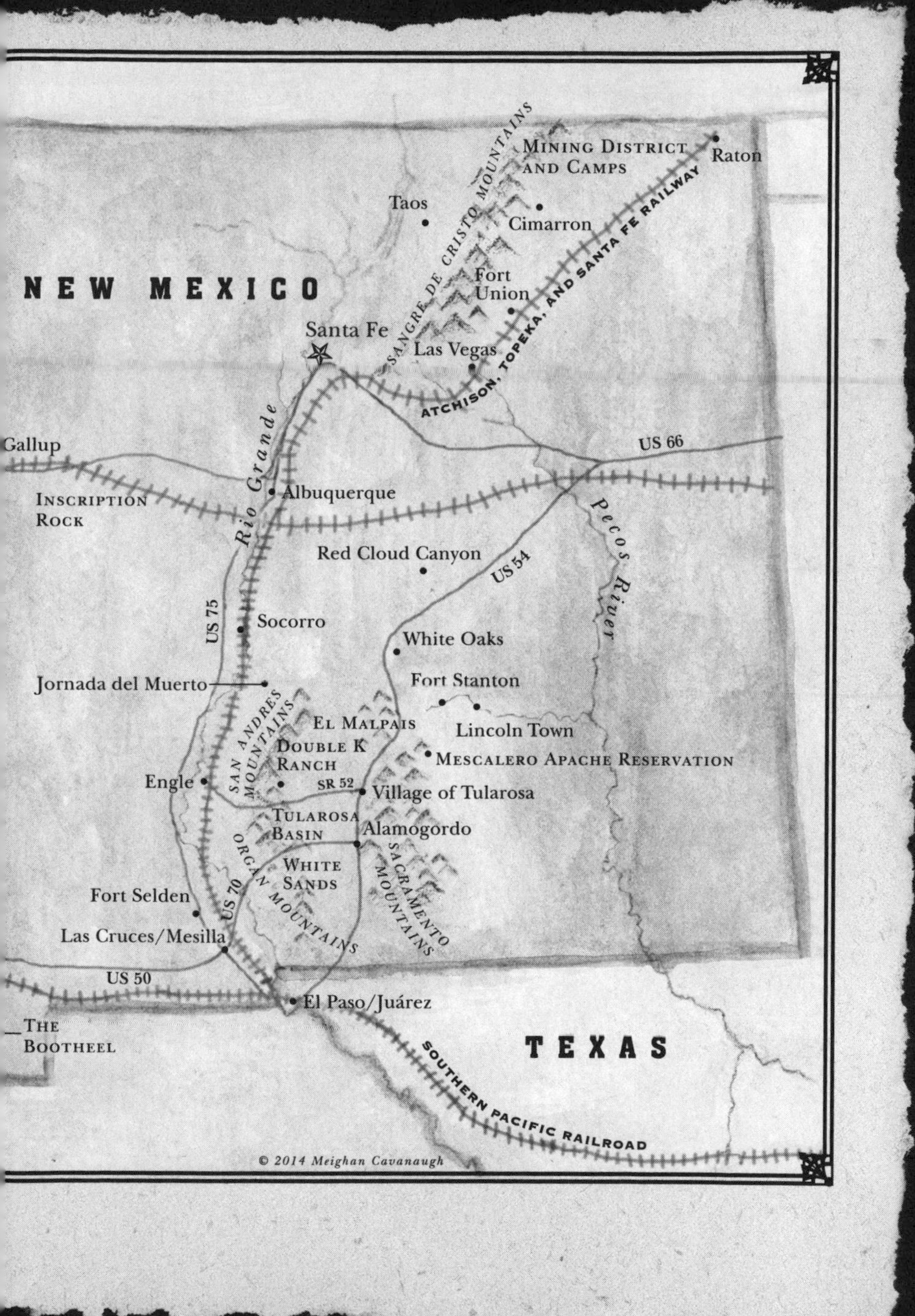

NEW MEXICO
Mining District and Camps
Raton
Sangre de Cristo Mountains
Taos
Cimarron
Atchison, Topeka, and Santa Fe Railway
Fort Union
Santa Fe
Las Vegas
Rio Grande
Gallup
US 66
Albuquerque
Inscription Rock
Pecos River
Red Cloud Canyon
US 54
US 75
Socorro
White Oaks
Fort Stanton
Jornada del Muerto
San Andres Mountains
El Malpais
Lincoln Town
Double K Ranch
Mescalero Apache Reservation
Engle
SR 52
Village of Tularosa
Tularosa Basin
Alamogordo
Organ Mountains
White Sands
Sacramento Mountains
Fort Selden
US 70
Las Cruces/Mesilla
US 50
El Paso/Juárez
The Bootheel
TEXAS
Southern Pacific Railroad
© 2014 Meighan Cavanaugh

❋ONE❋

Emma Kerney

1

Emma Kerney woke early. Not a sound could be heard outside: no cackling of chickens in the neighbor's backyard, no braying of the ancient donkey Mr. Roybal kept in the small field adjacent to his dilapidated adobe casita, not even a whisper of wind through the bare branches of the trees that lined still dark, quiet Griggs Avenue.

As she had every night since the onset of winter, Emma had gone to bed exhausted, half expecting to die in her sleep. And every morning, she opened her eyes to a deep fatigue that haunted her throughout the day. Her exhaustion was now so persistent she could no longer hide it from her eight-year-old son, Matthew. She could not conceal the gushing nosebleeds, the searing chest pains that doubled her over in agony, and the noisy, raspy breathlessness that came after all but the slightest bit of physical exertion.

There were days when she barely gathered the strength to mop a floor, cook a meal, or wash a dish. Often she had to rely on Matthew to finish her chores, and lately out of fear she might collapse on the short walk downtown, she'd taken to sending him off to the grocer's on Main Street to do the weekly household shopping. He had done all that she asked without complaint, never failing to oblige her with other than a worried look and a tight-lipped smile, old beyond his years. It broke Emma's heart to see her plucky boy give up so much time caring for her when he should be with his friends enjoying a fleeting, carefree childhood. It wasn't fair at all.

But this morning, Emma woke up feeling unusually rested. The sound of her pounding heart in her ears had subsided, her normally twitchy legs were still, and her mind was clear of worry. As she stretched her thin, fine-boned frame under the thick pile of blankets that covered her, she felt full of energy, as if the defective valve in her heart had miraculously mended. Not a bone ached, her legs felt light and limber, and her feet, normally cold no matter what the season, were deliciously toasty.

For a long minute she lay still, wondering if she was daydreaming, suspicious that if she moved another inch the feeling of endless weariness would return and squash the fantasy. Finally convinced that she felt wonderfully like her old self, she pushed away the covers, swung her legs over the side of the bed, and stood. There was no light-headedness, no touch of numbing listlessness, and above all, the snappish mood that had plagued her for weeks was gone.

Almost giggling with delight, she dressed quickly, hurried to the kitchen, stoked the embers in the cookstove, and added some wood before peeking out the window. Early dawn revealed a dusting of snow on the bare branches of the cottonwood tree in the front yard. Not a drop of moisture had fallen on the town of Las Cruces since late summer, and the welcome sight raised Emma's spirits. The start of the day was perfect. If she kept feeling lively and normal for a change, the entire day would be wonderful.

She swooped into Matthew's bedroom and roused her sleeping

son with a big hug just as Mr. Roybal's donkey announced the arrival of dawn with a long, honking bray.

"Let go," Matthew grumbled sleepy eyed, pulling away.

"Time to rise and shine, young man," she said, turning on the bedside lamp. "How about some hotcakes, eggs, and bacon for breakfast?"

Long and lean, with square shoulders like all the Kerney men and brilliantly blue eyes, Matthew squinted at his mother. "Are you feeling better?" he asked tentatively, searching her face.

Emma smiled and nodded. "Much better, and I've a great hunger for hotcakes. Now, shake a leg. You have chores to do before we eat."

"You're really better, no kidding?" Matthew asked again.

"For now," Emma said.

Matthew smiled. "Boy, I'm glad to hear that."

"So am I." She gave him a kiss on his cheek, which he quickly wiped away. Out of bed, he reached for his clothes, which were neatly folded on the top of the small dresser next to a framed photograph of his older brother, CJ, standing stiff and proud in his sergeant's uniform. It had been taken a few weeks before his death on a French battlefield during the Great War.

She couldn't look at it without having to stifle the sob that always rose in her throat. What a fine man he would have become if the madness of war hadn't claimed him.

She left Matthew to dress, returned to the cozy warmth of the kitchen, and set about mixing the batter, cutting thick strips of bacon, and heating the griddle. In a small Apache basket on the top of the kitchen cupboard Emma kept all the letters CJ had sent home from the army. Tonight would be a perfect time to read them again with Matthew.

Until her latest bout of illness, Emma had been writing letters for Matthew to find and read after her death. Mostly, she'd set down the happy times in her life and the people and friends she'd known, loved, and admired, so he would have some knowledge of her past and his family's history. She had never hidden the fact from him that her defective heart couldn't be fixed, and she didn't shy away from the subject in the letters. However, she had kept silent about the reality of her dying soon, which until now seemed wisest. Why burden a child with such cruel knowledge? But now, with her illness more than an occasional inconvenience once easily masked, and the undeniable suffering she endured and that Matthew had witnessed day after day for weeks, the subject could no longer be avoided.

She dreaded that conversation they soon must have. CJ's death still troubled Matthew, and he often became visibly gloomy at the mere mention of his brother's name. As for Emma, the clear-cut knowledge that she wouldn't live to see Matthew fully grown was a wrenching sorrow that made the idea of the conversation almost unbearable. Yet she had to prepare him for the inevitable, especially since it could no longer be ignored.

She would do it soon, she vowed, but not today. Today was for celebrating.

Matthew came into the kitchen followed by a blast of cold air, bundled in his coat, with an armload of wood for the cookstove. As always, he'd slicked down his cowlick in an unsuccessful attempt to tame it. His cheeks and nose were rosy from the cold.

"It snowed a bit last night," Matthew said as he filled the woodbin.

"I know," Emma replied. "How wonderful. How many hotcakes can you eat?"

"Four," Matthew replied as he shed his coat and hung it on the back of his chair. "No, maybe six."

Emma raised an eyebrow as she greased the griddle. "Six?"

Matthew nodded. "Yep, you haven't made hotcakes in a long time."

Emma paused, spatula in hand. "That can't be true. You'll eat them all?"

"Yes, ma'am, promise."

"Fair enough. Six it is. Pour yourself some milk and get the jug of syrup."

Bacon sizzled in the frying pan, to be done crispy the way Matthew liked it. She poured the batter and quickly made a stack of hotcakes she kept warm on a platter in the oven. When the bacon was done, she forked it onto plates with the hotcakes, fried two eggs, eased them onto the stacks, and brought breakfast to the table.

Matthew grinned at the plate of food placed in front of him. "This looks just swell," he said.

"Thank you kindly, sir," Emma replied. The look of pleased anticipation on Matthew's face raised Emma's spirits even higher. She watched as he broke the egg yolks, poured syrup on the hotcakes, and dug in with his fork.

He ate with such happy concentration that Emma didn't venture a word to interrupt him. She turned with gusto to her own meal and spoke only when he looked up from his empty plate.

"I think I'd like to walk with you to school this morning," she said.

Matthew looked startled. "Are you sure you should?"

"Am I acting poor and sickly?" Emma teased. Minute by minute, she was feeling better and better.

Matthew studied his mother's face and shook his head. "No, ma'am, not this morning, but you've been sick for quite a spell."

"And you've been a good sport, taking on so much work and being the man of the house."

"That's okay," Matt said, visibly pleased by the compliment.

"You deserve a reward." Emma got her change purse from the cupboard drawer and gave Matthew a dollar in quarters.

Matt looked at the coins in his hand and beamed. "Wow. Thanks."

Emma snapped the purse closed and smiled. "You've more than earned it. Now, I haven't stuck my nose outside for weeks. A walk to school with you will do me good. I'll clean up the kitchen while you make your bed and feed your pony."

Matt's happy expression turned serious. "Are you sure you can do it, Ma?"

Half convinced she wasn't fooling herself, Emma laughed and said, "Starting today, things are back to normal. Is that okay with you?"

Matt's smile returned. "That's aces with me."

"Then jingle those spurs. After school you can go downtown and spend your hard-earned money any way you like. I'll have a nice snack fixed for you when you get home, and we'll have an extra-special meal at dinnertime."

Matthew grinned, grabbed his coat, and flew out of the house to feed and water Patches.

* * *

A block away from the schoolhouse, Matthew ran ahead of Emma to catch up with two of his best chums, Jimmy Potter and Joe Pete Johnson, waiting for him at the corner. As soon as he got there, he turned and waved. Emma smiled in return, waved back gaily, and watched as the three pals raced the rest of the way to school, skidded to a stop in unison at the front of the tall double doors, and piled inside, three abreast.

It had started to snow on the short walk to school, dropping heavy flakes that made Emma smile with delight. A thin white blanket now covered the dirt road, and a low sky of dense clouds promised a lot more moisture to come throughout the day. Before turning for home, she watched the last few children hurry inside just as the school bell rang. It was good to be outside in the snow, good to see Matthew happy with his friends, and good to feel strength returning to her body.

On the way back, she set a steady pace, thinking she would freshen up and change into a nicer skirt and blouse before setting out to pay the monthly grocer's bill and make appointments to see her banker and lawyer. Sickness had forced her to let important matters go by the wayside, and now, while she felt rejuvenated, it was time to put things back in order.

At home, she washed up in the small bathroom that she'd had added to the rear of the house at the back of the hallway that separated the two bedrooms. Barely big enough to turn around in, it had a sink, lavatory, bathtub, and cold-water tap only, which meant bath nights required heating water on the kitchen stove and carrying it to the tub. Still, it was a great convenience compared to the old outhouse, which had been torn down and filled in to make room for the small stable that housed Matt's pony, Patches.

Over the sink was a small mirror and above it a single light fixture. Emma couldn't quite remember the last time she'd looked closely at herself, but what she saw this morning stunned her. She'd always been slender but never so rail thin. Her pale face was bony, almost gaunt, and there were dark circles under her eyes. Quickly she applied some face cream to hide the circles and bring out a bit of color on her cheeks, touched up her lips with a light lipstick, and darkened her eyebrows with a pencil. Upon inspection, she decided she didn't look too frightening after all, just a lot older than she wished.

Outside, the subdued winter snowfall of early morning had turned blustery, and a gust of wind rattled the small bathroom window above the tub. After changing into a brown skirt and a fresh, ruffled blouse, she snuggled back into her warm winter coat, pulled a wool cap down over her ears, put on her gloves, and stepped into a gale that was blowing wet snow sideways. After so many weeks of dust and drought, the moist air smelled marvelous. It might not be the best weather to be venturing out in, but she felt fine and it was but a few minutes' walk to the grocer and a few more steps from there to the bank.

She hurried down the road, snow-blown wind at her back, with half a thought to believe in miracles—she felt that good. Twenty years ago, she and her ex-husband, Patrick, had bought the house on Griggs Avenue after a doctor warned them of the risk of another miscarriage if she remained at their remote Tularosa ranch during her pregnancy. She'd given birth to CJ in that house, returned with him in her arms to the ranch, and remained there until her separation from Patrick and the divorce. Ever since, she'd lived in Las Cruces permanently, giving birth to Matthew at home there as well.

Over the intervening years, the town had grown some, especially with the recent completion of the Elephant Butte Dam on the Rio Grande eighty miles north, which created a farming and business boom all the way south to El Paso. But even with the growth, Las Cruces still gave way to open range along the wide, fertile river valley, and the small residential neighborhoods, from the modest to the most elegant, were still clustered around Main Street.

Few people were out in the bad weather, and only a single truck chugged down otherwise empty Main Street. Miles away to the east, across the rolling desert, the Organ Mountains were masked by a thick blanket of clouds that made the scale of the land seem less vast, more reasonable. The sky was so low, not even the prominent spires of St. Genevieve's Church or the smokestacks of the power plant were visible. As the winds eased and the snow squall diminished, everything looked tranquil and soft under a white mantle.

At the grocer's she stomped her feet to shake off the wet snow as Sam Miller came round the counter smiling broadly in greeting, his round cheeks bright pink as always.

"Why, Emma, you're up and about," he said jovially.

"And feeling fit as a fiddle," Emma replied.

"That sure is good to hear. What all do you need this morning?"

Emma opened her purse. "I came to pay my bill and set aside a few things to pick up later for dinner."

"Happy to oblige," Sam replied as he slipped behind the counter and reached for the account book he kept on a shelf beneath the shiny nickel-plated cash register. After he read off the amount Emma owed, he studied her carefully as she counted out bills and coins from her purse. She seemed smaller, swallowed up in her heavy winter coat, and her features, while still attractive, were sunken. She looked frail and worn in spite of her good humor.

Sam counted the money, rang it up on the cash register, and then helped Emma pick out what she needed to fix Matthew an extra-special dinner.

"No need to stop back by," he said as he wrapped up a freshly dressed chicken, several baking potatoes, and the fixings for a peach pie. "I'll have my boy bring the groceries by your house around the noon hour."

Emma smiled brightly. "Thank you, Sam. That will be perfect."

"You take care not to stay out in the cold for long," Sam said with concern as he entered Emma's purchases in his account book. Through the large plate-glass window, snow was blowing hard down Main Street again.

Emma laughed as she turned toward the door. "Don't you worry about me, Sam Miller. The bank is just a few steps away."

Sam watched Emma pass by the store's front window. Most everybody in town knew she was likely to die soon from a bad heart, and it was a damn shame. She'd suffered hardships, especially her divorce and the loss of CJ in the war, came through it all with spunk and spirit, and made a good life for herself and young Matt. As far as Sam was concerned, Emma Kerney deserved a far better hand than the one fate had dealt.

* * *

As a single young man, Henry Bowman had come to Las Cruces with his widowed father, George, after making a sizable amount of money selling tractors door-to-door to farmers across the upper Midwest during the closing years of the old century. Almost immediately upon their arrival, father and son bought majority shares in a struggling bank and quickly turned it into a successful enterprise by attracting both Mexican and Anglo merchants with attractive loan rates and personal service. With George Bowman's death five years ago, Henry took over as bank president and doubled the loan department staff to keep pace with the burgeoning real estate market. Initially, he'd moved into his father's old office without changing a thing other than placing a framed photograph of his dad on the wall above the tall wooden cabinet that held the files of the bank's most important clients. From his perch, George gazed down on his son and his clients with the look of a man who knew the value of a dollar and the importance of hard work.

Although the office furnishings were out-of-date, Henry liked the old-fashioned, ornate breakfront bookcase; the large writing desk, which held an inkstand and postal scale, placed there solely for ornamentation; and the two high-backed chairs for clients, which fronted the desk. His only concessions to change were a comfortable new solid oak revolving desk chair on casters and a mahogany standing coatrack conveniently placed next to the office door.

He rose quickly when Emma Kerney stepped into his office, helped her out of her coat, and ushered her to one of the high-backed chairs in front of his wide desk, where he joined her, scooting his chair sideways a bit to have a better look at her. In the two months since he'd last seen her, Emma's pretty blue eyes had grown paler, her face more aged, and her cheeks hollow. A woman with a small frame and long legs that made her seem taller than she really was, she now had a slight bend to her once perfect carriage.

Emma had enchanted Henry Bowman from the day they had first met almost twenty years ago, and the feeling hadn't changed one iota since. Although he'd never spoken of it to her, he felt certain that she knew.

"It's good to see you," he said with a smile.

"It's good to see you as well, Henry," Emma replied.

Over the years, Henry had become portly as a result of sitting behind a desk, and a moon-shaped bald spot had spread over the top of his head. He was a sincere, serious-minded man not given to lightheartedness or small talk.

"How is your family?" Emma asked.

"Everyone is fine," Henry replied.

"Give Martha my best," Emma said.

"Of course," Henry said, eager to move the conversation off the subject of his wife, whom Emma always made a point to mention. "I'm glad you stopped by. An interesting and profitable offer has been tendered on two of your commercial lots just west of the city limits. But before we discuss that, how are you feeling?"

Emma laughed. "First Sam Miller and now you. Seems everyone is concerned about my health. I'm fine today."

Henry shook his head sternly in rebuke. "Every soul in town who knows you knows how sick you've been with your heart condition. So again I ask: How are you?"

Emma paused. Over the years Henry had been a trusted adviser who had never pried into her personal life. When she was carrying CJ, he'd suggested it would be smarter to buy a house rather than rent while she lived in town during her pregnancy. After her divorce, he'd guided her into some wise investments and profitable opportunities. He deserved an honest answer.

"You're very kind to be concerned," she said, holding up a hand to stem a look of remonstration forming on Henry's face. "Today, honestly, I'm feeling much better, but I don't know how long that will last. Not long, I think, and my doctor agrees. He's told me time and again that any one of a number of things can kill me and that it's a miracle I've survived as long as I have. So let's talk business, instead of worrying about my ailments. I want to make sure there's enough money to see Matthew through after I'm gone."

"It's hard to imagine your passing," Henry said glumly. "Not a pleasant notion to consider at all."

Emma smiled. "Now, don't get all soppy on me, Henry. There's nothing to be done, no good reason for me to complain about it, and no need to be downcast. When I do go, I'd like it to be as quick as possible. The idea of being a helpless, bedridden invalid mortifies me. Now, tell me about the offer on my lots that you mentioned."

Henry composed himself, nodded, rose, and went to his desk. "In a moment. Have you put your legal matters in order?"

"I thought first I'd speak with you about finances and then visit with Wallace Hale."

"That's very wise." Henry reached for the telephone. "Let's see if Wallace can meet with us within the hour. By then we should know exactly how much your estate will be able to provide for Matthew's care, and he can advise you on the best way to legally ensure it will serve Matthew's needs only."

Emma adjusted herself in the chair. "That's exactly what I want. Please call him."

Henry placed the call, confirmed that Wallace Claiborne Hale would join them shortly, fetched Emma's file from his locked cabinet behind the desk, settled into his chair, and read aloud the particulars of the offer on the lots. When he finished, he suggested that the interested party might be willing to pay ten percent more than the asking price. If so, the net profit would be almost quadruple what Emma had paid for the land four years ago.

"The buyer wants to close quickly," he added. "Shall I approach him with a counteroffer?"

Emma nodded her agreement. "The timing couldn't be better."

"I'll see to it," Henry promised.

"With this sale and the income from my remaining properties, is there sufficient annual income to see Matthew through for at least the next ten years?"

Henry opened Emma's file, slid his chair in front of the adding machine at the corner of the desk, and began paging through documents, entering numbers. Emma Kerney owned three houses that were rented out, eighty acres of pasture near the river leased to a dairy farmer, two additional vacant commercial lots, and her home on Griggs Avenue. He ran a total of the projected annual income and deducted a reserve for taxes, upkeep, repairs, loss of rental income, and trust administration fees.

"I'm assuming you would want to sell the remaining commercial parcels and put the money into Matthew's trust," he proposed. "It could be used to make up any shortfalls in income that occur, and the balance will continue to earn interest."

"Should I do that now?"

"It might be best. The interested buyer plans on building an automobile dealership and a large garage on the lots. Once the sale goes through, I know several speculators who will be very interested in the remaining parcels at the same if not a slighter higher price."

"Sell them as soon as you can," Emma said.

"What about your home?" Henry asked. "Sell it also when the time comes?"

Emma's eyes widened at the unhappy thought, and she paused momentarily. "I'd like Matthew to keep it, if possible. After all, it's his home too. He can sell it when he's grown, if he has a mind to."

"Very well." He put the papers carefully back in order and closed the file. "Taking into account expenses, there's enough to provide Matthew an annual income of fifteen hundred dollars."

"Over the next ten years?" Emma asked, relieved to hear that her investments would yield enough to adequately support a whole family, not just a single person.

"Yes, but I'm assuming we'll have rent going into the trust from the Griggs Avenue property. Matthew can't live there alone after your passing, and there are no relatives to care for him other than his father."

Emma leaned forward and fixed Henry Bowman with an intent gaze. "After I'm gone, Patrick Kerney must have no rights to Matthew's inheritance or how the trust is to be used on his behalf. He can be a father to his son, if that's at all possible, but have no say-so about the money. Promise me that."

"I understand," Henry said soothingly. "But it could very well become contentious even with proper legal safeguards in place. That's what lawyers are for."

Emma bit her lip.

"What is it?" Henry asked.

Emma shook her head. She wanted to say how badly she wished for ten more years to raise Matthew, but it would only sound self-pitying. "Nothing," she said brightly.

A knock at the door and the announcement by Henry's clerk that Wallace Claiborne Hale had arrived saved Emma from further questioning. The clerk stood aside and Hale filled the open doorway, his curly hair damp with wet snow, the overcoat draped on his arm dripping snowmelt on the polished wood floor.

"It's a blizzard out there like I've not seen before," he announced in his booming courtroom baritone, smiling broadly at Emma. "You must allow me to drive you home after our meeting."

"Thank you," Emma said. "That would be very nice."

"Very thoughtful of you, Wallace," Henry chimed in, unhappy with himself for not having offered to do the same sooner.

Wallace Hale nodded in agreement as he sat next to Emma. "It will be my pleasure." A tall man with a thin frame and long legs, Hale had a narrow nose and thick, bushy eyebrows. He studied Emma's face. "I hope that seeing you up and about means that you are recovered from your illness."

"Not entirely," Emma replied.

Wallace smiled knowingly. "I thought not. Otherwise there would be no rush for the three of us to meet." He turned to Henry Bowman. "What is the issue I am here to address?"

"We have agreed upon a trust plan for Matthew that should

carry him comfortably through ten years after Emma's death. She wants Matthew's father to be barred from access to the trust."

Wallace leaned back. "That is certainly possible, simply by appointing someone other than Patrick as the trust administrator with the power of attorney to use the funds on Matthew's behalf within a specified scope of authorized expenditures. I can have a draft prepared within a few days."

He paused and waved a cautionary finger. "However, remember that as the surviving parent, Patrick Kerney will have full legal rights to raise Matthew as he sees fit. If he finds himself at odds with the conditions of the trust, he might hire a lawyer to contest it before a judge."

"Can't it be made ironclad?" Emma asked.

"Few marital and family legal issues are that clear-cut and tidy," Wallace replied. "As a result, courts and judges have traditionally more leeway when deciding upon matters pertaining to minors. I will promise you a trust document that legally meets your need to provide for Matthew according to your wishes, but I cannot guarantee the outcome of any future challenges brought to it in a court of law."

"This is not what I was hoping for."

Wallace smiled sympathetically. "Of course it isn't. But remember, your ex-husband has a good reputation as a rancher, businessman, and law-abiding citizen, which means mounting a challenge against the trust might succeed if he can convince a judge it would be in Matthew's best interest to do so."

Emma bit her lip. "Make it as difficult for Patrick as possible."

Wallace nodded. "It's too bad your ex-husband hasn't had any serious run-ins with the law. The court wouldn't look kindly upon that."

"I think maybe he did as a young man," Emma said.

Wallace raised his eyebrows. "Do you have specifics?"

Emma shook her head. "He never talked about it. That's no help, is it?"

"No," Wallace said as he checked his watch and stood. "I'm due to meet with a judge shortly. Let me get you home, if you don't mind my rush."

"Not at all," Emma said as Henry hurried to get her coat.

"We'll have something for you to review by the end of the week," Wallace said. "Think about whom you'd like to be a trust administrator."

Emma smiled at the men. "Both of you will do nicely, if you're agreeable. That way I'll be sure Matthew will be well looked after."

"As you wish," both men said simultaneously.

* * *

It was still snowing lightly when school got out. The heavy, wet stuff was perfect for making snowballs, so Matthew, Jimmy Potter, and Joe Pete Johnson battled their way against a gang of four older boys all the way to Main Street, until they broke off the fight and ducked inside Sam Miller's store, laughing and red-faced, where Matt bought a round of hard candy with some of the money Ma had given him that morning.

The three boys lived in the same neighborhood and had been friends forever. Jimmy was the bravest, Joe Pete the toughest, and Matt the smartest and the tallest, towering a good two inches above his pals. Because of that and his somewhat serious nature, most folks pegged him as older.

On the chance they might get waylaid, they waited until the four older boys were nowhere to be seen before splitting up. As Matt was leaving the store, Mr. Miller told him that his ma had been in earlier to buy the fixings for a special dinner she had planned for tonight.

"I was glad to see her out and about," Mr. Miller added.

"Me too," Matt replied with a big grin. "What's she fixing?"

Mr. Miller shook his head. "I'm not telling. You need to get on home to find that out."

"I will."

Hearing that Ma was still feeling better gave Matt a powerful good feeling. Maybe things could get back to normal again. Still grinning, he ducked into the drugstore, hoping to find the book he'd secreted at the bottom of the used-book bin under a thick volume of famous quotes by famous people. *With Flintlock and Fife: A Tale of the French and Indian Wars* was still there. He paid a dime for it and started home, eager to read it and find out what Ma had planned for dinner.

Although he was good at all his subjects in school, Matt loved reading best. Happily, the book report due in two weeks could be on any subject he wanted to write about, and *With Flintlock and Fife* was just the kind of story Matt liked: brave soldiers fighting for a worthy cause, just like his brother, CJ, had done in the Great War.

In his dresser, carefully wrapped in a leather pouch, Matt kept CJ's medals, which the army had sent home to Ma months after his death in France. The Victory Medal had a silver star for gallantry and the Meuse-Argonne battle clasp on the ribbon. The other medal was the Croix de Guerre, from the French government, awarded for feats of arms.

CJ had been a war hero. Just about everybody in Las Cruces knew the story of how he'd run away from home, lied about his age, and became the youngest sergeant in his regiment before shipping overseas. It always filled Matt with pride and sadness whenever folks talked about his brother. He intended to be a soldier like CJ when he grew up, but he knew better than to say anything to Ma, who would surely give him what for about it.

At home, although keen to learn what Ma was fixing for dinner, he checked on Patches first, laid down fresh straw, broke the ice on the water trough, and fed him a bucketful of oats. After dinner he'd muck out the stall before starting in on his homework.

He stepped inside and shucked his coat. The delicious smell of a roasting chicken made his mouth water and his stomach grumble. He called out to Ma but got no answer. She wasn't in the kitchen, but a fresh-baked, delicious-looking peach pie sat on the table. A slice had been cut out and left on a plate as a snack. He wolfed it down and looked for her in the sitting room and her bedroom. With his heart thumping with worry he called out to her again and knocked hard on the closed bathroom door.

"Ma, are you in there?" he asked, his voice rising.

"Yes, give me a minute."

Matt held back a sigh of relief. "Are you okay?"

"Yes. Go set the table for me."

Matt hesitated. She sounded okay, but should he ask again? Sometimes Ma said things just to keep him from fretting.

"Go on, now," Emma said from behind the closed door.

"Okay."

Emma smiled at herself in the mirror as Matthew's footsteps receded. She'd prettied herself up, brushed her hair, and changed into a fresh blouse for dinner. It was going to be a wonderful evening meal with Matthew, and not just because she was feeling so much better and so lively. The mail had brought an astonishing surprise that would surely delight him as it had her.

She glanced again in the mirror, pleased with the results. Ever since her divorce, CJ and Matt had been the only men in her life, although it wasn't for a lack of flattering attention from the likes of Henry Bowman and a few other married men about town she knew. If she'd lived elsewhere—in a big city such as New York—it might have been different and she could have taken a lover. That was impossible to do in Las Cruces without inviting harsh criticism. Still, even with that disadvantage, she had what most women lacked: the freedom to live independently, answerable to no man. So she'd schooled herself to be virtuous. Given her lusty nature, it had been no easy task.

Matthew had eaten his snack and set the table for dinner. She found him sprawled on his stomach across his bed, nose in a book.

"It's about the French and Indian Wars," he explained as she sat beside him, "for a book report."

"I'll want to know all about it once you finish."

Matt nodded as he looked up at her. "You look pretty."

"Thank you. Now will you stop worrying about me?"

"Maybe."

"Hungry?"

"Yep."

"Then let's eat. After dinner I have a surprise to show you."

"What is it?"

"You'll see."

* * *

Matthew devoured his dinner, topped off by two slices of the peach pie, which he praised with each bite, and left to tend to Patches. Emma busied herself with the dishes, impatiently waiting for his return. Finished, she took the magazine, letter, and book that had arrived in the mail, sat at the table, and reread the letter from Gene Rhodes.

Dear Emma:

This is not a letter—it's an apology. It took this old yarn spinner more years than he'd like to admit to whip "Emma Makes a Hand" into a good enough story to get published. But here it is, wrapped inside this issue of Sunset *magazine with a drawing to go with it of a young gal on horseback twirling a lasso by my friend Maynard Dixon that I swear looks just like you.*

My New Mexico friends—thugs, gunmen, and outlaws that they are—tell me you've been sickly and I am grieved to hear of it. I hope "Emma Makes a Hand" lifts your spirits. I'll surely always remember that trail drive on the Tularosa when you showed me and all those other boys what a heck of a fine hand you were.

I've also been told that you've got a son named Matt who likes to read, so I'm sending along a copy of my book, West Is West, *that I inscribed to him. Tell him to read everything.*

Yours truly,
Gene Rhodes

She thumbed through the magazine to the story and read the opening paragraph:

Thomas Wheeler Van Eaton, known to all on the basin as Van, drew rein in front of the Double K ranch house and gazed at the prettiest gal he'd seen in a long, long time. Freshly beautiful she was; sparkling and fair, hair curly, eyes bewilderingly blue, slight as a desert willow. He had heard of Emma Kerney, her frank and friendly

manner, her warmth and sweetness, but seeing her under
a cloudless sky, with a soft wind at his back and the sun
touching Rainbow Ridge, rendered him speechless.

She thought back to the day Gene had showed up at the ranch
with a badly swollen eye and puffy lips after a fistfight in a mining
camp, asking for a place to hide out in case the law came after
him. Over supper he told her he had written a short story about
her that had been turned down by a magazine editor. He promised to send her a copy if it ever got published.

Not long after, he moved back east to live with his wife and her
family. Over time he became a highly popular writer of Western
books and one of the best-loved cowboy storytellers of the Old
West. Tall tales still circulated on the Tularosa about Gene's con-
nections to infamous New Mexico outlaws and cattle thieves of the
territorial years. To many folks, that made him an intriguing character with a somewhat shady background, which only served to
build his reputation as a writer who truly knew the ways of cowboys
and desperadoes.

To Emma, Gene was a good man who kept his word, stood by
his friends, was more honorable than most of his trail-riding companions, and had always been a gentleman with the ladies. She'd
read all his books and many of his short stories, often wondering
what had happened to the yarn he'd written about her. Finally,
here it was in her hands for everyone in the country to read. Good
memories of living on the Double K flooded her mind and brought
happy tears to her eyes.

She closed the magazine and put it with the book and letter.
What a day it had been! For months she'd felt her life slipping
away, and now it was back, vibrant and exciting. She was beginning

to wonder if it was possible for a body to heal itself, for a heart to mend on its own. Nothing seemed impossible.

The back door slammed shut.

"What is that surprise you promised to tell me?" Matt asked as he stomped snow off his boots and hung up his coat.

"Come in here and I'll tell you a story," Emma replied.

2

The days following the arrival of "Emma Makes a Hand" were the most exciting in Matthew Kerney's young life. The *Sunset* magazine story about his ma had sold out all over town, as had a second batch of copies sent down by train from Albuquerque. Mr. Duncan at the drugstore said folks were clamoring for more and the magazine was sold out in El Paso as well. At the library on Water Street, run by the Women's Improvement Association, five dog-eared copies of the magazine were available for people to read, but you had to sign up and read it right there on the spot when your time came. The lady at the desk told Matt the waiting list ran to the end of the month, with folks who didn't normally come to the library putting down their names. She'd never seen so many people through the door in a week. The recent arrival of the latest Zane Grey novel didn't even rival it in popularity. She also told Matt that the story contained exactly forty-six hundred and twenty-seven words, not including the title. She'd counted every one of them.

One afternoon, the editor of one of the local newspapers interviewed Ma for an article about the veracity of the story while Matt sat quietly in a corner of the room and listened. Later, Ma told him that *veracity* meant *truth*. Matt filed the word away for future use.

The article came out with a portion of the letter Gene Rhodes had sent Ma included, except for the part about her having been sickly, left out at her request. The editor quoted Ma as saying the story about her "making a hand" was pretty much accurate as Gene Rhodes wrote it. That it was fact and not storytelling caused quite a stir among some folks in the community, who were still arguing about the suffrage movement and the recent ratification of the Nineteenth Amendment giving women the right to vote. Letters to the editor either praised Ma as an example of a modern woman or chastised her for unladylike behavior.

After school, when his chores were done, Matt sat at the kitchen table and read the letters in the paper. He couldn't quite figure out why folks were in such a huff about whether Ma was right or wrong to do a man's job on a roundup, until Ma pointed out that the town womenfolk, who made up the majority of her letter-writing detractors, came from back east and had never worked outside their own houses, while the ranch and farm wives, who made up the majority of her supporters, worked side by side with their men and knew for certain a woman's place wasn't just in the home.

"It's all about what kind of life a person lives," she explained.

Matt looked puzzled.

"And whether they think they know what's best for others," Ma added.

Matt nodded knowingly. "I know kids like that. Stuck-up and bossy is what I call them."

On the way to school one morning, Joe Pete told Matt that the magazine story had been the subject of the sermon at Sunday Mass, but he couldn't remember what exactly the priest had said except that it wasn't chaste for Matt's ma to have been out on a roundup and trail drive with men night and day for weeks.

"Edgar told me *chaste* means *virginal*," Joe Pete explained with a know-it-all air, referring to his oldest brother. "That means a girl hasn't started making babies yet."

"I bet the priest also said it's not a woman's place to work with men," Matt suggested, recalling Ma's comments on the letters in the newspapers.

"Yeah, he said that too," Joe Pete replied. "What do you think?"

Matt shrugged. "Doesn't matter to me what people say. She's the best ma in the world, except when I get one of those looks she gives me for doing something terrible wrong. That's scary."

"My ma can do that to me too," Joe Pete said, shaking his carrot-top head to ward off the thought of an impending spine-chilling look from his mother, or any other mother for that matter.

Later in the week, another newspaper, the most popular one in town, printed a longer article about Ma and Gene Rhodes's short story along with a reprint of their original news report of CJ's heroic death during his gallant action in the Great War. After that, more people took to stopping by the house, including some townsfolk who'd never even said as much as howdy to Matt or his ma before.

For several days, Matt came home from school to find every seat in the front room occupied by folks clutching copies of the magazine and the newspapers, treating Ma like she was a motion picture star and getting her to sign her name on the first page of the story or above the newspaper headline. Even several of his teachers showed up at the house and asked to see the inscribed, signed copy of *West Is West* Gene Rhodes had sent to him. Although they didn't say so exactly, they seemed mighty envious of Matt's good fortune to have such a treasure from a famous writer, and they repeatedly cautioned him to take good care of it.

As the brother of a dead war hero and the son of a woman made famous by Eugene Manlove Rhodes, Matt became the most popular kid in Las Cruces for a time—at least at his school and around the neighborhood. Even the older neighborhood bullies gave up on taunting, teasing, and chasing Matt and his pals for a spell, which was a welcome break from the daily nuisance they usually caused the trio.

Ma herself was doing fine and pretty much back to being like she used to be before she got sick, easing Matt's worry about her considerably. In fact, he was starting to believe Ma wasn't gonna die after all and he wouldn't have to get sent off to the ranch to live with his pa.

He liked the ranch a lot but didn't care for Pa all that much. He had a stern manner and never said much, even when he tried hard to be nice. About the only times Matt felt easy around Pa was when he was showing him how to do stuff, especially when they worked with the ponies Pa sold to other ranchers around the state.

Ma said people like Pa, who'd stopped drinking, had to be hard on themselves just to stay on the straight and narrow, and that made him seem gruff. But the way Matt saw it, he didn't think Ma liked Pa all that much either. When they were at the ranch, everybody worked real hard trying to get along, but it wasn't any fun and made no sense. Besides, Matt had been raised just fine by Ma on her own, and he didn't need another parent to ride herd on him or boss him around.

Winter gave way to spring, and during the weeks of Ma's sudden fame, she had all her energy and high spirits back, which freed Matt from having to do any extra chores around the house. After school, when the folks who showed up to visit with Ma had departed and Matt had tended to his chores, she shooed him outside to find his pals or go riding down to the river, where he'd take Patches on a good long gallop through the cottonwood trees.

Back home, dinner waited, with Ma serving up great meals, including delicious homemade soups with warm bread fresh from the oven, which Matt loved. Afterward, he'd rush through his homework and settle in to read another chapter in *West Is West*. It was such a good story, he decided to do his book report on it, rather than the one about the French and Indian Wars he'd originally selected. He'd already written out the introduction with Ma's help. The first sentence read: "Eugene Manlove Rhodes, the famous Tularosa cowboy and writer, tells stories filled with veracity." He thought it was a humdinger of a sentence.

One night, Ma got down CJ's army letters from the Apache basket and they took turns reading them aloud. Ma got teary eyed some, and Matt had to pause his reading once or twice from being choked up, but he never broke down. Neither did Ma.

Although Matt didn't say it, he figured being a sergeant in the army was about the best job a fella could have, starting out. If CJ had done it, someday so would he.

Before he went to bed, Ma told him to meet her at the bank after school and warned him not to forget or dawdle with Joe Pete and Jimmy along the way.

"Why do I have to go to the bank?" he asked.

"Because I want you to meet two men who are going to help us," Ma said. "Mr. Hale and Mr. Bowman."

"Are we broke?" Matt asked, thinking about Joe Pete, who had a lot of older brothers and sisters and lived poor in a crowded, run-down adobe that backed up to the scrub-grass foothills that ran to the mountains.

Ma laughed. "No. These men will help us make sure that doesn't happen."

Still not convinced it was something he really needed to do, Matt shrugged. "Okay."

* * *

At the bank the following day, a clerk showed Matt to a private office, where he got a steely look from Ma for being late because he'd poked along with Joe Pete and Jimmy Potter. With a frosty smile, she introduced him to Mr. Bowman and Mr. Hale. Both men smiled warmly and gave Matt hearty hellos as they shook his hand.

"Your mother wanted us to meet you," said Mr. Bowman, who looked a bit like Humpty-Dumpty behind his huge desk, "so you'd know who to turn to if need be."

"I've got Ma to turn to," Matt replied dubiously, glancing from Mr. Bowman to Mr. Hale, who sat on one side of him, Ma on the other. "We do just fine, the two of us."

"I'm sure you do, son," Mr. Hale said earnestly. "But from now on, we're here to help out just in case you need us."

Matt studied Ma, who no longer looked miffed. "Are you gonna get sick some more?" he asked.

"It's about you being taken care of by Mr. Bowman and Mr. Hale if I'm not around," Ma said softly, reaching for his hand.

Matt stuck his hand between his legs before she could grab it. "Are you getting sick again?" he demanded.

"It could happen," Ma replied, "and probably will. We need to be ready so you don't have to take care of me the way you did before."

"I didn't mind doing it most times, and you said I did a good job of it." Matt looked at the men. "What will they do if you get sick again?"

"Make sure you don't want for anything."

Matt stared at the tall man sitting next to him. "How are you going to look after my ma?"

Mr. Hale smiled at Matt. "I've heard you're a smart boy, and you've asked a smart question deserving an honest answer: I'll look after your ma by looking after you. That's the way she wants it. Mr. Bowman and I will be responsible for your welfare if she can't. We're meeting today so you know who we are, what we've been asked by your mother to do, and how to find us."

From behind his desk, Henry Bowman cleared his throat and gave Matt a kindly smile. "She wants you to be happy and well provided for. That will be our job."

"I can help my ma and look after myself," Matt declared, a sinking feeling filling his stomach. "I've already showed that I could."

"What if she gets really sick?" Mr. Hale asked gently.

"I said I can do it," Matt replied defiantly.

"No, you can't," Ma said with a sad shake of her head. "I won't allow it. You will not spend your childhood looking after me. That would make me miserable and unhappy and be awful for you. You know my sickness can't be fixed. We've talked about it before."

"But you're better now," Matt said.

"But not forever," Ma replied, "and maybe not for long. We can't change that."

"Are you going to send me away somewhere?" Matt asked, getting to his feet, his resolve to not act like a little crybaby faltering.

"I would never do that!" Ma said.

"Do I have to stay with these men when"—he forced himself to say it—"you die?"

"You'll go to the ranch and be with your pa," Ma said.

She had the saddest smile on her face he'd ever seen, like she was already saying good-bye to him. Somehow he knew he'd never forget the way she looked at that moment. His feet were frozen to the floor and he felt like sobbing, but he blinked away the tears. He didn't want to hear any more words, wasn't gonna start bawling baby tears in front of everybody. He wanted to run away. He wanted to hit somebody. He held his breath until the jumble of notions stopped thundering through his head, until he felt cold inside about everything and everybody, empty and all alone.

Finally, he shook his head. "I have to go feed Patches." The words tumbled out, his voice thin and far away in his ears. He ran out of the room before anyone could stop him.

* * *

Riding low, his cheek on Patches' neck, Matt raced his pony through the cottonwood trees along the bosque, not caring where he went or how long he was gone. Patches stretched out in a smooth, steady gait, hooves pounding on the soft turf of the early spring grasses that lined the riverbed. At a shallow river crossing Patches hesitated, and Matt urged him across the slow brown current, up the sandy bank, and west into the desert. On the horizon, sunset had turned to dusk. Already late going home, Matt continued west, keeping Patches at a steady lope, the tiny twinkling lights of Las Cruces receding at his back. On broken, rock-strewn ground he finally drew rein and turned around. Just a hint of moonrise light touched the tips of the mountains east of town, and even with a sky full of stars, the night was black.

Worn-out, Patches blew snot. Matt slid out of the saddle and started slowly afoot for town, more than a little leery to go home, not just for the scolding that surely awaited him, but because of the nightmarish fear that had haunted him since Ma got sick: One day he'd find her on the kitchen floor not breathing or lying cold in her bed.

He remounted Patches at the river, crossed, and trotted toward town, wondering what Ma would say or do to him once he got there. Only once before in his whole life, when he was six, had she paddled him for stealing coins out of the money jar she kept on the kitchen counter and lying about it. Maybe tonight he'd get a second walloping. The thought of it made him feel even more dismal.

At the house, Matt quietly unsaddled Patches, walked him into his stall, wiped him down, and gave him oats and fresh water. All the lights burning inside the house seemed a warning sign for him to stay away. Was Ma home alone, or were those men he'd met at the bank with her? He rubbed Patches' ear, which earned him a contented snort, wondering if he should go inside or just stay with his pony until Ma got tired of waiting for him.

But what if she wasn't alone? Or was out in the cold night looking for him? Or maybe getting deathly sick again like he feared?

The scent of woodsmoke from the chimney made the thought of a warm kitchen and a cozy bed more appealing than a thin covering of straw in his pony's stall. Besides, he knew Ma would stay on the lookout for him all night if need be. He squared his shoulders, took a deep breath, marched inside, and shucked his coat. Ma was alone, sitting at the kitchen table. She didn't look at him, didn't say a word as she got up and took a plate of warm food from the oven and carried it to his place at the table. Matt got a glass of milk and sat, his eyes fixed on Ma, who acted busy searching through her sewing basket, as if he wasn't even there.

"Ma, I'm sorry," he said.

She just shook her head and said nothing. Her jaw was clamped shut hard, and she had one of those icy looks in her eyes that Matt hated.

"You can switch me if you want," he offered.

Ma flicked a glance at him like he was a complete stranger.

Miserable but hungry, Matt lowered his head and ate his food in silence.

When he finished, Ma took his plate, watched as he swallowed the last of his milk, and said, "Go to your room and stay there."

He gathered his schoolbooks. "I said I was sorry."

Ma pointed toward his bedroom.

Matt waited for her to say something more, but she turned back to her sewing. Defeated, he trudged to his room, threw himself on the bed, and tried hard not to cry. Sniffling, he opened his schoolbook to the arithmetic lesson Mr. Savacool had assigned for tomorrow. It would have been better if Ma had walloped him.

* * *

Morning came, and Ma greeted Matt with silence until he was at the kitchen table staring unhappily at a steaming-hot bowl of oatmeal.

"Are you still planning to run away from home?" she asked as she placed a pitcher of milk next to his oatmeal.

Matt shook his head. "No, ma'am, and I wasn't really going to anyway."

"Don't you ever put a fright like that into me again," Ma said with a half smile.

Matt smiled back. "I won't, I promise."

Ma ruffled his hair and gave him a quick kiss on the cheek. "Did you finish your homework last night?"

"Yes, ma'am."

"Good. Eat your breakfast."

Matt poured milk on the oatmeal and picked up his spoon. "I don't want you to die," he said suddenly, the words spilling out.

"Hush now," Ma replied gently. "I'm still here and there's no need for such sorrowful talk so early in the morning."

Matt forced a smile, gave his ma a serious nod, and said, "Okay."

"It's a lovely morning," Ma said, "and a walk will do me good. Would you like some company again on your way to school?"

"Yes, ma'am," Matt replied happily, glad all was forgiven.

* * *

On the walk to school, Jimmy Potter rushed up. "Morning," he said to Ma as he careened to a stop next to Matt.

"Good morning, Jimmy," Ma replied.

He nudged Matt with an elbow. "I got something to tell you," he whispered low, almost bursting with excitement.

"What is it?" Matt whispered back, glancing up at Ma, who didn't seem at all interested in the conversation.

Jimmy shook his head. "I'll tell you at school."

Wise in the ways of boys and their secrets, Ma slowed her pace. "You boys go on ahead."

Jimmy grinned. "Race you!" he dared, breaking into full stride.

"No fair!" Matt yelled, chasing full tilt after him.

At the schoolhouse, the boys came to a panting stop in a dead heat.

"What's the big secret?" Matt asked after catching his breath.

"I saw a golden eagle down by the river yesterday and I found its nest high up in a big old cottonwood. It's huge—maybe four, five feet round and deep, real deep. Biggest bird nest I ever saw."

"You sure it was an eagle?" Matt asked.

"You bet," Jimmy replied, spreading his arms wide. "It was no more than a hundred feet above me, floating over the river, not even beating its wings. My pa says this is mating season, when they lay eggs, so there should be two of them, but I only saw one."

"Maybe it's just an old nest," Matt said, feeling a twinge of regret for being absent during such a grand discovery.

"Nope," Jimmy said authoritatively. "There's fresh rabbit fur and bones scattered at the base of the cottonwood. Gopher and prairie dog bones too. Even some snakeskin. We gotta go right after school."

"Count me in," Matt said.

"Nobody's to know except us two and Joe Pete," Jimmy cautioned.

"Mum's the word," Matt said. He knew Jimmy had a single-shot .22 rifle and sometimes went bird hunting with his father. "You're not gonna shoot it, are you?"

Jimmy shook his head. "Pa says not to. But I'd sure like to find some eagle feathers."

"Me too," Matt echoed.

"I'll bring along my pa's field glasses," Jimmy said.

Joe Pete caught up to Matt and Jimmy just as Mr. Savacool rang the school bell. As they hurried to their classroom, they told him about the after-school expedition.

"That's okay with me," Joe Pete said with a grin as he shoved Matt up against the crowded hallway wall.

"Get off me, you lug!" Matt hooted, shoving back.

During recess and lunch the three chums made plans for the adventure. According to Jimmy, the eagle's nest was a far piece outside of town, deep in the bosque. To save time, the boys agreed to travel by horseback, which would give them plenty of daylight to look for the eagle and investigate the nest. Joe Pete, who didn't have a pony, would ride double with Matt on Patches, and Jimmy would be on Blue, his roan mare. Matt volunteered to bring snacks and Joe Pete agreed to bring a canteen of water.

When school let out, the boys split up and raced home. Matt slammed inside the house, out of breath and flushed with excitement, and told Ma about their plans to go by horseback to look for an eagle Jimmy had spotted in the bosque.

"Jimmy's bringing field glasses, Joe Pete the water, and I'm to bring something to eat," he added. "Can I take some cookies?"

"Of course," Ma said, smiling at Matthew's bubbling enthusiasm. "I'll put up a bag of snacks for you and the boys while you change and saddle Patches."

"You're the best," Matt said with a grin.

"But I want you home before dark," Ma said, "and you must promise to be careful."

"I promise," Matt replied as he hurried to his room to change out of his school clothes.

He dressed in a hurry, had Patches saddled and bridled lickety-split, and came upon Joe Pete running down the road from his house, the canteen looped on his belt and bouncing against his hip. He gave him a hand up and broke Patches into a trot. Up ahead, past the last building on Main Street, Jimmy sat ahorseback waiting. They joined up, Jimmy took the lead, and soon they were past the last levee in thick bosque, dodging Patches and Blue around stands of brush and trees.

They broke into the open, crossed a wide, sandy channel where the river had once wandered, stopped under a stand of old cottonwoods heavy with buds on thick branches, and dismounted.

"We'll walk from here," Jimmy said in a low voice.

"I don't see any eagles," Joe Pete noted, his head craned skyward. "You made it all up, didn't you?"

"Did not," Jimmy replied, punching Joe Pete on the arm.

Joe Pete playfully shoved Jimmy to the ground.

"Stop horsing around," Matt said. "Where's the nest?"

"Yonder a ways," Jimmy replied as he brushed twigs and leaves off the seat of his pants.

"Let's go," Matt urged.

Once again, Jimmy took the lead, and soon they were at the base of a mighty cottonwood with a trunk wider than the smoke-stacks of the power plant in town. High up, an eagle nest lodged against the tree trunk, supported by two large lateral branches, the bottom bulging fit to burst.

"Holy cow," Joe Pete said.

A shadow flashed above the crown of the cottonwood, followed by a high-pitched scream of *kee-kee-kee,* and there it was, floating away, white at the wing tips, gold at the nape.

"Hot diggity," Matt said, pointing at a speck high above it. "There's another one!"

Mouths agape, the boys watched in silence as the majestic birds danced in the sky, swooping up, plummeting down, sweeping around each other in an ever-shrinking arc. Finally, the eagles cir-cled away, across the Rio Grande toward the rock-strewn Robledo Mountains northwest of town.

"I bet there are eggs in the nest," Jimmy said. "I'm climbing to see."

"Dibs after you," Matt called as he watched Jimmy hoist himself onto a low branch that curled almost to the ground.

Jimmy made his way quickly up the tree, pausing halfway to smile down at his pals. "Whoo-e," he hollered. "This is high. Any sign of the eagles?"

"Nope," Joe Pete answered. "I'm last, so hurry up. Otherwise it will be too dark for me to get a look."

"Just hold your horses," Jimmy said as he continued climbing.

"I'm starting up," Matt announced, swinging onto the low branch. He threw a leg over it, pulled himself upright, found his footing, and scrambled upward. Above, Jimmy had almost reached the nest.

"What do you see?" Joe Pete yelled.

"Nothing yet," Jimmy replied.

Matt was a good twenty feet above the ground when Jimmy crawled out on a branch that supported the nest and rose to take a look.

"It's empty," Jimmy reported as the branch cracked and gave way. He tumbled down, arms and legs flailing, crashing against the boughs, the eagles' nest disintegrating around him as it also fell. He landed with a thud, his head bouncing hard against an old log.

Matt scurried down the tree to Joe Pete, who was at Jimmy's side trying to rouse him. Blood gushed from a wound in the back of Jimmy's head, and he wasn't moving.

"Take Blue," Matt ordered. "Ride to town. Get help. Leave the canteen."

Joe Pete stood frozen, staring at Jimmy's bloody head and vacant eyes. "Is he dead?"

"Go on," Matt shouted. "Get!"

Joe Pete dropped the canteen on the ground and ran to get Blue.

Matt shucked his coat, took off his shirt, and tried to stem the blood from the wound, but it just soaked through the shirt and kept bleeding. He poured water on Jimmy's face to wake him, tried shaking him conscious, yelled his name over and over. Jimmy didn't move.

He lowered an ear to Jimmy's mouth. He wasn't breathing. He put his ear to Jimmy's chest. His heart wasn't beating.

Matt sank back on his haunches, tears rolling down his face. He kept Jimmy company without moving, shivering in the cold until Joe Pete and a posse of men with lanterns gleaming in the dusk arrived.

"I should have caught you," Matt whispered into Jimmy's ear as hands pulled him away. "I should have caught you."

It was the worst day of Matthew Kerney's young life.

3

Patrick Kerney slipped into one of the last remaining empty seats at the back of the church. Up ahead, the small casket containing Jimmy Potter's body stood in front of the altar rail. Except for soft organ music from the choir loft above, the occasional shuffling of feet, and a stifled cough or two, silence reigned. In the front pew Patrick could make out the broad back and big shoulders of Jimmy's father, Luke Potter. Luke had been a friend since his arrival in Engle some years back. He'd come from Kansas to supervise the vast freight yards built by the railroad to store and ship materials to the massive Elephant Butte Dam construction project on the Rio Grande. When the job ended, Luke got promoted and transferred to Las Cruces. Patrick hadn't seen much of him since then.

Luke's wife, Jeannie, sat next to him. She was a tall, thin woman, quiet by nature. Her sunny personality and intelligent brown eyes livened up her otherwise plain features. She slumped against Luke as if the spark in her had been permanently extinguished.

On the same aisle two rows back, Emma sat with Matt, her arm wrapped protectively around his shoulders. Patrick had long given up the notion that Emma would ever reconcile with him enough to let him back into her heart or into her bed. Instead, they had forged a tense, polite truce based on his promise to do his best to be a good father to the boy. Two years of trying hadn't done much to strengthen the ties that bind. Patrick accepted his share of the blame, but Matt had never warmed to him, and Emma always seemed to have one reason or another to cut short their ranch visits.

They'd settled into a routine of three ranch visits a year during Matt's school holidays. Although Patrick would never say it aloud, that suited him fine. He just didn't have much of a talent for fathering. He'd proved that long ago with CJ, the day he shot the boy's pony after riding it half drunk, getting bucked off, and crashing headfirst into the stubbing post. They scuffled over it, and CJ left the ranch that very day, never to come back.

That was the last Patrick saw of him. His sodden stupidity caused CJ to run off to the army and get himself killed in France. The memory of it pursued him daily, one of many dim-witted blunders he'd made over the years that had kept him drinking until Emma forced him to stop.

In the pulpit, the preacher cleared his throat, shuffled a few pages in his big Bible, and looked out over the congregation. Not one for religion or speechifying, Patrick stopped listening before the preacher's sermon began, his thoughts wandering to Matt. He'd heard tell that some folks held the boy responsible for the accident, saying he'd shamed and bullied Jimmy into climbing that old cottonwood tree to peek into the eagle's nest. Patrick didn't believe it and hoped Luke and Jeannie didn't either. But if they did, he'd stand behind Matt come what may, no matter where the balance of truth fell. Emma would rightly expect no less from him. The boy had to be hurting miserably over seeing his friend die before his very eyes. Patrick knew that feeling all too well from his experiences with the Rough Riders in Cuba.

Patrick couldn't tell how Emma was faring through the tragedy. He knew she'd been mighty sick until recently, with the folks in town who knew her best worrying about her and fearing the worst. But last week, his lawyer had sent a copy of the registered deed for two sections of homesteaded land in the San Andres Mountains backlands Patrick had bought from a hardscrabble sheep rancher. In a note inside it, the lawyer wrote that Emma was much improved and back to her old self again.

He didn't doubt it, looking at her straight back and square shoulders. She'd always been slender, but now she looked frail. He wondered if her latest recovery would hold true for long. So many times during their marriage, he'd seen her recover from a bad spell only to decline again into poor health. So many times, he'd heard the doctors warn her to take better care of herself or accept the inevitable that someday she'd become a bedridden invalid. So many times he'd gone to sleep next to her wondering if he'd wake up in the morning to find her dead.

He'd never stopped worrying about her. In spite of their breakup, all the harsh, bitter words that passed between them, and the times she'd driven him half *loco* with her ways, he'd never loved anybody more. He studied the line of her long neck, just visible above her collar, and yearned for their happier days together.

As the pastor read a lengthy passage of scripture, Patrick shook off his glum thoughts and mulled over what he planned to do with his newly bought two sections. The twelve hundred eighty acres were some distance away from his ranch holdings and mostly surrounded by marginal government land that drew few pilgrims willing to stake a homestead claim. It had been overgrazed by the sheep rancher but not chewed down to the roots. If the wet weather held through spring, the grasses would start to come back.

With the war over these last two years, the Brits no longer buying American beef to feed their army, and on-the-hoof prices falling, he had no intention of buying more cattle to pasture on his new acreage. After spring works, when his steers, the barren cows, and some of the culled yearlings sold, he'd pay his outstanding bills, fence the two sections, knock down the small shepherd's shack, sink a well near the live water source, and hold it in reserve for the next drought, which would surely come; of that he was certain. And when it came, a rested, high-country pasture with live water and good browse might mean the difference between the survival and the failure of the Double K.

The service ended and Patrick ducked outside to wait on the street for Emma and Matt. As the congregation slowly left the church, he wondered how she would greet him. He'd missed the wake, so would it be with stony silence or a cold reserve? Either way, neither mother nor son would show him much warmth, if any, and he had little of it to offer to them himself.

He waited with the ever-present twinge of uncertainty that always came over him just before he saw her. He never quite knew what to expect from her and often guessed wrong. Her looks, her smarts, her fierce emotions, and her strange ways had baffled him when they first met and still baffled him now.

As Emma and Matt emerged from the church and approached, Patrick removed his hat, ran a hand through his freshly cut hair, and nodded by way of a greeting.

Emma nodded back. "Say hello to your father, Matthew," she said.

"Hello," Matt replied dutifully, his voice hollow. He looked pained and miserable.

Patrick forced a smile. The boy mystified him. "It's good to see you, son. Are you holding up all right?"

Matt nodded stiffly. "Sort of."

Patrick patted Matt's shoulder. "That's the spirit."

Matt dropped his head and stared at his shoes, refusing to look up until Patrick removed his hand.

"Did you just get here?" Emma asked snappishly. "You weren't at the wake."

Patrick stifled a curt reply. "No, but I was in the back during the service." Emma's cheeks were rosy and her eyes bright, but somehow she looked fragile, although he couldn't say why. He looked at Matt, who had walked on ahead of them a few paces. "Are Luke and Jeannie blaming Matt for the accident?" he asked softly.

Emma shook her head. "No, they know it was Jimmy's idea from the start."

"That's good."

The low murmurings of the waiting mourners who'd gathered in tight groups drifted away to silence as the pallbearers carrying the casket emerged from the church, followed closely by Luke and Jeannie. Bells tolled from the steeple as the mourners slowly assembled behind the grieving couple for the short walk to the nearby cemetery.

"Walk with us," Emma whispered.

Patrick nodded and joined Emma and Matt as they stepped out to join the slow-moving procession.

At the grave site, the preacher said comforting words to console Jimmy's parents and then read a short prayer to lay the little boy to rest. With a final *amen,* the casket was lowered and folks began to disperse, leaving Luke and Jeannie standing alone, frozen, clutching each other at the foot of the open grave.

Matt turned away, walked to a nearby headstone, and stood with his back to the grave site.

"Her doctor says she can't have another baby," Emma whispered as she blinked away the tears in her eyes. "She's lost her only child."

"I didn't know that," Patrick replied, glancing at Matt, who hadn't budged from his spot a few feet away.

"That's so tragic," Emma added.

"I reckon so."

"I remember how eager you were for us to have children so I wouldn't leave you."

Patrick's eyes widened. "Don't go making things up, Emma. I never said anything like that."

Emma almost smiled. "You didn't have to. The fact that you never gave a hoot about being a good father is proof enough."

"Are you going to chew on me about that again?"

Emma took two steps in Matthew's direction and halted. "No, you made an honest attempt a time or two, when I asked, but it just wasn't in you. And I do appreciate you making an effort with Matthew as best you can."

"Well, ain't I just about a worthless wreck of a man," Patrick growled.

"Don't get in a dither, Patrick," Emma soothed. "I guess I should thank you for giving me Matthew. He's all I have to save me from Jeannie's fate. I don't think I could endure losing an only child. Burying Molly and losing CJ in the war were bad enough."

Patrick's jaw dropped a little. He searched Emma's face for any hint of mockery and found none. She'd divorced him after he'd forced himself on her, calling him a loathsome rapist and an incompetent father and compelling him to sign legal papers acknowledging Matthew as his natural son before the child was even born. Now she was thanking him.

"Do you mean that?" he asked.

Emma smiled slightly. "Don't take it as a full pardon of your behavior."

"There are no halfway pardons," Patrick noted emphatically.

Emma shrugged off Patrick's strong reaction. "I was just being snippy." She walked to Matthew, took him by the hand, and continued down the path to the street.

"What were you talking about?" Matt asked.

"Nothing important," Emma replied.

Matt frowned at her answer.

"She was telling me that I'm a damn fool who made too many mistakes," Patrick explained.

"Is that why you're divorced?" Matt asked.

"Yep," Patrick answered.

"I'm glad," Matt announced.

"I'm sorry to hear that," Patrick replied.

Matt shrugged and fell silent.

Emma yanked Matt's hand. "Don't be disrespectful, young man."

"No harm done," Patrick interjected.

"Sorry," Matt said obediently.

Emma sighed and shook her head in displeasure at Matthew as they turned the corner onto Main Street. "Come with us to the house. We have a lot to talk about."

"Such as?"

"Matthew's future," she answered. "Someday it will be in your hands. At least a part of it, and I want no misunderstandings between us."

Patrick's throat tightened. "Got it all figured, have you?"

"Why, yes, I think I do."

"I'm not going home," Matt said, yanking free from Emma. "I don't want to hear it, not ever." He clamped his hands over his ears and scowled at them.

Emma pulled his hands away from his ears. "Stop that."

Matt struggled, broke free, and covered his ears again. "I shoulda caught him!" he cried. "I shoulda stopped him. It's my fault Jimmy's dead."

"No, no, no," Emma said, reaching to embrace Matt, who turned and took off running full tilt down Main Street.

"That boy is hurting something fierce," Patrick said as he watched Matt dart around pedestrians on the sidewalk and disappear down a side street.

"It's not just that. Ever since the accident he's been asking me when I'm going to die. He hates the notion of it now more than ever."

"I hate that idea myself."

Emma raised an eyebrow. "Really?"

"Yes, ma'am. Aren't you going to fetch him back?"

Emma shook her head. "Let him go. Are you coming to the house?"

"I surely am. I can't wait to hear what you've got cooked up for the boy."

Emma looked up at Patrick and smiled. "The *boy* is your son, Patrick, and I'd appreciate it if you call him by his name."

"I'll surely try."

"Thank you. You probably won't like what I have to say to you."

"Well then, let's get it over and done with."

* * *

Patrick Kerney sat silently at the kitchen table over a cup of coffee as Emma skimmed through the general terms of the trust she'd established for Matt. It effectively cut him out from any say or control over how her assets could be used to benefit the boy. While she made it sound like it was all simply the best for Matt,

Patrick took it as a slap in his face. Her trust document might as
well have just come out and said that he was a scoundrel not to be
counted on to look after his own flesh and blood. It made him
plenty irate.

When Emma finished talking, Patrick took a long minute to
stifle his aggravation for fear she'd fall silent at any hint of displeasure and send him away before he learned more. Instead he asked,
"How much will there be to care for him?"

"Enough to see him to his eighteenth birthday," Emma replied.

"I didn't ask how long it would last. I asked how much."

"Why do you need to know that?"

"The boy will be living with me. It's helpful to know."

Emma took a moment to consider her answer. "It's money for
Matthew only."

"I understand that. I ain't gonna steal from him, Emma. How
much?"

"You've always put your own needs first, which is why I've made
these arrangements. He'll have fifteen hundred dollars a year."

"That's more than most ranchers earn," Patrick said, taken
aback. "The boy won't need near that amount to get by on."

"Then with luck there will be money left to give him a good
start on his own. Will you stop calling him *the boy*?"

"I meant Matt," Patrick amended. "So if Matt needs something,
I go hat in hand to the banker fella and your lawyer and ask for it,
correct?"

"It will only seem humiliating if you take it that way," Emma said
sharply.

"But that's the way it is."

"I don't care one smidgen about your wounded pride. Matthew's trust will be managed in confidence by two men I have full
faith in. I warn you not to raise a stink about it."

Patrick shrugged, galled by her attitude. "It's your hand to play."

"Yes, it is," Emma replied firmly.

Patrick pointed at the trust papers in Emma's hands and shook his head. "How did we get to such a sorry state with all of this rigmarole between us?"

Emma frowned at him, glared at him. "You know what I lived through as a girl. You saw it with your own eyes. Before we married, I made you promise never to raise a hand against me or take me against my will. Never, never, never, and still you did."

Patrick looked away. "Does Matt know?"

Emma's eyes widened in surprise at the question. "Heavens no, and he never will."

"Well, that's something, I reckon. Maybe he'll warm up to me in time."

"Promise me you'll do your best by Matthew."

"I swear to it," Patrick replied. "But I'd rather have you stay around to raise him up. That would be best."

Emma glanced warily at him. "I think you actually mean that."

"I do, in more ways than you know."

It earned him a genuinely agreeable smile, one he hadn't seen on Emma's face in years. It was too dangerous to say more; he might start begging for forgiveness. He reached for his hat. "I'll be going."

He said good-bye at the front door, heard it close slowly behind him, and walked down the street without looking back. He'd never felt so alone, not since he was a miserable young child in the goldmining camps of northern New Mexico, virtually abandoned by his lunatic aunt and her drunken lover. He'd survived by trusting no one, caring for no one, believing in no one.

Only with Emma had he come close to breaking free of the

suspicious, doubting nature entrenched in him since those harsh early days—but never for very long and never completely.

It pained him, angered him, to still love the woman who'd walked away from him, and it pained and angered him even more to relive time and again his shameful drunken idiocy that had caused it.

He walked down Main Street toward his hotel wondering how long it would be before a rider came to the ranch to report Emma's death. Or would he find out at the Engle post office the next time or two he collected the mail? Or maybe Matt would just show up one day in a Tin Lizzie accompanied by the lawyer and the banker with a copy of Emma's legal trust document in hand.

He had no doubt Emma wouldn't want him to know she was dying until the dying had been done. And he knew her well enough to know she was fixing to die. He could see the strain of staying alive etched on her face. It gave him a shiver, and a great thirst for a whiskey or two came over him. Hell, maybe he needed a whole bottle.

* * *

In his hotel room, Patrick changed out of the new duds he'd bought for the funeral service and went out for a meal. He found a Mexican cantina in a small adobe house off Main Street, walked quickly past the long bar, lined with customers, sat in the back dining room, and ordered a meal of enchiladas, beans, and tortillas. He stopped short of asking for a whiskey.

Although Prohibition had recently become the law of the land, it hadn't changed the behavior of hard-drinking New Mexicans much. They still frequented the saloons and cantinas, where bartenders now splashed liquor into coffee cups instead of glasses and kept the booze bottles out of sight so as not to rile any Anti-Saloon League members who might appear and cause a ruckus.

With truckloads of high-quality liquor smuggled day and night across the nearby Mexican border and nary an Internal Revenue agent in sight, customers and connoisseurs with a taste for good whiskey didn't have to settle for hundred-proof moonshine or rot-gut. Many establishments were quickly transformed into private clubs, and most customers practiced good behavior in order to keep from drawing attention to their God-given right to engage in the illicit consumption of alcohol. It got so civilized in bars that drinking became mostly a genteel pastime. In appreciation of im-proved community tranquility and fewer drunken brawls, local sheriffs and town marshals tended to look the other way.

Pleased with his self-restraint, Patrick finished his meal, re-turned to his room, stretched out on the bed, and tried to not think about how pleasant it would be to wet his whistle with an after-dinner whiskey. The thought of it made him too restless to stay still, so he worked with pencil and paper, figuring exactly how much barbwire he needed to fence the two sections. To save money, he'd cut juniper in the high country for the fence posts.

He tallied the cost and realized he had more than enough re-serve cash on hand to pay for the wire. All he needed was the time to cut the posts, haul them down from the high country, set them, and string wire. But with spring and fall works, routine ranch chores, caring for the cattle, and training the ponies, putting up the fence on his own could take several years.

More than once, the urge for a drink forced his mind to wan-der. Twice he almost stepped out to buy a bottle, reining in the impulse just short of putting on his coat. He shook off the desire by going over his calculations again, estimating how many fence posts he'd need to cut and how many wagon trips it would take to haul them down. He drew a map of the two sections from memory and sketched in areas where the fencing spanning a gully or running up the side of a hill would be more difficult to do.

Weary eyed and tired, he thought he'd licked the yen for a drink and was about to turn in for the night, when the craving came on stronger than ever. He tried to fight it off. Drinking a bottle of whiskey alone was a bad idea. Knowing that didn't keep his need for a whiskey at bay. He stopped and looked in the mirror above the washstand. He'd been sober for two years. Nursing one whiskey at the Mexican cantina bar wouldn't turn him into a drunk again. Reaching such a logical conclusion felt reasonable. He grabbed his coat and hat, jingled his spurs down the hotel stairs, and headed straight for the cantina.

* * *

Patrick finished his third whiskey at the bar and called for another just as a short, stocky man sidled next to him and nodded a greeting. Although the dim light and thick tobacco smoke made it hard for Patrick to see the stranger clearly, he nodded back and reached for his refilled coffee cup.

"I know you," the man said genially. "You're Pat Floyd."

Stunned to hear that name, Patrick put his cup down and studied the stranger. He had a chubby face and a button nose and looked vaguely familiar, but Patrick couldn't place him. "You're mistaken, friend. That's not my name."

The man smiled. "That may be, but I knew you in Yuma Prison as Pat Floyd. I guess that was your go-by name."

Twenty-five—no, twenty-seven—years had passed since his time in Yuma Prison, just about long enough for Patrick to mostly forget about it. He had no need to be reminded. "I've never been in prison," he said, "there or anywhere else."

The man laughed. "Well, I ain't gonna argue with you, but I swear we were cell mates. You had a bunk high up and I slept on a straw-tick mattress on the ground with the centipedes and spiders. Eight, sometimes ten of us crammed into those damn tiny cells. Hot as hell they were, couldn't sleep a wink in the summertime. Everybody called me Squirrel. Remember?"

Patrick shook his head. "Sorry, but you've got the wrong man."

The man shrugged. "Look, I ain't meaning to cause you any trouble or embarrassment. It was a long time ago and some things are best left behind."

"In spite of mistaking me for someone else, there's truth to that," Patrick replied, giving the man a closer look. His coat was ragged at the cuffs, his worn-down boots hand-patched with pieces of leather, and he needed a bath and a shave. "You said people called you Squirrel," he ventured.

Squirrel smiled. "Real name is Vernon Clagett, but I answer to Squirrel as well, although I don't like the handle much. Maybe I was mistaken."

"No harm done," Patrick replied, finally recognizing the skinny kid inside the body of the stocky, beat-down man. He'd earned his nickname in prison by selling and bartering goods the inmates needed, like tobacco, soap, and liquor. "Let me buy you a drink, and you can tell me what brings you to these parts."

Squirrel's smile widened. "I'd be obliged."

Patrick called for a whiskey and placed more money on the bar. "Are you just passing through?" he asked.

"I am." Squirrel eyed the bartender carefully as he poured the drink. He picked it up with a shaky hand and downed it in a gulp.

"That's if I can earn some money. I need work so I can go back to Texas, where I've got some family."

Patrick hid a smile as he motioned for the bartender to pour another. Squirrel was a drunk, no doubt about it, and when sober, drunks worked for whatever wages they could get. "Ever do any ranch work?" he asked.

"Yes, sir," Vernon replied, his eyes fixed on the bartender as he poured whiskey in the cup. "Farm work, mostly," he corrected as he reached for the drink. "I'm a fair handyman, not good at everything, but I can drive a wagon, mend fences, cut wood, tend to chickens, hoe a field, and shoe a horse—whatever is needed around a place."

"Where did you last work?" Patrick asked.

"I was a barn boy over in Willcox on a horse ranch."

Vernon knocked back his drink and kept talking. Patrick only half listened; he'd already decided to offer Squirrel work fencing the two sections. If the man agreed, and there was no reason to think he wouldn't, Patrick figured it would serve two purposes: The fence would get built and his prison record wouldn't get spread around town.

Three whiskeys had made Patrick light-headed but far from drunk. He'd made a point of not telling Squirrel his real name. He looked around the room and didn't see a soul who knew him. That was good. He looked back at Squirrel, who had stopped talking. Drunks were notoriously unreliable hands and required watching, but the risk was worth it. "I just may have some work for you," he said.

Vernon grinned. "I'd be much obliged if you did. I'll work hard, I promise you that."

Patrick clasped Squirrel's shoulder. "I believe you will. Meet me at the Engle train station the day after tomorrow at noon. It's a town northeast of here a ways on the main line. Not that far. If you show up, you have a job."

"I'll be there."

"Good, I'll see you then. Have another drink on me." He flipped a half-dollar tip to the bartender, put enough money on the bar to pay for two drinks, and left the cantina, happy with the turn of events. Squirrel would either show up in Engle or not. If he did, Patrick would stock the shepherd's shack with victuals, let Squirrel live in it while he built the fence, and send him on his way when the work was done. If Squirrel didn't show, Patrick figured he'd move on before too long and that would be the end of it. He doubted there was much of a chance his prison record and go-by name of Pat Floyd would catch up with him.

* * *

Patrick slept poorly and woke up early with a dry mouth and dull ache in his head reminiscent of his drinking days. Fully sober, he had no longing for a morning whiskey to chase away the cobwebs, and that was a good sign. Maybe he could have a few drinks every now and then without backsliding into being a drunk again. He also had a clear memory of meeting Squirrel and offering him a job. In thinking it over, he liked how he'd handled the whole situation.

The hotel boasted indoor plumbing, with a tub and hot water in the communal bathroom, and he made full, leisurely use of it, until a knock at the door made him get out and get a move on. He dried off, dressed quickly, shaved in his room, went to breakfast, and was the first customer to be served in the empty dining room. Over coffee, the dull headache receded and by the time he finished breakfast, he felt full of energy and ready to go.

A hardware store by the depot, no more than a few minutes'

walk from the hotel, always opened early and stocked the barbwire he needed. In no hurry, he paid the check, settled the bill for the room, packed his gear, left it with the desk clerk, and walked to Emma's house. Lights were on in the kitchen and smoke drifted from the chimney. He heard the back door slam and Matt's pony whinny, and walked behind the house to the small horse barn. The pony was in the corral eating a bag of oats while Matt mucked out the stall.

Matt heard Patrick's footsteps and looked out. "Ma's in the house," he said tonelessly.

"I came to see you and find out how you're doing," Patrick said.

"Fine," Matt replied before disappearing inside the stall.

Patrick gave Patches a careful look. "You take good care of your pony. I admire a man who does that."

Matt's movement inside the stall stopped.

"You can learn a lot about a man by his horse," Patrick continued. "Your pony tells me you'd be a good man to ride the river with."

Matt appeared in the stall doorway.

"I ever tell you about a man named Cal Doran?"

"Nope, but Ma has told me some about him. She says he was a good and generous man."

"That he was. He raised me up after my pa, your grandpa, died, and he had a pony named Patches."

"He did?"

"Yep, and he truly loved that horse. Sometimes a man's pony can be his best friend, the most important critter in a cowboy's life. You can never own a pony like that. They just kind of pick you out and let you join up with them."

"How do you mean?" Matt asked. Finished mucking, he set the pitchfork aside.

"It's hard to explain," Patrick answered. "Let me ask you this: What did you think when I first showed you that pony out at the ranch?"

"Like he was special," Matt answered. "The best-looking pony I'd ever seen."

"*That's* what I mean, and he took to you right away, just like you took to him."

Patrick stepped inside the corral, unhooked the empty feed bag, and handed it to Matt. Patches snorted, turned his head, and looked him in the eyes. "You bring him out to the ranch next visit and we'll work him into a top ranch pony. He's got the smarts and the heart for it."

Matt brightened. "You mean it?"

"I mean it."

Matt hung up the feed bag, put Patches back in his stall, and said, "You can come inside, if you like."

Patrick smiled. "I appreciate the invite, but I've got business to attend to and you need to get ready for school. Look after your ma and give her my best."

"Yes, sir, I will," Matt answered gravely.

"Adios."

Matt smiled. "Adios."

Patrick smiled in return and left, feeling almost buoyant, thinking there might be a chance to make friends with Matt after all. It put a spring in his step.

4

For a month, Vernon Clagett worked alone, cutting and hauling fence posts and stacking them at various locations along the perimeter of the pastureland Patrick Kerney owned. He saw Patrick about once a week at the shepherd's shack when he came to check on Vernon's progress and drop off supplies. On one visit, Patrick took him to Engle, where they picked up rolls of barbwire freighted by train from Las Cruces. While in town, he bought Vernon a meal but refused to advance him any money from his pay to buy a bottle of whiskey to take home to the shack.

Vernon's living quarters were sparse at best, consisting of a rough-fashioned plank-board bunk with a lumpy mattress, a small woodstove for heating and cooking, a shelf for provisions, a bucket for water, one hurricane lamp, and several wall pegs for clothes and gear. It had a leaky roof, drafty walls, and a smoky chimney and was home to numerous varmints and crawly critters that scurried across the dirt floor. Vernon offered no complaints. He'd lived in far worse conditions with little food and fewer prospects.

At the outset of his employment, especially at nighttime, Vernon got so desperate for a drink he considered riding two hours to town and selling Patrick Kerney's horse for a jar of rotgut. Only the knowledge that he'd likely never get away with it, and the fact he was too doggone exhausted to move, kept him from acting on the impulse. When the shakes, the sweats, and the blinding headaches came over him, he curled up on the bunk, laid low by the misery. Yet with each passing day he felt a little less sick and a little bit stronger, until finally the trembling in his hands stopped, his appetite improved, and he no longer stank from a putrid booze smell that oozed from his pores.

On payday Patrick came at dawn and put twenty dollars in Vernon's hand.

"You can pack your gear, walk to town, buy a bottle, get drunk, and you'll work for me no more," he proposed. "Or you trail along to the ranch and keep your job for a spell."

"What about fencing the pasture?" Vernon asked, staring at the greenbacks.

"That gets put off until I've got everything ready for spring works. When things are shipshape, you'll come back here and start stringing wire. If you stay sober, that is."

"I'm building fence by myself?"

"No, you'll have help."

"What do you want me to do at the ranch?"

"I got ponies that need to be shod, equipment to repair, a chuck wagon that needs a good greasing, and the like," Patrick replied. "I'll up your wages five dollars a month, but be warned, there's no liquor to be found on my spread. I don't allow it. A man with a big thirst has a far piece to go for a drink, and when he leaves he isn't welcomed back."

Vernon considered his options. The headaches, sweats, and shakes were gone and he felt better than he had in years. Plus,

he'd been told in Las Cruces that Patrick had one of the best outfits on the Tularosa, and he wanted to see it for himself.

Vernon put the folding money in his pocket. "I'll trail along,"

"I'll be back from town by early afternoon," Patrick said as he
mounted his pony. "Be ready then."

"You sure go to town more than any other country folk I know,"
Vernon said with a friendly smile.

Patrick stared him down. "Putting your nose into other folks'
business will get you sent down the road in a hurry," he snapped.
"You get my drift, Squirrel?"

Vernon blinked and backtracked. "I didn't mean nothing by it.
But I'd appreciate it if you didn't call me Squirrel anymore."

Patrick nodded. "Fair enough. See you after noon."

"I'll be ready," Vernon replied. He watched Patrick ride away,
thinking the man sure seemed to have more to hide than a go-by
name and a prison record. It made Vernon all the more curious
about him.

* * *

Started back in the territorial days by Patrick's father, John Kerney, and his partner, Cal Doran, the Double K was the oldest and
most remote outfit on the east side of the San Andres Mountains.
It was twenty miles to the nearest state road and about the same
distance to Patrick's closest neighbor. The ranch boundaries encompassed high-country meadows and foothill pastures that
spread onto the Tularosa Basin. The basin, an expanse that filled
the eye, stretched beyond blindingly brilliant sand dunes to the
south and dangerous, ink-black malpais to the north. Most days
the basin shimmered under crystal-clear skies, with mountains
looming and lurking in all directions.

Tucked into a shelf along the hillside of a meandering valley that dipped and rolled into soft foothills, the ranch headquarters was watered by a spring-fed pond and an intermittent stream that coursed to the basin and disappeared underground. The ranch house faced east, with a view of Sierra Blanca Peak towering over the Mescalero Apache Reservation in the forested uplift of the Sacramento Mountains forty miles distant. Most mornings brought brilliant sunrises that flung rainbow colors over the alkali flats bordering the Double K. Windbreaks and stands of cottonwood trees planted in the early days of the ranch gave it an inviting, comfortable feel, in stark contrast to the harsh desert landscape, ravaged by years of overgrazing and perpetual cycles of punishing drought.

Because of the location, the ranch had no electricity or indoor plumbing, telephone service was years away, and although the government promised rural free mail delivery, it was spotty at best, given frequent washouts, rockslides, bad weather, and the breakdowns of the mail car.

Every backcountry rancher with a motorcar or truck fastened cans of gasoline, oil, and water to their vehicles' running boards as a precaution against inevitable disasters. Patrick knew the automobile had come west to stay but refused to own one until the roads were safer and filling stations more numerous. Until then, a horse and wagon were much more reliable in the unforgiving, treacherous mountains and desert of southern New Mexico.

Patrick's weekly trip to Engle was the only consistent way to stay in touch with Emma. Sometimes she sent a note to his post office box, but most times not. When he didn't hear from her for a spell, he'd call her house from the Engle train station or send a telegraph wire asking about her health. She sounded chipper and fine when they talked, and she sent short, reassuring replies to his inquiries, but without seeing her face-to-face, Patrick continued to worry about her.

This week a letter from Emma awaited him at the post office. She wrote that spring school recess started in two weeks and they would be arriving in Engle on the Friday evening train the day school got out. Patrick mailed back a note that he'd be waiting for them at the station, turned, and bumped into Albert Jennings on his way out the door.

"Can't say I'm glad to see you," Al said dourly. Big-boned, with a jovial round face that matched his personality, Al was well liked by all his neighbors, except for Fermin Lucero, the sheep rancher who had sold out to Patrick. Al's blue eyes and curly light brown hair concealed from strangers his Hispanic blood, a heritage from a grandparent on his mother's side.

"That ain't very neighborly of you," Patrick said with a grin. Al owned a ranch on the west side of the San Andres, right next to the two sections that now belonged to Patrick.

"I guess it ain't," Al said with a smile. "How did you find out before me that Lucero wanted to sell?"

"You tried to drive that old boy and his sheep off his property so many times, he was hell-bent not to sell to you," Patrick replied. "So he came to me."

Al shook his head. "I should have known."

"That's what I mean about you not being neighborly, getting Fermin all riled up at you like that."

Al threw back his head, laughed, and slapped Patrick on the shoulder. "I'm about as neighborly as you are when it comes to sheep. Can't stand the critters. Let me buy you a meal and talk you into selling me that land. Hell, it's across the mountain and a far piece from your boundary. Too damn inconvenient for you to own, I'd say."

Patrick nodded in agreement, but only about the offer of a free meal. A sign outside the hotel advertised fresh eggs on the menu and the cook made a decent cup of coffee. "I'll let you feed me," he said, "but don't expect anything to come of it other than you being two bits poorer. I'm not selling."

Al grinned as he stepped off in the direction of the hotel. "That figures. Leastways, I'm hoping you'll tell me what you plan to do with that pasture. I've never known you to buy land for no purpose whatsoever."

"It's an insurance policy."

Al paused in front the general store. "Against what?"

"Look up and down the street," Patrick said. "What do you see?"

"Engle," Al replied, not bothering to look.

"Rootin'-tootin' Engle," Patrick said. "Right?"

Al paused and looked around. A barbershop, a saloon, and a dry goods store had closed in the last year, and the buildings remained empty. "Well, it ain't as rip-roaring as it once was back in the boom days when they were building the dam; I'll give you that."

"Someday when roads and cars replace trains, it's gonna dry up and blow away," Patrick predicted as he moved toward the hotel.

"Maybe so, but what does that have to do with Lucero's pasture?"

"His sheep eroded the soil but didn't kill all the grass. I'm gonna fence it, rest it, sow seed in some places, bring the grasses back, put in a well, and keep live water running in the springs. Next time a bad drought hits, I plan to put my stock on it and maybe keep the Double K from going under."

"You've got some good high-country meadows to graze cattle on in dry times," Al countered.

Patrick nodded. "So do you. Think there's enough browse to get you through a two- or three-year drought?"

Al shrugged as he stepped into the hotel dining room. "That's doubtful. How long you figure it will take to green up enough to use?"

"Three to five years," Patrick replied as he took a seat at an empty table.

"That's a long time to have land not working for you," Al said, sliding into a chair.

Patrick waved the waitress over. "We can't keep ranching by throwing our livestock on overgrazed pastures and praying for moisture. It's time we got a little smarter. Cutting back on the livestock and resting the land makes sense to me."

"You'll lose profits," Al cautioned.

"I'll earn less, but in the long run I may be able to keep what I have. If the land wears out, it's no good to anyone."

Al pushed his hat back and scratched his chin. "You've chewed on this a while."

"I have."

"Let's order," Al said as the waitress approached. "We can talk more about it over a plate of steak and eggs."

"Suits me," Patrick said.

As they dug into their meals, the two men traded worries over falling cattle prices and rising operating costs, before Al returned to Patrick's notions about resting his new sections. By the time they were ready to push back from the table, Al had thrown in on the idea, deciding to do the same with two sections that bordered Patrick's new land. Although it was higher up the mountainside and more heavily forested, there were several large meadows with good, reliable water. They agreed to keep the sections fallow for at least three years and consult with each other before putting any animals on them.

"I'll fence my sections after spring works," Al said.

"Good deal."

The friends grinned and shook hands.

"I didn't figure to come to town and get caught up in some conservation scheme that's gonna cost me money," Al said.

"You need to put that money you've got sitting in the bank to work," Patrick countered, tongue in cheek.

The thought of cash in the bank made Al chuckle. "Maybe I should, if you'll put on paper I get first offer to buy if you ever decide to sell."

"We don't need a paper for that," Patrick said. "Another handshake will do."

Pleased with their agreement, the two men shook hands again and parted company.

* * *

A week after arriving at the Double K, Vernon went with Patrick by wagon across the basin to the village of Tularosa. It was an all-day journey from sunup to sundown under a blue sky in a gusting breeze that now and then lashed dust into their eyes. They crossed a grim landscape of prickly pear cactus, mesquite, swales of yucca groves, stands of greasewood, and vast sandy beaches cut by wide arroyos. It was about as desolate a slice of country as Vernon had ever seen, impressive only for the vastness of the parched land and the mountains surrounding it. He thought it a harsh, unappealing country with little value.

But the village of Tularosa surprised Vernon. When they first raised it up, the town appeared like an oasis at the foot of stacked hills that strayed to high country. In town, under cottonwoods that arched with bursting leaves over low adobe houses, surrounded by irrigated fields along a narrow river, the basin vanished from view.

At a well-tended, large hacienda on a side road, Patrick stopped the wagon and called out in rapid Spanish to a young man busy removing a broken section of rim from a wagon wheel. The young man turned, smiled at Patrick, replied, and hurried inside.

Patrick handed Vernon the reins, got down from the wagon, and said, "Wait for me at the general store. It's the first building after the hotel on Main Street."

"Okay."

"Do you speak Spanish?" Patrick asked.

Vernon shook his head. "Hardly a lick. All I made out from what you said were the words for *mother* and *howdy*. I didn't understand that Mexican boy at all."

Patrick eyed him suspiciously. "You know what an *ardilla* is?"

"Nope. What does it mean?"

"I'll tell you later. Remember, you get drunk and you're fired. If you try to bring whiskey to the ranch, you're fired. *¿Comprende?*"

Vernon nodded. "I understand that Mex word."

"Good. Wait for me at the store."

The young man appeared in the hacienda doorway and motioned Patrick to enter.

"What's that other word mean?" Vernon asked again.

"*Ardilla?*"

"That one."

Patrick rattled something off in Spanish that made the young man in the doorway laugh.

"What did you say?"

"I said a man who is called Squirrel by others should at least know his nickname in Spanish."

"It means *squirrel?*"

"Yep. Now, get along," Patrick said as a handsome older Mexican woman brushed past the young man in the doorway and hurried toward him.

Vernon started the team of horses, wondering what had brought Patrick to Tularosa. Over his shoulder he saw the woman reach out, take Patrick's hand, and lead him into the hacienda. He wondered who the woman was and why Patrick had made him come along when any other boss would have left him at the ranch working on chores and such. It didn't make much sense.

After a stop at the post office to mail a letter to his sister in Texas, Vernon parked the wagon in front of the store and took a good look up and down the street. Across from the hotel a cantina attracted a lot of customers. Vernon sauntered over and found the place jammed with men crowded at the tables, lining the long bar, knocking back shots, sipping beer schooners, and filling the air with tobacco smoke. He doubted there was a Revenue agent any closer than El Paso and figured the sheriff had more important matters to attend to than interfering in the late-afternoon pastime of his voting constituents.

He licked his lips and hesitated for a moment before turning on his heel and walking away. At the general store, he spent some of his wages on a shirt, a pair of jeans, a cheap denim work jacket, and cigarette fixings, before heading back to the cantina, where he bought a bottle. Behind the cantina, he took a quick swig and then another before hiding the bottle in his bundle of new clothes, which he stuffed under the wagon seat.

Vernon was certain Patrick was concealing something, and he figured it was more than doing time in Yuma Prison twenty-some years ago. Sure, Patrick was tight-lipped and standoffish—a lot of bosses were like that—but what else did he want kept secret? Vernon recalled that Patrick had been locked up in Yuma for robbery.

Maybe after his parole, he'd returned to his stealing ways before trailing back to New Mexico. Maybe he'd arrived home with a sizable stake of other people's money he'd been using over the years to keep that pretty ranch of his operating in the black. There had been a number of lone-bandit holdups from the old days in Arizona and western New Mexico that as far as he knew had never been solved. Some were big paydays for the robber, if he recalled correctly.

The Double K sure looked like money, the way it was kept up and all. The room at the ranch house where Patrick had him bunk was nicer than any dingy two-bit hotel room, and a hell of a lot nicer than any tar paper shack or bunkhouse. And the herd of horses he owned were the finest cow ponies Vernon had ever seen.

He rolled a cigarette, lit it, contemplated what to do, and decided to have another drink of whiskey while he waited on Patrick. He took a long swallow, poured out the remaining liquor, kicked the empty bottle under the stairs to the general store, and smiled. His plan was simple: stay sober, find out what Patrick had hidden and where it was stashed away, and then steal it.

* * *

Teresa Magdalena Armijo Chávez sat at the table in the huge kitchen of her hacienda, hands busy with sewing while Patrick Kerney ate a bowl of stew and told her his worries about Emma. He spoke effortlessly in Spanish, which she'd taught him as a young boy. Even back then, he'd never been close to her, or anyone else for that matter. Not until Emma.

Miguel, her youngest child, now fully grown and soon to marry, sat next to Patrick. On the night Miguel was born, his father, Ignacio, dead these past five years, staggered home drunk in the company of Patrick and Cal Doran after a fistfight in a cantina with a gringo *pistolero*. Because it was the only time he'd ever come home drunk and because he had beaten the *pistolero* senseless with only one good hand, it became one of Ignacio's favorite stories to tell.

Teresa kept her eyes on her sewing. For the way he'd destroyed his marriage, she had little sympathy for Patrick. It saddened her to hear Emma's condition had worsened over the winter, and although Patrick reported that she'd recovered some, he sounded so discouraged about it that Teresa found no comfort in his words.

"Does she still refuse your help?" she asked.

"I can't do a darn thing for her," he said. "She's bringing Matt out to the ranch next Friday, and I'm looking to hire on a woman to cook and such during their stay and through spring works. I don't want Emma showing up trying to prove how much she can do around the place. Last time she got sick in Las Cruces, young Matt did the chores, and that isn't right. With somebody already there to do the work, I won't have to argue with her about it, and Matt won't have to care for her if she falls ill again while I'm away with the livestock."

More than slightly surprised by Patrick's intended thoughtfulness, Teresa looked up from her sewing. "I have a niece, Evangelina. I could speak with her. She's my oldest brother's only daughter."

"I'd appreciate that," Patrick said. He knew Teresa's brother Flaviano from years back when he visited the family with Cal Doran, but he didn't remember Evangelina. Because village girls married young, he asked her age.

"She's almost twenty."

He raised an eyebrow. "Not married?"

"No."

Patrick wondered if there was something not right with her but held his tongue.

Teresa ignored his doubtful expression and turned to Miguel. "Go ask your uncle Flaviano and Evangelina to come here right away, if they can."

Miguel got to his feet. "Should I tell them why?"

"Yes," Teresa answered.

Miguel left. Patrick waited for Teresa to say more. Instead she returned her attention to her sewing. Her hair had gone gray some, but not completely, her hips were a bit fuller, and she was a touch rounder from bearing four children. None of it took away from her intelligent, inquisitive dark eyes and her pretty oval face.

Never good at making small pleasantries, Patrick lowered his head and concentrated on finishing his bowl of stew. As he soaked up the last of the contents with a warm tortilla, Miguel returned with Flaviano and his daughter in tow. A slight girl with long, thick black hair, she stood partially behind her father, her face hidden. It wasn't until they joined him at the table that Patrick saw the large birthmark on the left side of her face. Pale, almost colorless in contrast to her olive complexion, it covered her cheek and circled above her eye, ending in a slash on her forehead.

Patrick looked away so as not to stare and concentrated on Flaviano.

"You seek a housekeeper, my nephew tells me," Flaviano said. Thick in the chest and big in the arms from years behind a plow, he had a soft, high-pitched voice and a bushy black mustache that covered his upper lip.

"Only for a time," Patrick replied, glancing with a smile at Evangelina. She kept her head lowered, face partially averted. Ignoring the birthmark was difficult, but Patrick saw a strong resemblance to Teresa.

"Miguel says she would look after Emma and your son while they stay with you at the ranch," Flaviano said.

"More to do the cooking, cleaning, and washing," Patrick corrected. "Unless she gets sick, Emma's not one to be looked after."

"She cannot be there alone with you or other vaqueros only," Flaviano stipulated.

"If you say so," Patrick replied.

Flaviano nodded. "I say so."

"That's okay by me. I'll pay her cook's wages for a month, guaranteed, even if Emma and Matt leave before the month is up. Either way, I'll get her right home to you. I need her to start in a week."

"That is fair," Flaviano said, turning to his daughter. "You will work for Señor Kerney."

"Yes, Papa," Evangelina said softy, glancing shyly at Patrick.

"Miguel and I will bring Evangelina to the ranch a day or two early," Teresa declared, clapping her hands together in delight. "And we'll make a fiesta for Emma and Matthew."

"There's no need to go to all that trouble," Patrick said, although the idea intrigued him. Perhaps a party at the ranch was exactly what was needed to soften some of Emma's bad memories.

Teresa laughed. "Ah, Patricio, you never were one for fun. But this time you have no choice. It has been far too long since I've seen Emma, so either we have a small fiesta to celebrate the reunion of old friends or I will ask Flaviano to forbid Evangelina to work for you."

Grinning, Patrick pushed back from the table. "You drive a hard bargain, Teresa. But if we're gonna do this, let's make it a surprise."

Teresa beamed with pleasure. "Yes, what a fine idea."

"Come in five days, so we can get everything ready," Patrick suggested. Feeling suddenly expansive, he turned to Flaviano. "You and your wife must also come. I have more than enough room."

Flaviano smiled warmly. "Gladly. We'll come the day before, and I'll bring my guitar."

"Good." He thanked Teresa for her hospitality, said his good-byes, and left the hacienda with a pleasant feeling of excitement and anticipation about the surprise party for Emma. The idea of it put him in such a good mood, seeing Vernon lounging on the steps in front of the general store didn't sour it at all. If Vernon was drunk, he was fired. If he was sober with a drink or two under his belt, Patrick just might keep him on.

"Have you been drinking?" he asked as Vernon scrambled to his feet.

"Some," Vernon replied, "but I ain't drunk."

"How much is some?" Patrick demanded.

"Two drinks since we got here," Vernon replied defensively.

"Got a bottle hid somewhere to carry back to the ranch?"

"Nope, I was planning to but changed my mind. Poured it out and threw it away. It's under the stairs."

Patrick took a look, gave Vernon fifty cents, and pointed to the diner down the street. "Get yourself a meal while I care for the horses and get some provisions. We're heading back home in half an hour."

"We ain't staying over in town?"

"That's right," Patrick answered as he swung up onto the wagon seat. "Jingle those spurs."

"I'm going," Vernon replied, setting off for the diner.

"Half an hour," Patrick called after him, "or I leave you behind."

* * *

Patrick kept the team of horses at a steady trot until nightfall. He stopped to make camp under a clear, star-filled sky, with a sliver of moon cresting the Sacramento Mountains, and had Vernon build a fire next to a large cairn on the west slope of a wide arroyo. Vernon had the coffeepot boiling by the time Patrick finished unhitching, watering, and hobbling the ponies for the night. He added a rock he'd picked to the cairn and warmed his hands at the fire.

"What's the marker for?" Vernon asked as he poured Patrick a cup.

"An old boy name George died here on his way home to the ranch during a big gully washer. Crawled under the wagon, went to sleep, and never woke up. Leastways, that's what I believe happened. His heart gave out on him."

"Is he buried here?"

Patrick shook his head. "We laid him to rest at the ranch."

"One of them graves up on the hill behind the ranch house?"

"That's right," Patrick replied.

"He must have been a good man for y'all to do that."

"He was."

Vernon threw a mesquite root on the fire and hunkered down on his bedroll. "Look here, I've been meaning to apologize for mistaking you for that Pat Floyd fellow."

"Pay it no mind," Patrick said. "From what you said, it was a long time ago when you knew him in prison. I don't envy you the time being locked up."

"Ain't no fun losing your freedom," Vernon allowed, stringing along with Patrick's charade. He wondered how far he'd take it. "I appreciate you giving me work, knowing I was in prison and all."

"You're earning your keep. Besides, there isn't a good man in these parts who hasn't stretched the law every now and then."

"Well, I didn't kill anyone," Vernon said, thinking Pat Floyd knew different. "How come you didn't ask me what I'd done?"

Patrick shrugged. "It isn't my place to ask."

"I reckon that's so," Vernon said, deadpan to keep from laughing in Patrick's face. "I was a clerk in a store and I got caught taking things. I'd never done anything like that before. I pled to petty larceny to get a lighter sentence."

"Bad luck," Patrick said.

"You could say that," Vernon replied.

Patrick finished his coffee and said, "I'm gonna turn in." He spread out his bedroll feeling good about hornswoggling Vernon, who'd been sent to Yuma Prison for manslaughter. As he recalled, it had something to do with a barroom fight that went bad. Vernon's lie was proof enough to Patrick that he had him fooled. "My son and his mother are coming out to the ranch in a week to stay a spell," he added, "and I'm gonna throw a surprise party for them."

"You gonna want me to make myself scarce and head back to the shepherd's shack?" Vernon asked.

"No reason why you can't stay and enjoy the fun," Patrick replied, feeling magnanimous. "I've hired a girl to keep house and cook while they're here, and folks will be coming in from Tularosa. Tomorrow or the next day I'll ride out and invite some neighbors, folks Emma liked when she lived at the ranch."

"She just lives in town now?"

"We got a divorce a while back," Patrick answered as he pulled off his boots and stuck them in the bottom of his bedroll.

"Sorry to hear it."

"Ain't something I like talking about. If you stay sober, I may keep you on for a spell. I know what liquor can do to a body."

"I guessed maybe you did, what with your rule against liquor at the ranch and your hard talk about it. How you gonna keep folks from drinking at the fiesta?"

"I won't even try," Patrick replied as he settled under the blanket. "But remember, you're the hired hand. Either you're man enough to avoid temptation, or you're not. Get drunk and you're fired."

"You're the boss."

Patrick grunted and rolled on his side. "We start early come morning."

Vernon covered up with his blanket and let his thoughts roam. He'd have a chance to take a real good look around the ranch when Patrick went off to invite neighbor folks to the fiesta. If he got lucky and found valuables, or better yet a sizable amount of cash money, he'd take it all, steal a pony, and skedaddle. If not, he'd keep looking when he had the opportunity.

Either way, he wasn't gonna leave the Double K with just wages in his pocket. His time working at the Double K was gonna cost old Pat Floyd a hell of lot more than that.

5

Emma fully expected to arrive in Engle and find Patrick ready to start out immediately on the lengthy wagon ride to the ranch. Consequently, she boarded the train with Matthew equipped not only with enough clothes for their ten-day stay, but with blankets, hats, scarves, and mittens to keep them warm on a journey that would last deep into the night.

Away from the bright green irrigated fields bordering the Rio Grande, the landscape hadn't changed much since the arrival of motorcars. Unpaved dirt roads, often rutted, petered out when further passage by anything other than a horse and wagon proved impossible. The train entered the Jornada, a sandy, waterless, twisted desert country hemmed in by the Rio Grande to the west and a string of mountain ranges that blackened the eastern horizon, interrupted by broken tablelands and tumbled hills.

The railroad tracks paralleled the old Camino Real, used by Spanish settlers traveling north to Santa Fe. For centuries the road served as the primary trade route between Mexico and remote New Mexico outposts. The small town of Engle, created by the coming of the railroad, sat in the middle of the Jornada and for a time had been an important commerce and shipping point for the large ranches, which often encompassed a hundred square miles or more, sprawling from the river to the mountains.

Now in decline, the town consisted of a few remaining shops, post office, hotel, livery, train station, school, and some small frame houses, all clustered on the flats along the rail line. Because the town had no marshal and the sheriff was miles away in the county seat of Hot Springs, Engle was an attractive haven for drifting cowboys, transients, vagrants, and a smattering of notorious outlaws encamped in the nearby San Andres Mountains.

On previous trips to the ranch, Matthew had always put on his sourpuss face during the journey, acting out of sorts for being forced to leave home during school vacations, thus abandoning his playmates and friends in Las Cruces. This time he seemed more agreeable, even somewhat eager to visit the ranch. Emma decided it had to do with escaping the aftermath of Jimmy Potter's death, which continued to dampen Matt's spirits.

She sat across from him in the half-empty passenger car, watching as he read for the third time the book Gene Rhodes had sent him. The train lurched forward slightly as it gathered speed, causing Matt to look up from his book.

"Are all the folks Gene writes about in his books and stories real people?" he asked.

"As far as I can tell, I don't think so," Emma replied.

"My teacher, Mr. Savacool, says that Gene shouldn't write about real people and call it fiction."

"Why is that?" Emma asked.

"He says it isn't a made-up story if you just write about real people and tell what they did. He said the story Gene wrote about you was just a fancy newspaper article about something that really happened."

"Do you think Mr. Savacool is right?"

Matt shrugged. "He knows a lot."

"Do you like Gene's writing?" Emma asked.

"Yeah, I do."

"Then that's what matters," Emma said. "I like his writing too. He knows what he's writing about and wraps it up in a first-rate yarn that makes places and people come alive. Only very good writers do that."

"That's the same way it is for me," Matt said.

Emma smiled. "Then we both agree that Mr. Savacool is wrong."

A worried look crossed Matt's face. "I can't tell him that."

Emma laughed. "You don't have to and probably shouldn't anyway."

Matt grinned. "I best not. Do you think Pa has read Gene's story about you?"

"I don't know. He hasn't mentioned it."

"I brought along a copy of it for him. Mr. Duncan at the drugstore had an extra one he gave me. You don't mind, do you?"

"No, I'd like him to read it if he hasn't already. It was a happy time for us back then." The train slowed and Emma glanced out the window. Up ahead she saw the top of the water tower at the Engle station come into view. "We're almost there."

Matt closed his book and scooted next to Emma for a look. "Do you see him?"

"Not yet." Emma stood quickly and reached for the bags. For a few seconds she felt dizzy and had to steady herself with a hand on the seat back. During the past week, her light-headedness had returned—not as severely or as consistently as before, but enough to be troubling.

She handed Matthew his satchel and looked out the window again. There was no sign of Patrick, and his wagon wasn't parked next to the station. "After the train stops, you go fetch Patches from the livestock car and I'll find your pa."

"Okay."

When they disembarked, Matt left his satchel on the platform with Emma and made tracks to the livestock car at the rear of the train. Except for the stationmaster and the conductor, the platform was empty. Worried thoughts tumbled through Emma's mind. Had something happened at the ranch? Had Patrick started drinking again?

She hoped not. He'd promised Matthew that they would train Patches to be a working cow pony, and that promise had helped Matt perk up considerably about the visit.

She glanced in Matthew's direction and relaxed. Patrick and the train brakeman were at the livestock car pushing a ramp against the door. Lickety-split, Matthew jumped on the ramp, pushed open the door, and disappeared inside. Within a few minutes he reemerged, leading Patches off the car. Even from a distance, she could see a big smile on his face.

She waited for them at the edge of the platform. Halter-led by Matthew, Patches came along a little skittish, eyeing the noisy locomotive suspiciously, with Patrick following a few steps behind.

"Where's your wagon?" she asked Patrick after he tipped his hat in greeting.

"At the livery, where we'll stable Patches," he answered, picking up her bag and Matthew's satchel. "I've taken rooms at the hotel for the night. I figure this young cowboy is old enough to want to stop sharing a room with his ma, so we each get one."

Matthew grinned. "Aces," he said.

Emma searched Patrick's face. "What's the occasion?"

"Nothing special," he replied as they ambled toward the livery.

"I brought you the story that Gene Rhodes wrote about Ma, and you're in it," Matt said.

"I've heard about that," Patrick said. "Is it a good story?"

"The best I've ever read."

"I'll take a gander at it after we eat. The hotel dining room is serving up a special pork chop dinner tonight and I'm hankering for a plateful. How does that sound to you?"

The idea of having his very own hotel room for the night *and* a plateful of pork chops at dinner made Matt pull Patches along to the livery in a hurry.

* * *

Vernon Clagett didn't care much for the Mexicans who'd showed up at the Double K. The first to arrive were three women and three men, including the young buck who'd greeted Patrick at the hacienda in Tularosa. To make room for them, Patrick had moved Vernon out of the casita behind the ranch house to bunk in the barn. Vernon didn't like being ousted by Mexicans—the idea of it went against the grain—and he found it mighty irritating that they jabbered to one another in Spanish all the time. He righteously believed people should talk American in America, and that included Mexicans. And although they didn't show him any disrespect, he didn't cotton to them acting like they were equal to a white man. That just wasn't right either.

After Patrick left to fetch his son and ex-wife from the train station in Engle, Vernon felt downright surrounded by the Mexicans. The feeling had worsened this morning, when four more of them showed up, including two children. It was about intolerable until two neighboring ranch families arrived with a passel of kids, all white folks as far as he could tell, which eased his mind considerably. All told, a crowd of some twenty people were busy preparing for the fiesta that was due to start the minute Patrick arrived with his ex-wife and his young button.

Before the first bunch of Mexican guests arrived with the temporary housekeeper, Patrick had left for a spell on two different days to invite some of the neighbors to the party. Vernon used the time to poke around for any valuables, gold, or money that might be hidden in the house or around the ranch headquarters. He found fifty dollars in greenbacks in a desk drawer he picked open, but nothing else worth stealing. He considered taking the money and leaving by shank's mare but decided not to risk Patrick riding him down before he got far enough away. Besides, he was still curious about what might be hidden somewhere on the ranch. In Las Cruces he'd heard stories about treasure in the San Andres Mountains, and the Double K covered a big slice of that country. There was a legend of a lost, rich gold mine worked by a priest and his congregation back in the old Spanish days, tales of vast Apache plunder taken during the Indian Wars concealed in sealed-up caves, and rumors of a fortune in Spanish gold ingots buried deep inside an enormous mountain cavern.

Maybe it was hogwash and had nothing to do with Patrick and the Double K, but Vernon wasn't finished snooping around and remained convinced old Pat Floyd had something more than fifty dollars in a locked desk drawer that he didn't want found.

In the tack room, the driest, cleanest part of the barn, Vernon had assembled a stout bunk bed out of scrap lumber and covered it with a thick straw mattress made up of gunnysacks sewn together. It was away from the constant chatter coming from the ranch house, so after he put out a fresh salt block in the horse pasture, he went back to the tack room, closed the door, and began cleaning and mending the reins, bridles, and halters Patrick wanted put in good repair. Spring works would start right after the woman and the boy returned to Las Cruces.

The room had saddles on built-in racks along one wall, with a row of pegs above for bridles and halters. A large trunk against the back wall held blankets, sheets, leg wraps, several worn-out Indian saddle blankets, and cloth scraps good for cleaning. On the very bottom was a smaller, padlocked army box with PVT. PATRICK KERNEY stenciled on the lid. Next to the big trunk stood an old Mexican cabinet made of thick pine on sturdy legs; it held grooming tools, spare bits, horse medicine, ointments, and a sewing kit filled with odds and ends of leather and rawhide good for patching. On top of the cabinet were some brand-new, shiny grain buckets.

Vernon removed the army box with Patrick's name on it and set it aside before getting to work. Patrick kept his tack, like his ponies, in top condition, so there wasn't much fixing for Vernon to do. He cleaned everything good and started in on the saddles, mending a small tear on one fender, a loose seam on a skirt, and the binding to a billet strap. Done with repairs, he put the sewing kit away, returned the saddles to the racks, and inspected the padlocked army box.

Born in a Brooklyn slum, Vernon had learned lock picking from his uncle, who'd used him as a lookout during burglaries before his parents moved the family west to Texas. It was a skill he'd honed over the years.

Inside the army box he found a Rough Riders uniform, a campaign hat, two Spanish-American War Campaign Medals, and a Rough Rider medal from Teddy Roosevelt. In a small oilskin pouch tucked inside the uniform shirt were some military papers and hospital records made out for Patrick Kerney along with a letter granting a full pardon to convict Pat Floyd signed by the governor of the territory of Arizona and the superintendent of the Yuma Prison, Thomas Gates. Tucked in with the pardon was a letter from Mrs. Dora Ingalls, who oversaw the prison library. In it she wrote that Pat Floyd's work as a trustee assigned to the prison library had been commendable and he deserved a second chance to become a law-abiding citizen.

Vernon smiled and put everything back in the box except the pardon, which he hid in the bottom corner of his gunnysack mattress. He was one up on old Pat Floyd now, he thought gleefully. How he was going to turn that into an advantage, well, he would have to cogitate on that some before playing out his hand.

* * *

Emma couldn't remember the last time she'd truly enjoyed Patrick's company, but it certainly preceded their divorce more than eight years past. Last night at dinner, he'd been almost charming, at ease with Matthew and attentive to her without his usual flashes of irritability or defensiveness. He completely captured Matthew's interest by talking about how they would train Patches during this visit to the ranch, and he utterly surprised Emma by telling her about some rangeland he had recently bought and planned to restore. Patrick was normally closemouthed about anything to do with the ranch, and never loquacious by nature, so his unusual behavior kept Emma awake and wondering about him for a while after she tucked in a sleepy, happy Matthew and retired to her room.

In the morning at breakfast, Emma half expected Patrick to revert to his typical distant ways, but he remained talkative, actually dawdling over his coffee after the meal, which she found amazing. Usually, he wanted everything done in a hurry so he could get on to whatever needed doing next.

They left Engle with the morning sun warming the day, a slight breeze wafting down the slope of the mountains, and Matthew riding Patches ahead of the wagon with orders from Emma to always remain within sight.

"He'd have to stray afar to get himself lost," Patrick said.

"Do you think I'm too much of a fussy mother hen?" Emma asked.

"I didn't say that," he answered. "But it isn't a bad thing for a boy to get lost once or twice. It can test his mettle and teach him a thing or two about life."

Emma glanced at Patrick. Was he talking about Matthew or himself? As a young boy, Patrick had often been alone and forgotten in the mining camps of northern New Mexico while his crazy aunt and her lover drank themselves into stupors.

She reached over and gripped his free hand.

"What's that for?" Patrick asked, astonished by her gesture. She hadn't deliberately touched him in years.

"You weren't lost as a child; you were abandoned."

Patrick slowed the horses. "I wasn't talking about myself."

"I think you were," Emma replied softly as she removed her hand. "And I think that's why you hated me for leaving."

Patrick stopped the team and turned to face Emma. "I've never hated you. You've hated me for what I did to you."

Emma bit her lip, shook her head. "I take it back. It hasn't been hatred for either of us."

"Then what is it?"

Emma paused, collected her thoughts, and sighed. "I'm just starting to make sense of it now. In different ways, I think neither of us ever counted on anything good happening in our lives, and we were dead certain if it did it wouldn't last."

"I'll admit to that," Patrick said as he flicked the reins to start the team. "But I don't see it in you, not with your spunk and boldness."

Emma smiled plaintively. Acting brave and strong kept at bay the constant reality of being imprisoned, raped, and abused as a girl. That was how Patrick found her, yet he couldn't or wouldn't see the hidden damage it had done. She wondered how many untold women endured rape of one sort or another, and how many legions of men believed it to be their right. For Emma, forcing Patrick to accept the wrongness of his act had been a defiant moral crusade, one she'd been proud to win.

"You never liked my boldness and spunk," she said.

Patrick glanced over at Emma. "That's unkind of you to say."

Emma laughed.

"So is laughing at me," Patrick added.

Emma laughed again. "I'm laughing because we've been talking, not squabbling, and you haven't lost your temper yet."

Patrick smiled. "That's true, ain't it?"

"Keep acting nice and I'll start to expect it," Emma cautioned.

Patrick snorted. "Don't count on it; I'm probably just off my feed."

"My goodness, are you showing a sense of humor?" Emma asked, feigning disbelief.

"Trying to, I reckon," Patrick answered with a grin.

"Did you read Gene's story about our roundup?"

Patrick nodded. "It got me remembering that there were good times between us—lots of them, as I recall."

"It wasn't all dreadful," Emma allowed. "And I don't say that to sting you."

"Just to keep me at arm's length," Patrick ventured. "I've finally got that one figured."

There was no hint of bitterness in Patrick's voice. Emma searched his face. "Have you?"

"Yep."

"It would be nice if we could stay friendly, especially for Matthew's sake."

"I'd like that," Patrick replied.

Up ahead, the fringe of the Jornada gave way to the upward slopes of the San Andres Mountains, a far gentler incline than the rugged eastern face of the mountains. In the distance where the road curved out of sight behind a grove of junipers, Matthew patiently waited on Patches.

"How come you've been just dillydallying along this morning?" Emma queried. "That's not like you. You're always in a hurry to get back to the ranch."

Patrick flicked the reins and the ponies picked up the pace. "I hired on a man to help me get ready for spring works," he explained. "No need to rush; he's keeping an eye on the place."

Not convinced of Patrick's truthfulness, Emma let it go by. "Still, I'd like to get there before nightfall," she said. "Are you ever going to get a truck or a motorcar?"

Patrick shrugged. "Maybe someday I will. A used army truck might do once the county gets around to building decent roads. I remember Cal telling me after he saw his first automobile that he didn't want to be part of a world where folks stopped riding ponies. I guess I feel the same way."

Emma giggled.

"What?"

"It's too late. That world is already here."

Patrick grunted disgustedly.

"Are you becoming a cantankerous old man?" Emma asked.

Patrick urged the ponies into a smooth trot. "There are worse things a man could become," he answered, thinking about the hard cases at Yuma Prison and Vernon Clagett at the ranch. Maybe it hadn't been smart to hire him on. "We'll hurry along for a spell, if that will please you," he added.

* * *

After a short, late stop for a lunch of ham sandwiches packed by the hotel's cook and a box of Barnum's Animal Crackers that Matt single-handedly devoured before loping ahead on Patches, they turned onto the ranch road for home. Emma always loved the way through the high country and the astounding view of Victorio Peak hovering over a hidden basin nestled inside mountainous folds. But she loved best entering the horse pasture those last few miles to the ranch, with the entire Tularosa stretched out below her. Today it seemed more beautiful than ever under a bank of high clouds lit by a sinking sun, long, drifting shadows on the ground curling across sugar-white dunes.

Although she'd lost sight of Matthew for some time, it caused her no worry. He knew his way along the ranch road through the pasture, and although he might tarry here or there, he wouldn't stray. She'd fallen silent since that first glimpse of the Tularosa, as had Patrick. Despite all their years living on the land, the grandeur of it still could make talk superficial, words inadequate. Emma let the joy of seeing it again soak into her.

A faint whoop and a holler carried along on the breeze, and the sound of approaching horses on the road captured Emma's attention. Patrick reined to a stop, and out of a swirling cloud of dust came Matthew and five riders, who quickly circled the wagon. She looked up to see Al Jennings, Juan Chávez, Earl Hightower, Flaviano Armijo, and Miguel Chávez smiling down at her.

"Look who I found at the ranch, Ma!" Matthew said, grinning with excitement.

"Señora," Juan Chávez said in Spanish, removing his hat in a courtly gesture. "We have come to escort you to a fiesta in your honor. Many guests await your presence."

Emma's heart fluttered in her chest. Never had anybody ever done such a thing for her. She looked at Patrick, who smiled and cocked his head in the direction of the ranch house.

"Want to ride in and see what all these gents are talking about?" he asked.

Emma nodded, almost speechless. "Lead on, if you please, gentlemen."

"As you wish, señora," Juan replied with another grand sweep of his hat.

The horsemen formed up around the wagon and the procession began. As they drew close, Emma saw Teresa waving from the veranda, along with Dolly Jennings; Addie Hightower; Juan's wife, Adelina; Cristina Armijo; and her daughter Evangelina. Everyone, including the children who lined the railing, called out greetings. Bunting and a dozen lanterns festooned the veranda. A cow roasted on a spit above the hot embers of a freshly dug pit.

To keep from crying, she reached out and grasped Patrick's hand. "Is this your doing?"

"Only somewhat," he replied quietly, reining in the ponies.

Surrounded by the women, who quickly spirited her away, she was given no chance to thank him.

6

The fiesta continued deep into the night. Flaviano started the party going with his guitar, and the dancing began when Juan, Teresa's oldest son, took out his fiddle. A late meal served by the women gathered everyone at long tables on the veranda, a full moon cresting the distant Sacramento Mountains, sprinkling the basin with a silvery glow. Platters of tender beef strips, bowls of frijoles, stacks of tortillas, plates of steamed cactus leaves that tasted like green beans, and tureens of green chili stew were passed around the table. There were hard-boiled eggs, roasted potatoes, and bread fresh from the oven. Everyone ate their fill and then some.

After dinner, the men remained at the table long enough to finish the last of the homemade wine served with the meal. The children scurried off to play before the women corralled them for kitchen chores. Caught up in conversation with women she dearly loved, Emma didn't worry about keeping an eye on either Matthew or Patrick. Occasionally Matthew whizzed through the kitchen with Al Jr., both boys enjoying a rare late night up with no bedtime and a seemingly endless supply of *biscochitos* and bread pudding to feast on. Down at the roasting pit, the men congregated around the warmth of the glowing embers, jawing between sips from flasks of bootleg whiskey. The notion of Patrick getting drunk gave Emma pause for a moment, but she shrugged it off, deciding not even that could spoil such a wonderful surprise party.

When the mealtime chores were almost done, Dolly Jennings and Addie Hightower shooed Emma and Teresa out of the kitchen. They adjourned to the living room and settled on a couch that faced the window overlooking the veranda. Reflected moonlight on the faraway white sand dunes sparkled like countless earthbound stars.

"I've been meaning to tell you that Evangelina will be your housekeeper until you and Matthew return to Las Cruces," Teresa said.

"That's ridiculous," Emma sputtered, completely taken by surprise. "I don't need any help. I can't allow it. Was this your idea?"

"No, it was Patrick's," Teresa replied with a smile, tickled as always by Emma's unflagging gumption to stay independent no matter what. "He came to the hacienda asking if I knew someone he could hire for the job, and I suggested Evangelina. He knew it would be best to arrange something before you arrived so you couldn't reject the notion, just as you are trying to do now."

Emma squared her shoulders. "Well, it's just unnecessary."

"I don't think that is so," Teresa replied with a gentle smile. "I can see you tire easily."

"Only a bit now and then," Emma grudgingly admitted. "Was it your idea to have a fiesta?"

"Patrick and I teamed up on it."

Emma raised an eyebrow.

Teresa laughed off Emma's doubtfulness. "I proposed it, *real-*

mente, but he needed no encouragement, and it was his suggestion that it should be a surprise."

"That I can almost believe," Emma said. "Although it's surely not what I'm used to from him."

"*Sí,* it is not Patrick's nature to think to bring gladness to others. I hope you will not disappoint Evangelina and send her away when we depart tomorrow. Before we left Tularosa, she told me how happy she would be to escape from her parents for a brief time. They are very strict with her."

"Well, I can't spoil it for her, can I?" Emma said with a sigh. "Besides, it will be nice to have the companionship of another woman here during our stay."

Teresa clapped her hands. "Excellent."

"She is a pretty girl if you look past the birthmark."

"Yes, but she does not believe that to be so," Teresa replied. "Flaviano has tried often to arrange an engagement for her but without success. So many of the young men have left the village, there are now only a few unmarried ones left. None of them have an interest in her as a wife. Some think her birthmark is a sign of a sorcerer. She has been shunned all her life by the village boys, and none of the gringos who show interest have honorable intentions."

"How sad," Emma said.

"Patrick insisted she should stay in the casita," Teresa said, "which pleased Flaviano. He is very protective of her. He thinks men try to take advantage because of her appearance, believing she might be willing to give away her virtue in the hopes of achieving marriage."

"Do you think she is inclined to do that?"

"Perhaps a bit," Teresa said with a small smile. "But she is neither silly nor stupid."

"Didn't we all have such foolish thoughts when we were young?" Emma conjectured.

"*Sí*, but luckily the boys didn't know it," Teresa replied. As a new bride, she'd lived for a year at the Double K in the casita her husband, Ignacio, had built for her. She remembered how frightened she'd been at first to be taken so far from home, and what a happy year it had been. "Do you miss this place?" she asked.

"Sometimes very much," Emma replied.

"It holds many good memories," Teresa said. "Tonight I think the children should do something special to remember this fiesta. The night is so beautiful and calm, perhaps we should allow them to sleep under the stars bundled up on the veranda."

"What a wonderful idea!" Emma said. "If I could, I'd sleep outside every night for the rest of my life."

Teresa laughed. "Always the maverick."

"*Bold* is what Patrick calls me, and not to flatter," Emma replied. "Tonight you'll share my bed. We'll pretend we are silly young girls and gossip and whisper secrets to each other into the wee hours."

"Yes," Teresa exclaimed. "It will make me forget how old I've become." Her lighthearted expression turned serious. "Let me start the gossip now by asking, who is that man who works for Patrick?"

Emma shook her head. "I don't know. I haven't met him, nor have I seen him at all tonight. Has he caused trouble?"

"No, but I find him not pleasant," Teresa answered. "Perhaps it is nothing."

"I'll keep my eye on him, especially around Evangelina, and ask Patrick to do the same."

"*Gracias,* my dear friend," Teresa said as she stood. "Now, shall we tell the other ladies of our plan? Morning will come soon enough, and it's way past time to put the little ones to bed."

"Let's," Emma said, getting to her feet. "What a wonderful day this has been."

"*Perfecto*," Teresa replied as she embraced her.

They stepped onto the veranda. Below, the women and the children had joined the men around the roasting pit, now a luminous, crackling fire lighting up the night. As if on cue, Juan began to sing "The Ballad of Reyes Ruiz," accompanied by Flaviano on his guitar. When the last notes faded away, a moment of warm silence prevailed. In that moment, the sight of Matthew and Patrick standing side by side, Patrick's hand resting gently on his son's shoulder, made the day flawless for Emma.

Her eyes filled with tears. "*Perfecto*," she whispered.

* * *

Before first light, Patrick found Vernon asleep in the tack room and shook him awake. "I want you to gather the wagon teams from the horse pasture and feed and water them before folks sit down for breakfast," he said. "They'll want to be heading home soon after they eat."

"Can't the Mexicans take care of their own livestock?" Vernon asked peevishly as he pulled on his boots.

"Those folks are friends and my guests," Patrick snapped, in no mood for back talk. His last drink of whiskey at the fiesta last night had given him a headache that hadn't let up. The right side of his head throbbed in sharp pain, his nose felt stuffy, and his blurry eye wouldn't stop watering. "Do as you're told or get off the ranch."

Vernon held up a hand to ward off more criticism and smiled weakly. "I meant no offense; I'm just tired is all. I didn't get much sleep last night what with the music, singing, and such."

"You could've joined in," Patrick said unsympathetically. Vernon's excuse made no sense. "I didn't see you once last night."

Vernon shook his head. "I don't much fit in with most of them folks. Besides, I didn't want to risk getting drunk and having you fire me, so I just stayed put right here, away from temptation."

Patrick held the lantern closer to Vernon to see if he'd been drinking. He looked back at him with clear eyes and a smug expression on his face. "There's a fresh pot of coffee on the stove, and Evangelina will fix you breakfast. Have something to eat and get to work."

"Is that the name of the Mexican girl who's staying on as a housekeeper?" Vernon asked as he tucked in his shirt. "I bet she don't get much male attention what with that awful mark on her face."

"Don't get any notions," Patrick said.

Vernon chuckled. "Keeping that one for yourself?"

"Get a move on before I kick you down the road by the seat of your pants," Patrick replied gruffly.

"Don't get all riled," Vernon sneered as he made for the door. "I'm going."

"When you finish with the horses, load the salt blocks on the wagon and drop them off where I showed you in the south cow pasture," Patrick added. "Don't put them where the grass is scant."

"You already told me that half a dozen times," Vernon replied.

Patrick followed behind, wondering why Vernon, who'd been meek until now, had suddenly become belligerent. He returned to the tack room and took a quick look around for a bottle stashed somewhere, thinking maybe booze was supplying Vernon with liquored-up moxie. There was no hooch to be found, not even under all the horse blankets and bandage rolls in the trunk. He eyed the old wooden army locker with his name painted on the top. It showed smudge marks on the lid. He jiggled the lock hard, but it held firm. Still, the smudge marks bothered him. He hadn't touched the locker since who knew when. Had Vernon been snooping? Patrick didn't doubt it. Where else had he been poking around?

As he crossed from the barn to the house, Patrick determined to be shucked of Vernon no matter what. He would pay him his wages and send him packing at week's end. The decision eased his mind considerably.

In the kitchen, Vernon sat at the table wolfing down a plate of *huevos* and beans, his eyes fixed on Evangelina as she moved around the room. A slender, well-formed girl, she moved with a natural ease pleasing to the eye. Patrick asked for some coffee and Evangelina brought it to him quickly, with a small smile on her face.

"I am very happy you gave me this job, Señor Patrick," she said.

Patrick took the cup from her and nodded. "And I'm glad you're here to help out."

At the table, Vernon smirked and wiped a sleeve across his mouth to try to hide it.

Patrick nodded at the kitchen door. "Get going."

"I'm hurrying," Vernon replied. He gulped his coffee, pushed back from the table, gave Evangelina a last once-over, and headed out the door.

"Was he bothering you?" Patrick asked. His headache had eased up and his eye had stopped watering.

"No, señor, I am used to such men. They look and I say nothing."

"Okay." Before he could say more, the kitchen filled with bustling women intent on rousing sleepy children out of their bedding on the veranda and getting started on the business of fixing breakfast. He studied Emma as she stoked the cookstove firebox.

She gave him a happy look and he smiled in return, pleased to see her in good spirits. Maybe it would last, maybe not. With Emma he never knew, but at least this visit had started out as the best ever since their divorce. He hoped it would stay that way.

* * *

Except for Teresa and her youngest son, Miguel, who—much to Emma's delight—would stay over another day, everyone departed before midmorning. As the last wagon left, Matt plucked at Patrick's sleeve and reminded him of his promise to start training Patches right away.

"It's a promise I aim to keep," Patrick said, turning to Miguel, who'd sought out his company as a safe haven away from the womenfolk. "Are you disposed to climb on a pony and go ahorseback riding with me and my boy?"

Miguel grinned. "I'd like that."

"I already know how to ride," Matt said, frowning in disappointment.

"Sure you do," Patrick replied. "But we need to start slow with Patches and see what he knows, what his habits are, before we start working him. Maybe he's got a wrong idea or two in his head that needs fixing, or maybe he gets out of sorts if asked to do something that upsets him."

"He's not like that at all," Matt said defensively. "He's a good pony."

"I believe it," Patrick replied. "But I need to see him in action with some cows, savvy?"

Matt brightened at the idea of working Patches with cows. "I know he'll do just swell with them."

"Then let's give him a chance to prove himself," Patrick said with an appraising glance at Miguel, whom he knew to be farm raised but no horseman. "I've got an easy-riding buckskin that might suit you, unless you'd like a pony that's a bit more lively."

"The buckskin is best, I think," Miguel replied.

"Good choice," Patrick said, clapping his hands together. "Let's stop wasting time, cut out our ponies, and get them saddled. It's a good hour's ride to the south cow pasture."

After promising to return in time for dinner, they left with lunches of thick beef sandwiches fixed by the women and packed in their saddlebags. As they moseyed along, Patrick talked horses—a subject he loved—especially cow ponies. He praised Calabaza, the pumpkin-colored cayuse he rode, as one of the three smartest cutting horses he'd ever owned. He described how Calabaza could spin and dart quickly to separate a calf from an angry mother or keep a wild-eyed, snot-snorting steer from bolting the herd.

He'd put Miguel on a calm, gentle twelve-year-old gelding named Stony, a pony best suited for night work on the trail after the herd bedded down.

"A skittish pony can easily make cattle nervous, restless, prone to run at night," Patrick explained as he drew rein halfway across the pasture. "Old Stony here stays peaceful no matter what. Nothing much bothers him."

"You have many ponies," Miguel said. "I count over fifty in this pasture."

Patrick nodded. "A few of them are poor stock—too old to work and too muleheaded to learn. I don't know why I keep them. If you have need of a worthless pony with bad manners, I'll sell you one at a good price."

Miguel laughed. "I think not."

"You're a wise man," Patrick said. Up ahead, Matt was a good quarter mile away, making horse tracks for the cow pasture. "Best jingle our spurs, before young Matt gets too far ahead of us."

"Should we gallop to catch up?" Miguel asked.

"No need. The only time to run a horse hard is in an emergency. Matt will stay in sight."

They reached the gate to the south cow pasture just as Vernon arrived on his way back from putting out the salt blocks. He told them there were about twenty head of cattle at the dirt tank over the next rise two miles distant.

"Turn the wagon around and follow us," Patrick said. The idea of Vernon at the ranch house alone with three women just didn't sit right.

"You got something else you need me to do out here?" Vernon asked cantankerously.

"I'll let you know if I do," Patrick said evenly. "Turn the wagon around."

Vernon shrugged. "You're the boss."

Patrick turned to Matt. "Get on over to the tank and take a look. We'll catch up."

Matt grinned and spurred Patches into a fast canter, heading up the rise, kicking up dust.

Patrick slow-trotted along, accompanied by Miguel, Vernon rattling behind in the wagon.

"I thought galloping was to be done only in an emergency," Miguel said.

"A boy on a fast pony might not agree with that notion," Patrick said with a chuckle as Matt disappeared over the first rise.

He spurred Calabaza into a fast lope and soon came upon Matt at the hilltop overlooking the dirt tank. Twenty-three cattle lounged nearby. A quarter mile away, two steers and a yearling were at one of the salt blocks Vernon had put out.

Patrick knew every animal in the bunch. He'd cut each of them from the herd and thrown them into the south pasture, where they would stay until after spring works. None of them had wintered well. About a third were scrubby calves and yearlings abandoned by their mothers, another third were dry stock no longer fit for breeding, and the rest were a mixture of old steers and anemic half-wild heifers Patrick had chased out of their high-country hiding thickets.

Spring works was for branding, not selling. Typically, Patrick would hold these animals over as feeders until fall, fatten them up, and sell them to the packers along with the rest of the beeves. But this year, with the grasses scant over the winter, a dry spring, and falling cattle prices, reducing the size of his herd now made sense. He'd rest some grassland and build the herd back up next year if the rains came.

"What are we gonna do, Pa?" Matt asked impatiently, pulling Patrick back to the moment.

"Walk Patches real slow down to the cows so as not to spook them."

"Then what?"

"Ride him in and out of the bunch a couple times. Pick out a critter and see if Patches is interested in nudging it over to the salt block yonder."

"How do I do that?"

"Keep Patches pointed right at the cow. That's his target. Don't let him lose sight of the animal. When it tries to scamper, move Patches sideways, turn him fast, back him up, or draw rein if you have to. The idea is to get Patches thinking it's a game. If he likes what you're asking him to do, he'll catch on."

Matt looked uncertain.

"You can do it," Patrick said. "You're a good rider." Behind, he heard Miguel and Vernon approaching.

Matt set his jaw, nodded, and walked Patches down to the tank. The bunch stirred, backed up, and scooted away when he got close. He rode a wide circle around the cows before urging Patches toward a small group of yearlings, which quickly scattered. His attempt to move a bellowing heifer toward the salt block ended in a draw when the heifer charged and Matt retreated. He drew rein and gave Patrick a frustrated look.

"Is the cow dangerous?" Miguel asked Patrick in a whisper.

"Any critter that big can hurt you if it has a mind to," Patrick replied. He cupped his hands and called out to Matt. "Try again. Forget about the salt block. Pick one cow and follow it wherever it goes. Get as close to it as you can."

On the next try, Matt chased a gaunt yearling a good half mile around the dirt tank. Although he struggled some to stay in front of the bobbing animal, it was clear that both horse and rider liked the chase. With little urging on Matt's part, Patches stopped and turned quickly, but when the yearling unexpectedly veered and darted away, Matt tried to cut it off by wheeling Patches too abruptly. The pony balked and dumped Matt into a fresh cow pie. He was on his feet and brushing himself off when Patrick and Miguel got to him.

"Patches never did that to me before," he said sheepishly. His pony stood quietly nearby.

"Wasn't his fault or yours," Patrick replied as he slid off Calabaza. "Are you all right?"

Matt nodded. "Yes, sir."

"Are you willing to try again?" Patrick asked.

Matt dusted his hands and nodded bravely. "Yes, sir."

"Let's put you on Calabaza this time," Patrick added. "He'll give you a real good idea of what a top cow pony can do."

Matt looked uncertain but game. "Okay."

"Once you've got your critter picked out, all you'll need to do is give Calabaza a hint of what you want to do. A light touch of the rein will tell him direction. If you want him to run hard, raise the reins."

He put Matt's saddle on Calabaza and gave him a leg up. "Ready?" The bunch, including the sorry-looking yearling that had caused Matt's wreck, had carelessly reassembled halfway between the dirt tank and the salt block.

Matt smiled and touched spur to Calabaza. The pony broke into a fast lope and Matt headed him at the largest steer, closing fast. The steer snorted, ducked, twirled like a whirligig, and darted away. Calabaza spun, drew even, and nipped the steer's shoulder. Angry, it blew snot and turned. Calabaza cut it off. Three more attempts to elude Calabaza left it head down, panting and motionless.

Matt rode back to the watching men with a grin a mile wide. "Jeepers, that was aces."

"You ride real good," Miguel said admiringly. "Better than me, *cabrón.*"

"Thanks."

"You'll make a hand," Patrick said with a smile.

"But Ma wants me to go to college," Matt replied, relishing the compliments.

"A man can be book smart *and* still make a hand," Patrick replied. "We'll give those critters a rest for a spell while we have our lunch. Then you can take a couple more cracks at that steer before we head home."

Matt dropped out of the saddle. "Do you think Patches can be as good as Calabaza?"

"He's got the makings, if you're willing to work with him," Patrick replied.

"I am," Matt said as he stroked Patches' neck. "I sure am."

* * *

After lunch, Patrick and Matt mounted up and worked the steer together while Miguel and Vernon watched the show from the top of the rise. Patrick hazed to keep the steer running straight so Matt could cut the animal from the bunch without difficulty. After three rounds, Matt was getting good at using Patches to pester the critter into submission, and pride of accomplishment shone on his face. The boy looked so downright happy, Patrick didn't think it necessary to mention that the poor, bedraggled steer was just plum wore out.

They watered and rested their ponies before starting for home. On the way, Matt asked how long it would take to get Patches trained.

"It depends on how much time we have to work with him," Patrick answered. "If you stay at the ranch this summer, we could get it done before school starts."

"All summer?" Matt asked.

Patrick nodded. "His true test as a cow pony will come at fall works, when we gather for market. Then we'll know how good a job we did with him."

"Ma won't want me to miss the start of school."

"She's persnickety about your schooling; that's for certain," Patrick agreed. "But if Patches is gonna be *your* top pony, you have to be the one to ride and work him. Besides, you haven't come out for fall works yet. Best you see what gathering a herd is like before motorcars, trucks, filling stations, and paved highways change the world forever."

"I'll ask her right away."

"Wait a spell," Patrick suggested. "Let her first see how serious you are about doing this."

Matt nodded. "That's a good idea. I had fun today."

"Me too," Patrick replied, wondering if he had finally found a way to make friends with his son. It was a cheerful thought. Over his shoulder Vernon and Miguel lagged a quarter mile back. To the west, the sun signaled plenty of time left to get home for supper. Half a mile up ahead, the gate to the horse pasture marked a thirty-minute ride to the ranch house.

"I'm dusty and hot," Patrick announced. "How about you?"

"Me too," Matt said.

"Let's make for the stock tank in the horse pasture and take a cool dip while the sun is still high."

Matt grinned. "That sounds swell. What about Miguel and your hired man?"

"They can do as they like."

"Race you to the gate," Matt said, spurring Patches forward, giving him his head.

Patrick kept Calabaza in check, stayed behind, and ate dust all the way to the finish. Matt bragged on his pony all the way to the stock tank.

* * *

Invited by Patrick to join everyone in the kitchen for dinner, Vernon ate in silence as the young button talked about his afternoon adventure with his pa chasing cows on his pony. The boy's ma and the older Mexican woman carried on like sisters, and Vernon took to wondering if Patrick's ex-wife was Mexican herself or maybe a half-breed.

Although the food was good and he was plenty hungry, he turned down a second helping. Eating with Mexicans just didn't sit right with him. He eyed the young housekeeper with the big birthmark on her face, wondering if she'd give him a poke if he showed up at the casita real quiet-like later on. The way she moved sure told him it would likely be a good poke, and he sorely needed one. Vernon gave her a big smile as he pushed away from the table, stood, and made his thanks for the meal. The bitch ignored him.

"Before you call it a day, chop some wood for the cookstove," Patrick said.

"Can't it wait until morning?" Vernon asked.

"Nope, and we're low on kindling too."

Vernon nodded. "Okay."

He went to the tack room first, removed the governor's pardon from the mattress, and hid it in a space behind the thick plank nailed to the wall that supported the saddle racks.

Vernon didn't think Patrick was onto him, but there was no reason to take any chances. He had cogitated on a plan of blackmail and decided if Patrick wanted the pardon back, it would cost him wages due, the fifty dollars locked in his desk, one good saddle horse, and two ponies.

That was more than enough to get him to his sister's place in Texas.

Tomorrow after the two Mexicans left, he'd get Patrick alone and play his hand, and if he turned him down, he'd kill them all. Maybe not the housekeeper; leastways, not right away.

At the woodpile, he sharpened the ax, split logs, and carried enough firewood to fill the big woodbox in the courtyard. Then he cut a big bundle of kindling and brought it to the kitchen, where the three women yapped away in Spanish as they washed the dishes.

He gave the Mexican housekeeper another big smile as he left, and again the bitch ignored him. Riled by her swellheaded ways, he pondered dropping the blackmail scheme, killing them all on the spot, and taking whatever he wanted.

He warmed quickly to the idea. In Arizona he'd murdered two nesters asleep in their bed for a mule, a wagon, and two silver dollars. He could leave here tonight with a hell of a lot more in his pocket than that. He'd get his pistol from the tack room, find and shoot dead Patrick first, and then hunt the rest of them down.

With moonrise yet to come, he crossed from the house to the barn in the darkening night. He lit the lantern that hung just inside the barn door and carried it to the tack room, where he found Patrick waiting for him, an angry look on his face and a ball-peen hammer in his hand.

"Where is it?" Patrick demanded.

"What are you looking for?" Vernon asked, sounding as confused and innocent as possible. "Didn't I put something away like I should have?"

"You sorry son of a bitch," Patrick replied through clenched teeth. "You broke into my army locker. Now, where the hell is the pardon?"

Vernon smiled meekly, dropped his shoulders, and turned his empty hands palms up. "Look, I was just gonna fun with you; that's all. Torment you a bit about the fiddle-faddle you tried to pull. I knew you was Pat Floyd from first we met, but I just wanted to prove it for sure. I meant no harm by it." He could see Patrick wasn't buying it.

"What else of mine have you been pawing through?"

"Nothing." Vernon raised a hand skyward. "I swear to God."

"Give me the damn pardon."

"Sure," Vernon said, sidestepping around Patrick to the head of the bed, where he kept his gunnysack. "Let me get it for you right now. Like I said, I was just funnin'.'' He could either take a beating and get sent away afoot and flat busted or leave with money, guns, and ponies.

With his back to Patrick, Vernon pulled the pistol from the gunnysack, turned, and felt his head explode. He fell to the floor dead.

Patrick dropped the ball-peen hammer. He'd smashed Vernon's skull wide open and done murder. There was blood everywhere: on the saddles, the wall, the old Mexican cabinet, the dirt floor, and the bed. He could feel blood on his face, see the splatter on his hand.

He couldn't say a word about what had happened; it would ruin the best time Emma and Matt had ever had at the ranch and probably expose him as an ex-convict. He needed to hide Vernon's body fast. He cleaned his hands and face, emptied the trunk, stuffed Vernon inside, and doused the lantern. After everybody went to bed, he'd come back, wipe up the blood, move Vernon's body, and search for the pardon.

Outside, Miguel, Teresa, Evangelina, Emma, and Matt were sitting on the veranda, the lamplight shining through the living room windows, casting them in silhouette.

"Join us," Emma called merrily. "We're telling Matt stories about the ranch, and it's your turn."

"I'll be there as soon as I clean up," Patrick replied.

7

After midnight, when all fell quiet at the ranch, Patrick saddled Calabaza, tied Vernon's body to a pack animal, and made rapid horse tracks for more than two hours. He stopped at a low mesa that jutted abruptly onto the barren alkali flats, remote and far away from any trail and road. He hid the body in a shallow cave at the foot of the mesa that he'd found years ago while tracking a marauding mountain lion that had been killing his calves.

He returned home at first light to find Evangelina alone in the kitchen, starting breakfast. A fresh pot of coffee boiled on the stove. Dog tired from his all-night effort, he eased into a chair at the table.

"*Buenos días*," Evangelina said pleasantly. She handed him a cup of coffee and glanced at the kitchen door. "Does your hired man want breakfast?"

"He quit me last night and left as soon as I paid him," Patrick answered wearily.

Evangelina shrugged and turned back to the pot of beans simmering on the stove.

"No loss," Kerney added, reading her reaction.

Evangelina gave him a quick smile over her shoulder.

"I didn't like him much either," Patrick added, and wished he'd held his tongue. Seeing as he'd killed Vernon, saying anything scornful about him wasn't very smart. He didn't need to talk himself into trouble.

Evangelina laughed. "You will hire someone else?"

"Eventually. When do we eat?"

"I can make breakfast for you now, if you don't want to wait for the others."

Patrick shook his head, finished his coffee, and stood. "Teresa and Miguel are leaving for home today, so I'll wait and break bread with them. Give me a holler when it's time."

"As you wish, señor," Evangelina said gaily.

Evangelina seemed downright pleased and happy to be cooking and caring for the place. It made Patrick wonder if her life in Tularosa wasn't very agreeable.

Back at the barn, he fed Calabaza some oats, gave him fresh water, rubbed him down, and put him in his stall. He did the same for the pack pony before turning it out in the horse pasture. He carried his saddle into the tack room, mulling over what still needed to be done to make all traces of Vernon disappear. He couldn't risk the unlikely chance that some pilgrim lost on the basin might stumble upon Vernon's body. He decided to return to the cave later in the day, bury Vernon deep, burn all his belongings, collapse the opening with dynamite, and make the rubble look like a natural rockfall. Once that was done, he doubted Vernon's remains would ever be found.

He had killed the man in self-defense, but if he reported it and got let off scot-free, the truth that he'd been a convicted felon was sure to come out. He couldn't abide that, couldn't stand the idea of neighbors and folks knowing he was once a common thief. He had only his good name and the Double K to take pride in, and he wasn't about to lose either.

He took his army locker out of the trunk, set it on the floor, wrapped up Vernon's bedroll, mattress, and gunnysack in a horse blanket, stuffed the bundle in the trunk, and closed the lid. Calabaza's soft whinny from his stall made him turn just as Matt stepped into the room.

"Morning," Patrick said.

"Morning, Pa," Matt said, glancing at the bare and empty bedframe. "What happened to the hired man?"

"He didn't like it here, so he quit me last night and struck out for Texas, where his sister lives."

"Ma said Tía Teresa didn't like the look of him at all," Matt said.

"Well, Teresa always has had a good eye when it comes to reading folks. When did she take you on as a nephew?"

Matt's expression clouded at the thought that maybe Pa didn't like the notion. "She said I should call her *tía*. Ma said it was okay; she said that Teresa was like a sister to her."

Patrick smiled. "No need to worry on my account, boy. If your ma and Teresa made a private treaty, then you're part of the Chávez family clan for certain."

Matt's expression cleared. "I never had an aunt before. Next to Ma, she's the nicest lady I know."

"I agree with you there, old son," Patrick said.

Matt stared at the footlocker with Pa's name and rank painted on the lid. "Ma told me about how you fought in the Spanish-American War as a Rough Rider."

"I did."

"Can I look inside?"

"Sure." Patrick unlocked the box and opened it. "There's nothing important to see, just old army stuff."

Matt sat on the floor, carefully picked up Patrick's squashed campaign hat with the crossed-sabers insignia, and put it on his head. It sank below his ears.

"It's a mite big," Patrick said as he hunkered down. "But it looks good on you."

Matt took out the folded uniform shirt, the pants, the boots, and the leggings and inspected each item before picking up Patrick's medals. "Ma gave me CJ's medals to have," he said. "I keep them in my room."

"You can have mine if you like."

Matt grinned with pleasure. "Thanks. That's swell." He turned each medal over in his hands and studied them. "I'll put them on my dresser with CJ's." He looked at Patrick with wet eyes. "Sometimes in my bedroom, Jimmy and me would pin CJ's medals on our shirts and pretend we were brave soldiers getting decorated by a general. I miss him a lot."

Patrick nodded. "I know how that is. I lost a pal in the Rough Riders and I still think about him to this day."

"You do?"

"Yep."

"I'm gonna go into the army when I grow up."

"I figured as much, but don't tell your ma that."

Matt nodded wisely. "I already know not to. She'd scalp me. Are we going to work Patches some more today?"

"We will, later on. With Vernon having quit me, I've got some range work that needs doing that can't wait."

"Okay."

From the veranda, Evangelina called out in Spanish that food was on the table and people were waiting for their company.

"What did she say?" Matt asked.

"Breakfast is ready. Best you start learning Spanish if you're gonna have a *tía*."

"Who taught you?"

"Your *tía* Teresa," Patrick replied. "Put those medals in your pocket and let's go get some grub."

"Can I wear the hat?"

"You sure can."

* * *

At breakfast, Patrick announced Vernon's sudden departure from the Double K and it caused nary a stir. No one raised an eyebrow, asked any questions, or showed the slightest remorse about his leaving, which relieved Patrick of the need to make up a tall tale about his going.

Emma was downright high-spirited at breakfast, making plans with Teresa to travel to Tularosa for Miguel's wedding later in the year and arranging for Teresa to visit her and Matt in Las Cruces before the wedding. She had a glow that put color on her cheeks and a sparkle in her eyes. Patrick hadn't seen such a frisky, happy look about her in years, leastways not when she was in his company.

"Miguel will be the last of my children to marry, so you must come help us celebrate," Teresa said to Patrick.

"You must," Miguel echoed. "It will be a grand fiesta. Many friends and relatives will be there. It will seem like the old days in Tularosa."

"I reckon I can't miss it," he answered, glancing at Evangelina as she circled the table, clearing away dishes. Her smile didn't hide her sad eyes. "Are you ready to hitch up your team?" he asked Miguel.

"*Sí*, my friend," Miguel replied. "It is time to take my mother home so she can pester me about all that I must do before the wedding."

"Can I help with the horses?" Matt asked eagerly, putting the Rough Rider campaign hat on his head.

"Come along," Patrick replied. "We'll show you how to hitch a team to a wagon."

Matt looked at Ma for permission.

"Go on, gentlemen," Emma said with a smile, and she shooed them out the door.

* * *

Soon after Teresa and Miguel departed, Patrick announced he had work to do out on the flats and made horse tracks to where he'd buried Vernon. Once at the cave, he worked hard and fast but carefully. When he was finally certain no one would ever suspect a body had been buried at the foot of the mesa, he started for home. He'd covered all the bases save one: the missing Yuma Prison pardon. He had to find it.

He dozed in the saddle on his return to the ranch, turned Calabaza out to pasture, and spent a fruitless hour searching the tack room. He pulled everything away from the walls, looked under the trunk and the bunk bed, searched shelves, cubbyholes, and saddlebags, and stopped looking when exhaustion and frustration took over. The pardon could be hidden anywhere on the ranch headquarters. He would make a more thorough search after Emma and Matt returned to town.

He put everything back where it belonged and found Matt astride Patches at the hitching post, impatiently waiting to start the next session.

"Where's Calabaza?" Matt asked as Patrick approached.

"We don't need his help today," Patrick replied. So far, everything he'd done with Matt had been purely to see how the boy sat a saddle and handled his pony. He was a natural on horseback, but pleasure riding was vastly different from working a top cow pony. The real training of the horse and rider was about to begin.

"Head on over to the corral," Patrick ordered as he stepped off toward the big circular corral bordering the pasture.

"What are we gonna do?" Matt asked.

Patrick stopped and explained to him that Patches was about to start learning three things: how to keep his head down; how to turn with his head, not his shoulder; and how to back up.

"That's all?" Matt asked, hoping for more cattle chasing.

"For today." Patrick opened the corral gate and waved Patches inside. "It takes plenty of time and schooling to finish a top cow pony. You best be sure this is something you really want to do before we get started."

Matt nodded. "You bet I do."

Patrick swung the gate closed. "Okay, then. Gallop him around the corral until I say stop."

Matt spurred Patches into a gallop. It didn't take but a half dozen turns for Patrick's campaign hat to fly off Matt's head. Patrick retrieved it and called for him to rein in.

"What do we do first?" Matt asked as he drew rein. He looked over Patrick's shoulder and waved.

Patrick turned to see Emma smiling and watching from the closed gate.

"Back him up slowly," Patrick said, happy to see Emma standing there with the sun on her face, looking so alive and healthy.

He worked with Matt and Patches for an hour, and Emma stayed to watch the whole time. She opened the gate for Matt, and he rode through, beaming down at her as he trotted his pony to the barn.

"I don't think I've ever seen him happier with you," she said as Patrick latched the gate.

"He'll make a hand, if ranching is something he decides to do."

"Is that what you want for him?" Emma asked.

Patrick hesitated. "I don't know. But the Double K will belong to him someday, if drought and the bank don't take it from me before I die."

"We should talk about his future. I've made some plans for him."

"Haven't we already gone through that?" Patrick asked.

"Not completely. When I pass, you're going to have to take him in and be his pa until he's grown."

"I know that, but your passing isn't a subject I care to discuss much. What else have you got up your sleeve?"

"Can we take a moonlit ride together tonight and talk about it then?"

Patrick smiled. "Now, that's something we haven't done in years. Are you still able to sit a horse?"

Emma laughed. "Why would you doubt it?" She touched his arm. "This has been our best time at the ranch since we started coming. Matt hasn't groused once about missing his friends in town, and I'm totally spoiled having Evangelina here to take care of everything. Thank you."

"No need to be thanking me," Patrick said, thrown off stride by her warmth, remembering how tender she could be. Unwilling for Emma to see his longing for her, he turned quickly on his heel and headed for the barn. "I've chores before dinner."

"Pick out a gentle saddle pony for me," Emma called after him.

"I already got that figured," he called back to her. He'd put her on Stony, the twelve-year-old gelding he had given Miguel Chávez to ride.

* * *

With the moon as clear as crystal and the sky awash with stars, they rode first to the small family cemetery on a hill overlooking the ranch so Emma could visit for a spell. Patrick hung back to give her time alone for private thoughts.

Four graves with markers, enclosed by a picket fence, over-looked the basin. Here Patrick's father, John Kerney, was buried along with his best friend and partner, Cal Doran. Next to him was Cal's friend and hired hand, George Rose, and in the smallest grave, Baby Molly, Emma's firstborn.

Emma had never known John Kerney, who'd carved the ranch out of wilderness, but she knew the story of how he'd searched and found his young lost son and brought him home to safety. What he did for Patrick had always touched her heart. Cal and George were family to her: Cal dearer than flesh and blood, the wisest and truest friend; George steadfast and kind, whose friend-ship never wavered. And Molly, beautiful Molly, born out of so much pain and suffering.

Knowing what he knew, would any other man but Patrick have taken up with her and Molly? She gasped at the thought that per-haps she'd been too unfair, unyielding, unforgiving, with him. With tears for all the good and bad memories, she returned to Patrick, who waited with the horses.

"You've kept it very nice," she said as he gave her a leg up.

"That's our history."

Emma nodded. "Except for CJ buried in France."

"With his comrades, as he should be," Patrick noted.

"Yes, I suppose so, although I'd rather have him here at home," Emma said. "Promise you'll bury me next to Molly."

"I won't listen to that kind of talk."

"Promise," Emma prodded.

"Is that your wish?"

"Yes, but not yet," she replied with a laugh, and she spurred Stony to a trot.

They rode in silence up the canyon to a small meadow cut by the stream that meandered down to the ranch house. The basin, partially muted in the gray and brown of a dry winter under a night sky, ran to a darker hue against the Sacramento Mountains. A light breeze rustled through the mesquite and floated up to them like a whisper. Electric streetlights in the town of Alamogordo forty miles away winked like mysterious heliographic Morse code messages.

"Do you remember how angry you were when you learned Cal had willed the ranch to both of us?" Emma asked.

"Why open that old wound now?" Patrick replied.

"Because I don't want you snarling at me about what I want you to do for Matthew."

"Are you fixing to tell me something that will rile me?"

"Before this visit, I'd say yes," Emma replied. "But now I'm not so sure."

"I'll hold my tongue," Patrick said gruffly. "Say your piece."

"After Matthew finishes grade school, I want you to promise me that he'll go on to high school and graduate."

Patrick looked at her in stunned disbelief. "How in the hell can he live here at the ranch and go to high school in town at the same time?"

"He can board with a family in town during the school year," Emma answered. "There will be money to pay for it."

"What if he doesn't want to go to high school?"

"He will."

"You're cocksure of that?"

"Yes."

Patrick shook his head in wonder. "Well, if he's anything like you, he's already smarter than me by a mile."

"You'll do it?"

"Have you put something in writing with your banker and lawyer?"

Emma nodded.

"It figures."

"What does that mean?"

"I'm trying to hold my tongue like I promised, but it chafes me to know you don't trust me to do right by him."

"What I'm asking is no different than what I'd be demanding if we were still married, living here on the Double K, and raising Matthew together."

"And you'd hound me about it until you got your way," Patrick added.

Emma smiled. "Probably."

"You'd like him to go on and be a college man, wouldn't you?"

"That's my dream."

"There's nothing wrong with that, I suppose. Are we done talking about what's gonna happen after you die?"

"Why does it trouble you so?"

"It just does," Patrick said, stifling the impulse to tell Emma he loved her, always had, always would.

The chill of the desert night had deepened, and a shiver ran up Emma's spine. She started Stony down the canyon and called over her shoulder, "Are you coming?"

"Yes, ma'am," Patrick responded.

Emma had bundled up for the ride, but it didn't keep the cold from numbing her arms and legs on the ride home. By the time they arrived at the ranch house, her hands tingled, her feet were freezing, and the wind against her face felt like pinpricks. She dismounted feeling weak, dizzy, and short of breath but determined to care for her pony without Patrick's assistance.

He took the reins from her hand. "You look done in."

"I am," she admitted, her resolve weakening.

"Go on," he ordered, nodding toward the house, feeling done in himself. "I'll care for the ponies."

"Thank you. Good night."

"*Buenas noches.*"

He watched her walk to the house before attending to the ponies. By the time he had Calabaza and Stony in their stalls, the light in Emma's bedroom was out. He walked softly past Matt, who had taken to sleeping on the veranda every night. Scrunched up under a pile of blankets with only the top of his head showing on the pillow, he looked peaceful and innocent. In his bedroom, Patrick took off his boots, stretched out, and pulled a blanket up to his chin. He'd been this weary many times before; ranch work often demanded it. But tonight his heart felt worn-out. He was tired of being alone; tired of being without a family; tired of his failures as a husband and father, which had put him in such a wretched state.

He had almost gotten Emma back tonight. He'd sensed it, felt it on their ride. Now it was too late. He fell asleep thinking *almost* was a useless word.

8

For three days, Emma was able to hide her failing health only because Patrick and Matthew were away from the house much of the time. They worked with Patches, fixed fences, cared for the ponies Patrick hoped to sell, and moved cattle from the higher pastures closer to ranch headquarters in anticipation of branding during spring works.

At mealtimes and in the evenings, she marshaled enough energy and cheerfulness to convince them she was simply fighting a mild springtime cold. She wanted nothing to spoil the good time Matthew was having with Patrick. He loved every new adventure with his pa and came home tired and ravenously hungry. In the evening, he chattered on about the events of the day, wolfed down his dinner, and before last light was deep in sleep wrapped up in his bedroll on the veranda. It made Emma's spirits soar to see Patrick and Matt getting along so well.

On one morning over breakfast, Patrick said, "If Matt wants it, he'll be a stockman from the heels of his boots to the crown of his hat, and a damn good one too."

Matt's grin lit up his face.

"Is that what you want?" Emma asked Matthew.

Matt shrugged. "Maybe."

"Would you want it enough to give up your schooling to be a rancher?" she prodded.

"Why would I have to do that?" Matt asked, his grin fading to a frown.

"You don't have to," Emma said, hiding her relief. "You can learn all your pa can teach you by coming to the ranch during school vacations and summer recess." Emma turned to Patrick. "Isn't that right?"

"I reckon so," Patrick said.

"I'd like that the best," Matt replied. He finished the last bite of his second stack of hotcakes and stood. "May I be excused?"

"You may," Emma said with a nod.

"I'll be with you shortly," Patrick said. He waited until Matt scooted out the door before turning his full attention to Emma, searching her face intently. "Seems you're more than just sick with a springtime cold."

"Why do you say that?"

"You haven't been outside once since Matt and I rode in yesterday evening. You don't stay lying about unless you're really wore down."

"I'm fine," Emma protested in a hurt tone of voice. "If I've spent too much time inside it's because this place deserves a good cleaning from years of your neglect. I've been helping Evangelina, and that has tired both of us some. Ask her."

"Is that true?" Patrick asked, looking at Evangelina, who'd been listening at the dish tub.

"*Sí*, it is true," Evangelina fibbed, as she promised to do if Patrick questioned her about Emma's health.

"I didn't bring you out here and pay you wages to put Emma to work."

Evangelina blushed. "I am sorry, señor."

"Don't you snap at Evangelina," Emma cautioned sternly. "I help her because I enjoy the company *and* this house needs our attention."

Patrick glanced from woman to woman and figured there was no purchase in pursuing the subject further. He made his excuses and headed out the door.

Evangelina waited at the window until Patrick entered the barn before drying her hands and joining Emma at the table. "You must tell him you are not well," she counseled in Spanish.

Emma shook her head and replied in Spanish. "He knows I'm dying. So does Matthew. I want them to have these last few good days together before we go home to Las Cruces without worrying about me."

"Why are you no longer married?" Evangelina ventured. "He seems to care about you greatly."

Emma shook her head as though to ward off the question.

Evangelina dropped her gaze. "Forgive my intruding."

Emma took her hand. "No, please don't apologize. He does care about me a lot, except when I rile him, which is frequently. He married me when no one else would have me."

Evangelina's eyes widened. "Truly?"

"Truly," Emma replied. "You like it here, don't you?"

"Very much. I feel I am my own person, not just my parents' unmarried, old-maid daughter."

"But you're not old, and being unmarried isn't a curse."

Evangelina's smile didn't hide her melancholy. "Everyone in my family believes I will be an old maid forever."

"Do you think so?"

"*Sí*. Are you happy living alone?"

"Do you think only old maids and widows should live alone?" Emma asked.

Evangelina ran a hand across her birthmark. "No, just women who are ugly."

"You are not!" Emma said.

"Tía Teresa says the same, but I know better. But you did not answer."

"I love my independence, every minute of it," Emma replied.

"You don't miss being close to a man?"

Emma nodded. "Sometimes a little bit, sometimes a lot. But that is not as important as my freedom."

"You are fortunate. In two days my father will come for me and what little freedom I have known will be gone forever."

"Only if you give in."

"Give in?" Evangelina began polishing a water spot on the table with her dishcloth.

"Let your parents govern your life," Emma explained.

"Disobey my father?" She studied the spot on the table and rubbed harder with the dishcloth.

Emma took the dishcloth from her hand. "You're of age. It has nothing to do with defying Flaviano."

"I am not like you. I have no way to get by, no means of support except from my family."

"You could stay here and work for Patrick. I could see to it."

Evangelina shook her head. "Impossible."

"Because of what Flaviano believes you might do," Emma challenged.

Evangelina dropped her gaze. "He thinks I might give up my virtue because of my disfigurement. I must be carefully watched so I do not stain the family honor."

"You are not disfigured, branded, or deformed," Emma said. "You have a birthmark, nothing more. Is your virtue truly at risk?"

Evangelina covered her mouth and giggled.

"Why is that funny?"

"No one has ever asked me that before. Sometimes I think I should prove my father right. You were lucky that Patrick married you."

"I lived with him for well over a year before we married," Emma said with a playful smile. "I guess you could say I suffered from a prolonged fit of weakened virtue." A heavy coughing spell came over her, racking her body before it subsided.

"You must rest, señora," Evangelina said. "Let me take you to your room."

Red-faced, out of breath, and weak in the knees, Emma said, "No, take me to the casita. I can hide there."

Taking Evangelina's steady hand, she walked slowly across the courtyard to the casita and stretched out on the bed. "You must stop calling me señora," she said.

"As you wish, Emma," Evangelina said tentatively.

"That's much better." Suddenly she felt drained of all her strength. The pounding of her heart was an erratic drumbeat in her ears.

"Rest now."

"Yes."

"If you are not better by dinner, I will have to tell Patrick you are sick," Evangelina warned.

Emma shook her head in protest. "I'll be fine. If they ask, tell them I am busy sewing."

"I will come back often," Evangelina said.

"I'll be fine after a nap," Emma replied, gasping for air.

* * *

After a morning session working with Matt and his pony, Patrick left the boy behind to practice some on his own and made tracks for the south pasture. Yesterday, a rider from Earl Hightower's spread had come over to tell Patrick that a traveling cattle buyer with a small crew was visiting outfits on the Tularosa, buying up culls to ship to Mexico. He'd be stopping at the Double K midday next.

The penny or two per pound Patrick would lose selling to the buyer was worth the time he'd save trailing the stock to town after spring works. Plus it would put some cash money in his pocket and he'd be able to rest the south pasture a bit longer with the animals gone.

He found the scrawny critters clustered at the dirt tank and the salt lick block. He rounded them up without difficulty and moved them slowly homeward, chasing an upstart yearling or two and a disorderly steer back to the bunch every now and then.

He had been with company of one sort or another almost constantly since the day he fetched Emma and Matt to the ranch, and he welcomed the solitude, except when the killing of Vernon Clagett still preyed on his mind.

The day was mild with a touch of moisture in the air, but not enough to promise rain. Small puffy white clouds drifted up the Tularosa Basin, blocking the sun for fleeting seconds, pausing to hang suspended over the malpais. It made a pretty picture. Farther north at the railroad town of Carrizozo, a small spit of virga draped below a lonely, thin gray cloud, evaporating in the late morning sunlight. He couldn't remember a day when the basin failed to show him a fresh view of things. It was a slice of the world where *ordinary* had no meaning.

At ranch headquarters, he threw the stock in the corral and

went to the kitchen for some grub. Matt was at the table alone, working hard on a bowl of chili and beans.

"Where's your ma and Evangelina?" he asked.

"They're in the casita," Matt replied between bites.

"Doing what?"

Matt spooned in another mouthful. "Evangelina said they had some sewing to do."

The sound of an approaching rider kept Patrick from going to investigate what the women were up to. He stepped out on the veranda as the rider drew rein at the hitching post.

"Patrick Kerney?" the man asked.

"Who might you be?" Patrick replied as Matt scooted out the kitchen door to see who'd arrived.

"Makiah Whetten," the man answered. "You might not remember me, but I bought some cows for my boss from you and Cal Doran down in Mexico some years back. I'm here to buy what livestock you got to sell."

"I do remember you," Patrick said. "Light. We've got coffee and some good chili and beans."

"I'd be obliged for a cup," Whetten said as he stepped down from his pony and came spritely up the stairs.

It had been more than twenty-five years since Patrick had seen Whetten. Back then he'd been in his prime, a Mormon cowboy with three wives and a passel of kids who worked for the biggest stockman on the biggest ranchero in Chihuahua, Mexico. Whetten was an old man now, still slender, a little stooped, with a bushy white mustache, but still vigorous in his manner.

"It's been a while," Patrick said, shaking Whetten's hand. "I didn't expect to see you again, not with that revolution going on down your way."

"Ten years of killing are about over," Whetten replied with a sad shake of his head. "Since nineteen and ten, a million dead and the rangeland empty. It's time to restock."

"Are you still ramrodding for old Emiliano Díaz?"

"His son, Delfino," Whetten explained. "Emiliano got himself killed late in the war for supporting the wrong brand of revolution. Unfortunately, he left a lot of land and very little money, so I'm forced to bargain hard for the best prices I can get."

"Hard times can do that, I reckon," Patrick said. He introduced Matt to Whetten and told him to take Patches and pester the livestock in the corral while he talked business. Matt grinned, hightailed it to his pony, and jigged Patches to the corral.

Over coffee on the veranda, the two men caught up. Patrick kept it short, mostly about how Cal died after getting mauled by a bear, and how the stockmen in the basin were toughing it out now the war in Europe was over and the Brits had stopped buying horses and beef.

Whetten told of staying put with his family in Mexico during the heavy fighting between factions while many Mormons fled back across the border to the United States. His uncles and cousins were now homesteading along the Gila River in southwestern New Mexico. He had held on to his small ranch for as long as he could, but the revolutionary government took it away from him a year ago and gave it to a high-ranking general's son.

"They had to move us off at gunpoint," Whetten added. "It scared my wives half to death that we'd be shot. We're living on the ranchero now; my oldest boys and their families have stuck with us. The rest are married and have moved on. Emiliano's son has been good to us."

Patrick nodded. "I'd have done the same to try and save my spread." The road from Mexico where he'd met Makiah Whetten had taken him through the gates of Yuma Prison and more recently to the killing of Vernon Clagett. He wondered if an invisible noose from the past had settled around his neck.

"Good coffee," Whetten said, setting down his cup. "Let's take a look at your cows."

"Livestock inspection is tight at the border," Patrick noted as they stepped off to the corral. "How do you plan to cross them without getting quarantined?"

Whetten smiled. "I'll teach them to swim the river, just like you and Cal did."

At the corral, Whetten eyed the cattle carefully before quoting Patrick a dollar figure for the lot. Patrick haggled for a quarter cent more on the pound and got an eighth. The small wad of bills in his jeans pocket felt good.

"Two vaqueros will be here soon," Whetten said, checking his pocket watch. "We'll move the cows to the Hightower outfit, where I have another small bunch bedded down."

"You'll trail them to Engle from there and load them on cattle cars to El Paso, I reckon," Patrick said.

Whetten nodded. "After a stop at Al Jennings's Rocking J."

"He'll have a few to sell," Patrick predicted.

Out in the horse pasture, several colts whinnied and kicked up their heels as two approaching riders threw dust in the air. Patrick remembered back to the days when CJ rode his pony to school at the Hightower Ranch. It was in part of the San Andres Matt hadn't seen. They could make it there and back before dinner.

"Mind if my boy and I ride along?" he asked.

"I welcome the company," Whetten replied.

Patrick called to the house for Evangelina and Emma. Evangelina quickly appeared at the courtyard wall, and Patrick told her of his plans.

"Okay, señor," Evangelina replied with a wave.

"Pretty girl," Whetten noted.

"Yes, she is," Patrick agreed. He went to the fence and whistled Calabaza in from the horse pasture.

* * *

While Pa and Mr. Whetten lazed behind, jawboning, Matt rode with the two vaqueros, helping them chase an occasional cow back to the bunch. The vaqueros didn't speak much English, but one of them, who had a star on his front tooth, said that Patches was a real good *caballo*. That made Matt feel proud. He couldn't wait to tell Pa and Ma as soon as they got home.

At the Hightower outfit, cows were spread out grazing and loitering in a large open pasture between a ranch house and a one-room school. A rope corral under a stand of trees enclosed a small remuda of cow ponies. At the nearby chuck wagon, the cook worked fixing grub for dinner. Matt spotted one cowboy busy caring for the ponies and another two out with the stock. Mr. Hightower waved his hat as he rode out from the ranch house to greet them, and Matt waved back, thinking this was the best day he'd ever spent on the Tularosa. Maybe he'd be a cowboy rather than a soldier when he grew up. Or both, like CJ and Pa.

Earl Hightower drew rein next to Matt just as Patrick and Makiah Whetten came up.

"Gents, my wife wants y'all to stay for dinner," he said.

"It would be my pleasure," Whetten said.

"We'll eat early so you and young Matt here can get back to the Double K by dark," Earl said to Patrick.

"We're obliged," Patrick replied with a smile. "No sensible man can refuse a turn at Addie's table."

Addie Hightower kept chickens, and at supper she served Matt a juicy thigh from a plump roasted bird and a pile of dumplings smothered in gravy. The youngest of the Hightower girls, Nellie, still lived at home. A tall, serious young woman who wore eyeglasses, she taught at the school and had eleven students this year. She questioned Matt about his school in town, what he studied, and what subjects he liked best. Finally and almost reverently, she asked him if it was true that he had a personally inscribed copy of one of Gene Rhodes's books.

"Yes, ma'am, I do," Matt said proudly. "It's a copy of *West Is West*. He sent it to me along with the story he wrote about my ma."

"I think everyone in New Mexico has read that story," Nellie said. "Your ma is famous."

Matt blushed with pride.

"I'd surely like to see that story," Mr. Whetten said.

"I'll fetch you our copy to read," Addie Hightower said, rising from the table.

After Mr. Whetten read "Emma Makes a Hand," a discussion started about Gene Rhodes, his life on the Tularosa, and the various facts and fictions of his supposed outlaw past. Patrick told the story of how Gene came to the Double K with the law on his trail after getting into a brawl in a mining camp. Mr. Hightower told of Gene hiding out in the San Andres with the two men accused of killing Albert Fountain and his young son, a crime that remained unsolved. Stories about Rhodes's bronco-riding skills, his love of the game of baseball, and his habit of eating only other ranchers' beef kept folks anchored at the table for a good amount of time. When the conversation slowed, Earl Hightower eyed the remaining daylight outside the kitchen window and invited Patrick and Matt to stay the night.

"We appreciate the invite," Patrick replied, "but we'll mosey on home."

With thanks to Addie and Earl for a fine meal and good company, and a farewell handshake with Makiah Whetten, Patrick and Matt left, jigging their ponies to a fast trot to take advantage of the fading daylight. At dinner, Patrick had had an anxious moment when Whetten reminisced about first meeting Patrick years ago, but thankfully he'd steered clear of any mention of the trouble Patrick had caused in a Juárez whorehouse. His shameful behavior and quarrelsome nature that day cost him a beating and almost lost him Cal Doran's friendship and the Double K.

The lag between nightfall and moonrise slowed their progress, and when they raised up the ranch house, Matt was asleep in the saddle, his head bobbing against his chest. Lamplight spilled through the kitchen window, but all was quiet when Patrick dismounted at the hitching post. He carried his sleeping son to the veranda, pulled off his boots, wrapped him gently in his bedroll, and tended to the horses before returning to the house. In the kitchen, slices of bread and thick slabs of beef had been left out on a covered plate. Next to it was a note from Emma.

> *We waited up late for you two cowboys to come home and*
> *finally decided you either stayed over the night at Earl and*
> *Addie's or got in a wreck on the way back. If you got in a*
> *wreck, don't wake us unless you need patching up. If you're*
> *hungry, have a bite and put your dirty dishes in the tub.*
>
> *Emma*

He put the note in his pocket, carried the lamp into the living room, and paused for a moment at Emma's bedroom door to listen. All was silent. He suppressed an urge to look in on her, went to his room, shucked his clothes, and sank down on the bed. He could still work hard day and night and spend long hours in the saddle, but now there were aches and pains in his joints and muscles that sometimes kept him awake. He fell asleep within minutes, only to be roughly shaken awake by Evangelina, who hovered over him, the lamp in her hand shining in his eyes.

"You must come," she said, the words spilling out of her. "Come now. Emma is very sick."

He sat bolt upright, his head sluggish. "What's wrong?"

Evangelina grabbed his hand and yanked him to his feet. "She can't breathe. I'm afraid that she is dying."

9

In the morning, Emma sat propped up in bed and in a raspy, breathless voice asked Patrick to take her and Matthew home to Las Cruces.

"I'm not carting you anywhere," Patrick countered. He'd spent the darkest hours before dawn with her, wiping sweat from her brow and listening to her labored breathing.

"I'll see my doctor as soon as you carry me home," she promised.

"I'll fetch him to you," Patrick countered.

"You don't have to do that." Emma stroked Matthew's cheek as he snuggled close to her. "We'll be fine once we're home. Isn't that right, Matthew?"

"You should do as Pa says," Matt said sternly.

Emma wrinkled her nose at his disloyalty. "Bringing the doctor here won't do me one bit of good."

"Then why did you say you'd see him in town?" Patrick demanded.

Emma quit arguing. "How long do you plan to hold me hostage?"

"Until the doctor says you're well enough to travel."

"It will take a day or more to bring him here."

"Evangelina can care for you." He turned to Evangelina. "Will you?"

"*Sí*, for as long as you and Emma wish," she replied.

"That seals it. Do you agree?"

Emma nodded her acquiescence.

"Good," Patrick said. "Matt, you stick close, help your ma with whatever she needs, and do what Evangelina asks while I'm gone. You savvy?"

"Yes, sir," Matt replied solemnly.

"I'm making horse tracks."

Emma grabbed his hand. "This really isn't necessary," she said softly, looking him squarely in the eyes, hoping he'd realize fetching the doctor was pointless.

"Can your sawbones sit a horse?" he asked, fully aware of her meaning, refusing to believe it.

"I don't know."

"I'll take old Stony along and tie the doctor to the saddle if need be," Patrick announced with a grin. "You take care, old girl. I'll be back as soon as I can."

Emma smiled back. "I'll see you then." Patrick left, and tears filled her eyes.

"Are you crying, Ma?" Matthew asked.

"No, I'm not," Emma answered with a sniffle. "It's just this darn cold." But that wasn't the case at all; it was the astonishing realization that Patrick truly did love her.

* * *

For several hours after Patrick's departure, Matthew sat at the foot of Emma's bed reading a Western called *Arizona Nights*, a book of old cowboy stories told around a campfire, with some really super illustrations in it by an artist named N. C. Wyeth. It had been published in 1907, five years before Matt was born.

"Are you going to sit there with your nose stuck in that book all day?" Emma asked.

"Pa said to stay close," Matt replied. Last night, he'd dreamt that he'd grabbed on to Jimmy as he was falling out of the tree and they both crashed to the ground dead. The fright of it woke him up. "Besides, I'm worried about you feeling so poorly."

"There's no need for that." Emma smiled and swung her twitchy legs to the floor. "It's too nice a day to be cooped up inside. I'm going to sit on the veranda. In fact, you know what I'd like even more? If you and Evangelina will carry my mattress and bedding to the veranda, I'm sure the fresh air will help me clear my lungs. I can rest there while you show me all the tricks you and your pa have taught Patches."

Matt closed his book and nodded eagerly. "Wait until you see what he can do."

"Before you jingle your spurs, I want you to know I've decided to ask Evangelina to come home with us. Is that okay with you?"

"You bet," Matt said. "I like her a lot."

Very slowly, Emma stood. "Good. Now, I'm going to the *baño* and then to the veranda. You do know what a *baño* is, don't you?"

"Everybody knows that word," Matt groaned as he left to find Evangelina.

Alone in the privy, Emma coughed up thick brown phlegm from her waterlogged lungs. Every breath caused pain; every cough singed her throat. She was burning up, sweating profusely. She coughed until it turned into a rough, dry hack and finally, gratefully subsided. On the veranda, her mattress and bedding were laid out with her pillows plumped against the wall.

She stood for a moment marveling at the Tularosa: the wind-rippled sands, the flat-bottomed arroyos, the fingertip lava flows touching soft, narrow sand hills decorated by scattered squaw-bushes, thickets of yucca with stalks ten feet high, the gray, empty alkali flats, all framed and enclosed by majestic mountains.

She'd once read that treasure appeared only to those who did not seek it. She decided the same could be said of the stark beauty of the Tularosa. It always took her by surprise and capti-vated her.

Below, at the hitching post, Matthew sat mounted on Patches, ready to begin his demonstration. Emma called for Evangelina to join her, and together they watched, applauding each successful maneuver Matthew accomplished. When he finished, Emma sum-moned up a whistle that left her breathless and Evangelina shouted, "*¡Muy bueno!*"

Matthew grinned with pleasure, took his bow still ahorseback, and walked Patches to the corral.

"He's a fine boy," Emma said. "He'll need someone besides Patrick in his life to care for him after I'm gone."

"What are you saying?" Evangelina asked.

"When Patrick asked, you said you would care for me as long as I wished. If I guaranteed your wages, would you do the same for Matthew?"

"I would not work for Señor Kerney?"

"Yes, you would. But I'd arrange for the money to be there so it would never be a burden on Patrick for you to stay on."

"How long would my job last?"

"As long as you, Matthew, and Patrick want it to."

Evangelina hesitated. "I'm not sure."

"You must decide now," Emma urged. "If you agree, I'll send Matthew off to the mailbox with a letter to my banker."

"My father will be angry."

"But you will be an independent woman earning your own wages."

Evangelina covered her mouth and giggled like a schoolgirl at such an outlandish idea.

"Well?"

"I will do it."

"Thank you," Emma said with great relief.

At Patrick's desk, she found pen, paper, and an envelope and stamp and quickly wrote to Henry Bowman. She sealed the envelope, gave it to Matt, and told him to take it to the mailbox at the end of the ranch road.

"Pa said I'm supposed to stick close to you," he argued.

"Out here on the Tularosa, anywhere less than a day's ride is close," Emma rebutted. "If you make horse tracks at a lope, you'll be back soon enough."

Matt balked.

"Please do as I ask," Emma said politely.

"Okay," he said. He kissed her check and hurried out the door.

Emma turned to Evangelina and said, "I think it would be a very good idea to clean out the chicken coop and ask Patrick to buy some hens and a rooster."

"It is not too late to start a small garden," Evangelina proposed.

Emma beamed her approval. "An excellent idea. Let's make a shopping list for his next trip to town. There are staples you desperately need for the pantry."

With Evangelina's help, Emma prepared a shopping list and then wrote to Patrick informing him of her wish to have Evangelina care for Matthew and her arrangement to have his trust pay her wages.

She handed the letter to Evangelina and said, "Make sure he gets this."

"You can give it to him upon his return," Evangelina proposed.

"I may forget," Emma replied, pushing the sealed envelope back into Evangelina's hand. If she did get to see Patrick once more, she didn't want talk of money to tarnish the visit.

* * *

Patrick returned in the morning with Emma's doctor, David Mead Sperry. With great effort she was able to pull herself to a sitting position and put on a bright smile before they dismounted and reached the veranda.

"I didn't think you'd make it," she said to Patrick.

His eyes searched her face. "You should know better than that."

"I do." She turned to Dr. Sperry. "Now that you're here, please tell Patrick I can go home."

"Not so fast," Sperry replied cheerily. Tired, sore, dusty, and hungry, he smiled at Emma as he dropped to one knee, took a close look, and said to Patrick, "Give us a minute or two alone, if you please."

"I'll have Evangelina fix you up some grub," Patrick said as he reluctantly walked to the kitchen.

Sperry felt Emma's forehead. She was burning up, emaciated in the face, and flushed pink from her neck to her cheeks. Her pupils were dilated and of unequal size, a worrisome sign of a stroke.

"I'm a tough old bird, Doctor," Emma said weakly.

"So it seems," Sperry replied as he felt her pulse. It was rapid and erratic. "Your ex-husband is a very persistent fellow."

"I told him not to bother fetching you."

"He obviously didn't pay attention." Sperry listened to her heart and her lungs and took her temperature. She had a high fever, a collapsed lung, fluid in the other lung, and a heart that could stop beating at any second. "Did you faint or fall recently?"

Emma nodded. "Yes, last night. I just collapsed. When I came to, Evangelina helped me back to my bed."

"Have you lost feeling anywhere?" Sperry asked.

"My left side is numb and my vision is blurry."

"Okay." Sperry took her pulse again. Her heartbeat slowed, spiked, paused, and spiked again.

"I'm dying, Doctor," Emma whispered. "I can feel my body leaving me."

"Did you sleep at all last night?"

Emma shook her head.

"You'll sleep soon," Sperry said gently. "It won't be long now."

"Good."

Sperry rose. At the kitchen door he called everyone to the veranda.

Emma closed her eyes and smiled, remembering that when Cal lay dying she'd sent Gene Rhodes to fetch a doctor. Cal had argued it was a waste of time and money and proved himself right by dying two hours before Gene and the doctor arrived.

Willpower last night had kept her alive waiting for Patrick's return. Now she could let go. She wanted to let go.

She opened her eyes. Patrick, Matthew, and Evangelina surrounded her. Patrick and Matthew held her hands. She barely felt their touch. Holding a rosary, Evangelina silently prayed. A fuzzy shape in the background against the Tularosa sky might have been Dr. Sperry.

For an instant she panicked at the thought that she had something important to say, but words—all language—flitted from her mind. She smiled, closed her eyes, and vanished.

❧ TWO ❧

Matt Kerney

10

Former Lincoln County sheriff John William Owen, known to all as Jake, ranched on a small spread outside Corona that barely broke even in a good year. As sheriff, Jake had gained a name for himself as a crackerjack investigator. After leaving office, he'd parlayed his reputation into a moneymaking proposition that helped keep the ranch afloat by hiring out as a private detective on cases that caught his interest.

Most of his work came by way of district attorneys, judges, and sheriffs around the state who needed someone to take on tough investigations no one else could handle. It was 1925, but the caliber of police work in New Mexico was still mired in the territorial years of the last century, except now most sheriffs rode in cars, not on horseback.

Jake's current case hadn't come to him through the usual sources. Edna Mae Bryan, a woman from Mitchell County, Texas, had asked him to search for her missing brother, Vernon Clagett, who'd last contacted her by letter in 1920 while working at a ranch on the Tularosa. In it, he'd mentioned meeting a fellow named Pat Floyd, an old pal he'd known in Arizona, and his plans to return to Texas for a visit as soon as he saved some money.

Because she hadn't kept the envelope and couldn't remember where it had been mailed from, Jake decided to start from scratch in Las Cruces, where Vernon had mailed an earlier letter to her.

According to Edna Mae, her brother was an ex-convict, a drunk, and—due to the recent death of an aged uncle—sole heir to a hundred and twenty acres of land in West Texas, where an oil boom was making millionaires out of dirt farmers. In '23 a well called the Santa Rita #1 in Big Lake had started it all. Chances were good that Vernon's quarter section was oil rich, so he needed to be found alive or proved dead so Edna Mae could get on with the job of making herself and her kin wealthy.

That was all the information Edna Mae had supplied, but Jake had done some letter writing to prisons in the Southwest and learned that thirty-some years ago Clagett served time in Yuma Prison for robbery and manslaughter. In with a copy of the prison records sent to him was a photograph of young Vernon, looking mean and tough.

He began the search for Vernon in Las Cruces, showing his picture around at stores, speakeasies, hotels, and diners, but nobody remembered him from five years back. Likewise, the Pat Floyd moniker rang no bells. He tried the towns of Engle, Alamogordo, Tularosa, and Carrizozo with the same results before returning to his Corona ranch, where he outfitted himself for a tour of every ranch on the basin.

In truth, he wasn't at all hopeful of finding Clagett or Pat Floyd, who was most likely a drifting drunk like Vernon. Both were probably buried in unmarked graves somewhere in the West, never to be heard from or seen again. But Edna Mae was paying him top dollar, and she deserved his best effort to find the man or prove him dead.

Jake knew the basin better than most men but was also wise enough to know that there were hideaways, cabins, old homesteads, and remote ranches he'd miss completely if he failed to get information and directions from stockmen along the way. He also knew using a motorcar to take him where he needed to go would be pure folly. The old trails and wagon roads would simply be too much for such a vehicle. So he began his journey in the midsummer heat ahorseback, riding along the eastern edge of the Tularosa traveling south, zigzagging back and forth from high country to flats, up and down canyons, stopping wherever folks lived to ask about Clagett and Floyd. After two weeks with half the job done and no results, he returned home, out of supplies and out of steam. He rested his ponies for a few days, caught up on chores, reequipped, and set out again, this time drifting toward the western slope of the basin.

He made several stops at ranches on the northern fringe, crossed the malpais to the low hills that ran up against Workman Ridge, rode south for a spell, and veered west to Estey City, a copper-mining settlement struggling to survive despite a lack of water. He questioned residents without success about Clagett and Floyd before turning south to camp for the night at Mills Ranch, nestled at the toe of the Oscura Mountains.

In the morning, he crossed to Mockingbird Gap in the San Andres Mountains and began working his way down the eastern slope. At Dick Gilliland's spread he was treated kindly to lunch, reminisced with Dick for a time about the cattle wars in the old days, and went on his way empty-handed, feeling less and less positive about finding Edna Mae's missing brother. He rode into the Hightower Ranch headquarters late in the afternoon, weary from a long day in the saddle, and got invited to dinner.

Addie Hightower served up her famous beef-and-bean casserole with homemade bread to soak up the juices, and Jake just couldn't say no to seconds. Over coffee on the porch, Earl recalled that Patrick Kerney at the Double K had taken on a hired man some years back who might have been Vernon Clagett. Earl remembered the year, 1920, because he'd seen the man at the Double K the day Patrick had given a party for his ex-wife, who'd died soon after.

Jake showed him Vernon's photograph. After studying it for a while, Earl couldn't decide if it was the same man or not but guessed it just might be. Jake raised Pat Floyd's name to Earl, but it didn't ring a bell. Nevertheless, Jake turned in for the night encouraged to have his first inkling of a lead since he'd started spending Edna Mae's greenbacks to find her brother.

* * *

At the chicken coop pen, Matt stopped cleaning bird droppings and watched the approaching rider. He was astride a pretty calico pony leading a sorrel packhorse. Because he had his hat pulled low, casting a shadow on his face, Matt couldn't make him out. He looked lean and wiry and sat easy in the saddle.

Pa had left home early to deliver some ponies to Engle for rail shipment to a ranch in Cimarron and wasn't due back until evening. Matt called up to the house that a rider was coming and walked to the horse pasture fence to greet the visitor.

The man drew rein at the gate, pushed back his hat, nodded, and said, "Howdy, I'm Jake Owen and I'm looking to speak with Patrick Kerney." He had a bushy white mustache that covered his upper lip, a high forehead, and thick ears that stuck out from his head.

"I'm Matt Kerney," Matt replied. "My pa's not here right now, but light and sit a spell."

"Thank you kindly." Jake eased out of his saddle. At the house, a pretty Mexican woman holding a toddler stepped onto the veranda. Jake tipped his hat and the woman waved in return.

"When will he be back?" he asked.

"In time for dinner," Matt answered. "Are you looking to buy some ponies?"

"After passing by some fine-looking colts in the pasture, I'm mighty tempted to do just that," Jake answered genially. "No, I'm trying to find a man who hasn't been heard from for some time, name of Vernon Clagett."

Matt nodded. "I know him. He worked for my pa, but not for long."

"You're sure of that?"

"Yes, sir."

"About five years ago?" Jake asked.

"That's right. He wasn't too friendly around folks. Kept to himself mostly. He took off one night."

"You saw him leave?"

"No, sir. My pa said he asked for his wages and left."

"He just rode out at night?"

"He didn't have a horse, so he walked, I reckon," Matt replied.

Jake paused. Why would a hired man without a horse quit at night and just walk away, especially from a remote ranch miles from anywhere? He'd save that question for Patrick Kerney. "Are you sure of all this, son?"

The question peeved Matt. He inclined his head in the direction of the woman on the veranda. "There's no reason for me to lie. Ask her, if you don't believe me."

"I'm not doubting you," Jake said soothingly. "But remembering something from five years ago can make facts get hazy."

"Are you the law?" Matt asked.

"I used to be the sheriff of Lincoln County," Jake replied. "Now I do private detecting work. Mind telling me who the lady is?"

"Evangelina, my pa's wife," Matt answered. "She was here when Vernon quit and left."

"Mind if I water and rest my horses?"

"Go ahead. There's coffee on the stove when you're done."

"Thank you kindly."

Matt returned to cleaning the chicken coop and pen, a job he truly despised, wondering what was so dang important about finding a man who left the Double K five years ago. From what he recalled about Vernon, he couldn't think of one good reason anyone would want him found in the first place.

He'd read novels about private detectives but had never met a real one before. As he watched Mr. Owen water his ponies, tie them to the hitching post, loosen their cinches, and climb the stairs to the veranda, Matt determined to find out more about this mystery.

* * *

Based on his recent travels, Jake decided the Double K was one of the nicest-looking outfits on the western slope of the Tularosa. The well-built, large house sat on the shelf of a hill overlooking the basin, with a barn, a windmill, a water tank, several outbuildings, and the corral below near a narrow streambed. A small, mud-plastered adobe casita sat behind the main house, enclosed by a courtyard wall connected to the house. The barn was weathered but bigger and more solidly constructed than any Jake had recently seen, and everything, including an old chuck wagon parked beside the barn, appeared to be in apple-pie order. Beyond the house, higher up on the hill, a small family graveyard surrounded by a low picket fence looked out on the Tularosa. It was about the prettiest resting place Jake had caught sight of on the basin.

With the kitchen door open, a cooling breeze coursed through the room. Over a cup of good, hot coffee, Jake spoke to Evangelina about Vernon. She attested to what the boy had said.

"He wasn't a nice man," Evangelina added. "I was happy when he left."

"Wasn't nice?" Jake echoed, trying not to let the pale birthmark that covered most of her cheek and part of her forehead distract him. It didn't hide her prettiness. Under the table at his feet, the little button was playing with a miniature cast-iron horse on wheels and a toy Model T Ford coupe. A boy of two with blue eyes, he didn't look one bit Mexican. He pushed his toys back and forth on the floor, scooting along behind, making motorcar and pony noises and talking to himself in Spanish.

"How so?" Jake asked.

Evangelina shrugged. "Just with the looks he gave me and the way he smiled. I think he would like to do mean things to women. Why do you search for him?"

"His sister in Texas wants to find him. Where did he bunk when he worked here?"

"In the tack room in the barn."

"Mind if I take a look?"

"There's nothing of his there, not even the bunk, but you can look if you wish."

Jake drained his coffee and stood. "Much obliged. What's your little boy's name?"

"Juan Ignacio Kerney," Evangelina replied, smiling with obvious pride, "but we call him Johnny. Will you stay for dinner?"

"I will, and thank you kindly." On the veranda he came upon Matt. "Mind showing me the tack room?" he asked.

"Why do you need to see it?" Matt asked.

"Maybe Vernon left something behind that will help me find him."

"I doubt it," Matt said as he opened the barn door. "Things get lost around here and never found."

"Why do you say that?" Jake asked.

"Pa's been looking for some papers he misplaced years ago. I think he's been through every nook and cranny on the ranch. He hasn't found them yet."

Jake held his tongue as he stood in the middle of the tack room, although he was suddenly mighty interested in knowing what Patrick Kerney had been searching for over such a long time and if it had anything to do with Vernon Clagett. He took a quick look around. Saddles, bridles, halters, and ropes were all in their proper places, neatly put away. A big old Mexican cabinet stood against a wall next to a large chest. The boy sat on the chest watching Jake closely.

"Are you looking for a corpus delicti?" Matt asked jokingly.

"No, I'm not," Jake answered. "But you're a smart young fella to know what that is."

"I'm moving to town when school starts so I can go to high school," Matt replied with a touch of self-conscious pride.

"High school," Jake repeated, raising an eyebrow. "That sure is ambitious. I bet your pa is proud."

"Not so much," Matt said. "He'd rather keep me on the ranch helping out."

"That's what most boys your age do, I reckon."

"I know, but I'm not ready to quit my schooling. Do you know my pa?"

It intrigued Jake that such a young lad would stand so openly against a father's wishes, but it wasn't any of his business. "I've made his acquaintance a time or two," he answered.

"Aren't you gonna search for evidence?"

"I don't see a need to. Where would you look?"

"Anywhere that isn't obvious, like behind and under things."

"That's good thinking," Jake replied as he turned to the door.

"Why do you want to find Vernon?" Matt asked.

"His sister needs him at home in Texas," Jake answered. "Family business and such. Think your pa will let me bunk here for the night?"

Matt nodded. "But the casita is a lot nicer. It even has a chamber pot and a washbasin."

"This will do me fine," Jake replied, eager to take a closer look at the tack room without any company.

* * *

Several miles from home, Patrick was intercepted by Matt, who'd ridden out on Patches to bring exciting news that a private detective named Jake Owen was at the house looking for Vernon Clagett.

Patrick's pulse quickened. "What did you tell him?" he asked as indifferently as possible.

"That he'd worked here for a little while," Matt replied as he rode alongside.

"It was so long ago, I'd almost forgotten about Vernon," Patrick lied. "Why is Jake looking for him?"

"Because Vernon's sister hired Mr. Owen to find him."

Patrick forced a laugh. "Why would anyone want to find that no-account?"

"He didn't say."

"Well, no matter. I'll tell Jake what I know and he'll be on his way. Has he been invited for dinner and to spend the night?"

"Yep," Matt replied. "Evangelina's holding supper until you get home, and I'm plenty hungry."

"That won't do." Patrick spurred his pony to a trot, his head racing with all the possibilities of what Jake Owen's visit meant.

* * *

As soon as Patrick arrived, put away his pony, and washed up, he greeted Jake and sat down for dinner. "My boy says you're searching for Vernon Clagett," he said after his first mouthful.

"I am," Jake said. The aroma of Evangelina's enchiladas had his mouth watering in anticipation. "But I'm not about to get up from this plate of good food to go find him."

Patrick laughed. "And I sure ain't about to go with you."

Although anxious to know what Jake knew, Patrick stuck to small talk throughout the meal. It wasn't until they were alone at the kitchen table that Jake returned to the subject of Vernon Clagett.

"I heard from your wife and boy that Vernon didn't work for you long," he said.

"About a month all told, maybe a few days more," Patrick answered. "I'd hired him for a temporary job of work, and truth be told I planned to let him go anyway. He quit me before I could fire him."

Jake scratched his head. "But why did he leave by shank's mare at night?"

Patrick shrugged. "I don't know what was in his mind. He wanted to leave right away, so I gave him his wages; he packed up and left. If you ask me, that old boy was a little weak between the ears."

"Did he leave anything behind?"

"I don't think so. Why do you ask?"

Jake smiled. "Drifters like Vernon land someplace for a while and often squirrel away what few valuables and private papers they have. Sometimes they forget when they move on. If Vernon got scatterbrained and did that, whatever he left behind might help me find him."

"If he did, I would have kept it for him in case he came back looking for his property. He left nothing here as far as I know."

"He didn't steal from you?" Jake asked, probing around Matt's statement that his pa had been searching for some lost papers for years.

"Not a dime," Patrick answered. "He was just an unreliable, hard-drinking man."

"How did you come to hire him in the first place?"

Patrick grimaced. "Jake, you're plumb wearing me out with these questions and I was tired already. Now, Matt says you want to bunk in the tack room, and I won't hear of it. Evangelina has the casita all made up for you. If you have more to ask me, we can finish this up in the morning."

"You're right." Jake pushed back from the table and stood. "That's mighty kind of you and the missus. I'll get my bedroll. *Buenas noches.*"

"Good night," Patrick replied.

Jake stopped at the door. "Did Vernon ever mention a fella named Pat Floyd?"

The flickering lamplight couldn't hide the color that rose on Patrick's cheeks, and he swallowed hard before answering. "I never heard of the man."

"I'll see you in the morning," Jake said, wondering what soft spot he'd just niggled.

He got his bedroll from the tack room and ambled to the casita, feeling Patrick Kerney's eyes on him all the way.

In the morning after breakfast, Jake brought up Pat Floyd one more time. "Maybe I should be looking for this Pat Floyd fella in order to find Vernon Clagett."

Patrick's jaw tightened and his back stiffened. "You're doing the detecting work, Jake, not me."

Jake sighed as he walked to his saddled and waiting pony. "And I'm not getting anywhere with it; that's for certain. It's likely I ain't ever gonna find old Vernon. Maybe he fell off a cliff and broke his neck or got lost in the basin and died of thirst, his bones scattered by a mountain lion or coyotes. I've got half a mind to write his sister and advise her to call off my search."

"Do what you think is best," Patrick said, tension easing from his body.

"Thanks for making this old boy welcome," Jake said as he put a leg up and eased into the saddle.

"Stop by anytime."

"I appreciate that," Jake said, now more determined than ever to learn more about the mysterious Pat Floyd. But not yet; he had a few more outfits to visit south of Rhodes Canyon where Clagett might have sought a rancher's hospitality after quitting the Double K.

* * *

In the five years since Emma Kerney's death, Wallace Claiborne Hale and Henry Bowman, exercising their duly appointed responsibilities as trustees for Matthew's inheritance, made semiannual visits to the Double K ranch to check on the boy's welfare and progress. Always politely but never warmly received by Patrick Kerney, they left satisfied that Matt was content living on the ranch, got along quite well with his father, and excelled in his studies at the rural, one-room school he attended on a nearby ranch. Matt had also made it clear during their visits that he planned to continue his education after grade school, in keeping with his mother's wishes.

Today, a troubled Wallace Claiborne Hale traveled alone to make an unscheduled visit to the Double K. Three months past, a sudden heart attack had killed his good friend Henry Bowman, and Wallace's impromptu trip was provoked by a letter he'd just received from Patrick Kerney. In it, he wrote that Matt was needed at the ranch and would not be permitted to live in town to attend high school. Why Patrick had decided to go against Emma's express wishes, spelled out in the trust document, puzzled Hale. Until now he'd expressed no opposition to Matthew's desire to continue his education.

Prepared and willing to do battle with Patrick about his decidedly wrongheaded decision, Wallace kept the horse moving at a steady pace on the dreary ride from Engle. A city-raised boy from the East, he liked the comfort and orderliness of town life, loved driving his automobile, and actively lobbied the state legislature and county commission to build more highways. He found no aesthetic inspiration in the stark desert and desolate mountain landscapes of the Tularosa, and today he especially missed Henry's congenial company and lively conversation, which had made the previous bone-jarring trips to the ranch tolerable.

There were no clouds in the sky to temper the blistering, blinding sun. Gusting, swirling winds coming from every direction had coated his face and hands with fine dust and sand. Most creatures were wisely hiding from the noonday heat, except for a few stray cows, standing as stationary and silent as statues, and several large, dangerous-looking snakes stretched out like broomsticks in the middle of the road. Only once did he encounter another soul, an old cowboy with a bushy white mustache who mumbled howdy as he trotted by leading a packhorse.

He arrived at the ranch parched and cranky but determined to put on a pleasant face and hear Patrick out before making his argument on Matt's behalf, if indeed the boy hadn't changed his mind about continuing his schooling.

The Double K had a reputation for being one of the nicest outfits on the Tularosa, and in comparison to the hardscrabble ranches surrounding it, that was indeed the case. But in Wallace Claiborne Hale's opinion, it still came up short, lacking the basic amenities of indoor plumbing, electricity, and telephone service. It was so primitive that water for household use had to be hauled by hand from a well, and so remote that an expedition had to be mounted to go to the mailbox.

Matt was at the corral watching his father ride a large horse that didn't seem too eager to cooperate. As Patrick tried to turn the animal to the left, it balked, snorted, bobbed its head, and kicked its rear legs. Each effort Patrick made to turn the beast caused the same aggressive behaviors.

Hale had never understood why anyone got pleasure sitting on the back of such potentially dangerous creatures. He saw nothing romantic about it whatsoever. He stepped down from the buggy and greeted Matt with a wave and a smile. The boy had sprouted since Hale's last visit. He was now a gangly juvenile, all arms and legs, with his father's square shoulders and his mother's blue eyes.

"Hello, Matthew," he said as the boy drew near.

"Howdy, Mr. Hale. I got your letter about Mr. Bowman dying. Sorry to hear it. I liked him."

"So did I, Matthew," Hale replied. "He is missed by many folks."

"What brings you to the Double K?"

"As the sole remaining trustee of your estate, I thought it best to give you and your father a complete report."

"Have we run out of money?" Matt asked, worry creeping into his voice.

Hale chuckled. "On the contrary, Mr. Bowman made some wise stock investments on your behalf. I'll go over it in detail with you and your father. You haven't changed your mind about high school, have you?"

Matt glanced in his pa's direction. "Nope, but Pa has dug in his heels about me going. He wants me to stay put and help out here. Says I don't need more schooling."

Wallace patted Matt's shoulder. "Let me see what I can work out with him."

Matt smiled anxiously. "I sure hope you can do something."

Wallace handed Matt a wrapped package. "I've brought you two books: *Babbitt* by Sinclair Lewis and *One of Ours* by Willa Cather. *One of Ours* is about a farm boy who goes off to fight in the Great War. It won a great literary prize. I hope you'll like both of them."

Matt tore open the package and inspected the books. "That's swell of you. Thanks, Mr. Hale."

"You're welcome," Hale replied, grabbing his bag from the buggy. "Mind if I wash some of the dust off?"

"Shucks no," Matt answered. "Pardon my manners. You go on and get settled in the casita. I'll take care of your pony."

"Thank you." Hale waved to Patrick Kerney in the corral, who'd dismounted and was now slowly walking the pony in circles, for whatever reason Wallace couldn't begin to imagine. Patrick nodded slightly in return.

Grateful to get out of the sun, Wallace went straight to the casita, drenched his face in the cool water of the washbasin, changed into a fresh shirt, and went to the kitchen, where Evangelina greeted him with a warm smile. She put a finger to her lips and pointed to her young son, asleep on a pile of blankets under the window. On the veranda, Hale asked how she was.

"We are all fine, Señor Hale. It is a nice surprise to see you here again so soon. How sad for you to lose your friend Señor Bowman."

"Yes, very sad." Wallace carefully studied Evangelina. He knew Patrick Kerney's mistreatment of Emma had caused her to divorce him; thus, he always looked for any visible sign that the same might be happening to Evangelina. She seemed in perfect health. "How is young Johnny?" he asked.

"Ah, such a handful," she replied. "I chase him everywhere. Only when he sleeps do I rest." She looked back into the kitchen. "Tonight I will fix a beef stew for you for dinner."

"That sounds delicious," Wallace said, not at all pleased at the prospect. "Are you happy and well?"

"Oh, *sí*," she answered, but there was no joy in her voice or merriment in her eyes.

* * *

Wallace Claiborne Hale had practiced to perfection the ability to appear cordial and disarming in the most demanding circumstances, until he gauged it was time to strike on a client's behalf. At the dinner table, he kept the conversation centered on topics important to ranchers: the weather, range conditions, beef prices, and in Patrick's case, the weak market for cutting horses and cow ponies. After dinner, in the living room, he began with a straightforward recitation of the trust's financial particulars—what was devoted to real estate, bank deposits, stock—and the total current net worth, which showed a healthy growth in liquid assets.

"I'm therefore happy to report that new earnings have erased all expenses paid to date on Matthew's behalf and added a nice profit to the trust," Hale concluded.

From the chair behind his desk, Patrick simply nodded and said nothing.

Wallace turned to Matthew, who sat next to him on the couch. "Your mother would be pleased. If we continue to see such satisfying results from Mr. Bowman's investments, you'll be handsomely provided for well beyond your eighteenth birthday."

"Is there enough now for Pa to hire help so I can go to high school?" Matt asked.

"There certainly is," Wallace replied.

"High school ain't gonna teach you how to run this ranch," Patrick said sharply to Matt. "And that's what's important. You get along to bed now."

Matt didn't move from the couch.

"Go on," Patrick ordered.

Matt stood with his back straight, his eyes locked on Patrick, and with only the slightest quaver in his voice said, "Yes, sir, I'm going. But I've been looking forward to high school and maybe college afterward for a long time, and I'm not being sassy about it. It's what I want to do and what Ma wanted for me."

He took a deep breath, turned to Wallace, and said, "Good night, Mr. Hale."

"Good night, Matthew," Wallace said, admiring his gumption.

Patrick waited to speak until he heard Matt's bedroom door close. "Like I wrote in my letter, Matt stays here, and that's the end of it."

"Not quite, Mr. Kerney," Wallace replied amiably. "When you married Evangelina, the trust ceased paying her a salary, but at your request it agreed to send the same monthly allotment directly to you for Matthew's upkeep."

"What's your point?"

"These past three years, we've not asked for an accounting of those expenses from you," Hale replied. "Legally, the trust is entitled to such an accounting and can, if it is found to be reasonable, demand the repayment of any funds you've received that were not specifically spent for Matthew's benefit."

"I've put a roof over his head and food on the table for him," Patrick blustered.

"Which the state and the law expects of you as his father," Hale noted without rancor. "Certainly you can't think that Matthew's trust should reimburse you for doing what every responsible parent does for a child."

"Of course not," Patrick said, glaring at Hale.

"I didn't think so. Should I request an accounting?"

Patrick leaned forward in his chair. "You do that and I'll hire a lawyer to ask the court to put me in charge of Matt's trust. I'm the boy's pa, and by thunder that counts for something in the eyes of the law."

Hale nodded. "That's true enough. But if you choose to take such action, I will do my very best to convince a judge to be sympathetic about a dying mother's last wishes for her son and unsparing in his censure of a father who misused money she left specifically for that child."

"You're bluffing."

Wallace smiled engagingly. "No, Mr. Kerney, I welcome the challenge."

Patrick snorted and leaned back in his chair.

"Perhaps we can compromise," Hale suggested. "If you allow Matthew to attend high school in Las Cruces, the trust will increase the monthly stipend you receive to cover the additional expenses incurred for you to visit him regularly and ensure his well-being.

I'll make all the arrangements for the trust to hire suitable adult supervision for Matthew during the school year. He'll stay at the Griggs Avenue house. I'll have the renters vacate and make sure it is furnished and in good order for Matthew before he arrives."

"How much of an increase?" Patrick asked.

"The trust will send you sixty dollars a month starting when Matthew begins school." It was a generous offer. Over the course of a year, Patrick would receive seven hundred and twenty dollars, nearly twice what a typical ranch hand earned.

Patrick stared at Hale hard for a full minute, working his jaw as though he was chewing over the offer. Finally, he said, "Okay."

Hale got to his feet. "Excellent. I'll put our agreement in writing and have it for you to sign in the morning. Good night, Mr. Kerney."

"Good night." Happy with the outcome, Patrick watched Hale leave before he allowed himself a smile. He needed the money and Matt wanted more schooling, so they both would profit. It was a good deal all the way around.

* * *

Matt crept quietly across the veranda, climbed through his open bedroom window, and stretched out on his bed. He'd heard every word between Mr. Hale and Pa and didn't know whether to whoop for joy or blubber like a baby. Maybe both, he reckoned. He had to be worth more to Pa than money, didn't he? They got along okay, mostly because Matt tried real hard to please him. And on Pa's part, although earning praise from him was rare, he'd never raised a hand to Matt yet. They both shared a love of horses, and over time Matt had come to cherish ranch life, but other than that, he didn't think Pa cared about him much at all.

From what he could tell, Pa was the same with Johnny. He never really played with him or showed much interest in all the new things little kids learn at that age, no matter how much Johnny pestered him for attention. Pa was Pa and probably never would change.

No matter, he was going to high school after fall works, and that was something to crow about! He couldn't wait.

11

To Jake Owen's way of thinking, the fact that Vernon Clagett walked away from the Double K five years ago, never to be seen again, meant he'd probably met with foul play. He reasoned that Vernon had to know the basin some from his time at the ranch and likely would have stayed on the public road that cut across the heart of the Tularosa or taken one of the ranch roads that wandered to canyon or high-country outfits and homesteads. In either case, if Clagett left the Double K alive, as Patrick Kerney said, and wasn't laid low by some bandit, within twenty-four hours he would have showed up somewhere looking for a meal, a place to lay his head, a job—or maybe all three.

Asking folks to remember something from five years back tested their recollection, but everyone Jake questioned swore that a stranger afoot at their door would have been impossible to forget no matter how long ago it had happened. Jake believed them simply because if he'd encountered anyone traveling by shank's mare through the remote backcountry of the Tularosa, it would have been a jaw-dropping experience etched firmly in his mind.

The additional fact that Clagett had planned to travel home to

Texas and never made it further fueled Jake's reasoning that he got held up and killed. He sorely doubted Clagett had traveled cross-country through the badlands and lost his way. That would have made him dumber than a village idiot.

Yet with all his deducing, Jake remained frustrated, with no answers. He'd visited ranches south of Rhodes Canyon, ridden the radius of a day's hike from the Double K looking for bleached human bones along the way, asked about the mysterious Pat Floyd, and gained no advantage whatsoever for his efforts.

Before starting out from his ranch on his second swing, Jake had written Edna Mae Bryan to report no progress. It sure looked like he'd be sending the same news to her in his next letter, and he didn't like that notion one bit. There was one spread left on his list to visit, the Rocking J, owned by Al Jennings; then he'd drift homeward bound. He glanced quickly skyward; it was getting on to midmorning. He'd raise up the Rocking J long before dinnertime.

* * *

He arrived at the Rocking J to find Al Jennings and a traveling blacksmith shoeing ponies outside a slat-board horse barn next to a squat windmill on a wooden tower that creaked as it whirled in a steady breeze. Sheltered in a forest meadow, the horse barn and a small, four-room ranch house of stone and mud-plastered adobe faced west, with a view through the trees of the dry, dusty Jornada tablelands below.

While unexpected visitors were never obliged to lend a helping hand, it was always neighborly to do so. Jake pitched in, and well before dinnertime all Al's ponies were freshly shod, and the blacksmith, who was due at a ranch on the Jornada early in the morning, had packed up his gear and gone on his way. Jake and Al loitered on the porch while Dolly and Al Jr. studied the Sears catalogue at the kitchen table in anticipation of an upcoming supply trip to town.

Jake asked Al about Vernon Clagett.

He slapped his knee and guffawed. "He was a piece of work, I'll tell ya. I only met him a few times after Patrick hired him to fence his pasture. Last time was when we went to that surprise party Patrick threw for Emma at the ranch. He was an oily kind of fella, toadying around Patrick, but in a needling way. Patrick said if I wanted to get his dander up to call him Squirrel. It was a moniker he hated. He sort of looked like a squirrel too. Right off, I couldn't understand why Kerney hired him."

"He told you Clagett's nickname was Squirrel?" Jake asked, thinking if Vernon disliked the handle that much, why disclose it? That made no sense, unless maybe Kerney knew Clagett from an earlier time and a different place.

Al nodded affirmatively. "That old squirrely fella just mostly stayed to himself. He wasn't a friendly sort."

"When did Kerney hire him to fence a pasture?" Jake asked.

"I don't recall exactly," Al replied. "But it wasn't long before the party. Patrick set him up at an old shepherd's cabin for a time before he brought him over to the ranch to help out before spring works."

"Where might that cabin be?"

"Head southeast from here about six miles on the ranch road," Al directed. "You'll see a gate on your left. The place is pretty much caved in. Why are you looking for him?"

"Clagett just might become a Texas oil millionaire if I can find him," Jake replied. "At least that's what his sister hopes. He owns a quarter section next to a top-producing oil field."

"If that's true, the Almighty sure works in mysterious ways," Al remarked sardonically.

"Amen to that, brother," Jake chuckled.

After they filled their bellies at dinner, Jake and Al traded stories, talking of livestock, bloodlines, and times of drought until it was time to turn in. Eager as he was to search the shepherd's cabin come morning, Jake fell asleep quickly and slept soundly on a soft bed of straw in the horse barn.

* * *

In a cool morning drizzle from a big cloud parked over the west slope of the mountains, Jake searched the ruins of the shepherd's cabin. Finally he decided anything once hidden had long ago decayed to dust or been carried away by rats or crows. The rain cloud blew to the north, the sky cleared, and in the heat of the day he made tracks across the basin to the village of Tularosa, where he sent a telegram to the state of Arizona superintendent of prisons requesting additional information about ex-convict Vernon Clagett, including his nickname and known associates in prison, and a record search for a former inmate with the handle of Pat Floyd. He asked that the reply be sent to him care of the Lincoln County sheriff's office in Carrizozo.

He stabled his ponies, rented a hotel room, paid for a bath, and spent a good, long time soaking his bones in a tub before dressing and stepping out for a drink of whiskey at the best speakeasy in town, which also served up a good, thick beefsteak dinner. Inside the town's grandest hotel, the speakeasy was a wide-open, walk-in establishment that had once been the most popular bar on the basin, with thespian companies staging popular plays of the day, dance hall girls putting on burlesque shows, and wagering tables filled with cowboys, tinhorns, and locals gambling away their money.

He ordered a whiskey at the ornate bar, thinking maybe Prohibition was the law only in the other forty-seven states of the U.S. of A., because it sure didn't seem that way in New Mexico. He ate a leisurely meal capped off with a piece of warm apple pie before strolling down a lane under tall, cool cottonwoods to a rambling adobe near the river.

Jake had talked to everybody who'd been at the Double K the night Clagett disappeared, except the Chávez family members. He knocked at the open door and was greeted by a very pretty dark-eyed little girl no more than four years old who stared up at him and said nothing.

Behind her, Teresa Chávez quickly appeared. She'd aged over the years since he'd last seen her but was still a handsome woman.

Jake tipped his hat. "I'm Jake Owen, señora," he said. "I don't know if you remember me, but sometime back I was Lincoln County sheriff, and your husband's cousin, Edmundo, was a deputy of mine. You were kind enough to feed and put us up a time or two when we were traveling through on official business."

Teresa smiled and stood aside. "*Sí*, Sheriff Owen, come in."

The large room, with a huge fireplace at one end, served as the kitchen, dining room, and family parlor. A long table stood squarely in the middle, surrounded by benches and chairs. Hand-carved cabinets and chests rested against a two-foot-thick outer adobe wall with three small windows that looked out on the courtyard.

"Are you hungry?" Teresa asked as she picked up the little girl.

"No, ma'am, but I appreciate the offer. I'm here to ask about a person I'm looking for, a fella by the name of Vernon Clagett. You met him some years back at the Double K."

Teresa sat with the little girl at the table and motioned for Jake to do the same. "The strange man Patrick hired years ago?"

"That's right," Jake said as he removed his hat and took a seat across from Teresa.

"I can tell you nothing about him."

"Do you remember him leaving the ranch?"

Teresa nodded. "That is what Patrick told us. I did not see much of him."

"He quit and left the night of the fiesta."

"That is what I understand."

"Your son Miguel was with you at the ranch."

Teresa smiled and nodded. "Yes, as was my brother Flaviano and his wife, Cristina. They are in Albuquerque and won't return until the end of the week." She patted the little girl's cheek. "This is Miguel's daughter, Carmelia, my youngest grandchild. He and Bernadette are expecting another baby any day now."

"Well, that's mighty fine," Jake said. "Where is Miguel now?"

Teresa nodded at the open door. "You'll find him at the casita across the meadow waiting anxiously for the baby to come. Carmelia's birth was difficult, so he hasn't been in the fields for two days."

"Do you know a Pat Floyd?" Jake asked.

Teresa's smile faded. "Who?" she asked unconvincingly.

"Pat Floyd," Jack repeated.

Teresa shook her head. "No, I do not. Do you seek him as well?"

"I'm looking for anybody who may have known Vernon Clagett," Jake replied. "Pat Floyd's name came up."

Each time he'd said the name, Teresa seemed uncomfortable. Jake dropped the subject. "Last I heard, Edmundo was still living in White Oaks; is that right?"

"*Sí,*" she answered with some relief. "Have you been to the Double K recently?"

"I surely have."

"How are they?" Teresa asked. "How is Evangelina? Juan Ignacio? Matthew? It's been months since I've seen them."

"They're all doing just fine, as far as I can tell."

Teresa's smile returned, but a bit forced. "*Bueno.*"

"Have you ever known Patrick Kerney to use another name?" Jake asked.

Teresa stiffened. "I have known him since he was a little boy, and he has always been Patrick Kerney. Why do you ask me such questions?"

"Sorry, ma'am, to have made you uncomfortable," Jake said as he stood. "But I think you know the name Pat Floyd, and it would be a boon to me if you'd answer truthfully. I ain't looking to cause the man trouble, just find out what he knows about Vernon Clagett."

Teresa walked Jake to the door. "*Buenas noches,* Sheriff."

Jake shook his head sadly. "This isn't about the law, señora. Vernon's family wants him found and sent home safe and sound if possible. They don't know whether to grieve or continue to hope. They're counting on me to help. It must break a body's heart not to know the whereabouts or the fate of a loved one."

"Such pain that would bring," Teresa said sympathetically. She touched her heart and took a deep breath. "I know nothing for certain, only an old rumor my husband once told me long ago. Speak to your former deputy, Edmundo. He may know more about this person you seek."

"*Gracias,* señora." Jake tipped his hat and walked through the meadow, scattering a small herd of grazing sheep, wondering why worry was in her voice when she'd asked about Patrick Kerney's family and why she had failed to mention him.

He called out for Miguel Chávez at the lane in front the casita, under the branches of tall cottonwoods that concealed him in shadows. He moved closer to the house and was met by a nervous-looking man at the front door.

"I'm Miguel Chávez," Miguel said anxiously. "I saw you coming from my mother's casa. Did she send you over here?"

"Yes, she did. I'm Jake Owen and I'm looking to find Vernon Clagett."

"Ah, Sheriff Owen, I remember you from a long time ago when I was very small," Miguel said.

"I hear your wife is about to have a baby, so I won't take much of your time."

"I have nothing but time," Miguel said sheepishly. "I am banished to the kitchen while my wife's mother and sisters are with her, with orders to race over and bring my *madre* when told to do so. The women say that is all I am good for right now. Who do you look for?"

"Vernon Clagett."

Miguel nodded. "The Squirrel. That's what Patrick called him when they came here from the ranch. You look for him?"

"I do," Jake answered. "His sister wants to find him."

"He quit the night of the fiesta for Emma. I have not seen him since. At breakfast, Patrick told us he'd walked away, but I thought surely he'd ridden away."

"Why do you say that?"

"There were too many people staying the night and not enough room in the ranch house, so I slept in the wagon next to the barn. Late in the night, I woke up to the sound of horses leaving."

"You're certain of that?"

"Well, I thought so, but it could have been a dream."

"How many horses?" Jake asked.

"Two, I think, but it must have been a dream. I'm sure it was."

"Most likely," Jake said.

"You say his sister is searching for him?"

"She needs him at home in Texas," Jake replied.

Miguel nodded knowingly. "One cannot escape family."

Or death, Jake thought. "I reckon so," he said. "Good luck with the baby and all."

"*Gracias.* It will be a boy; I am sure of it."

* * *

In 1903, Jake's first term in office as Lincoln County sheriff had lasted less than a year when his opponent won a court fight and took over in August. At the time, Carrizozo was nothing more than a railroad terminus with a few slat-board saloons and cafés, some of them half-tent affairs. It had no schools, no bank, no streets to speak of, and one hotel that skinned folks a dollar a night for a room.

In 1905, Jake got elected again and served until a new sheriff took office in 1909. By that time Carrizozo had a church, a school, a bank, several fancy houses, two livery stables, a depot and round-house, half a dozen stores, and a good hotel or two. Many of the businessmen had moved their establishments from White Oaks, a nearby gold-mining town that had fallen on hard times when the railroad bypassed it.

During all the years Jake served, Lincoln had been the county seat. That changed in 1913, when a court fight to move the county seat to Carrizozo succeeded. The local politicians who backed the move were so sure of victory, they started building a new court-house before the case got decided.

The courthouse had been finished the same year, and it was the most imposing building in town. Made of red brick, it soared two stories on a stone-and-mortar foundation, with a broad stairway leading to a high, arched entry. Above the entry rose neoclassical columns that framed arched windows and a low balustrade, topped off by a square cupola with a flagpole. Behind the entry, a hipped roof with parapets continued the formal façade. Large windows on both floors looked out at a parklike setting with benches and cottonwood trees. It proclaimed to all that Carrizozo was a community on the rise.

Jake got to town after the county workers, including the sheriff, had gone home for the day. The front entrance to the courthouse was unlocked, so he put a note saying where he would be staying on the sheriff's office door, put his ponies up at the livery, paid extra for oats, and had a drink at the Stag Saloon before ambling to the Carrizozo Eating House and Hotel, where he'd spent many a pleasant hour visiting with old friends while in town from the ranch.

Built and operated by the railroad, the hotel had steam-heated rooms, electricity, indoor plumbing, and an elegant dining room, where good food was served around the clock. He got a room and washed up but felt too restless from long days in the saddle to stay still. He stretched his legs on a walk around town, wondering where the search for Vernon Clagett would finally take him. He turned the corner to the hotel to see Tom Sullivan, the current Lincoln County sheriff, step up onto the porch.

A battlefield veteran of the Great War, Tom had returned home and joined the New Mexico Mounted Police, serving until it was abolished by the state legislature in 1921, which left the citizens of New Mexico without a statewide police force. A native of Lincoln County, he'd amassed one of the state's best arrest records as a mounted police officer, which had helped get him elected sheriff four years back.

Inside, Jake spotted Sullivan at the registration desk with his back to the front door, talking to the room clerk.

"There he is," the clerk said, nodding at Jake.

Tom turned. "Howdy, Jake. I've got a telegram for you at my office out of Arizona about a fella named Vernon Clagett."

"What's it say?" Jake asked as he shook Tom's hand.

"It's a long one," Tom replied. At six-two, he made Jake feel undersize. "Best you come and read it."

"Let's mosey on over," Jake replied. "If I like what it says, I'll buy you dinner."

Tom grinned. "Then I'm a shoo-in for a free meal."

* * *

Jake settled into a chair next to Tom Sullivan's office desk in the county courthouse and read the telegram from the Arizona authorities. Vernon "Squirrel" Clagett had been a cell mate of Pat Floyd, who in 1893 had been tried and convicted in Cochise County for stealing a saddle and sentenced to serve two years at the Yuma Territorial Prison. Upon the recommendation of the prison superintendent, Floyd had been pardoned by the governor and released early.

Additional disciplinary reports about Clagett showed he'd been in solitary confinement three times for smuggling, twice for insulting an officer, and once as the prime suspect in the murder of another inmate, who'd died from a knife wound. No charges were filed against him. Considered dangerous, Clagett had his sentence extended after being convicted of selling contraband cigarettes and liquor to other inmates. He'd served a total of eight years.

There was only one infraction for fighting on Pat Floyd's record, which caused him to be assigned to breaking rock on the trouble-makers' crew. But he had then been transferred to the prison library, where he worked as a trusty up to the time of his pardon.

"Does the name Pat Floyd ring a bell with you?" Jake asked.

Tom shook his head. "Nope, would have told you if it did."

"I make it to be a go-by name," Jake ventured.

"Could be," Tom said. "Most boys who use one pick a name close to what their mamas gave them. But trying to find somebody who used a go-by name thirty years ago might be as hard as scratching your ear with your elbow."

"Pat for Patrick," Jake suggested.

"That's likely," Tom agreed. "Got somebody in mind?"

"Patrick Kerney of the Double K down on the east slope of the San Andres," Jake replied. "But I want firm proof. If you'll ask Arizona to send you a photograph of Pat Floyd, that just might help cinch it for me."

"I'll send a request by telegraph in the morning. It might take a while to get it by mail. Why are you hunting these rowdy old boys?"

Jake folded the telegram and put it in his pocket. "I'm looking for Clagett because his sister wants him found and Pat Floyd because maybe he knows where Clagett is or he killed him. I'm figuring Vernon to be dead."

"Why so?" Sullivan asked, lighting a stogie.

Jake gave a Tom a quick summary of what he'd learned on his search.

"Clagett may have deserved killing," Tom said, sliding a piece of paper to Jake. "Take a look at this."

It was a year-old telegraph out of Willcox, Arizona, advising all county sheriffs in Arizona and New Mexico that Vernon Clagett was wanted for the theft from a ranch of two pistols and a long gun, which he'd pawned in Bisbee.

"Seems like old Vernon didn't go straight and narrow after prison," Jake allowed.

"There's more about that old boy you might want to know," Tom said with a sly smile. "His name rang a bell with me from my days with the mounted patrol, so I did some searching in the old files and came up with the pièce de résistance, as the French like to say. Clagett is also wanted on murder charges out of Graham County, Arizona. Seems in 1920 he killed a man and his wife asleep in their bed and stole their mule and wagon."

He handed Jake the old wanted poster. "There's a five-hundred-dollar reward for his capture."

Jake read the poster. "Well, I'll be damned."

"I telegraphed the Graham County sheriff," Tom said, handing Jake a Western Union message, "and here's his reply. Clagett drove the wagon to Duncan, sold it to a livery owner, and disappeared into the Gila high country. Told folks he was going searching for gold. The murdered couple had a grown son who homesteaded near their place. He identified the wagon, the mule, and Clagett, who'd been hired on to help his father cut and haul firewood to sell in the neighboring towns. Find him alive or prove him dead, and you're five hundred dollars richer."

"That would be a nice piece of change," Jake remarked. "Would you ask Cochise County to send the court proceedings on the Pat Floyd trial? That might tell me something about the man."

"I sure will." Tom snuffed out his stogie and stood. "Are you happy with what you've learned?"

Jake got to his feet. "Hell, I'm almost giddy."

"That's good, because the idea of you springing for a meal at the hotel has given me one hell of an appetite. They're serving up oysters that came in fresh on the train, and I mean to have me a plateful."

"You're gonna love what I have to tell you about why Vernon's sister is looking for him."

"Tell me now," Tom said as he locked his office door.

"Nope, I don't want to waste a good dinner story," Jake replied.

* * *

Jake Owen's story of the hunt for Vernon Clagett and Pat Floyd so intrigued Tom Sullivan that he got up early the following morning and knocked on Jake's hotel room door.

"How about I buy you breakfast," Tom said when Jake opened the door. "Then I'll drive you out to White Oaks to see old Edmundo Anaya."

"I'll meet you in the dining room," Jake replied. "Order me two fried eggs and some biscuits and gravy."

Over a final cup of coffee after breakfast, Tom slid a five-star Lincoln County deputy sheriff's badge across the table to Jake. "I've been thinking that you may need the law on your side," he said. "Especially if Clagett turns up alive and wants to make trouble, or Pat Floyd does the same. Do you swear to uphold the Constitution of the United States and the laws of New Mexico?"

"I do," Jake said, slipping the badge into his shirt pocket.

"You're duly sworn," Tom announced. "Pay is a dollar a month, just to make it legal."

Parked at the curb outside the hotel was a new Model T Ford coupe with SHERIFF in white letters painted on the doors. Jake climbed aboard as Tom slid behind the wheel and cranked the engine with the electric starter button on the floorboard. It caught right away.

"It cost two hundred and forty dollars," he said. "It's got twenty horsepower and a top speed of forty-five miles an hour. I had to talk the county commission into spending the money on it, but I'll tell you, old son, with almost five thousand square miles to cover, it saves me time going from one place to another."

"Unless you get stuck, or need to go somewhere a car can't," Jake ventured.

Tom nodded. "There's that, but it's convenient when the weather is good and the roads don't run out."

The Ford bounced along the dirt road to the old gold-mining town of White Oaks at a good clip, throwing up more dust than a herd of wild horses. Sheltered in a small valley surrounded by hills and mountains, the town had fallen on hard times. It had once been a busy town of twenty-five hundred souls, but when the gold played out and the railroad bypassed it, most folks left. Now no more than a few hundred remained, with the number dwindling every year.

Many houses stood abandoned. Empty stores, including the two-story bank building, looked out on quiet streets. Up by the mines, idle stamp mills silently rusted. The schoolhouse tucked into a gentle hillside, the whitewashed church on the valley floor, and several of the stately Victorian homes with lovely grounds still looked cared for, but where neat rows of modest homes had once stood, now there were only piles of rubble, forlorn sections of picket fence in front of empty lots, and weathered, boarded-up houses with collapsed porches.

Edmundo Anaya lived with his wife in a dilapidated cottage on Jefferson Street near an old placer site on the outskirts of town. Now nearly blind, and crippled badly with rheumatism, Edmundo greeted them in the small, cluttered front room while his wife made fresh coffee in the kitchen.

"It is not often my old friends come to visit," he said to Jake as he rose slowly from his chair and offered his hand. "What brings you and the sheriff to my home?"

"I've been negligent about visiting," Jake said as he shook his hand, shocked by the sight of his old deputy. His body was bent and twisted, and thick spectacles accentuated his washed-out, runny eyes. Both men were of the same generation, and while Jake had his aches and pains, his complaints about his health were nothing compared to Edmundo's frailties. "For that, I apologize."

"There is no need," Edmundo replied, settling back into his chair.

"We're here to ask you about a man named Pat Floyd," Tom Sullivan said.

"Pat Floyd," Edmundo repeated, staring in Sullivan's general direction. "I don't know him. Does he live here in White Oaks?"

"Teresa Chávez told me you might have known him," Jake said.

"Who?"

"Teresa Chávez, your cousin Ignacio's widow," Jake clarified.

Edmundo shook his head. "I don't know her either."

"Yes, you do," Jake urged. "Teresa and Ignacio would put us up when we traveled together through Tularosa on official business."

Edmundo nodded. "Ah."

"Do you remember now?"

Edmundo gestured helplessly. "Only a little."

"Do you know Patrick Kerney?" Tom Sullivan asked.

"From long ago?" Edmundo asked.

"Yes," Jake answered.

He made a small space between his thumb and forefinger. "*Un poco,* I think. I forget so many things. You tell me, did I know him when I was your deputy?"

"Probably not," Jake said as Edmundo's wife came into the front room with mugs of strong coffee. It was time to stop asking any further questions. "That coffee sure smells good."

Edmundo smiled. "*Sí.* We always have good coffee. It is one of the few things I tell my wife I always must have, no matter what—good coffee."

As he drank his coffee, Jake hoped Edmundo's memory might improve, so he made small talk about their days sheriffing together. Edmundo recalled some of the more notorious *bandidos* he'd arrested, though he easily confused the crimes, the dates, and the places. At one point he seemed to think it was still 1908. When Jake asked about his children, Edmundo talked about a dead son, killed long ago in a tragic wagon accident, as though he were still alive.

They left with nothing to show for the visit other than the sadness of seeing a once proud, strong man laid low and in such poor circumstances.

"I do believe Teresa Chávez bamboozled me into believing that I'd talked her into giving up Patrick Kerney's secret past by sending me to see Edmundo," Jake said as Tom wrestled the Ford down Jicarillo Street on the way out of town.

"Maybe she didn't know Edmundo had gotten so frail and forgetful," Tom suggested.

Jake laughed at such an absurd notion.

"Now what?" Tom asked.

"I wait and hope Arizona has a prison photograph of Pat Floyd."

"And if they don't?"

"Old Patrick Kerney doesn't need to know that, does he?"

* * *

For two weeks, Jake faithfully rode to his mailbox hoping to find a letter either from the Arizona prison authorities or one from Tom Sullivan containing the proof he needed to confront Patrick Kerney. What finally arrived left him with conclusive evidence that

Patrick Kerney had used the go-by name of Pat Floyd when he'd been tried, convicted, and sent to Yuma Prison.

Although Arizona had been unable to find a photograph of Pat Floyd, the district court in Cochise County had sent a copy of the trial transcript, which included his sentencing statement to the judge. In it, Floyd told the judge he stole the saddle because it had originally belonged to him, that he'd lost it in a card game, and that he badly wanted it back. He swore the saddle had been given to him on his fifteenth birthday by a man named Cal Doran, who had raised him up after his pa died. It was a double-rigged, hand-tooled stock saddle with wool-lined fenders and a nickel-plated horn and had so much personal and sentimental value that he got drunk one night and foolishly decided to steal it back. He apologized for his grievous error in judgment and asked for leniency. His youth and remorsefulness got him a reduced sentence of two years.

Tom had circled Cal Doran's name and added a note on the margin of the page that Doran had been a Lincoln County deputy before the turn of the century and a partner in the Double K Ranch with John Kerney, Patrick's father.

Tom had also enclosed a personal letter:

Dear Jake:

> *I sent a passel of telegrams to sheriffs in New Mexico asking if either a Pat Floyd or Patrick Kerney were known or suspected criminals and all the answers came back in the negative. Of course that doesn't mean anything definite. I've discovered Kerney served in the Rough Riders in Cuba and was cited in one of Teddy Roosevelt's dispatches for volunteering as a runner during a battle and getting the*

message through in spite of being wounded in action, so he's
got some grit.

One notion continues to plague me about Kerney. Seems
any man who has made so much of an effort to keep a part of
his past a secret for so long just might become dangerous
when faced with the truth.

Since I put a badge in your hand and am now your boss,
I propose to go with you on your next visit to the Double K.
Consider it a direct order. I close with my good wishes.

Sincerely,
Thomas Sullivan, Sheriff
Lincoln County
State of New Mexico

Early in the morning three days later, Jake Owen and Tom Sullivan, well supplied and on sturdy ponies, rode out of the town of Carrizozo, drifting along a trail that would take them to Malpais Spring, where they would camp for the night on their way to the Double K Ranch.

* * *

From his ma's grave site on the hillside above the ranch, Matt watched two riders approach from the northeast. He'd walked up from the house when Pa had started yelling at Evangelina about Johnny getting into the henhouse and breaking the eggs. Matt felt particularly bad about it because he'd been the one to discover Johnny covered in egg yolk coming up the stairs to the veranda with a big grin on his face, holding the last egg in his hand. It didn't seem to matter to Pa that Evangelina had been in the *baño* for only a few minutes while Johnny did his mischief in the henhouse. He yelled at her anyway. He always held her to blame for anything around the house that went wrong or upset him. It made Matt miserable to see it, and Evangelina was always glum and wretched for days afterward. Even little Johnny went around like a hang-tail puppy for a while after one of Pa's temper fits.

As the riders got closer, Matt recognized Mr. Owen. The other man was a stranger, but both of them wore badges on their shirts. He scrambled down the hill in time to reach them at the hitching post just as Pa stepped out on the veranda.

"Howdy, Mr. Owen," he said as the two riders stepped down.

"Matt," Jake replied.

"I didn't know you were the law."

"Just sometimes," Jake said, looking up at Patrick on the veranda. "Best you let the sheriff and me have a few words in private with your pa."

"What's going on?" Matt asked, hopeful Mr. Owen and the sheriff were chasing an outlaw loose on the basin.

"Never you mind," Pa boomed. "Bring in that gray gelding from the pasture and put it in a stall. It's showing some lameness in the right forelimb. Git, now."

Disappointed, Matt threw a leg up on Patches. With Pa riled already, there was no chance he'd change his mind. He went through the gate and put Patches into a fast lope, hoping to be back with the gray in time to find out what had brought the law to the Double K.

* * *

"What brings you here with the law and a badge pinned to your chest?" Patrick asked Jake as he stepped off the veranda.

"I guess you know Sheriff Sullivan," Jake replied genially.

"I know who he is," Patrick replied, his gaze fixed on Jake. "I asked you a question."

"Vernon Clagett," Jake replied.

"I already told you what I know," Patrick replied.

Jake scratched his chin and shook his head. "I've been trying to figure the best way of saying you ain't been telling the whole truth. I was gonna mention I know two horses were heard leaving late the night Clagett supposedly took off from here by shank's mare, and that somehow you knew Clagett's prison nickname, and that there is no way in hell that Clagett could get off the Tularosa alive without somebody seeing him."

"Is that what you were gonna say?" Patrick replied sarcastically.

"Yep, I was, until I got proof that you're Pat Floyd, and Vernon Clagett was your cell mate at Yuma."

"You know that for sure?" Patrick hissed.

Jake nodded. "I surely do. You gave yourself away when you threw yourself on the mercy of the court in Cochise County, Arizona Territory, and got a reduced sentence for stealing that nice saddle Cal Doran gave you that you lost gambling."

Patrick's expression turned grim. "So I lied to you. A man has a right to his privacy and you weren't the law."

"But if you lie now, it's gonna be a lot harder on you," Tom Sullivan warned.

"You can't arrest me for something I ain't done yet," Patrick retorted.

"That's true," Jake answered. "But before I ask you again what happened to Vernon Clagett, you might want to know that if I can't abide your answer and prove you wrong, I'll make sure every citizen on the Tularosa knows you're a liar, thief, and ex-convict."

"That's big talk, old man, with a star on your chest and a pistol on your hip."

"But maybe I don't have to tarnish your good name with those facts," Jake said, unperturbed by Patrick's snappishness. "We know Clagett liked to work for folks, find out what valuables they had, kill them, and steal what he could carry away. Last time it happened was in Arizona some years back. There's a murder warrant out for his arrest."

"Did that happen to you?" Tom Sullivan interjected.

Patrick bit his lip. "What if it did?"

"Man has a right to protect himself and his property," Tom answered.

"Let's say a man did that; what would the law do?" Patrick asked.

"Swear to it that it was self-defense, and if the law believes you, no district attorney will prosecute," Jake replied.

"But in this particular situation, we have to be fussy," Tom said, "and ask you to produce a body."

"Why is that?"

"Jake's put in too much hard work to let it go all for naught," Tom answered. "He has Clagett's sister to answer to, and she needs physical proof he's dead."

Patrick fell silent. "What would I have to do exactly?" he finally asked.

"Tell us exactly what happened, take us to where Clagett is buried, and make a sworn statement of fact to the district attorney," Tom said. "If we back you up, it will end right there, guaranteed."

"No court, no judge, no trial?"

"That's right," Jake said.

Patrick sighed. "I'm not going back to prison."

"No need to worry about that," Jake counseled.

Patrick nodded. "Okay, I'll talk."

In the heat of the day under a sun beating down on them, Tom Sullivan and Jake Owen listened as Patrick Kerney told them a story that began in 1893 in Tombstone, Arizona, with the theft of a saddle and ended in 1920 with the death of Vernon Clagett on the Double K.

* * *

Matt spent considerable time trailing the slow, lame gray back to the ranch, and he was still a good mile from home when Pa rode up with Mr. Owen and Sheriff Sullivan.

"I'll be gone for several days," Pa said gruffly. "You take care of that gray and look after things."

"Where you going, Pa?" Matt asked.

"We're looking for someone and your pa is scouting for us," Jake replied.

"An outlaw?" Matt asked, his eyes lighting up.

"A real bad one," Sheriff Sullivan replied.

"Can I come?"

Pa shook his head. "I need you here. Head on home, now."

Jealous and unhappy to be left behind, Matt watched them ride away. Sometimes it was not fair to be a kid. Not fair at all.

12

Drought parched the Tularosa in 1926, and by the end of the year Patrick was forced to sell all but his breeding stock and most of his cow ponies. Only his scheme to fence the pasture he'd bought adjacent to the Rocking J as a hedge against drought had saved him from having no grass at all. But he'd borrowed against the land, and unless he got the loan extended, he'd lose it and be forced to bring the animals back to the lower pasture near the ranch house and purchase expensive feed for them.

With no money coming in from ranch operations, the monthly checks Wallace Claiborne Hale sent from Matthew's trust account kept Patrick from going further into debt. For that he was grateful.

A month ago at a stockmen's meeting in Alamogordo, the talk was about drought and how to deal with it. A professor from the agricultural college in Las Cruces who came and spoke to the group applauded Patrick's strategy of resting grasslands as an example of good ranching practices. A rancher with a small outfit pointed out that Patrick's scheme worked only if you had the land to spare. To pay the bills and keep creditors off his back, the man hired on as a logger in the Sacramento Mountains when work was to be had, while his wife and two young sons looked after the ranch in his absence. In many families it took everybody pitching in to keep kith and kin together, while out on the range their few remaining animals starved.

Patrick hoped for early winter moisture and lots of it. But it stayed bone-dry and the Tularosa remained a hazy, choking patchwork of dull, dusty colors during the daylight hours. The land was mostly burned brown, with puffy, finely granulated dirt on top of hardpan. Bunchgrass had withered and died to the point that he could kick it out of the ground, roots and all, with the toe of his boot. Winds rose late in the morning and persisted deep into the night, buffeting both man and beast. Stands of desert-hearty fourwing saltbush drooped thirstily, scorched by an unrelenting sun. The once-abundant wildlife that had left countless critter tracks on sandy shelves, arroyo bottoms, and alkali flats virtually disappeared. Although winter had arrived on the calendar, only cooler days, colder nights, and long shadows signaled the change. Everything on the ground crackled dry underfoot.

Drought and hard times in the Southwest weren't big news back east. Fat cats were making fortunes in the stock market, city folks were buying fancy cars, radios, record players, and refrigerators for their modern, stick-built homes, and all the politicians were proclaiming far and wide that prosperity for everyone was just around the corner.

Good fortune hadn't completely bypassed New Mexico. Patrick saw it each time he went to town or during one of his rare visits to Albuquerque. More streets had been paved, curbs and sidewalks put in, street signs thrown up, and electric light and telephone poles erected. Wires ran every which way down streets and alleys. New houses filled once-vacant land fit only for rattlesnakes, lizards, jackrabbits, and scorpions. On Central Avenue in Albuquerque, every new office building, hotel, and merchandise store had electricity, indoor plumbing, radiator heat, and telephones. It all made for easier living, Patrick reckoned, and while he appreciated what towns and cities had to offer, he never liked them much.

He remembered seeing a nameless spot on the road at the foot of the Sacramentos transformed into the blossoming railroad town of Alamogordo almost overnight, complete with a train station, hotel, stores, and blocks of homes on a neatly laid-out street. The first time he saw it, he'd been trailing a herd of cattle from the ranch down the Chalk Hills with Emma, Cal Doran, and Gene Rhodes, skirting the undulating, shifting white sand dunes, paralleling the wagon road. They stopped at the crest of a small rise to rest and water the critters, and there before them a town appeared, shimmering in the distance like a desert mirage. The somber beauty of the untouched tableland with the long, unbroken uplift to the easterly hills where widemouthed canyons spilled from high mountains capped in thick forests had been changed forever. It seemed at first unsightly to Patrick. But with the passage of time, he could barely remember how that spit of land had looked before the hand of man transformed it.

Patrick loved the Tularosa and gladly survived in its harsh beauty far away from town life. What he made in a year rarely equaled half of a city worker's salary. He lived without the modern conveniences and comforts many people took for granted, on a solitary frontier where even in a drought livestock outnumbered people. He kept a shaky hold on marginal land that provided meager subsistence and fought drought, floods, wildfires, and disasters without a thought of ever willingly giving it up. The basin held him in place like a powerful, unbreakable magnet.

On Christmas morning, he sat alone at his desk in the empty and quiet ranch house, tallying his expenses and debts for the year. Evangelina and Johnny were in Tularosa with her parents and relatives for the holidays. They'd been gone for a week, and he wouldn't fetch them home until after the first of the New Year. Matt was in Las Cruces staying with Wallace Claiborne Hale over Christmas. He hadn't been at the ranch since fall works and wouldn't return until spring break.

Patrick didn't miss any of them. In truth their absence relieved him of any need to put up with their ways for a time. Johnny was a whirling dervish, never still for a moment, constantly underfoot, impossible to find, hard to discipline. When he gave his mother fits and Patrick threatened to take a switch to him, she turned hard faced and angry with him. There were days they hardly spoke to each other. Even when they did, there was no joy between them.

Matt was no easier to deal with. His schooling in town had turned him into a know-it-all. He paid attention to Patrick only when it came to something to do with horses. Otherwise, he kept his head buried in books. He did his chores without complaint and minded his manners, but his heart wasn't in the ranch. Patrick figured the day would come when Matt would be gone from the Double K for good.

A howling wind made the prospect of working outside unappealing. Chilled, he rose and put a log in the fireplace and poked the embers until they ignited into long, flickering tongues that burst into flames. Reminders of the ghosts from the graveyard on the hill were all around him. An old pair of Cal's spurs was on the fireplace mantel with John Kerney's hunting rifle mounted above. George Rose's Navajo saddle blanket was draped over the back of the couch, and on the floor in front of it was the flowery hooked rug Emma had made years ago, now faded and worn. He felt no sadness, no lingering grief about their passing, just an empty weariness about life.

He got another cup of coffee, laced it with a liberal shot of whiskey from a bottle he kept in a bottom desk drawer, shrugged off the chill, and returned to tallying his expenses in the ledger book. After he got all the figuring done, he'd hunker down for the day, fry up a beefsteak and warm some beans, and search some more for the governor's pardon from Yuma Prison that Vernon Clagett had stolen out of his Rough Rider's footlocker. Maybe he'd even get drunk after he finished the afternoon barn chores and put feed out in the chicken coop. It amounted to a day off.

* * *

The day after Christmas, Evangelina sat with her *tía* Teresa at the big table in her hacienda. It was the first time since her visit that she'd had an opportunity to be alone with Teresa, and she was relieved to be away from her harping mother, who seemed intent on browbeating her into having more children. Evangelina had no desire to do so, nor did she wish to explain why. Knowing she would be chastised as ungrateful, she'd said nothing about her unhappy marriage to her parents or any of her relatives.

Her son, Juan Ignacio, as Teresa insisted on calling him, was across the meadow at Miguel's house, happily playing with his cousins. The rest of the family had scattered to their own homes after breakfast, and in the peaceful quiet, the women began sorting through a large pile of serviceable children's clothing Teresa routinely collected from family members and stored in a large wardrobe.

As her grandchildren, grandnieces, and grandnephews multiplied, so had Teresa's assortment of dresses, pants, shirts, blouses, sweaters, socks, undergarments, coats, and hats in all possible sizes. She inspected, repaired, washed, ironed, and folded each item before carefully putting it away. Over the years, the wardrobe had come to be known as Grandmother's Closet. There were children in the family who were the third or fourth beneficiaries of items from Grandmother's Closet.

When the sorting was done, Juan Ignacio Kerney would return to the ranch with enough clothing to more than replace the few decent pairs of pants and shirts he had left to wear.

"*Gracias,*" Evangelina said. "These will last him all year."

"It is nothing," Teresa replied. "The drought has made all of us even more frugal than before. With no cattle to sell and nobody buying his ponies, I'm sure Patrick is having a hard time making ends meet."

"It has been difficult," Evangelina agreed.

Teresa took a brown paper parcel from the chair next to her and passed it Evangelina. "This is for you."

"What have you done? Christmas was yesterday."

Teresa smiled. "Open it."

Evangelina quickly untied the string and peeled back the paper to reveal two housedresses, one a light blue with a zigzag seamed bodice, and the other a pretty yellow frock with a rickrack trim.

"These are brand-new," she said, her eyes sparkling as she fondled the material. "How wonderful you are to be so generous."

Teresa reached across the table and patted her hand. "I don't see enough of you. Can't you come with Juan Ignacio to visit more often?"

"He needs me at the ranch," Evangelina said regrettably. "There is no help."

Teresa sighed at the inevitability of Evangelina's response. "Then I must come to visit you. I will bring your parents with me, your brothers and their wives, and some of the younger children, who can entertain Juan Ignacio. It is time for another fiesta."

Evangelina brightened. "I'd love that."

"*Bueno,* it is settled. Let's pick some dates."

Evangelina's expression clouded. "I should ask him first."

"Nonsense," Teresa countered. "We will all come to the ranch when the two of us decide it is best."

Evangelina put a hand to her mouth to stifle a laugh. "*Sí,* let us decide."

They talked of family matters and village gossip for an hour or more before Evangelina left to help her mother prepare a special dinner to honor Father Eduardo Morales, who had traveled from El Paso to conduct holiday services and hear confession. Both the Armijo and Chávez families would be in attendance, filling the hacienda with more than forty adults and children.

Wrapped in a shawl against the chill, with the comforting scent of woodsmoke in the thin, cold air of winter, Teresa stood in the courtyard and watched Evangelina hurry across the meadow to fetch Juan Ignacio, bundles of clothing tucked under her arms.

Teresa had held back asking her about her life with Patrick at the ranch, although it was clear that all was not well between them. A woman who truly cares for her husband will naturally and warmly speak of him to others by his given name. Over the course of their morning together—in fact, ever since Evangelina's arrival—never once had Teresa heard her do so. And although Evangelina had always been shy and hesitant because of her birthmark, now she simply seemed defeated.

She'd married Patrick quickly outside of the church, believing, perhaps rightfully, it was her only chance to find some affection and escape the likelihood of a dreary life as an old maid.

But was she better off for it? When Patrick had come looking for a temporary housekeeper, had it been a mistake to suggest Evangelina? How could she have possibly known Evangelina would stay on at the ranch after Emma's passing and marry Patrick? Should she have tried to stop it? Only Evangelina's parents, blind to her misery, seemed happy with her circumstances, pleased that she had married and had given them at least one grandchild.

Teresa's thoughts turned to Emma. Oh, how she missed her bold, fierce, independent ways. She wondered if the day would come when all women would be more like her.

* * *

Father Eduardo Morales sat with Evangelina in the front pew of the quiet, empty church. Last night after dining at her parents' hacienda, she'd asked to meet with him for pastoral advice. He readily agreed, knowing that she had married a nonbeliever, failed to have her child baptized in the cradle, and basically abandoned her faith. He found it bewildering that the daughter of such devout parents could stray so far from the sacraments of her religion, but Satan constantly worked against the teachings of the church in so many different ways.

"What troubles you, my child?" Father Morales asked softly, studying Evangelina's birthmark, which some villagers thought branded her as a witch. Did evil lurk in her? How much of a sinner was she? How far had she fallen? Concerned for her soul, he smiled benignly, warmly, at her.

"I don't know what to say, Father," Evangelina said with embarrassment. "I'm afraid of what you will think of me."

Morales smiled. He often heard such comments from the truly sinful, those more concerned about the outward show of appearances than the sins they'd committed. Sinners such as these often needed discipline and punishment. "Do not concern yourself with such needless apprehensions," he said. "Say what is in your heart."

"I have no happiness in my life, Father, outside of the joy my son brings me," she replied, studying her hands, clasped in her lap, to avoid his serene gaze. "I married knowing my husband didn't love me. I thought I could be content with that. He was the only man who would have me as a wife, and I was grateful, wanted to please him. But I'm nothing to him. No matter how hard I try, I do nothing right. I am no more than his housekeeper."

Father Morales arched an eyebrow. "Surely you are more than just a housekeeper if you have given him a son."

Evangelina blushed. "He has his needs."

"You cook for him, take care of his house, raise his child, share his bed," Morales enumerated. "You do all these wifely duties."

"Yes."

"And you do so without complaint?"

"I do not argue."

"Yet what he provides is not enough to comfort you?"

"We live in isolation far from town, Father. Rarely does he allow me to visit my parents, my brothers and sisters, or my many relatives. We see few people at the ranch and have no friends. He drinks at night and goes to sleep without saying a word. I am so lonely."

"How old is your son?" Father Morales asked.

"He will be four soon."

"Were you a true Catholic, I would tell you to have more children to bring comfort to you and eventually help this man you live with, but you are not," Morales said sternly. "I know that you were confirmed in the church, so you must remember your catechism. You must know that your marriage is not sanctified, not recognized in the eyes of the church. You might as well be a whore living with this man."

Evangelina gasped, lowered her head, and sobbed into her hands.

"Your tears cannot erase the truth of what I say," Morales said without a hint of sympathy. "Does this man beat you?"

Evangelina shook her head.

"Has he ever told you your child could not be raised in the faith?"

Evangelina shook her head again. She thought of telling Father Morales about the money that was to be paid to her through Matthew's trust, the money she never saw either before or after her marriage, the money Emma wanted her to earn to secure her own independence, but she knew it would make no difference to the priest.

"You have no reason to complain," Morales concluded. "Although he is not Catholic, he gives you and your child food, shelter, and clothing and does not raise a hand against you. He asks only that you do what any man reasonably expects from a wife: to serve and support him. If you are lonely, pray to Jesus Christ to give you back your faith. Pray the rosary every day. Ask the Virgin Mary to guide you. Teach your young son the catechism and raise him in the true faith of our holy church. Confess your sins when you have the opportunity to do so."

"Yes, Father."

"Are you ready to confess now?"

"Yes, Father."

In the confessional, completely broken, her hands trembling, her lips barely moving, her eyes blinded with tears, Evangelina crossed herself and said, "Bless me, Father, for I have sinned."

* * *

Matthew Kerney's Christmas vacation had been the best one ever since his ma had died. Usually, he'd be at the ranch counting the days until his return to town, but this year he was the guest of Wallace Claiborne Hale, staying at his grand house on the north side of Pioneer Park, a lovely square in the middle of the nicest neighborhood in town.

Many lovely houses faced the square, all of them decorated for the holidays. Wallace's house—he insisted Matt call him Wallace—had been built early in the century in what was called the Tudor style. It had a steeply pitched roof, massive chimneys crowned by decorative chimney pots, a stucco exterior, and tall, narrow windows that ran in groups of three around the front and sides of the structure. False timbering around the upstairs windows gave the house a medieval look.

Wallace had furnished the inside of the spacious two-story home with large, comfortable, overstuffed chairs, soft couches, and feathery beds, all topped off with the touches of a confirmed bachelor. There were framed hand-colored wildlife prints on the walls of the living room, which contained both a floor-standing Victor Victrola record player and a radio.

In his study, a rack of expensive pipes and tins of fine tobacco sat on a sideboard. A wall-to-wall bookcase was filled with old and rare tomes, and a large oil painting of an elegant, regal-looking woman, Wallace's great-grandmother, hung in a gilded frame behind his desk. Nearby, a beautiful, ornate gun chest held his collection of prize shotguns.

A coal-fired furnace in the basement heated radiators in each room, and there was hot and cold running water in the kitchen and both bathrooms. A Frigidaire electric refrigerator kept perishable food fresh, and in a laundry room behind the kitchen there was an electric washing machine.

Matthew had never lived in such opulence. Each morning, Mrs. Teller, a widow who was Wallace's live-in housekeeper, would wake

him with a gentle knock on his door and a cup of freshly brewed
coffee served on a tray. After coffee, he'd meet Wallace for breakfast in the paneled dining room, where they would plot their day's
agenda. Wallace had closed his law office for the holidays, and
over the course of the last two weeks, they'd attended several holiday gatherings at the homes of Wallace's friends and legal associates and taken long drives in his new Chrysler touring car, which
could go eighty miles an hour. They'd also been to the new Rio
Grande Theater on Main Street to hear a traveling musical company play and sing popular songs of the year, including crooner
Gene Austin's "Five Foot Two, Eyes of Blue" and "Yes Sir, That's My
Baby."

On New Year's Eve, Wallace threw a dinner party and all the
town bigwigs came with their wives, including the mayor, the
county sheriff, two judges, the minister of Wallace's Methodist
church, the district attorney, and the president of the New Mexico
College of Agriculture and Mechanical Arts, who invited Matt to
apply for admission as soon as he finished high school. Already
advanced a grade, Matt would graduate at the age of sixteen.

It was a sit-down dinner in Wallace's large dining room at a
table decorated with daffodils, pussy willows, and asparagus ferns
and set with fine bone china and sterling silver flatware. Mrs.
Teller served shrimp cocktails, chicken soup with noodles, a crown
roast of lamb, mashed potatoes, peas, butter rolls, and marmalade
pudding for dessert. The wine and after-diner cordials flowed freely
from Wallace's well-stocked liquor cabinet. Not a word about Prohibition was mentioned by the assembled guests. With their unan-
imous consent, Mrs. Teller served Matt his first cordial, a fine,
sweet Portuguese almond liqueur in a very small glass. He found
it delicious.

On New Year's Day, Matt and Wallace returned to the Rio

Grande Theater for the movie matinee and in a packed house watched *What Price Glory,* a new motion picture starring Victor McLaglen and Dolores del Rio. It was about two marines in France during the Great War vying for the attention of an innkeeper's daughter while fighting in the trenches. It was both funny and sad and made Matt think about his brother CJ. He still missed him very much.

They returned to Hale's home in the Chrysler in time to take Mrs. Teller to the train station and see her off on a weeklong visit to her daughter in California.

As the whistle blew and the train chugged out of the station, Wallace clasped a hand on Matt's shoulder and said, "Well, chum, it's just the two of us for the rest of your stay. Can you cook?"

"I can, if you like fried, well-done steak and beans," Matt said with a laugh.

Wallace made a face as he got in the car. "I think we'll be dining out nightly for the week. When we get home, I want to go over your trust account with you. You're old enough to know the particulars, and I think you'll be pleased with what I have to say."

"Tell me now," Matt urged.

"Don't be impatient, lad," Wallace lightheartedly chided.

At the house, Mrs. Teller had left them a light supper of cabbage rolls, cold cuts, potato salad with mayonnaise, and a fresh raisin cake. As they ate in the dining room, Wallace gave Matt the good news about his trust account.

"By all reasonable expectations," he said, "you'll be a very well-off young man when you start college. I've an old college friend who works for an investment house on Wall Street, and I've been putting a portion of your assets into blue-chip stocks that he recommended."

"How much?" Matt asked.

"Actually, not that much," Wallace replied. "I've leveraged the stock by buying it on margin, as my friend recommended. That means putting up only ten percent of the stock's value at the time of purchase. You receive full dividends and can sell it for a hefty profit when the value goes up. I'm doing the same with my own stock portfolio."

Wallace brought a new bottle of Portuguese liqueur to the table, uncorked it, and poured two small glasses. "With the money the trust will make over the next few years, you'll likely become the most eligible young bachelor in town."

"If there's enough to pay for college, that would be fine with me," Matt answered as he raised his glass.

"More than enough," Wallace predicted. "I brought a case of this liqueur back on my last trip to the Continent, and this is the last bottle. Let's plan to finish it together before you return to your casita at the end of the week."

"That's okay by me," Matt replied.

They sipped their cordials in the living room, listening to phonograph records by Louis Armstrong and Bessie Smith that Wallace picked from his collection. He poured a second cordial and played new recordings by Duke Ellington and Jelly Roll Morton, all music new to Matt's ears that he liked very much. He thought himself very sophisticated.

When the last record ended, Wallace plucked the empty glass from Matt's hand and ordered him off to bed. "We'll scheme up something to do tomorrow over breakfast," he announced.

"I'll clean up the kitchen before I turn in," Matt countered.

"Nonsense," Wallace said. "No guest of mine does housework. Off you go."

Matt nodded. "Thanks for a swell day. The whole vacation has been the berries."

"It's not over yet, me lad," Wallace replied in a bad Irish brogue.

He waved Matt off to bed and then tidied the kitchen and did the dishes as slowly as possible. All day long he'd been tortured by the idea of being alone with Matt. The boy was everything Wallace desired: handsome, smart, beautifully proportioned, on the cusp of a special kind of manhood. Not touching him except for a quick hug or a manly clasp of his shoulder had taken enormous willpower.

With the last plate put away, Wallace poured another liqueur, retreated to his study, and tried to occupy his mind with a book. Within minutes he put it aside. If he could sneak just one peak at Matt asleep, that would satisfy him.

He ran the idea through his mind. It was harmless enough, nothing more than a host checking on his young guest. Quietly, he climbed the stairs, paused at Matthew's bedroom door, took a deep breath, and silently turned the doorknob. He could hear Matthew's slow breathing in the darkened room. He crossed carefully to the foot of the bed, his eyes adjusting to the darkness. Stretched out under crumpled blankets, his naked right leg exposed, Matthew was fast asleep.

Wallace told himself to back up and leave the room, but the sight was irresistible. He sat down ever so gently on the bed and slowly leaned back until he was side by side with Matthew. Holding his breath, he reached out and caressed Matthew's exposed leg up to his thigh.

"What are you doing?" Matt shouted in panic, pushing Wallace's hand away, sitting bolt upright.

Wallace scrambled off the bed. "Nothing," he blustered. "Tucking you in; that's all. Please, go back to sleep. I'm sorry I disturbed you."

"Get out!" Matt yelled. "Get out!"

Wallace's stomach tightened like a vise as he backed up to the door. "Yes, yes, I'm going. Don't be upset, Matthew."

Matt stood, pushed Wallace out the door, and slammed it shut in his face. "Don't you come back in here," he called.

"No, no, never," Wallace said, sensing he'd just destroyed his world. "I'll see you in the morning. We'll talk then."

"No, you won't," Matt replied, his voice cracking with alarm and anger.

Shaking uncontrollably, Wallace went to his study and sat behind his desk with the door open, listening intently to the silence. In a few minutes, he heard Matthew's footstep on the stairs, and then the front door slammed shut. With his heart pounding, he went back up to Matthew's room and turned on the light. All the lovely presents he'd given Matthew for Christmas were in a jumbled heap on the bed.

Knowing that what had happened couldn't be undone, Wallace Claiborne Hale sank to the floor and buried his head in his hands.

13

Matt ran home through empty, dark streets. Once inside, he turned on every light and locked the front door. He lived alone, but Nestor and Guadalupe Lucero, hired by the trust to look after him during the school year, were close by, next door. Nestor took care of all the maintenance and repairs on the Griggs Avenue house and the rental properties, while Guadalupe cooked his meals, did the laundry and grocery shopping, and kept the place tidy. It was better than boarding with another family or having a live-in housekeeper. Matt got teased by kids at school for living like a swell, but he did his own chores and helped Nestor with anything that needed fixing around the house.

The notion that Wallace might follow him home spooked him. For a moment he considered waking the Luceros. Instead he got a baseball bat from his bedroom and put it by the front door. That made him feel safer.

An older couple, Nestor and Guadalupe had two grown sons with wives and children who lived nearby. Matt frequently got home from school to find Guadalupe babysitting some of her grandchildren or being kept company by her daughters-in-law.

Matt didn't mind. He enjoyed having them around and they treated him like family, inviting him for a Sunday meal, taking him along on weekend picnics at the river when the weather was nice, and correcting his Spanish until he was fluent.

He'd gone rabbit hunting a bunch of times in the foothills of the Organ Mountains with Guadalupe and Nestor's two sons, Roberto and Felipe, and trekked with the entire clan into the San Andres to cut wood, returning after dark with wagonloads enough to last through the winter. The closeness and affection the Luceros had for one another reminded him of Tía Teresa and her family in Tularosa.

The neighborhood had changed a lot since his ma's death. Many of the Anglo families had moved away to newer, nicer houses on the other side of Main Street, where Wallace Claiborne Hale lived. The Griggs Avenue neighborhood was now an older, less desirable part of town, with mostly working-class Mexican families barely getting by. Some of the houses were a little run-down, but the residents did what they could to brighten their casitas with whitewash and vivid splashes of color on picket fences, window trim, porches, and doors. Matt joined in by painting the doors and window sashes on his house turquoise blue.

In the evenings when the weather was mild, folks gathered outside to visit back and forth, the men smoking and swapping stories in their front yards while the womenfolk gossiped on the house porches. A kids' baseball game in a vacant lot would last until dark, with some of the younger girls keeping score. Occasionally there was music and singing, and once in a while a scuffle or argument would break out, but mostly the neighborhood was friendly and peaceful. It was never boring, and Matt liked being part of it all.

The phone rang repeatedly over the next few hours, but he refused to answer it. He had nothing to say to Wallace, never wanted to see him again. For years Matt had secretly wished his pa was more like Wallace: smart, interesting, witty, sophisticated, and worldly. Not anymore.

He'd never thought twice about why Wallace was a bachelor, and as far as Matt knew, no one else did either. He squired attractive single women to the many social and cultural events in town, belonged to all the right clubs, and was considered quite the ladies' man. It was all a big fat lie.

Matt fretted over what Wallace had done until he finally fell asleep on the living room couch. At midmorning the telephone brought him out of a dream where he was lost somewhere in Las Cruces on a street he'd never seen, surrounded by towering buildings that filled the skyline in place of the Organ Mountains. He answered without thinking.

"Good morning, sport," Wallace said cheerily.

"I don't want to talk to you."

"Please let me explain," Wallace pleaded. "I drank too much and had a silly notion to tuck you in; that's all. I didn't mean to startle you."

"That's not what happened," Matt snapped. The memory of Wallace's hand traveling up his leg made him shudder. "I don't believe you."

"You must," Wallace said pleadingly. "I was tipsy and silly. Forgive me."

"Just let me be."

Wallace sighed. "I've upset you. What can I do to make amends?"

"Nothing," Matt snapped.

"There must be something," Wallace urged.

"Nope. Just be glad my pa isn't here, or I'd tell him what happened."

"There's no cause for you to do that," Wallace implored.

"Leave me alone and I won't."

"As you wish," Wallace said, his voice filled with resignation. "I'm going to my office and won't be home until dark. I'll leave the back door open so you can come and get your things. You won't be bothered, I promise."

"Maybe I'll do that," Matt replied.

"Matthew."

"What?"

"I'm sorry. I was a real sap. I raise my hand and swear on a Bible to never again drink while in your company. Does that reassure you?"

"It doesn't matter," Matt replied. "I don't plan to come anywhere near you ever again."

His hand shaking, Matt hung up. He suddenly felt trapped inside a house that was too quiet, too empty. He ran outside and knocked on Nestor's front door. Guadalupe answered, smiling at him, her round face a delight to see. He almost hugged her.

"Matthew, are you back so soon from staying with Señor Hale?" she asked, stepping aside to let him enter.

"I have lots of studying to do before school starts again," he fibbed. The warm glow of the fireplace, the smell of green chili, and the sound of happy chatter coming from the kitchen made him feel safe and protected. "But I'm not here to ask you to come back to work early or to feed me, only to visit for a spell," he added. "I can take care of myself for a few days."

"*Bueno*. Everyone is in the kitchen. Come join us."

* * *

Wallace Claiborne Hale tried hard to occupy his mind with work, but attacks of dread interrupted his concentration time and again.

He stopped working on a breach-of-contract brief that required his full, undivided attention and kept busy organizing documents and placing them in the correct case files. Even so, the mind-numbing routine of putting his paperwork in order didn't erase the absolute panic that came upon him, making his hands shake and his pulse race.

Through his own stupidity, the career and reputation he'd carefully built since coming to Las Cruces were in danger of being destroyed. Up until now, he'd acted on his sexual preference for boys and young men only far away from Las Cruces, but he'd showered attention on Matthew over the past few years without a thought of hiding it. If Matthew decided to expose him, there would be no way to salvage things and escape being ostracized by the community. Matthew was too well liked and too highly regarded to be easily dismissed or ridiculed as a fabricator.

Although it was early evening, Wallace resisted the impulse to go home. He wanted to give Matthew as much time as possible to retrieve his belongings without being disturbed. Meticulous by nature, he began compulsively tidying his office. He arranged everything on top of his desk just so, lined up the books in his bookcases, squared up the row of file cabinets behind his desk, and adjusted his framed diplomas on the wall. Finally he sorted the pens in his desk drawer by size and then centered his chair exactly behind the desk. Satisfied that everything was as it should be, he turned off the lights and went outside to his car.

At home he found the Christmas presents he'd given Matthew on the living room floor, including a leather-bound copy of *The Life of Samuel Johnson* he'd bought in a London bookshop, a brown driving cap purchased at a Fifth Avenue department store, a stainless steel Hamilton wristwatch with MK engraved on the back, and two Levi's work shirts for wear at the ranch.

It was a clear message that all was not forgiven and never would be. Wallace picked everything up, stuffed it in the kitchen trash bin, and left. Realizing there was no chance of redemption, he got behind the wheel of the Chrysler and sped out of town. Up ahead on the gravel road, a new two-lane bridge with thick concrete pillars and railings crossed a narrows of the Rio Grande.

The bridge appeared in his headlights. Wallace floored the accelerator, pointed the car at the bridge bulwark, and at the very last instant before impact closed his eyes.

14

Patrick didn't learn about the auto accident until a letter from Matt came a week later. It arrived just as he was about to leave the Double K to freight some cow ponies by rail for the Diamond A in the Bootheel. The ranch manager was meeting him in Lordsburg to take delivery.

In Patrick's mind, the only issue of importance surrounding the death of Wallace Claiborne Hale was who would take over as the administrator of Matt's trust.

He trailed the ponies to Engle, loaded them on a livestock car, and changed the ticket so he could lay over with his ponies in Las Cruces for a few hours. In Las Cruces, he hurried downtown and immediately hired Alan Lipscomb, the lawyer who had handled his divorce from Emma, to find out what he could about the status of Matt's trust.

"That won't be a problem," Lipscomb promised, running a hand through his thinning hair.

"Good," Patrick said. "Now that both of the men Emma appointed to dole out Matt's money are dead, I want to know if there's any legal mumbo jumbo that bars me from taking over."

The Diamond A had agreed to a good price for the ponies and Patrick felt flush. He counted out some greenbacks and slid them across the desk to Lipscomb. "Let me know if you need more."

Lipscomb smiled. Cash was always welcome in his practice. "I'll get right on it."

"I'm freighting some ponies to Lordsburg and I'll be back the day after tomorrow."

"I'll have something for you by then," Lipscomb replied, pleased with the amount of Kerney's retainer.

"Let my boy know that I've asked you to make sure everything is gonna be okay with the trust. Tell him I'm delivering some ponies to a buyer and will see him soon. That's all you need to say, savvy?"

"I'll tell him exactly what you wish," Lipscomb vowed.

Patrick nodded and left.

The next day at the probate court clerk's office, Lipscomb got a copy of Emma's will and the trust document, and after a careful reading of both documents, he prepared his analysis and paid a visit to Hale's clerk, who was in the process of shutting down the practice. When Kerney returned the following day from his business trip to Lordsburg, Lipscomb reported that no provision had been made to name a successor in the event of the death of both trust administrators. Furthermore, the most recent last will and testament Hale had filed with the court did not mention the trust, much less state a preference as to who should manage it in the event of his death.

"That's what I wanted to hear," Patrick said. "I want to be put in charge of the trust. How do we do it?"

"As Matthew's father, you can expect a judge will look favorably upon your petition to assume fiduciary control of the trust on your son's behalf until his majority," Lipscomb replied.

Patrick groaned. "You can't just do some paperwork to get it done?"

"I'm afraid not," Lipscomb replied. "It will take a court order made on behalf of Matthew Kerney, a minor child, to change the trust document. It's not a lengthy process, but we will need to appear before the court and answer any pertinent questions the judge might have."

"What kind of questions?"

Lipscomb shrugged. "Nothing of great consequence, I would imagine. He'll be interested in knowing your current living conditions, your ability to adequately care for your son, your reputation and character—that sort of thing. He'll likely want to visit with Matthew in chambers and also speak to your wife."

"Is all that necessary?" Patrick snipped.

"I'm not sure if it is or isn't," Lipscomb answered, ignoring Kerney's querulous tone. "It depends on the judge. But it's best to be prepared."

"When can we see a judge?"

"Soon, I hope. Hale's clerk told me only Hale had the authority as trust administrator to write the checks and pay the bills. I'll cite economic hardship for creditors and workers who are owed money by the trust and ask to have your petition heard as soon as possible. It will take me two or three days to have the petition ready. It's best that we go over it together before I submit it."

Patrick snorted. "I suppose I can stay in town a day or two longer. Can you have it ready for me to look at day after tomorrow?"

"Fine," Lipscomb said, seeking to avoid being browbeaten by a man in a hurry. "We'll meet day after tomorrow here at my office, same time. You might want to bring Matthew along so he's fully aware of what you're doing on his behalf."

"There's no need to trouble him about all of this," Patrick replied. "Do you know if Hale was taking any money for himself out of the trust?"

"I don't have access to the actual financial records," Lipscomb replied. "But it's normal practice for a trust administrator to be reimbursed for any legitimate expenses that are incurred."

"So he probably did," Patrick ventured.

"I would imagine so. It's perfectly ethical."

Patrick cracked a tight smile and stood. "I'm obliged."

Lipscomb got to his feet and walked Kerney to his office door. "The sheriff told me that Hale drove straight into the bridge at a high rate of speed. He didn't swerve or brake to avoid something in the road. Don't you find that interesting?"

"Was he drunk?"

"The sheriff said he didn't appear to be."

"You're saying the man wanted to kill himself?"

"Apparently," Lipscomb replied. "But those of us who knew him are baffled as to why. The sheriff reported the cause of death as an accident."

"You got a point in telling me all this?"

"When I spoke to Matthew on your behalf, he mentioned he was Hale's houseguest over the holidays. It struck me that he might have an idea of what was troubling Wallace."

"The man's dead," Kerney replied tonelessly. "I say let him rest in peace."

Lipscomb's cheeks flushed pink as he accompanied Kerney through his outer office. "Yes, of course. I'll see you the day after tomorrow."

Patrick nodded and stepped out into a cold, dry wind. A curtain of dust was bearing down from the west. He moved at a fast clip down Main Street with a few other pedestrians, hurrying to beat the blast of sand soon to engulf the town, and made a quick

stop at a bank before turning onto Griggs Avenue. He reached the
house and knocked on the door just as a high wind began to whistle through the bare branches of the tall cottonwoods that lined
the street.

"It's blowing fierce out here," he said as Matt opened the door
to let him in. The boy had grown at least an inch or two in the time
since Patrick last saw him.

"Mr. Lipscomb told me to expect you sometime today. Have
you seen him yet?"

Patrick nodded. "I just came from his office. He says you, me,
and Evangelina are gonna have to go before a judge to get everything squared away. Seems old Wallace Hale didn't plan on dying,
so there's nobody who can take legal care of things until a judge
decides. With only three years until you turn eighteen, Lipscomb
thinks the best thing to do is put me in charge until then."

"Why is that?" Matt asked.

"For a couple of reasons," Patrick replied. "Appointing someone else could take a lot more time, and unlike Hale, I won't be
taking money out of the trust as a paycheck for managing it."

Matt stiffened. "Hale did that?"

Patrick shrugged. "That's what Lipscomb said."

"That's balled up," Matt snapped.

"Don't take it hard," Patrick counseled. "Most all of these lawyer fellas always find a way to look after themselves first."

Matt shook his head in disbelief. "How long does Mr. Lipscomb
think it will it take to get things settled?"

"I don't know yet. I'll see Lipscomb again day after tomorrow."

Matt scowled. "That's not fair to Nestor and Guadalupe. They
haven't been paid for two weeks. Hale really took money from the
trust?"

"I reckon," Patrick replied. "Ease up worrying about Nestor and

Guadalupe. I'll pay them out of my own pocket until we get this settled."

"That's jake," Matt said, his stern look vanishing. "Thanks."

"Lawyer Lipscomb thinks you might have some idea about why Hale killed himself, seeing as you stayed at his place over the holidays."

Matt's jaw tightened. "He said it was suicide?"

"What he told me was the sheriff called it an accident, but in fact old Hale drove straight into the bridge without stopping."

Matt took a breath and held it. "That can't be," he finally said.

The mortification on Matt's face made Patrick pause and wonder if he knew something about Hale he wasn't telling. "It could be just a lot of gossip," he said reassuringly. "Don't put any stock in it."

Matt recovered quickly. "Yeah, you're probably right."

"How about we step next door and settle up with Nestor and Guadalupe. With the wind now eased up some, we can walk over to that new diner on Main Street and have a meal. I hear the food is good."

"I'd like that," Matt said with a grin.

"Well then, jingle your spurs," Patrick urged.

* * *

During dinner, Matt managed not to ask Pa if he'd learned anything else from Lipscomb about Wallace Hale's death. The notion that Hale might have killed himself made Matt's guilt about Jimmy Potter's death bubble to the surface like hot lava burning in his mind. Images of Jimmy falling, falling, falling, out of that cottonwood tree, his arms flailing, his face frozen with fear, his mouth open in a silent scream, prowled inside Matt's skull most every day like a bad dream.

He should have stopped Jimmy from climbing that tree, or climbed it first. Now he had Wallace Hale's death weighing on his conscience.

With his head bent over a bowl of peach cobbler, he squeezed his eyes shut as the newspaper photograph he'd seen of Wallace's smashed car crumpled against the highway bridge floated into his mind's eye. It made him shiver. If he'd accepted Wallace's apology on the telephone, would he be alive today?

Matt wanted it out of his mind forever, but he knew it wouldn't go away. He swore silently that he'd never say a single word to Pa or anyone else about what Hale had done. Never, ever.

He glanced at Pa, who was busy finishing his bowl of cobbler, running his spoon along the rim for that last bit of sweet peach filling. Pa was never one for conversation at mealtimes, and Matt's silence at the table went unnoticed. About the only thing that would raise Pa's curiosity would be his untouched cobbler bowl.

Matt got to work on it. After his last bite, he thanked Pa for dinner and for paying Nestor and Guadalupe's back wages out of his own pocket.

"I was glad to do it," Pa replied. "Maybe it's best old Lawyer Hale is gone. There won't be any more of this taking your money for his own use. I'll look after what your ma left for you; I promise you that."

"He told me there's enough to pay for college," Matt said.

"You need to get yourself through high school first, before you have any highfalutin ideas about college."

"I know I can do it."

"Maybe so," Pa replied. "But don't get to thinking you'll become some smart-ass, high muckety-muck if you do spend a little time being a college boy."

Matt colored at the insult behind Pa's words. "I ain't like that."

"Maybe not," Pa retorted as he dug into his pocket for money to pay the bill. "Just don't get your hopes up."

* * *

Outside the diner, Matt grumbled good night, not caring if Pa heard the annoyance in his voice, and walked home alone. Not once in his life had Pa ever spent the night at the Griggs Avenue house. That hadn't changed since Ma died. Matt figured it had something to do with their divorce. The way he'd heard it from Ma, they'd bought the house together so she could stay in town while she was pregnant with CJ. Maybe Pa figured Ma's getting the house wasn't fair. Or maybe he couldn't stand to stay in the place where Ma had gone on to make a good life without him. From what Hale had told him, Ma's money savvy put her way ahead financially of what Pa had done with the ranch. Could be that he was just downright jealous.

Matt figured he'd never know the truth of what happened between his parents that caused Pa to be so uncomfortable at the house. But he didn't mind a lick that Pa stayed at a hotel when he came to visit. That was especially true tonight. The idea that Pa didn't seem to think he had the sand and the wits for college made Matt boil with anger.

At home, he plopped down at the kitchen table with his schoolbooks and stared blankly out the window at the dark, moonless night. Once again he got angry at Ma for dying and leaving him alone, and then the tears came.

15

Two weeks before the start of spring works, Patrick, Matt, and Evangelina met in chambers with Alan Lipscomb and Judge Horace Van Patten. In chronic pain from gout and with a highly publicized murder case about to go to trial, Van Patten had no desire to waste time going over the details of what was clearly a legitimate request by a responsible, law-abiding father to assume control of a minor child's rather considerable trust.

Spectacles perched on his nose, Van Patten quickly satisfied himself that the new trust document honored the intent and purpose of the original document drawn up for the boy's mother before her death. He looked up and smiled at Lipscomb and his clients, who stood silently at the front of his desk, and let his gaze fall on young Matthew Kerney, a fine-looking lad indeed.

"Do you plan to graduate from high school and continue on to college as your mother wished?" he asked.

"Yes, sir, I do," Matt replied. "I'm to graduate next year and start college in the fall."

Van Patten beamed with approval. "Excellent." He signed the

petition with a flourish, handed the documents to Lipscomb, and smiled at Patrick Kerney. "You've a son to be proud of, Mr. Kerney."

"He's a good boy," Patrick replied with a nod.

"Thank you, Judge," Lipscomb said as he tucked the documents away.

"Yes, yes," Van Patten said, distracted by his bailiff, who signaled from the private entrance to the courtroom that all parties had convened to present their pretrial motions.

Outside the courthouse, Patrick and Lipscomb departed for the lawyer's office, while Matt and Evangelina went to get Johnny, who was happily being looked after by Guadalupe. On the way, Evangelina urged Matt to come to the ranch for spring works.

"I hadn't planned on it," Matt replied as they strolled along. "I've got studying to do for exams."

Evangelina stopped him with a hand on his arm. "*Por favor,* come. Your *tía* Teresa will be visiting and I promised her you'd be there. She insists we are going to have a fiesta."

"Does Pa know about this?"

Evangelina nodded. "He tried to say no, but Teresa wouldn't hear of it. She is bringing my parents, some cousins, and a few of the little ones to play with Johnny. He gets so lonely with no other children around."

Matt searched Evangelina's sad face. "And you?"

"*Sí,* me *también,*" Evangelina admitted with a cheerless smile. "We have few visitors at the ranch, and many times when he goes to town he leaves us behind."

"He's a thickheaded old man who only cares about himself," Matt blurted, still stung by Pa's insinuation that he might not be smart enough to succeed in college. The barb stuck in him like a cactus thorn.

"You will come, *por favor*?" Evangelina pleaded without uttering one word in defense of her husband.

Matt nodded. "For you, Johnny, and Tía Teresa, I will." He pulled her along by the arm. "Let's get Johnny and go to the drugstore for a soda pop."

"I have no money," Evangelina said apologetically.

"It's my treat," Matt replied, jingling the coins in his pocket.

Evangelina smiled. "I am so happy Johnny has you for a brother."

"Come on, let's get the little rascal," Matt said, hurrying her along.

* * *

Anticipating that Judge Van Patten would approve Kerney's petition, Lipscomb had arranged a meeting at the bank that held the trust fund assets on deposit. The bank president and majority stockholder, Edgar Worrell, late of Chicago, Illinois, had poured a great deal of his wealth into the institution. A former member of the Chicago Board of Trade, Worrell had made his fortune during the Great War buying and selling grain commodities. He'd relocated to Las Cruces two years ago and quickly built a reputation as the banker to see for the most profitable ways to make money in the booming stock and real estate markets. Lipscomb had recently been appointed to the board of directors by Worrell and served as legal counsel.

A man with a thin face, long neck, and thick eyebrows, Worrell was a confirmed Anglophile who had adopted a formal Victorian manner that suited his status as a successful financier. He greeted Lipscomb and Kerney with a warm smile as he ushered them into comfortable office chairs.

"By your presence here, gentlemen, am I to assume the petition to administer the trust has been granted by the court?" he asked in a flat midwestern accent.

"Yes, indeed," Lipscomb replied as he presented the document to Worrell for his inspection.

"Excellent," Worrell commented as he scanned through the petition and set it aside. He removed a file from a desk drawer and handed it to Patrick. "Here are the financials for your perusal, Mr. Kerney. You'll find a summary report on top. Please note the trust grew twenty percent in the eighteen months since your predecessor, Wallace Hale, transferred the account to us. We would very much like you to consider keeping the trust with us."

"It says here in the summary some property got sold," Patrick said, reading the summary. "Why was that?"

"We felt the annual income from the agricultural land under lease was simply too inconsequential to justify retaining it in the trust portfolio. Mr. Hale agreed. He liquidated the asset and used the proceeds to buy a sizable block of stock on margin that continues to perform quite well both in terms of share value and strong earnings. That transaction alone generated over fifteen percent of the net worth increase in the trust."

"That makes sense, I reckon," Patrick said. "But I personally don't cotton to the notion of selling a good piece of land."

Worrell smiled appreciatively. "I understand your point of view completely."

Patrick ran a finger down the summary page. "I didn't know there were any mortgages on the rental houses."

Worrell smiled. "Only two that were recently taken out by Mr. Hale and are serviced by us. The proceeds have yet to be disbursed and are in an interest-bearing savings account. Wallace intended to use the funds to make additional investments in the stock market. You'll notice that the rental income on both properties slightly exceeds the monthly mortgage payments."

"I'm not sure I like the idea of borrowing against property when there's no real need for it."

Worrell nodded agreeably. "A worthy sentiment I fully share, but in this case the risk is at most negligible and the rewards substantial."

"I'll need to study on this more," Patrick said, tapping the file with his finger.

"Of course," Worrell said as he slid a paper across the desk to Patrick. "If you'll sign this authorization, you will have immediate access to the funds in the accounts. Feel free to consult with Mr. Lipscomb or myself should you have any financial questions or wish our guidance."

"I'll do that," Patrick said as he signed the form.

"Do you require any immediate cash?" Worrell asked as he retrieved the form.

"I surely do," Patrick replied.

* * *

Matt returned to the Double K two days before Tía Teresa and the others were due to arrive. He found Pa in a foul mood about the fiesta soon to be foisted on him, and Evangelina cleaning every nook and cranny of the house to avoid him and to get ready for her guests. The two weren't talking, and when Pa sulked back silently from his after-dinner chores he went straight for the whiskey bottle.

While Evangelina was off putting Johnny to bed, Matt sat with Pa in the living room watching him sip his whiskey.

"When did you start drinking again?" Matt asked.

Pa scowled at him from behind his desk and put the glass down. "Don't get your back up about something that ain't your business," he snapped.

"You haven't told me anything about my trust account," Matt replied, skirting the issue, thinking he didn't care if the old man drank himself to death.

"Old Wallace Hale did right by you," Pa replied. "There's enough money to get you through high school and then some. Hell, you might just be better off than me when you turn eighteen."

Matt almost said that would be okay with him but thought better of it. Instead, he asked, "How come you're mad at Evangelina?"

"Never ask a man about his personal troubles with his wife," Pa retorted. "It ain't polite."

"Because I'm part of this family, I can ask," Matt countered.

Pa shook his head in disgust. "I swear I should take a switch to you. Tomorrow at first light, be ready to ride. We need to fix the windmill at the north canyon. It's been broke since last fall, but with no cattle to water I haven't bothered with it until now."

Matt, eager to avoid any further clashes with Pa, allowed he needed to look after Patches and his tack if he was to be in the saddle most of tomorrow. He left Pa to his whiskey and at the pasture fence he whistled for his pony. In the soft light of dusk he watched Patches come to him at a fast trot, head high, tail in the air. Just the sight of him took away the disagreeableness of being with Pa.

Matt opened the gate and Patches pranced through. Fearing his schoolwork wouldn't give him time to care for him, Matt had left Patches behind at the ranch after fall works. He silently vowed not to do that again.

"Miss me, old boy?" Matt asked, rubbing the pony's nose.

Patches snorted a reply.

"I missed you too," Matt said. "Come along to the barn and I'll give you a good brushing."

In an empty stall, Matt brushed Patches down, prettied up his mane and tail with a comb, checked his mouth and teeth, and cleaned his hooves.

"You've been lazing around," he chided as he ran a hand over Patches' belly. "Not getting enough exercise. We'll fix that tomorrow."

Patches nodded.

"I'm fifteen soon. Three more years and we'll be done with all this," Matt whispered. "Ain't too long now," he added wistfully.

He left Patches in the stall and by lamplight spent some time cleaning his saddle in the tack room. Finished, he doused the lamp and hung it on a hook by the open barn door. A half-moon hanging over the Sacramentos gently illuminated the dark and quiet house. As he climbed the stairs to the veranda, the thought struck him that the only time there was ever any peace at the Double K happened at night, by accident, when people were sleeping—and maybe not even then.

* * *

When Pa concentrated on work and wasn't fuming about this or that, he was tolerable to be around. Matt studiously avoided topics he knew would set him off, which kept things calm right up to the time Tía Teresa and her entourage appeared, spreading laughter, conversation, and good cheer. It threw Pa into such a funk, he grumbled his greetings and stomped off, not to be seen again until folks had settled in.

When the women got busy in the kitchen, Flaviano, Miguel,

and Miguel's older brother, Juan, tracked Pa down in the barn with a bottle of liquor and enticed him to stop hiding.

The whiskey improved Pa's disposition enough that he did a fair job as host over dinner, snapping only once at Evangelina for not making his favorite empanadas for dessert. Silence around the table and Teresa's fierce look of disapproval stopped him from voicing any further criticism. Matt wiped his face on a napkin to hide a smile.

After dinner the first storm of the year chased the party into the barn. Bolts of lightning flashed across the San Andres, thunder rumbled and roared, and big, wind-driven raindrops pelted the ground. For a time everyone stood in the open barn door, silently mesmerized by the sight, faces turned skyward, breathing in the sweet scent of rain, listening to the rat-tat drumming on the roof.

When the downpour slackened a bit, the men moved the wagon out of the barn and stacked the hay in empty stalls while the women swept the dirt floor clean. Miguel hoisted Matt on his shoulders to hang lamps from the rafters, and under the flickering lights the music began, accompanied by the crescendo of the deepening storm.

Everyone danced, even the little ones, who twirled around the legs of their parents. Johnny did an improvised jig with Miguel's daughter, Carmelia, who was trying to keep him off her toes. Tía Teresa gracefully swirled in the arms of her oldest son, Juan. Even Pa had an arm wrapped around Evangelina as they took a turn around the floor. Matt didn't see one unsmiling face. It was as if the storm had brought along with it a magic concoction of merriment.

The fiesta didn't stop until the storm ended. Under a clearing sky in half-moon light, the ground was muddy, puddles filled wagon-wheel ruts, rainwater dripped off the sloped veranda roof, and the bone-dry empty streambed that coursed through the horse pasture from the high country roared full throated with water.

Except for Pa, folks hugged, said good night, and went off to bed. After his dance with Evangelina, he'd retreated to his whiskey, loitered for a few minutes, and then snuck away. Before turning in, Matt checked Pa's bedroom, but he wasn't there.

* * *

Teresa retired to the casita pleased with the success of the fiesta but deeply worried about Evangelina. Patrick had destroyed one marriage and was on a path to ruin another. He was a drunk who neither liked nor respected Evangelina and who seemed to care not a speck for their son, Juan Ignacio.

The reality of Evangelina's situation made Teresa shiver. How horrible to live that way. Yet, she knew of other women in similar circumstances who stayed and endured ill treatment by cruel men. Was Evangelina one of those women unable to break away? If so, what would become of Juan Ignacio? Teresa couldn't abide the notion of her grandnephew growing up in such misery.

Or was Evangelina like Emma? She wasn't sure. In recent conversations with her, not a bad word had passed between them about Patrick or her marriage. If she had the strength and desire to leave him, Teresa had yet to see it. And if she encouraged Evangelina to rid herself of Patrick, would Flaviano, who considered his daughter's marriage to Patrick a godsend, ever speak to her again? Without hesitating, Teresa shrugged off that trifling concern. Flaviano's disapproval mattered little compared to saving mother and son from a life of constant sorrow.

It came to her as she slipped out of her dress and prepared for bed that if Evangelina lacked the nerve to leave Patrick, perhaps Juan Ignacio could be saved. He could live with her, see his cousins every day, go to school, attend church, and have a normal life. Surely, Evangelina would see the wisdom to such a plan and be willing to consider making such a difficult but necessary sacrifice for the sake of the boy.

She brushed her hair in the mirror, the dim lamplight nicely softening the wrinkles and creases of her face, and slipped into her nightgown just as a soft knock came at the door. She peeked out to see Evangelina about to turn away.

"*Venga,*" she said, opening the door wide.

"No," Evangelina said nervously, "you are in your *camisón* and ready for bed."

"Don't be silly," Teresa said as she took Evangelina by the hand and brought her inside. "I have been thinking about you and hoping we would have a chance to talk again, like we did at Christmastime."

"You were so kind to me," Evangelina said in a weepy voice, as though it had been an uncommon event.

Convinced that it was exactly that, Teresa said, "Come sit with me." She patted the settee in the small sitting room and waited for Evangelina to join her before continuing. "Have I told you I spent the first year of my married life living right here in this casita?"

Evangelina nodded.

"Of course I have," Teresa said with a smile. "I'm becoming a forgetful old woman."

"Oh, no, Tía, there is nothing old about you."

"Not in my heart, I suppose," Teresa replied. "Did you see how happy Juan Ignacio was tonight, playing with his cousins and dancing with Carmelia? What a joy it was to see. It made me wonder if you might let him come home and stay with me for a while. It would be good for both of us, I think."

Evangelina began to sob.

"What is it?"

"I have nothing here," she gasped. "No life is worth living with a man who doesn't care. I would be better off as a servant in town working for room, board, and a few dollars a month. At least I'd feel alive."

"He gives you none of the money Emma arranged to have you paid?"

Evangelina shook her head. "Not since we married. And now he controls all of Matt's money she left for him. He had us stand before a judge to make it legal. Although Father Morales said I must, I cannot live like this. He cares not for me or for Juan Ignacio. Not even Matthew matters to him."

"Does he beat you?"

"Only with words and looks, never with his hand."

"You must leave him."

She wiped tears from her cheeks. "I have nowhere to go."

"You and Juan Ignacio will live with me. That will make me very happy."

"My father will be furious with me," she replied with a sniffle.

"Only for a little while," Teresa said as she wrapped her arms around Evangelina. "I had feared you would not be strong enough to do this. How I've misjudged you."

"I'm scared," Evangelina admitted.

"Every brave thing we do comes with misgivings. Tomorrow you and my grandson will go home with me."

"*Sí*, we will."

In the quiet of the night, Teresa held her niece and thought about Matthew. Patrick had caused both of his wives to flee from him. He deserved neither. Now that he controlled the trust, would Matthew be the next to be driven away?

* * *

Matt got roused out of bed early by Pa, who told him to hitch the wagon to a team, load it with hay, and meet him in the far horse pasture by the salt lick.

"Aren't we gonna have breakfast first?" Matt asked.

"We can eat later," Pa replied. "Besides, I've no reason to waste time dillydallying at breakfast with Evangelina's relatives."

"That isn't polite," Matt said.

"Don't try to school me in manners, boy," Patrick snapped. "Ranch work doesn't stop when visitors come calling. You should know that by now. Get a move on. I'm gonna need two loads of hay hauled out to the shed by the salt lick, and I want it done pronto."

"Yes, sir," Matt grumbled as he reached for his clothes.

The storm had turned the rutted road through the horse pasture into a muddy mess, with standing water in deep puddles. Matt got the first load through all right, but on the second trip a front wheel sank axle-deep and the team couldn't pull the wagon free. With Pa out of sight a good two miles away, Matt had no choice but to unhitch one of the horses and ride bareback to tell him that he needed help getting the wagon unstuck.

"You're just about useless," Pa growled as he climbed on his pony and rode back toward the wagon.

Matt followed, and at the crest of a small rise he saw three riders approaching the wagon from the ranch house at a slow trot. He jigged the horse into a fast lope and caught up with Pa as he drew rein next to Tía Teresa, Juan, and Miguel.

"What brings you out here?" Pa asked, worried-like. "Is something wrong?"

"We're leaving for home," Teresa said, "and Evangelina and Juan Ignacio are coming with us."

"What the hell for?" Pa demanded.

"They are leaving you, Patricio," Teresa explained.

Pa looked at Juan and Miguel, who stared silently back at him. "Is that right?" he asked boldly.

"It's what Evangelina wants," Teresa answered calmly.

"And you brought two of your boys with you to back your play to take my family from me."

"That is insulting," Teresa said. "You cry of an injustice, yet the truth is you care nothing for them."

Pa snorted and scowled at her for a long minute before sneering. "You're right. Take them with you and be damned. Now, get off my ranch."

"Adios," Teresa said, smiling sadly at Matt.

"Adios," Matt replied. His heart sank as she turned and rode away with Juan and Miguel, wondering if he'd ever see her or Evangelina and Juan again.

"Okay, Matt, let's get this wagon unstuck," Pa said.

"No, sir," Matt said, half afraid that Pa would take a stick to him for disobeying. "I'm leaving too, back to Las Cruces."

"You're under my care," Pa thundered, "and you'll do as you're told."

"No, sir," Matt said. "This ain't my home and never was."

He started the pony toward the ranch house, expecting Pa to run him down, but there was only silence behind him. When he was far enough away, he turned and looked back. Pa had dismounted and was hitching his pony to the wagon. As he watched, the hard, bare truth that Pa truly didn't care a lick about him— never had and never would—felt like a kick in the stomach.

He hurried the pony along, eager to be rid of Pa and the Double K forever.

16

For several months after returning to Las Cruces, Matt worried that Pa would come to fetch him back to the ranch or quit paying for his upkeep through the trust. Neither happened, but when school recessed for the summer, he stopped sending Matt his monthly ten-dollar allowance and paying Guadalupe's salary. Pa's explanation came in a terse note, telling him to either come back to the ranch or get a job in town.

Figuring ahead of time that Pa would likely give him some sort of ultimatum, Matt had rented out the spare bedroom to Boone Cavanagh Mitchell, a college man from Detroit, Michigan, who was studying engineering and working as a mechanic at a garage on Main Street. Matt used the rent money from Boone to pay Guadalupe's salary. To earn pocket money, he started working part-time at Sam Miller's store, clerking and delivering groceries.

Boone and Matt became friends over the course of the summer. At six feet two, Boone was four years older and stood four inches taller, but either Matt's new blue jeans were magically shrinking or he was catching up fast. During their free time, he taught Boone how to horseback ride. Boone repaid the favor by teaching Matt how to drive his jalopy.

On those evenings when they felt too lazy or worn-out to go horseback riding or motoring up and down Main Street in Boone's car, they stayed home and flirted with the pretty neighborhood señoritas or played baseball with the girls' brothers in a nearby field. Matt's favorite gal was Juanita, who was teaching him how to kiss in the alleyway behind her house.

On a Saturday morning in early August, Pa knocked on the door with whiskey on his breath to tell Matt the trust had increased in value another ten percent and he was going to use that profit— and only the profit—on things that needed fixing at the ranch.

His hair had turned gray around the temples and his jaw sagged a bit, drawing the corners of his mouth into a permanent scowl. A lifetime out in the desert sun had burned Pa's face permanently brown, and there were deep wrinkles at the corners of his eyes that looked like miniature furrows. Matt didn't exactly know Pa's age, but he sure looked more and more like an old-timer.

Pa explained that Matt would get full value back when he inherited the ranch. It would be Matt's alone to have. He'd divorced Evangelina and given her cash money to drop any future claim on the ranch by her or Johnny. She had signed a paper to make it legal. Matt thought it was downright cheap and mean of Pa to do such a thing but said nothing.

With the trust fund in the black and the future looking rosy, he was putting Matt back on his monthly allowance right away and raising it ten dollars a month. He'd hired the lawyer Lipscomb on a retainer to visit Matt regularly to make sure he was all right. Finally, he supposed Matt wouldn't be coming back to the ranch anytime soon. Matt allowed that was right. Pa nodded nonchalantly and said that it was jim-dandy with him if Matt wanted to stay in town.

Matt watched from the front porch as Pa strode off on his long legs. He still looked bull strong, with his wide back, but he stooped a bit now and wasn't so upright with his shoulders squared the way they used to be.

Pa never turned to look back, but Matt watched him until he was out of sight. When Boone got home from his job at the garage, Matt proposed that they take a couple of days off and drive over to Tularosa to visit his *tía* Teresa, Evangelina, and his kid brother, Juan Ignacio Kerney. Flabbergasted, Boone thought the idea was jake. He wanted to know more right away about the astonishing revelation of Matt's secret Mexican family.

"Never was a secret," Matt replied with a laugh. "And never will be."

* * *

The drive to Tularosa got slowed by a flat tire at the bottom of Chalk Hills on the east side of the San Andres. Matt volunteered to change the tire, and he set about the task while Boone wandered down the gravel road a piece. Matt finished to discover that Boone was nowhere to be seen. He waited a few minutes for him to reappear and then tooted the car horn several times. Boone popped over a low northerly rise and waved.

"I've never seen anything like this place," he called, his voice filled with wonder. "It goes on forever. Mountains everywhere and the valley is so enormous you can't see the end of it. You lived out here?"

Matt nodded. "Folks from here call it a pretty slice of country."

"*Pretty* isn't the word," Boone replied as he opened the passenger door. "It's awe-inspiring. You're driving. I've got too much to look at."

In Tularosa, Evangelina and Juan Ignacio rushed out of Tía

Teresa's house to greet them as soon as Matt stopped the car. Teresa appeared in the doorway, waving and smiling. There were hugs and kisses and lots of chatter in Spanish from Evangelina and Juan Ignacio that left Boone, who knew maybe a half a dozen words in Spanish, smiling in bewilderment.

They were hurried inside the house, where more merriment erupted as soon as Teresa's children and grandchildren arrived to greet Matt and his amigo. All the warm, happy, smiling faces made Matt's spirits soar, and the next few hours were filled with gossipy family small talk and lots of good, spicy Mexican food. Boone occupied his time repeatedly filling his plate with enchiladas and beans and flirting wordlessly with Evangelina's sixteen-year-old cousin under Tía Teresa's watchful eye.

The conversation soon turned to a widower by the name of Porter Knox, a carpenter in town, who was courting Evangelina. Originally from Iowa, Knox had lost his wife and baby during childbirth and had recently moved west to make a fresh start. He was ten years older than Evangelina and considered a nice man by all the women present. Teresa described him as thin and not too tall, with brown hair and a ready smile. But of more importance, Knox had taken up learning Spanish soon after meeting Evangelina. Because of this exceedingly favorable omen and the happy knowledge that Porter Knox was a practicing Catholic who attended Mass regularly, the Chávez and Armijo womenfolk were already surreptitiously planning a wedding *baile*.

In the cool of the evening after the festivities ended, Matt and Evangelina walked to the river. Leaves rustled softly in the trees and the sweet, soothing sound of flowing water was a welcome change from the boisterous chatter and laughter they'd left behind at Teresa's hacienda.

"Pa told me what he did to you and Juan," Matt said as they

paused under a big cottonwood. "Giving you some money and cutting Juan off from any inheritance to the ranch was just plain mean of him. I wish I could do something about it."

Evangelina patted his arm. "No, no, don't you worry, it's all right. He had nothing I wanted other than my freedom."

"But Juan shouldn't be cut off like that."

"Juan Ignacio has you as his brother and a loving family here in Tularosa. That is far better than having a father who doesn't care for him at all."

"Maybe he'll have more brothers someday, and a sister or two," Matt suggested.

"He would like that," Evangelina said with a happy lilt to her voice. "So would I."

"You seem so happy."

"*Sí*. Tía Teresa says that I am proof that every misfortune in life is replaced by joy. And you?"

"Since Pa got hold of my money, he pretty much lets me be. He's using some of it for improvements at the ranch, he says. I've only seen him once since you left him. I got on Patches that very day and vamoosed myself. I don't miss him; that's for certain."

"Will you continue in school as Emma wished?"

"Just watch me. Next year I'll start college in the fall. Will you invite me to your wedding?"

"*Sí*, if there is one," Evangelina replied coyly.

Matt laughed. "From what the womenfolk in the family are saying, I'm betting on it."

Evangelina squeezed Matt's arm and kissed his cheek. "We're both making your mother proud, no?"

"I reckon we are," Matt replied with a grin.

* * *

Two weeks after school started, Clementine Callaway, recently from Kentucky, joined Matt's senior class. She was, without a doubt, the most beautiful girl he'd ever seen. Small and slender, with sparkling, intelligent green eyes and long dark brown hair, she had an oval face and a narrow nose and carried herself with a sophisticated air. Her soft southern drawl only made her more alluring.

Simultaneously smitten and tongue-tied, Matt did his best not to blush whenever she came near. Although she was polite to everyone, Clementine chose the company of the girls in the class and had little to do with the boys during recess or lunch hour or before or after school. Within a week, some of the other guys, including Jeff Kyle, decided she was stuck-up and took to taunting and teasing her. Jeff soon became the worst of the bunch, sometimes going so far as to harass Clementine on her way home. A stocky boy who liked to pick fights and push other kids around, Jeff had been kept back a grade for failing math twice. He often walked behind Clementine, mocking her for being a southerner, calling her snooty, and tossing pebbles at her. Twice Matt saw Clementine run away from Jeff, clutching her schoolbooks tightly, as she darted across Main Street.

The next time it happened, Matt grabbed Jeff by the arm and pulled him into the alley behind Main Street. "Leave her alone," he ordered.

"Says who?" Jeff growled, breaking Matt's grasp. "You'd like that skirt all to yourself, wouldn't you?"

"Maybe she isn't stuck-up, just scared of you," Matt ventured.

Jeff sneered. "She's got her nose in the air and treats folks like dirt because she thinks she's better than everyone else."

"Just let her be," Matt repeated.

"Stay out of my way," Jeff snapped, "or I'll give you a good licking." He turned on his heel and walked away.

The next day after school, Jeff and his three pals glared hard at Matt as he passed by. They fell in behind him and silently followed him to the corner of Griggs Avenue before veering off. That night, Matt told Boone what had happened and asked for his advice.

"Is this Jeff fella the ringleader?" Boone asked.

"Yep," Matt replied.

"Describe him to me."

"He's chunky and shorter than me. He's not too bright and he likes to pick fights. I think I can take him in a fair fight, but not him and his pals all at once."

"Whip him and your troubles should be over," Boone said. "You just need to get him alone."

"How do I do that?"

"Do you think they'll follow you home tomorrow?"

"It's likely."

"Here's the plan; I'll leave class early tomorrow and wait for you in the alley on the corner. When you pass by, give a whistle to let me know they're following, and then stand pat. I'll occupy Jeff's pals while you teach him a lesson. Do you know how to fight?"

"I've never been in one before."

"After dinner I'll give you a few lessons, and we'll practice again tomorrow before you go to school."

In the early morning, Matt fed Patches, gave him fresh water, cleaned out his stall, and went back into the house mulling over what Boone had taught him last night. While Guadalupe made breakfast and shook her head in dismay at their antics, Matt got another fisticuff lesson from Boone. He practiced throwing quick, stinging jabs and putting his hips and shoulders into landing a hard right hand. To test him, Boone held a pillow against his chest and had Matt practice his one-two sequence until he was satisfied.

"It's one, two," Boone reminded him, demonstrating the

punches one last time. "If he wants to fight dirty, kick him in the balls; if he tries to bear-hug you, bite his ear. Remember, I'm not going to break it up if you get in trouble."

"Where did you learn all this stuff?" Matt asked.

Boone grinned. "On the streets of Detroit City before a kind-hearted judge suggested that I move far away to New Mexico. Tell me what Jeff looks like."

"Enough!" Guadalupe said as she brought food to the table. "Stop your he-man silliness and eat your breakfast."

At school, Matt could tell the fight with Jeff was brewing. Before classes started, Jeff scowled at him and made a fist. At lunch recess, he swaggered up to Matt with his pals and said, "Get ready for a whipping after school."

Instructed by Boone to act scared, Matt timidly said he didn't want to fight. If the ploy worked, Jeff would feel cocky and over-confident when the fisticuffs started.

"I'm gonna have fun whipping you," Jeff crowed triumphantly.

Matt forced himself to stay calm, but for the rest of the school day he worried that maybe he didn't have the grit to fight. When school let out, Jeff was waiting with his gang. Matt squared his shoulders and remembered what Boone said to do as soon as Jeff drew near: say nothing, drop his books, throw the jab, and follow with the right hand; repeat if needed. He started for home with the gang on his heels.

He saw Boone waiting in the alley and whistled as he passed by. He turned when the footsteps behind him stopped. Jeff and his gang were frozen in place, staring up at Boone, who had a tire iron in his hand.

"You go on ahead, Jeff," Boone said genially, tapping him on the chest with the tire iron. "Me and the boys will wait here for you until it's over. Good luck."

Jeff curled his lip, smacked his fist in his open palm, and strolled toward Matt. When he came within arm's length, Matt dropped his books, threw the jab, and hit him with his right as hard as he could. Jeff didn't get a lick in. He fell with a thud, faceup. Matt leaned down and hit him again with a solid right for good measure.

"Show's over, boys," Boone announced cheerfully to the gang, who looked astonished by what they'd witnessed. "Take your hero home. He's gonna have two big shiners by dinnertime."

They got a groggy Jeff vertical and walked him slowly away.

"You okay?" Boone asked.

"My hand hurts like hell," Matt replied, his heart thumping in his chest.

Boone took a look. "Bruised; that's all. You did real good."

Matt grinned. "I did, didn't I?"

* * *

Word of the fight spread fast, and at school the next day Clementine approached Matt before the bell rang. "I heard what you did and I want to thank you," she said. "You're a true gentleman, as we say back home in Kentucky."

She turned and walked away, and Matt's heart soared. But she didn't speak to him again that entire day and only nodded a brief hello when they saw each other during the rest of the school week. Over the weekend, Matt complained to Boone about Clementine's lack of interest in him.

"Look, she may be toying with you," Boone said. "Don't make any moves. See if she comes to you."

It was hard to follow Boone's advice, but Matt kept his distance from Clementine. Several weeks passed before she approached him again, to ask him to walk her home after school. Along the way, she questioned him about other boys in their class, particularly Warren Bristol, son of the richest man in town. Matt told her Warren was a good guy and left it at that. He went home deflated by the realization that she wasn't interested in him at all. Two weeks later as he sat with Boone in the Rio Grande Theater waiting for the matinee to start, Clementine walked in accompanied by Warren. Matt pointed her out to Boone.

Boone gave her a careful once-over. She had a face perfect for the ads in the ladies' fashion magazines and wore a stylish skirt that showed her legs nicely.

"She's a looker; that's for sure," Boone said. "But she's not right for you."

"Why not?" Matt grumped.

"Because you ain't the richest boy in town," Boone replied with a laugh.

* * *

On December 1, 1927, a letter came from Tía Teresa announcing the date of Evangelina's marriage to Porter Knox and telling Matt he must come and bring that handsome Boone along with him. With the wedding scheduled to be held on New Year's Eve, Matt figured the *baile* was going to be one hell of a party. He wrote back that he'd be there for certain but sadly without Boone, who would be traveling back to Detroit to visit his family over the holidays.

A week before Christmas, Matt drove Boone to the station for his journey home to Detroit.

"Now, don't you sulk over my absence while I'm gone," Boone chided, punching Matt on the arm. "And don't wreck my car either."

"Good riddance," Matt shot back. "I won't miss you at all."

Boone cuffed him on the arm again. "Take care, sport. See ya next year."

Already beginning to feel dismal, Matt stayed on the platform until the train left the station. Christmas fell on a Sunday and he wouldn't leave for Tularosa until midweek. He wasn't about to go to the ranch to see Pa for Christmas; that would be pure agony.

Nestor and Guadalupe had invited him for Christmas dinner, so he wouldn't be completely on his own. Still, he felt lonely, which was different from being alone in a way he couldn't quite figure out.

17

Matt bought new clothes to wear at Evangelina's wedding, packed a bag, and drove through a rare, dense snowstorm to Tularosa. The slushy gravel road made for slow going, but Matt didn't mind. There was almost no traffic, and until a weak sun finally broke through the slate-gray sky, it felt like traveling through a huge, silent, mesquite-studded cocoon.

At Tía Teresa's hacienda, the wedding and *baile* preparations had all the womenfolk occupied. After a round of welcoming hugs and kisses, Matt was sent off with Juan Ignacio to pick up grommets at Champion's Hardware Store that were needed to hang the wall decorations for the *baile*. He held Juan on his lap and let him steer the car and gleefully beep the horn on the short drive to Main Street. Juan was now four years old and had sprouted some since Matt last saw him. With his curly hair, oval eyes, and slightly turned-up nose, he looked more and more like his mother. He seemed calmer now that he wasn't living at the ranch.

At the store, they picked up the grommets, which were paid for, bagged, and waiting, and walked hand in hand to the drugstore, where Matt bought Juan a Coke at the soda fountain.

"What do you think about getting a new pa?" Matt asked as Juan blissfully sipped his soda.

Juan smiled. "I like it. He's nice."

"That's swell," Matt said. "Do you ever miss the ranch?"

"No," he answered matter-of-factly. "My real father doesn't like me, and he didn't let me have a puppy."

"Do you have one now?"

"*Sí*, Porter Knox got me one. I named him Pelo because he's so furry. He's going to adopt me; that's what Mama says."

"Who? Pelo?" Matt asked jokingly.

Juan kicked his feet and laughed. "No, you *loco*—Porter Knox. Mama says I have to call him *papá*."

"Is that okay with you?"

Juan shrugged. "*Sí*."

"Why do you call him Porter Knox?"

"Because that's his name," Juan answered, eyeing Matt as though he was really dumb. "We're moving to Albuquerque."

"When?"

Juan shrugged. "I don't know."

"I'll miss you."

Juan sucked down the last of his soda through the straw. "It's not that far away," he said, sounding very worldly for a four-year-old. "Tía Teresa showed it to me on a map. Can I have some candy?"

"Pick out what you want," Matt said.

"Chocolate," he announced.

Back at the hacienda, Evangelina confirmed the move to Albuquerque. Porter had been hired as a carpenter for a construction company building new houses near the university and was already on the job. He would leave early Friday after work in order to make it home for the wedding but was expected back on the job

Monday morning. He'd rented a small house in the Old Town part of Albuquerque, but it would be up to Evangelina to make the move, which she looked forward to with great anticipation. Matt had never seen her so zestful and excited about the future.

"Just so you know," she added, "when Porter adopts Juan, we plan to legally change his name to Juan Ignacio Kerney Knox. I don't want him to ever forget he's part of your family."

"There's not much of my family left," Matt noted. "But I'm obliged. I doubt I'll ever have another brother."

* * *

Bad weather slowed Porter Knox's return to Tularosa, but he still got back in time for Flaviano and all the men in the Armijo and Chávez families to carry him off to the best speakeasy in town for a drink or two. Invited to come along, Matt used the opportunity to size up Porter. Small in stature, as Tía Teresa had noted during Matt's last visit, Knox had a congenial disposition and a calm manner. A bald spot crowned his round head, and a neatly trimmed mustache made his lips look thinner, but his smile was warm and friendly. Knox was now able to get by in Spanish, and his effort to learn the language to please Evangelina had also paid dividends with the men of both families, who celebrated the upcoming nuptials with many long-winded toasts to the couple's happiness. Glasses were also raised in unison to the frequent and blessed prospect of babies, which began another round of toasting, until Matt realized he was too drunk to understand what was being said. When the party broke up, Teresa's oldest son, Juan, guided him slowly on his wobbly legs back to the hacienda.

"On the night my baby brother, Miguel, was born, your father was bringing home my very *borracho* father from a cantina where he'd gotten into a fight," he said, leaning Matt against the hacienda courtyard wall.

"No fight at the bar tonight," Matt protested, trying to focus. "I think."

"*Sí*, no fight," Juan agreed, not completely sober by any means. "But here we are repeating history."

"No babies being born either," Matt corrected, shaking his head. "Leastways not yet."

"*Sí*, no babies yet," Juan agreed. "You are very *borracho*."

Matt shook his head again and wagged a finger at Juan. "I resent that remark."

"Are you always so contrary?"

Matt nodded. "But only when I drink. Otherwise I'm obliging."

"How many times have you been drunk?"

Matt held up a finger. "Once, and I don't think I like it. I need the *baño*."

"No, you need the bushes, my amigo," Juan said, guiding him to the cottonwood tree across the lane.

* * *

A sober, fully recovered Matt loved every minute of the wedding ceremony and the *baile*. Time and again throughout the afternoon and night, as he watched Porter and Evangelina he'd substitute an image of himself dancing with Clementine, but it was wishful thinking and he knew it. He still smarted over her rejection.

He danced with all the women, including Evangelina's cute cousin, who harassed him for not bringing Boone to the wedding, and Tía Teresa, who made him promise to invite her to his high school graduation in the spring.

"Your mother would want me to be there for her," she said. "Also, I must come because you are family to me and always will be."

"I want you to come," Matt replied earnestly, suddenly realizing that without her he'd have no family there at all to celebrate the occasion.

"Then it is settled," Teresa said, smiling, as the music ended. "Now, go dance with all the young señoritas again. They cannot take their eyes off you."

He danced with the girls until the music stopped, a final toast was raised, some bawdy comments were made by Evangelina's drunken brothers, and the bride and groom departed amid much hooting and hollering.

In the morning, before the revelers who were staying with Teresa awoke, he shared a quiet breakfast with her, said good-bye to Juan Ignacio, who raised his sleepy head from his pillow to give him a kiss, and left Tularosa.

At home, too restless to stay put inside all alone, Matt saddled Patches and went for a long ride, letting his pony stretch out at a fast lope along the Rio Grande. It was the first day of 1928, and come spring he planned to be the high school valedictorian, and come fall a college man. He thought about figuring a way to needle Pa for trying to grind him down about having unrealistic expectations and decided it wasn't worth the effort.

Thinking about Pa began to sour his mood, so instead he thought about Boone's return from his visit to his family in Detroit. A week wasn't that long to wait, and the prospect of having his best friend return home raised his spirits considerably. About the only thing lacking in the New Year was getting out from under Pa's thumb.

Bending forward, he whispered into Patches' ear, "Only two more years," and spurred him into a gallop toward Robledo Mountain.

* * *

The Saturday before school break ended, Matt filled in for a sick clerk at Sam Miller's store. Boone was due in on the two o'clock train, and Matt had left a note at the house letting him know what he was doing. He fully expected Boone to saunter into the store around three, but the hour came and went with no sign of him. At ten minutes past four o'clock, Boone breezed in with a big smile on his face, hand in hand with a young woman he introduced as Mrs. Boone Cavanagh Mitchell.

"But she goes by Peggy," he announced.

Matt could barely speak. "Well, I'll be," he blurted. "Congratulations." She was a tall girl, with long brown hair and a thin but pretty face that matched her narrow frame.

"Boone says you are a dear friend," Peggy said. "I hope you'll be mine as well."

Matt smiled. "I'd like that."

"Surprised?" Boone asked, grinning from ear to ear.

"Flummoxed," Matt said.

"It happened in a hurry," Boone said with a laugh as he slapped Matt on the back. "Mind if we camp out with you until we can find a place to rent? Peggy promises to cook you up some fine meals in return for your hospitality."

"I'm a good cook," Peggy added. "You won't be disappointed."

"You can stay as long as you like," Matt replied.

At home after work, Matt found the front room filled with neatly stacked luggage of various sizes, one large steamer trunk, and several packing crates. The smell of baked ham came wafting from the kitchen.

"Sorry for the clutter, but Peggy couldn't bear to leave anything behind," Boone said. "We walked from the station, got the car, and then made four trips to haul everything over from the freight room. I guess she's planning to stick with me for a while." He grinned and added, "She's fixing us a good dinner."

"I didn't even know you had a girl," Matt said.

"I didn't either until I went home," Boone replied sheepishly. "We'd called it quits just before I moved here. But you know women—they can change their minds."

"What are you going to do about college?" Matt asked.

"I'll finish the semester, but I've got a wife to support now," Boone answered. "Mac at the garage might take me on full-time, or maybe I can go to work at the Ford dealer. I was wondering if we could rent one of those houses owned by your trust."

"I'll ask Mr. Worrell at the bank."

"That would be jake. But no matter what, I promise we won't intrude on you for long, and I'll keep paying you my rent. You can up it if you want."

Matt shook his head. "Nope, I don't want your money. You and Peggy are my guests until you get settled."

"You are one hell of a friend, even if you are still just a kid."

"Drop the kid stuff, or I'll change my mind about letting you stay," Matt warned.

"It's permanently dropped," Boone promised.

Peggy called them into the kitchen for dinner and served up baked ham, cauliflower with a cheese sauce, and green peas with melted butter dribbled on top. It was delicious. Over dinner, Peggy described the mad rush that occurred once they decided to get married. It had been a whirlwind marathon to get a license, find a judge to perform the ceremony, arrange for parents and nearby relatives to attend, get everything packed for shipment, and finally make it to the train station on time.

"We rode coach all the way from Detroit to Las Cruces," she added with a smile. "It was exhausting."

"I've promised her a real honeymoon someday, when we can afford it," Boone said.

"At least you got her a wedding ring," Matt said, looking at the gold band on Peggy's ring finger.

Peggy held up her hand and laughed. "It's my mother's. Something borrowed."

"I've promised her a ring of her own too, someday real soon," Boone added shamefacedly. "I sort of ran out of money."

Matt laughed. "This is like a love story out of one of those ladies' magazines."

Peggy snuggled close to Boone. "Pretty romantic, I think."

Boone gave her a kiss as Matt started to clear away the dishes.

"Don't you dare do that!" Peggy commanded, breaking away from Boone. "We'll take care of the dirty dishes."

"Best do as you're told," Boone said, reaching for Matt's empty plate.

Matt yielded with a grin. "I'll tend to Patches," he said, thinking Boone was one helluva lucky guy.

18

On graduation day, Matt gave his valedictory speech to the families, friends, and guests gathered to celebrate the Las Cruces High School class of 1928. As expected, Pa didn't come, but Tía Teresa arrived the day before, accompanied by Juan Ignacio, who would spend the summer with her in Tularosa. Boone and Peggy attended as well, as did Nestor, Guadalupe, and Matt's boss from the grocery store, Sam Miller.

Boone and Peggy threw a swell graduation party for Matt in the backyard of the house they rented from the trust. His favorite high school teacher, Mrs. Elizabeth Pickett, came with her daughter Nell, who was the smartest girl in Matt's graduating class. They had been dating since early spring, much to the dismay of Lester Nichols, his best friend from school, who came to the party red-faced, tipsy, and glum after drinking moonshine at another graduation party. When Matt's party wound down, he thanked Boone and Peggy, said good-bye to Tía Teresa and Juan Ignacio, and slipped away to Nell's party. There he found Lester mooning over Nell on the front porch and Mr. Pickett serving up his renowned barbecue brisket and German potato salad to a line of hungry guests. After dark, the celebrating continued at Lester's house, where the class of 1928 gathered with their dates to dance to records, sneak a drink or two, smoke cigarettes, talk about the future, and pet and smooch in the far reaches of the backyard, away from the flickering party lanterns. Darlene Fox, considered the class Goody Two-shoes, helped Lester overcome his unrequited love for Nell with some heavy petting behind a big cottonwood tree. It was the best party of the day.

Starting out, Matt had been miffed that Pa didn't make the effort to attend his graduation and offer his congratulations. But the next morning, he awoke without a twinge of annoyance about Pa's absence. If Pa didn't care a lick, it wasn't worth Matt's time worrying about it. It was as simple as that.

Over the summer on an early July evening, Pa paid a quick visit to inform Matt he'd once again taken the annual profit from the trust to use for the ranch, this time to buy new breeding stock to rebuild the herd he'd been forced to sell during the drought.

"Are you coming out to the ranch this summer?" he asked.

"What for?" Matt replied.

"Nothing, I guess," Pa answered. "It has pretty much dried up between us, ain't it?"

"Appears so," Matt said.

Pa turned on his heel and walked away without saying another word.

Matt planned to keep working part-time clerking for Sam Miller when he started the fall term at New Mexico College of Agricultural and Mechanical Arts. But once classes began, he found the classwork more challenging than he'd imagined and had to quit the job. He'd enrolled in science and mathematics courses, thinking to pursue an engineering degree, and hadn't counted on such a heavy homework burden. He kept to a rigorous study schedule, never missed a class, and by the middle of the term had high grades on all his papers and tests.

For a short time, Nell wrote to him from the University of Chicago, where she was studying archaeology. He faithfully wrote back, but by the end of October he stopped hearing from her. Soon after, Nell's best friend, Ava Tumble, told him Nell had found a new boyfriend. Matt had figured as much and didn't let the news get him down.

On the day after Thanksgiving, he sat on the back step of the house Boone and Peggy rented and listened to the first lusty cries of their newborn son, Kendell. As soon as Peggy and the baby had been made presentable by the midwife, Boone whisked Matt into the bedroom.

"We'd like you to be Kendell's honorary godfather," he announced.

"What does this high office require of me?" Matt asked as he grinned at the tiny pink baby wrapped in Peggy's arms.

"I'm not real certain," Boone replied with a grin of his own. "But it starts with us having a drink to celebrate the occasion."

"You two better not get drunk," Peggy warned, her voice weak with exhaustion, her face still red from the effort of giving birth.

"We wouldn't dare," Matt promised.

The arrival of Kendell quickly changed the nature of Matt's friendship with Boone and Peggy. They were fully occupied with the baby, and as time passed Matt saw less and less of them. When Peggy got pregnant again in the early spring of 1929, he hardly saw them at all. That summer, they made a whirlwind move to El Paso so Boone could start a new job as a senior mechanic for the Southern Pacific Railroad. Matt helped them pack and waved good-bye as they drove away in a brand-new Dodge Boone had bought to celebrate his advancement.

On July 4, Teresa Magdalena Armijo Chávez died unexpectedly in her sleep. In Tularosa, Matt grieved with the family, who had arrived from all parts of the state for the services and burial. True to form, Pa didn't show.

Matt sat with Juan Ignacio, Evangelina, and Porter Knox during Mass and walked with them in the procession to the cemetery, where Teresa was laid to rest next to her husband, Ignacio. It was a solemn, sad occasion made more melancholy by the tolling church bell and the mourners' despondent faces. Teresa had been dearly loved.

On the return to the hacienda, where food and drink awaited, Matt wondered when he'd see his six-year-old kid brother again. Would he see any of them again? Tía Teresa's passing cut his strongest link with her family, and he'd learned the hard way to accept the fact that even the best of friends and the people you care about the most can leave, never to return.

Although it had been sudden, the loss of Tía Teresa didn't sting Matt with a feeling of bitter loneliness. Instead he felt a sudden urge to make a pilgrimage to Ma's grave. He decided that tomorrow he'd journey to the Double K for that visit.

* * *

In the morning he had breakfast in Teresa's quiet house with Porter, Evangelina, and Juan Ignacio, and they told him of their new life in Albuquerque. Juan had just finished the first grade and had found many new friends at school. Porter had bought a house with some irrigated acreage outside of town in the North Valley and had plans to plant crops after he fixed up the old adobe. Evangelina had a vegetable garden started and was raising a small flock of chickens and selling eggs to make a little extra money for the family. She was pregnant, with the baby due in six months, and hoped for a girl to name Teresa. They were happy and excited about the future. They were a family exactly the way Matt thought a family should be.

After promising to visit them in Albuquerque someday, Matt said good-bye, walked to a garage on Main Street, and used the telephone to call Sam Miller in Las Cruces to ask for a few more days off from his summertime job. He'd hitched a ride to the service on a delivery truck and had planned to hitchhike home right away to return to work. But when he explained why he wanted some extra time, Sam gladly gave his permission.

Matt rented a sturdy pony at the Tularosa livery, bought a small sack of packaged and canned food to tide him over on the long ride to the Double K, and started across the basin. The old wagon trail had been transformed into a graded and graveled state road all the way to the eastern foothills of the San Andres Mountains, where the improvements ended and passage turned rough and rocky in the higher terrain. But when he reached the ranch road, he found it was also much improved. It had been graded, crowned, straightened, and rerouted to avoid some of the dips, curves, and gullies prone to washouts and erosion. Tire tracks showed the frequent passage of a vehicle, which made Matt wonder if Pa had spent some of his trust profits on a truck for the ranch.

He passed through the gate at the horse pasture, to be greeted by some yearlings and colts that trotted over for a closer inspection. Apparently Pa had restocked more than just the cattle he'd mentioned in their last conversation. He likely had the cows grazing on one or more of the high-country pastures.

Eager to see what else Pa was up to, Matt loped the pony across the horse pasture, topped the last rise, and drew rein. A new Chevy stake-bed truck capable of carrying at least a dozen bales of hay or several calves sat parked next to the freshly painted barn. Pa's pony, Calabaza, and a packhorse were in the corral, saddled and ready to go. Matt dismounted and called out to the house. Pa appeared on the veranda and silently watched Matt tie his pony to the hitching post. He was wearing chaps, spurs, and gloves and had his saddlebags slung over a shoulder.

"The place is looking good," Matt said by way of greeting.

"What brings the college boy out to the backlands?" Pa replied, never one for subtlety.

"Tía Teresa died. We buried her yesterday."

"I know it," Pa replied as he walked past Matt to the corral. "Are you staying the night?"

"Yep, I came to pick up some of my things."

"I threw out most of that stuff a year ago," Pa replied as he put a leg over Calabaza. "What's left you'll find in a box in the tack room. Fix yourself some grub when you get hungry. You know where to find it. I'm heading up-country to throw the cattle into fresh pasture."

Matt thought about questioning Pa about all the recent money spent on the ranch and decided it wasn't worth starting a spat. "Adios," he said.

Trailing the packhorse, Pa nodded. Matt closed the corral gate behind him and watched as he trotted up the canyon. He waited until he was certain Pa was out of sight before visiting Ma's grave. Half expecting to find it overgrown with weeds, he was pleased to find it neatly tended. He sat by Ma's resting place thinking about how much he missed her. He talked to her for a long time, until the last golden rays of the setting sun cast deep shadows across the basin.

Back at the house, he fed and watered his pony, fixed a plate of beans and bacon, and ate his supper on the veranda. He'd forgotten how quiet, serene, and calming it was and how splendid the basin and the distant Sacramento Mountains looked from the veranda.

He took a quick tour around the house. It was the same as when he left. There was no electricity or indoor plumbing, and while the rooms were untidy, the place wasn't dirty. He didn't see any whiskey bottles around, which made him hope Pa had stopped drinking again. There was no sign that Pa had taken on a hand to help out, which didn't surprise him. Pa was always stingy when it came to hiring help. But to be fair, from what Matt saw, Pa had been telling the truth about putting the annual profits into the ranch operations. That was reassuring.

When dusk turned to dark, he carried a lantern past the empty henhouse to the barn tack room. In a small box on top of the big trunk he found the few things of his that Pa had saved, including the extra copy of "Emma Makes a Hand" Matt had given Pa, two old, dog-eared dime novels, a penknife Ma had given him when he'd turned six, his first pair of spurs, and a notebook filled with drawings he'd made at the ranch the year Ma died. In it were sketches of Ma, Pa, Patches, the ranch house, and views of the basin from the veranda. All in all, they were nothing to crow about, but Matt thought they were fairly decent drawings for a kid. It made him smile to look at them.

One end of the board attached to the wall that held the saddle racks in place had pulled loose, exposing the tattered edge of a yellow, weathered piece of paper. Matt eased the paper free. It was a pardon dated and signed by the governor of the territory of Arizona given to Pat Floyd, an inmate of the Yuma Territorial Prison. Who was Pat Floyd? Why was his pardon hidden away in the Double K barn?

He remembered Mr. Owen, a former lawman who'd come to the ranch years ago asking questions about Vernon Clagett, the hired man who'd quit and walked away around the time Ma had died. Did the pardon have something to do with him? Maybe Pat Floyd was an alias he'd used. If so, why did he hide the pardon? It didn't make any sense.

He thought about leaving the pardon on Pa's desk along with a note asking for an explanation but decided to keep it instead. He wasn't sure why, other than feeling just plain ornery about the way Pa had greeted him when he arrived. He tucked the tattered pardon into one of the dime novels, bundled everything up to carry home in the morning, and headed back to the house, ready for a good night's sleep.

* * *

Fascinated by the pardon, Matt's thoughts returned to it time and again after he got home to Las Cruces. Finally, he decided to talk to Mr. Worrell at the bank and the lawyer Alan Lipscomb to see if they knew anything about Pat Floyd. Besides, he would turn eighteen in ten months and it was time for him to get better informed about the trust.

Matt first met with Edgar Worrell at the bank, who smiled at him from behind his office desk, cleared his throat, and said, "Normally, I'd direct you to speak to your father about the trust, but since I know you to be a smart, well-educated young man and the time does draw near for you to take control, I'll answer your questions."

"May I see the actual document so you can go over it point by point with me?" Matt asked.

"Why, yes, I suppose you can," Worrell replied. From a file cabinet he brought a thick document packet and placed it on his desk. "Let's start with the assets."

Within the hour Matt knew that all the rental properties were heavily mortgaged, with the proceeds used to buy stock on margin through a Wall Street broker. Since assuming control of the trust, Pa had approved each new transaction recommended by the broker. To Matt's untrained eye, it all seemed reasonable. Rental income covered the monthly mortgage payments, and the stocks held by the trust were paying a good annual return as well as increasing in value. He was also happy to see that Pa had been using only annual profits from the trust for ranching operations, as he'd promised, not the principal. Even with those costs and what it took to cover Matt's living expenses, including his college tuition, the value of the trust stood at slightly more than twice Ma's original investment.

"You'll be a very well-off young man when you turn eighteen next year," Worrell predicted.

"I reckon so," Matt said. He'd noted a provision in the trust prohibiting any loan to be made against the Griggs Avenue house without his written permission. "Is my house free and clear of any debt?" he asked, wondering about the exception.

"Indeed," Worrell answered. "As I understand it, your mother felt strongly that the property should remain yours unless you decided otherwise. In effect, she wanted to ensure that you always had a home."

"She never told me why she divorced my Pa."

"It was before my time," Worrell replied, "but I believe the divorce was less than amicable, which is unfortunately too often the case."

"Would Mr. Lipscomb know why they split up?"

"I image he might; he represented your father in the proceedings. I believe such records are public, so he should be free to tell you what he knows."

"Did either of my parents ever mention a man named Pat Floyd?" Matt asked. "Or do any business with him?"

Worrell looked perplexed. "Not to my knowledge. Of course, with all the past trust transactions over the years, it would be almost impossible to answer your question with complete certainty. But I've never heard of him. Who is Pat Floyd?"

"I don't know," Matt replied. "It's just a name I recently came across." He stood and shook Mr. Worrell's hand. "I appreciate you taking the time for me."

"Not at all," Worrell said. "I'll write your father about our conversation. I'm sure he'll be pleased to learn you're taking such an active interest in your financial future."

"I'm sure he will be," Matt said, not giving a hoot what Pa thought.

* * *

The night before he was to meet with Alan Lipscomb, a bad dream woke Matt just before dawn. In it he was a little kid at the ranch alone with Pa and they were playing a game of hide-and-seek that started out as fun but suddenly changed when Pa began stalking him, making an ugly face, lunging at him with murder in his eyes, and refusing to stop when Matt, terrified, begged him to. The dream gave him the willies and brought back a vague recurring memory of being with Ma and CJ when he saw Pa for the very first time. He had a telescopic image of Pa roaring drunkenly at them to get out of his way and Ma pulling him to safety. How he wished Ma and CJ were alive to tell him if that had really happened. He went through the day wondering whether any of his memories from that time were real or if they were all just imagined.

Although Matt had made an appointment in advance, Alan Lipscomb kept him waiting twenty minutes, and when he did usher him into his office, he did so with a serious look and a tight-lipped smile.

He sat behind his desk, gestured for Matt to sit in a straight-back chair, and said in a grave tone, "Mr. Worrell informed me of the purpose of your visit. I must tell you I have no desire to occasion a rift between you and your father."

Matt smiled sympathetically. "I sure don't want to put you in that situation, Mr. Lipscomb. As you probably know, I've never been close to my father or him to me, but I have nothing to gain by getting into a quarrel with him. I reach my majority soon and plan to finish college here and then perhaps move away. I'd like to part ways with him agreeably, if possible."

"If that is truly your intention, why bother digging up old history?" Lipscomb asked.

"Because it's *my* history, and I've a right to know it," Matt replied. "Since my ma died I've spent a lot of time pondering what made her divorce Pa, move to town, and raise me on her own. I've always wondered what happened."

"I doubt you'll find those answers here," Lipscomb warned.

"Maybe not," Matt replied. "But at least I might learn something I didn't know before."

Lipscomb tapped his fingers together before responding. "I cannot show you the file, but I will tell you this: Your mother gave up a sizable stake in the ranch to make a fresh start on her own. It was a brave act."

"What did Pa do to her to get her so riled?" he asked.

"Only your father can tell you that," Lipscomb replied. "But in a divorce, children and property are often what most parents fight about. Your parents reached an accommodation that was best for all concerned, including you and your brother CJ. Again, I suggest you ask your father these questions."

"I plan to do that," Matt said. "Did my Pa ever mention a man named Pat Floyd to you?"

"No, the name is unfamiliar to me."

Matt stood and shook Lipscomb's hand. "Thank you for your time."

"You've a bright future, Matt," Lipscomb prophesied. "Don't dwell on the past. It serves no good purpose."

"I won't," Matt answered. "Good day."

Outside, Matt walked home under cool, billowing clouds that masked the hot summer sun. Lipscomb had said Ma had been brave to break free and start fresh. Maybe that was all that really mattered.

Matt lengthened his stride. Soon he'd be free and able to make his own fresh start, just like Ma had. There was a whole world to explore and he would have the means to do it. The mere idea of it made him feel downright carefree.

19

When Matt was five, CJ had given him a cheap alarm clock to play with. He took it apart, put it back together, and got it ticking, but much to his frustration he never got it to keep the right time no matter how hard he tried. In spite of his failure, it didn't dampen his enthusiasm for taking things apart, to the point of getting into big trouble with Ma for attempting to disassemble her trundle sewing machine. To keep him away from such mischief, she presented him with a brand-new Erector set, which came in a red wooden box complete with a variety of different steel parts and nuts and bolts he could build stuff with. The set was a source of constant enjoyment, and he spent many contented hours on the living room floor constructing drawbridges, cranes, water towers, windmills, airplanes, and the like.

His more recent experiences helping Boone fiddle around with his old jalopy had reminded Matt how much he enjoyed working with his hands, so in his first semester of college he'd taken a mechanical arts course that consisted of learning how to disassemble and repair a variety of gasoline-powered motors, including an unusual twenty-four-horsepower horizontal automobile engine. The classwork also consisted of making detailed diagrams of engine components, which rekindled Matt's interest in drawing. It became his favorite course in his first semester.

Pleased with what he'd learned, in his second semester he shifted to an emphasis on applied science, with classes in drafting and basic welding and a calculus course to improve his math skills. He also signed up for an elective course in military science, taught by a veteran of the Great War. Matt enjoyed it so much, it got him to thinking he might consider the army as a career if he could serve as an officer in the Corps of Engineers.

But not yet ready to settle on a path his life should take, he figured to explore different courses in his sophomore year, including botany, a class in modern writers, and a land-surveying class, which would be useful in both agriculture and science. Classes started in six weeks and he was eager to begin.

When he wasn't at his part-time job clerking in Miller's store, he rode Patches several miles to the college outside of town, situated on the upper shelf of a wide tableland that extended beyond the Rio Grande far into the desert. With the permission of his mechanical arts professor, Augustus Merton, he'd parked a 1925 Studebaker Standard Six Roadster with a blown engine he'd bought at a salvage yard in an empty shed on campus. He hoped to have the roadster rebuilt and running before classes resumed so he could motor to and from college.

Three days of unusually cool and rainy weather had turned the gravel road to the college muddy and the surrounding land a brilliant green. He stopped at the campus gate and cleaned Patches' hooves before continuing on the horseshoe drive past ornate buildings with hipped tile roofs, arched windows, and domed towers that housed the gymnasium, classrooms, and administration offices. Science Hall and Agricultural Hall, the two most imposing, eye-catching structures on campus, soared over the desert land-scape and looked down on agricultural fields divided and fenced to grow a variety of experimental crops. They also towered over the new athletic field, the college's most important feature for town residents who filled the stands on football game days.

Matt drew rein at the shed, turned Patches loose to graze on tender new grasses, opened the shed door, and ran a hand over the roadster's dusty right front fender. The shed was soon to be demolished to make way for the construction of a new men's dor-mitory, and Matt was in a hurry to get the car running before the wrecking crew showed up. Happily, he was almost finished.

He was on his back under the Studebaker inspecting the en-gine mounts with a flashlight when he heard footsteps and saw a shadow on the dirt floor. Assuming it was Professor Merton drop-ping by to check on his progress, he poked his head out and in-stead saw Pa staring down at him. Matt pushed out from under the car and stood.

"How did you find me?" he asked, clicking the flashlight off.

"You really have turned into a citified college boy, asking a dumb question like that," Pa said scornfully. "I followed your horse tracks."

"What do you want?" Matt asked briskly, studying his father. Pa had lost a tooth and had a week-old beard, and his hair looked straggly under his cowboy hat.

"I'm looking to get back something of mine I reckon you have."

Matt laughed. "Now, that's a switch, seeing how you've been using my trust money to keep the Double K running."

"I've told you where every damn cent goes," Pa snapped. "Best you understand that."

"What I understand is you don't give a tinker's damn for me and never have," Matt retorted. "The only reason you wanted to get your hands on my money is to look after yourself, not me. So if you came to tell me you're taking more money, say it and go. Next year you won't get a dime from me."

"Most men would serve up a good beating to a son for that kind of lip."

"Son?" Matt snorted. "That's a joke. You've got no sons, old man, except by blood alone, and that doesn't count a lick."

The punch caught Matt flush on the mouth and knocked him back into the fender. He shook it off and swung a roundhouse right with the flashlight that hit Pa in the temple and put him on his ass. Pa sat motionless in the dirt, his hat knocked off, head lowered, breathing hard.

"Don't ever hit me again," Matt warned, tasting the blood in his mouth. His hand shook from the sheer fright of what he'd done. He dropped the flashlight.

"I didn't plan to hit you in the first place," Pa said, slowly getting to his feet and reaching for his hat. There was an ugly welt on his temple. "I've heard from Worrell and Lipscomb you've been asking about Pat Floyd, and I want that paper you found at the ranch."

"Is that what you've been searching for all these years?"

"Give it to me and I'll be on my way."

"Who's Pat Floyd?" Matt demanded, struggling to maintain his composure. If Pa hit him again, he'd fall apart.

"That ain't your business," Pa replied, rubbing his head.

"It is if you're gonna fight me about him," Matt said. "Who is he?"

Pa shook his head. "He's a ghost, a nobody, a good-for-nothing I knew a long time ago; that's all."

"He's you," Matt guessed. "Otherwise you wouldn't give a damn about the pardon."

"I ain't saying that," Pa said.

"You don't have to. Why did Ma divorce you? What did you do to her?"

"That's a private matter."

"Is there any one damn thing about you that isn't a secret?" Matt pushed. Pa was shrinking in his eyes, no longer terrifying, just an old worn-down cowboy. He felt in control of the situation and, for the very first time, in control of Pa.

"You're done with me, I can tell," Pa said. "I make no apology for who I am. Get me that pardon and I'll trouble you no more. The ranch and whatever else I have will be yours once I pass on. It's all I have to give and you're all the kin I've got to give it to."

"Except for your other son, Juan Ignacio," Matt chided. "I'll mail the pardon to you. I have no cause to go to the ranch."

"That'll be fine."

"You look like a whiskey-sodden old bum," Matt added.

"I've been feeling poorly, if you care to know," Pa replied. "Haven't had a drink in six months. Doc says all my teeth are rotten and have to be pulled."

Matt had no sympathy to give. He stared at Pa until he turned and walked away. When he was sure Pa wouldn't return to resume the fisticuffs, he picked up the flashlight and crawled back under the Studebaker chassis. In the dim light, with the damp dirt floor soaking his shirt, he remained motionless, his mind churning, until he heard approaching footsteps again. He scrambled out, expecting Pa had returned, only to be greeted by Professor Merton.

"Are you ready to give it a go?" Merton asked, peering into the engine compartment.

"I need to seat the spark plugs, adjust the carburetor, and install a new fan belt," Matt replied.

Merton nodded, took the flashlight from Matt's hand, and looked more closely at the engine. Universally liked by his students, Augustus Merton was a small man in his late forties with a mop of curly light brown hair, a round face that beamed goodwill, and lively brown eyes. He had a habit of softly commenting to himself when inspecting students' work, and no one liked hearing an unacceptable *oops* or *oh my* fall from his lips. Matt held his breath against the bleak prospect.

"I think you may have done it," Merton said, clicking off the flashlight.

"I'll finish tomorrow," Matt said, beaming with pride.

"Why not today?" Merton countered, rolling up his sleeves. "Come, I'll give you a hand. We'll have this fine motorcar running in time for you to drive it home, clean yourself up, and present yourself at my house for a celebratory dinner."

Matt grabbed the new fan belt from the dashboard. "That's very kind of you, sir."

Merton selected a screwdriver from the small worktable Matt had built. "My first Ford was a lot less complicated to work on than this Studebaker. How times have changed."

Two hours later they rolled the Studebaker Standard Six Roadster out of the shed into the bright late-afternoon sunlight. Matt fired it up and the engine responded with the reassuring steady sound of the pumping pistons.

"Off you go, then," Merton said with a kindly pat on Matt's shoulder. "When you get home, put some ice on that split lip. It will help the swelling go down. We'll see you for dinner."

"Thanks, Professor," Matt said, face lowered to hide a blush of embarrassment, and with Patches roped to the rear bumper he drove slowly homeward.

Augustus Merton waved as the departing Studebaker bumped

over uneven ground toward the campus gate, the pinto pony trotting easily behind. He'd overheard a good bit of the tense alterca-
tion inside the shed before returning to his office in Science Hall
for half an hour in order to allow Matt time to recover. That had
prompted him to invite the lad to dinner. A meal with folks who
weren't at odds with each other seemed just the medicine the
young man needed. If nothing else, it might keep his lifted spirits
high. He hurried to his office to call his wife, Consuelo, and let her
know about their unexpected dinner guest.

20

At home, Matt parked the Studebaker in front of the house, put Patches in his stall with fresh water, and went inside to clean up and change for dinner. He'd been to Augustus and Consuelo Merton's hacienda once before to attend the annual late-spring gathering the professor and his wife held for students enrolled in his mechanical arts classes. They lived in the village of Mesilla, a few miles south of Las Cruces.

Mesilla had been part of old Mexico until the middle of the nineteenth century, when the federal government bought almost thirty thousand square miles of borderlands to accommodate the construction of a railroad to Southern California. Much like Tularosa, it had remained a mostly Hispanic settlement.

Built by Consuelo's grandfather, Santos Mendoza, the thick-walled adobe hacienda was half a block away from the Catholic church, which had towering twin belfries that dominated the village plaza. Like many old adobe homes, it rambled on from room to room, with low-beamed passages that conked the heads of the unsuspecting, and finally opened onto a large, high-walled courtyard with an outdoor kitchen shaded by cottonwood trees. Stone-

and-mortar flowerbeds filled with brilliant summer blooms lined the courtyard walls, and a fenced vegetable garden with a hearty abundance of flourishing corn, squash, and tomato plants thrived in a sunny corner. Flagstone paths led to comfortable benches and chairs, and several well-placed birdbaths under low branches attracted darting, fluttering, singing, squawking robins, wrens, and warblers.

During his first visit, Matt had passed a pleasant few minutes in the courtyard with Señora Merton, who complimented him on his command of Spanish and asked how he'd come to speak it fluently. Without mentioning Pa or the ranch, he gave full credit to Tía Teresa, the Luceros, and Evangelina. Señora Merton, in turn, told him the story of meeting the professor at a dance when he was a student at the college and how he won her heart by reciting love poems to her in Spanish he'd learned as a child living in Barcelona. She merrily warned Matt to tread lightly on the hearts of the local señoritas lest a likely fate befall them. Señora Merton's dark hair and pretty eyes reminded Matt of Tía Teresa, as did her easy charm and grace. He had warmed to her immediately.

Matt and his classmates knew a little bit about Augustus Merton and his family because the professor often drew on his past experiences as an engineer when lecturing. The Mertons had lived in Mexico for many years during the professor's successful prior career designing and supervising the construction of bridges and tunnels, before returning to teach at the college. The couple had one son, Lorenzo, a recent West Point graduate serving at a fort in Oklahoma.

At the appointed time, shaved and wearing freshly ironed trousers and shirt, Matt tapped the heavy iron door knocker on the tall, hand-carved hacienda entry door. As he waited he gazed with smug satisfaction at his Studebaker, parked in the lane. A duplex roadster model, it came with a steel roof, four-wheel brakes, and a fifty-horsepower, six-cylinder engine. He'd added new bumpers front and back, a spare tire, and a sunscreen over the windshield, essential in the harsh New Mexico sunlight. When new, it had sold for almost twelve hundred dollars. Matt had bought it for three hundred from wages he'd earned at Sam Miller's store.

On the drive to Mesilla it had handled like a brand-new motorcar. Matt itched to take it on a long trip on one of the new oiled or paved highways. It was dusty from sitting idle in the shed for several months, and he hadn't had time to wash it, but tomorrow it would shine after he gave it a good cleaning.

The hinges on the massive door creaked open and Matt turned, expecting to see either the professor or his wife; instead, a petite, blue-eyed, redheaded girl with creamy skin, a ridge of freckles across her nose, and a stunning smile greeted him.

"Uncle Gus told me that if a young man with a split lip arrived at the front door driving a Studebaker, I was to let him in," she said in a breathy voice. "You must be Matt."

"You have me at a disadvantage, miss," Matt replied, trying to sound sophisticated. She was the prettiest girl he'd ever seen, far prettier than Clementine.

"I'm Beth Merton, Uncle Gus's favorite and only niece. Come in. He's already opened a bottle of wine to let it breathe. I don't know what that means, but since I'm not allowed to have any it doesn't matter. You've been here before, so find your way to the library. I'm helping Tía Consuelo in the kitchen."

Matt nodded and followed her into the house, appreciating her girlish figure until she disappeared into the kitchen hallway. In the library Professor Merton sat in an overstuffed chair, wineglass in hand. Although it was a hot summer evening outside, the thick adobe walls kept the hacienda comfortably cool.

"Good evening, Matt," Gus Merton said, rising to shake his hand. "Are you a drinking man? I've opened a good red that has a hint of raisin and almond. May I pour you a glass?"

"Yes, thank you."

"Excellent. Did Beth behave like a lady or try to disarm you with her quick wit and saucy attitude?"

"Both, I believe, much to my enjoyment," Matt replied.

"She's irrepressible," Merton noted, gesturing for Matt to sit.

"Is she here for a summer holiday?" Matt asked hopefully, thinking *irresistible* was a more suitable depiction.

"Alas, no," Merton answered. "Unfortunately, Beth has a troubling case of consumption, and her father, my younger brother Darcy, sent her to us from Cleveland for the dry climate. We've arranged for her to be admitted to a tuberculosis sanatorium that has just opened on the Alameda. She's to be examined by a doctor on Tuesday."

"She looks perfectly fine to me," Matt said.

"Indeed she does, and equates the sanatorium to jail, which I can understand, although it's a pleasant enough facility, with spacious rooms, a wide veranda that catches the breeze, and an excellent professional staff. If she pleads and begs for you to help her run away, you must decline."

"Perhaps as an alternative, I can take her for a ride in my Studebaker," Matt proposed.

Professor Merton smiled. "That's entirely up to the two of you."

At dinner, Matt sat across from Beth, and as the meal progressed he learned she was eighteen, had suddenly taken ill near the end of her sophomore year of college, and had plans to become a medical doctor.

"My unfortunate illness—as Uncle Gus refers to it—should prepare me well to enter the medical profession," she added flippantly. "At the very least I'll be good at diagnosing at least one disease. Don't you agree?"

"At the very least, it might make you more sympathetic to those who are very sick," Matt replied, thinking of Ma and all she'd endured.

His comment caught Beth by surprise. "What a perfectly splendid observation. Uncle Gus said you were a very bright young man."

"What I said to Beth was that you are not one to flaunt your intelligence and that I appreciate that quality in a person," Augustus Merton explained.

Matt turned away from Beth's dazzling smile. "Thank you, sir. But I must ask: Have you told her everything about me?"

Merton laughed. "I've only briefly touched on those facts and qualities about you that I have at my disposal. Any serious flaws or dark secrets you may have are yours to reveal or keep as you see fit."

"I'm greatly relieved to hear that," Matt replied.

"He's hopeful I'll take you as my beau," Beth said in mock seriousness.

Consuelo Merton stifled a laugh. "Stop it, Beth. You're incorrigible. He said no such thing."

Augustus Merton pounded the table in response. "There, sir! I am innocent. My words are easily twisted by the women in this house. Look to them for any evidence of romantic collusion, not me."

"Enough of this, you two," Consuelo scolded cheerfully. "Stop before Matt decides we're all lunatics and bolts for the door." She smiled reassuringly at Matt and added, "Beth knows no one here. We're hoping that you might find some time to keep her company while she's resting and recovering at the sanatorium. That is, if it's not an imposition."

"I'd like that," Beth said straight on.

"I'm told such places can be pure tedium," Augustus added. "As high-spirited as my niece is, she'll need some occasional distraction, if you'd be so inclined."

Matt glanced from the professor to his wife to Beth. All smiled at him with genuine good humor and goodwill. He felt incredibly at ease and comfortable, as though he was spending an evening with dear, lifelong friends. "I'd be more than happy to oblige."

"Excellent." Augustus raised his glass. "We are most grateful to you."

* * *

After dinner, Matt invited Beth on a stroll around the village plaza, and they left the hacienda with a promise to their hosts not to be long. With a cooling breeze and a lovely sky of puffy clouds tinged pink and orange by the sun low on the horizon, they entered the plaza, where a few *viejos* were clustered around a bench smoking and quietly telling stories while much louder sounds of merriment emanated from the open door of the corner speakeasy.

"Consuelo tells me you speak Spanish," Beth said. "Will you teach me?"

"Sure."

She pointed at the men at the bench.

"*Viejos*. Old-timers, or old men."

"*Viejos*," she said.

She pointed at a tree. "What's that?

"*Árbol.*"

"*Árbol,*" she repeated as she pointed at the church. "And that?"

"A church," Matt said.

"A church," Beth said with perfect elocution.

"Actually, it's *iglesia* in Spanish," Matt said.

"*Iglesia*. There, I know three more Spanish words besides *tía, señora*, and *adios*. My vocabulary has doubled with your help. Uncle Gus says you live alone. Are you a rich orphan?"

"What else has the professor told you?" Matt asked snappishly.

"Oh, please don't hate me," Beth pleaded, reacting to his tone of voice. "I don't mean to be rude. Sometimes people think I'm ill-mannered when I'm only trying to be amusing. It gives my mother fits. It happens when I try too hard to be liked."

The notion that Beth wanted Matt to like her brought a smile to his lips. "It's okay."

She hooked her arm in his. "Thank you. You must understand that Gus and Consuelo feel they must do everything possible to protect my virtue, safeguard my welfare, and promote my speedy recovery while I'm here. They are worse worrywarts than my parents. I think they spent days before my arrival arranging and planning every itty-bitty detail of my life in Las Cruces, selecting the sanatorium, deciding on the best doctor to treat me, and picking the perfect, most trustworthy young man to squire me around when it is allowed. You may be my only chance for any freedom."

"I've promised the professor not to help you escape."

Beth smiled jubilantly. "See? You've made my point exactly. But I'm glad they picked you to be my escort."

"So am I." Matt slowed at an empty bench away from the noise of the speakeasy and the *viejos*. Beth immediately sat down.

"It seems so much like a foreign country here," she said, gazing around the plaza. "So different from Cleveland, I hardly believe I'm in the United States. Do you dream of traveling the world?"

Matt sat beside her. "Sometimes, but mostly now I concentrate on my studies. It's a promise I made to my mother. You asked if I was an orphan. I'm not."

Beth put a finger to Matt's lips. "Hush. I'm sorry I asked such a thoughtless question. You don't have to answer."

He took her hand away, held it for a second, glancing at her eyes. He reluctantly released her hand and said, "I don't mind telling you."

He told her about Emma, her defective heart, which had ended her life much too soon, how she parlayed her divorce settlement into smart investments that put enough money in a trust to support him for years, and his home in town, where he'd lived mostly since the day he was born. He saved for last the tale of the short story Eugene Manlove Rhodes wrote about his mother making a hand on a Double K cattle drive back in the days before statehood.

"I know I would have loved her," Beth said emphatically.

"And she you, I bet," Matt allowed.

"Are you a cowboy as well as a scholar?"

Matt laughed. "Some might disagree with that notion, but I can sit a horse fairly well and know my way around cattle. I have a pinto named Patches. He's a fine pony."

"You must take me riding, and out for a jaunt in your motorcar. And will you lend me the story to read?" She stopped, out of breath.

Matt laughed. "Of course, whenever you like."

"Wonderful. You haven't mentioned your father or if you have any brothers or sisters."

At the far end of the plaza in the last light before dusk, Augustus and Consuelo Merton appeared, arm in arm. Matt stood to greet them, glad to be distracted from her sobering inquiry. "We've been spotted."

Beth sighed. "By my kindhearted jailers. When will I see you again?"

"I'll bring the Gene Rhodes story to you tomorrow, if you wish."

Beth stood on tiptoe and brushed her lips on his cheek. "Perfect."

Matt silently agreed as they strolled to meet the professor and his wife. The evening had been perfect.

* * *

Matt saw Beth twice more before she entered the sanatorium. As promised, he dropped off "Emma Makes a Hand" the following afternoon and spent an hour in her company before Consuelo whisked her away to shop for essentials she would need at the sanatorium. To his relief, not once did Beth question him any further about Pa or his family. Early the next morning, he took her for a jaunt in his Studebaker to see some of the countryside before she had to report to "jail." They drove to the base of the Organ Mountains, skirted along the foothills over rocky dirt roads to the state highway, crested the San Andres Pass, and stopped at a turnoff that gave a panoramic view of the Tularosa Basin. Beth took it all in with eyes wide in wonderment. Under a clear blue sky, with the desert in full bloom from the recent rains, the white gypsum dunes sparkled like diamonds and the Sacramento Mountains rose in sharp relief, hard and foreboding against the horizon, with the distant Sierra Blanca shimmering through the heat waves rising from the basin floor.

"It's magical," she proclaimed in a reverential whisper. "I want to see all of it. Why, you could drop Cleveland in the middle of it and it would be lost forever. Is there any water?"

Matt shook his head. "Hardly any."

"Can we drive on a bit farther?"

"A little ways, before it gets too hot."

At the bottom of the Chalk Hills he stopped again to point out the distant alkali flats that pressed against the north-south rib of the rugged eastern face of the San Andres Mountains. He described the winding, tortured pass through Rhodes Canyon, the high-country forests that capped the faraway peaks, the vast valleys and wide pastures hidden in the mountains, and the narrow canyons, musical and moist from live water trickling down rock streams kept cool by the shade of supple desert willows.

Without pause, he told her how the Double K sat poised in a low valley overlooking the basin, the toe of the rangeland touching desert scrub, the headlands rising to the tall pines, and how the ranch house with its wide veranda perfectly perched on a shelf gave a view that seemed to stretch to the ends of the earth.

"My ma is buried on a hill above the house," he concluded. "It's about the best spot in the whole world to be laid to rest."

"Does your father still live there?" Beth asked.

"He does," Matt answered shortly. "He's pretty much a loner who doesn't cotton to folks easily."

"Is that the nicest thing you can say about him?" Beth asked pointedly.

Matt hesitated. "I guess so."

"Will I ever meet him? Or see the ranch?"

"Someday, maybe." He wondered if a city girl could thrive in such a remote place, far from everything modern, no matter how beautiful the sunsets and the azure skies.

"Promise you'll take me there before I leave."

The notion of Beth someday leaving New Mexico felt like a stab wound. "I promise."

On the drive back to town, Beth told Matt about a pamphlet she'd been given that explained all the services at the sanatorium. She called it "The Rule Book for Inmates." She was to have no visitors for the first thirty days, take an hour a day of natural sunlight, practice breathing exercises to strengthen her weak lungs, take special vapors to refresh her sinuses, and read for no more than thirty minutes at a time, so as not to exhaust herself. X-rays would be taken routinely, her doctor would examine her weekly, and most important, she would be required to take the salubrious desert air twice a day on the veranda, once in the morning and again in the evening.

"Will you drive by on the road once in a while, honk the horn, and wave so that I know you're thinking of me?" she asked.

"As often as I can," Matt promised.

* * *

It took all of Matt's willpower not to drive by the sanatorium twice a day or more. He kept to a once-a-day routine, alternating between mornings and evenings, driving very slowly past the whitewashed adobe building with a high-pitched roof that had once been the private residence of a prominent Mexican merchant who had made a fortune in Juárez. The front porch was deep and screened, making it difficult for Matt to see in. But every time he passed by, Beth would be stationed in the same lounge chair waving madly at him as he tooted his horn.

At the end of Beth's first week of confinement, a note from her came in the mail complaining about the gruel her keepers passed off as food at mealtime and warning him that she would likely waste away from starvation long before consumption claimed her. She ended with a caveat not to write back, as she would miss him too much if he did so. After that, a new note arrived every few days containing humorous vignettes about her fellow inmates. There was Miss Lucy Monroe from Boston, who blushed at the mere mention of Dr. Brandt, the senior physician; Abigail Landis, who started a glee club for the inmates and sang contralto badly off-key; and Susana Martinez, a housekeeper who had taken to teaching Spanish to an old soldier everyone called Captain Mighty Fine because of his constant use of the phrase at every possible opportunity.

Her notes had him start counting the days until her mandatory confinement ended and he could see her up close, talk to her, be with her. The world seemed dull without her. He was more than besotted. In spite of her admonition, he wrote to her anyway, reporting on his horseback rides along the river, a recent dinner with her uncle Gus and *tía* Consuelo, where her company was sorely missed, his busy days clerking at Sam Miller's store for an employee who'd taken vacation. He didn't dare try to turn a clever phase or attempt to be witty. He feared that he lacked the necessary ingredients to be an entertaining correspondent. His best hope, he decided, was to remain attentive and pray it might compensate for his lack of sophistication.

On the first day Beth was allowed visitors, Matt went to the sanatorium with Gus and Consuelo, as they insisted he call them. After hugs for her aunt and uncle and a warm smile for Matt, Beth took them on a quick tour of the building and grounds, including the enclosed pool house, used for hydrotherapy treatments, and a lovely green lawn where patients who'd been approved for physical exercise could play croquet and badminton. She had a private room with big airy windows that gave a pleasant view of the lawn and several large cottonwoods and a private entrance that led to the flagstone walkway around the lawn. The room was furnished with a twin bed, a writing table and chair, and a tall chest of drawers. On top of the bureau were framed photographs of Beth's parents and her younger sister, Emily, along with a half dozen books, mostly novels.

Consuelo raised an eyebrow. "Let me bring you a few things from home to brighten your room up."

"That's very kind of you, Tía, but please don't," Beth replied. "I don't expect to be here that long. In fact, I've improved so much I'm now allowed to take my meals in the dining room with the other inmates and play croquet, in which I'm undefeated."

"Have all your symptoms abated?" Augustus asked hopefully.

"I haven't had a fever in weeks, and my appetite is back." Her sunny look turned stubborn. "All that's left to do is gain a few pounds and banish my cough. It's worse at night but getting better."

Consuelo smiled and hugged her. "*Maravilloso.*"

They visited for a time on the porch, interrupted every few minutes by curious patients stopping by, including the contralto who sang off-key, the old soldier, who shook Augustus's and Matt's hands and said it was "mighty fine" to meet them, and the Boston spinster who pined for Dr. Brandt and wanted to know if Matt was Beth's "young man." Both of them blushed, Matt a shade redder.

As they were leaving, Beth pressed a note in Matt's hand. He stuck it in his pocket and didn't look at it until after he said good-bye to Gus and Consuelo and drove away from their hacienda. It read:

*Meet me under the cottonwood behind the pool house at 8
tonight.*

At ten minutes to eight, he parked the Studebaker a hundred yards from the sanatorium. In deepening darkness he skirted the lawn to the cottonwood tree. Disappointed that Beth wasn't there, he waited. One by the one the lights inside the patients' rooms went out. After what felt like an eternity, Beth finally arrived, breathless and coughing into a handkerchief pressed against her mouth.

"Thank goodness you're here." She grasped his arm to steady herself.

Her touch electrified Matt. "I'm here," he managed.

"I am so tired of being banned from this, prohibited from that, prevented from doing something else." The words spilled out of her. "There is no one my age to talk to. I'm going insane. Take me for a ride in your car, please. I need to break the rules and feel like an outlaw, or I'll just shrivel up and turn to dust."

"Are you sure?" The notion of an illicit summer's night drive with Beth enthralled him.

"Yes, yes, yes."

They drove out of town into the desert, a million stars above in the sky, Beth with her head out the window and the wind blowing through her hair. He slowed the car at the turnoff to the Arrington Ranch.

"Don't stop," she pleaded.

"Okay." He drove on. "There's a place nearby called Sleeping Lady Hills. You can't see it at night, but from a certain angle it looks just like a woman sleeping."

"Can we go there someday?"

"We can get to it by horseback through the Rough and Ready Gap."

Beth laughed. "I love the names you have for places. Promise you'll bring me."

"As your riding buddy or your beau?" He was startled by his boldness.

"I think I'd prefer beau," Beth replied as she scooted closer to him.

21

Matt started the fall 1929 term of college in love. Beth's thirty-day quarantine had ended with her health so improved, the doctors allowed her to take weekend furloughs and gave her permission to have occasional evenings off the grounds during the week. Although she stayed at the hacienda on the weekends, most of her time—much to his delight—was spent with Matt. He kept his promise to take her horseback riding through the Rough and Ready Gap to the Sleeping Lady Hills, and when they weren't out roaming the countryside in his Studebaker or ahorseback, they attended an occasional evening concert in the park, went to a Sunday movie matinee at the Rio Grande Theater, and dined frequently with Gus and Consuelo at the hacienda. When they could, they slipped away to Matt's house, where they would pet so passionately it left them trembling and breathless in each other's arms. More than once they almost went all the way, but Beth's hushed *no* always brought Matt to a stop.

In early October, the local newspapers began running Associated Press stories from New York and Washington about falling stock prices caused by a speculative orgy on Wall Street. The papers also published editorials quoting financial experts who argued low interest rates and strong retail trade were proof the economy was growing and there was no need for investors who stayed the course to worry. When the market plummeted and many rushed to sell, bigwig eastern millionaires stepped in to shore it up. That caused talk of a panic to subside, although stocks continued to sink in value.

Far removed from the financial shenanigans of Wall Street, most New Mexicans—other than the bankers and a few fat cats—were more concerned about the lingering effects of drought and lower prices for livestock and farm produce than the ups and downs of the stock market. The news was interesting but not very relevant to folks who'd never had a bank account and weren't exactly sure what a share of stock was anyhow.

When the stock market plunged again and the deep-pocket millionaires did nothing to stop the bleeding, Augustus Merton predicted that millions of people would be thrown out of work. He recalled seeing tough times in Mexico during the height of the revolution, with peasants begging for food on the streets and whole families wandering the countryside, homeless and destitute. That experience had impressed on him the need to always be prepared for an emergency. He suggested that Matt would do well to keep some cash on hand to weather any uncertainties.

"Unless you can take care of the basics, you stand to lose everything," Augustus counseled. "Food, shelter, and cash money are essential in good or bad times. Never forget that."

Matt didn't disagree with him but figured Augustus was being overcautious. After all, living through a bloody revolution in a foreign country and surviving some economic hardship in America were two completely different things.

Later that evening, at home and alone, Matt thought more

about Augustus's advice. If hard times came, the house was his, free and clear, he had enough firewood to get him through the winter, and his tuition was paid for the full year. Still, the idea of keeping some cash on hand for emergencies made sense. Ma had always done that, and so had Pa. They also made sure the cupboards were well stocked with victuals. He decided to take some cash money out of the bank and go grocery shopping at Sam Miller's store tomorrow. That would cover the basics Augustus had talked about.

The next morning, after a trip to the bank and Sam Miller's store, Matt put the groceries away, hid his emergency cash in an empty coffee tin, and promptly forgot about the economy, his mind occupied with his course work and Beth. But in early November he was brought back to reality by an early-morning telephone call from a clerk at the bank asking Matt to meet with Mr. Worrell as soon as possible.

He arrived at the front door an hour before the bank was due to open and was let in by a worried-looking cashier who directed him to Worrell's office. After a tight-lipped greeting, Worrell wasted no time giving Matt the bad news: a margin call had been issued on the stock owned by the trust, which had completely wiped out all the cash assets. Worrell was in the process of calling in the mortgages on the rental properties, which needed to be sold to help cover the remaining market losses. It likely wouldn't be enough to cover everything the trust owed, but Worrell guessed the creditors would take what they could get and be happy with it.

"There is no more income from the trust," Worrell announced. "Any expenses you incur from now on will be your father's responsibility until you turn eighteen. In fact, we have no funds to pay last month's bills."

"I've got nothing left, right?" Matt asked, kicking himself for not taking all his personal funds out of the bank instead of just two hundred dollars.

"You have your house and all your personal possessions, but no cash. There is no money to pay for any of the outstanding expenses incurred on your behalf. I've informed your father by letter but have yet to hear back from him."

Matt got to his feet. "He'll show up, especially if he stands to lose the Double K."

"I'm afraid everyone will suffer in this disaster." Worrell extended his hand. "Good luck, Matthew."

"Thank you, sir."

Matt walked home calculating how far two hundred dollars would last him and came to the grim conclusion that it would barely stretch through to the end of the semester. At the house he threw off his jacket, got the cash out of the coffee tin, and spread the bills out on the kitchen table. Unless he did something about it, Guadalupe and Nestor wouldn't get paid for their work and Sam Miller would be left high and dry. To keep the money and not settle up wouldn't be right. Ma had taught him better than that.

Then there were the electric and telephone bills, feed for Patches, gas for the Studebaker, and money for food when the victuals in the cupboards ran low. He could do without the telephone and get by without electricity if he had to, but even cutting back that much wouldn't take him very far if he had no money. If he could sell the Studebaker, that would help, but he couldn't bear the notion of losing Patches. Finally, he could forget about completing his sophomore year or even finishing the current semester.

Questions, doubts, and anxious worries about what might happen to him and to Beth tumbled through his mind. What if he couldn't find work? What if Beth was forced to return to Cleveland? What if the bank tried to take the house away to pay debts owed to the stockbroker? Aside from finding a job and seeing if he could get some of his tuition money refunded, he wasn't sure what else to do. But he knew for certain he wasn't going to ask Pa for any help.

He took a deep breath to calm down, counted out the cash he needed to pay what was owed, put the remaining thirty bucks in the coffee tin, grabbed his jacket, and went to knock on Nestor and Guadalupe's front door. He returned home an hour later to find Pa sitting in his truck in front of the house.

"What are you doing here?" Matt asked as Pa climbed out to meet him.

"I came to town to get my false teeth put in," Pa said, clicking them together. "Mouth's a little sore, but the dentist says I'll get used to them soon enough. Glad I bought and paid for them before the crash. I stopped in to see Banker Worrell. He says we're both broke."

"Are you gonna lose the ranch?" Matt asked as he gave Pa a quick once-over. His new false teeth made him look almost respectable, his hair wasn't all raggedy under his hat, and his eyes were clear.

"Not if I can help it," Pa answered. "But the bank is gonna take the pastureland next to the Rocking J unless I can get Al Jennings to buy it at twenty-five cents on the dollar. I think he will. Then if I sell my ponies and cattle at a loss, I'll save the Double K."

"How did you get in such a fix?"

"I borrowed against that land to buy stock on the margin. I figured if Wall Street was making you good money in that trust, it could damn sure make me some. Dumbest thing I ever did."

"What do you want from me?"

"Nothing, just came by to say howdy and ask how you're gonna get by."

Matt shrugged. "I don't know yet."

"Come out to the ranch. I know we can scratch out a living together and keep the Double K from going under."

"Doing what?"

"Cut cordwood to haul to town and sell. And catch mustangs
out on the basin we can gentle and sell. There's gotta be hundreds
of wild Spanish ponies out there nobody owns to round up. But
I'll need a hand to do it and you're a damn fine wrangler."

Pa's compliment barely registered. Thinking of Beth, Matt
shook his head. "I'm gonna stay put right where I am."

"Not interested?"

"Not right now," Matt replied.

"Then I'd best be on my way."

"If I bring Patches out to the ranch, will you look after him?"

Pa nodded. "Don't see why not. I'll put him in with Calabaza
and Stony; they're the only two I plan to keep, other than a packhorse or two I might need. I'll be moseying."

"I got pork and beans I can heat up on the stove," Matt offered,
surprised by his blurted invitation.

Patrick stared at the house that had kept Emma away from him
for years; CJ and Matt too, for that matter. "Thank you kindly for the
offer, but I've a hankering for a sit-down meal at the hotel while I
still have a silver dollar or two in my pocket. Want to tag along?"

"I got somewhere to be soon," Matt lied. He wouldn't see Beth
until tomorrow evening and had nowhere else to go.

"Bring Patches out to the ranch anytime. I'll look after him."

"I'm obliged." Matt stood in the street and watched Pa's truck
disappear around a corner, glad to see him gone and at the same
time wondering why he couldn't hate him.

* * *

The next day Matt withdrew from his college classes and got a small tuition refund check, which he cashed at the bank right away. Boone Mitchell was on his front stoop with two suitcases in hand when he got home. He'd been let go from the El Paso rail yards and used his last paycheck to send Peg, who was about to have another baby, and Kendell to live with his parents in Detroit until he found a job. He had a thirty-day pass from his old boss to ride the freights so he could look for work up and down the line and was leaving on the morning train for California, where he'd been told that mechanics were being hired for a new trucking company just starting up.

"I just need a place to hang my hat until I get back on my feet, if you don't mind my freeloading for a while," he added. "I'm strapped for cash."

"Make yourself at home," Matt said. "Are you hungry?"

Boone grinned. "Boy, am I. I'm trying not to spend a penny if I don't have to."

"You're welcome to join me for a baked bean sandwich and some canned soup."

"Sounds like a feast."

After they ate, Boone did most of the talking. The new baby was due any day. They'd been about to buy a house when he got laid off, and the seller refused to give back the earnest money deposit. He'd tried to peddle their furniture, but no one was buying, so he just packed his suitcases and left it all behind. He'd sold his car for almost nothing and was using the money to see him through until he found work. If he couldn't find a job in a month, he'd join Peg and Kendell in Detroit and hope that his father could get him work at the Ford plant where he was a maintenance supervisor.

He asked about jobs in Las Cruces. Matt told him he'd heard things were bleak although he hadn't started making the rounds himself. Boone sighed, pulled a hip flask from his coat pocket, and took a big swig. Matt had never known Boone to drink hard liquor before. He wondered if he'd made a mistake in agreeing to let him stay.

In the morning Boone left early to catch the westbound morning freight. On his way out the door he announced that if he got a job, he'd send Matt the money to ship the big suitcase he left behind. If not, he'd be back by the end of next week.

Matt wished him luck, fixed a breakfast of coffee and oatmeal with a bit of butter on top, dressed, and spent the day going to every store and business, looking for work. He tried the downtown filling stations, car dealerships, livery stables, warehouses, freight yards, and most of the stores up and down Main Street. He returned home late in the afternoon, weary, unemployed, and hungry. He'd saved the twenty-five cents lunch would have cost, knowing he'd be offered dinner with Gus and Consuelo when he carried Beth to the hacienda for her weekend stay.

He washed up and headed for the sanatorium, mulling what he could say to convince Gus and Consuelo to let Beth accompany him when he took Patches to the Double K. He wasn't even sure if he could talk Beth into the idea, but he was determined to try to get her out of town and on her own in the hopes of finally wearing down the last of her resistance. His idea was that they'd take the train to Engle and stay over at the hotel for the night before traveling on to the ranch. But Matt wouldn't mention the stay-over part to Gus and Consuelo. He knew the scheme was a long shot, but it was worth a try. He was tired of being so doggone honorable. It had become painful.

He sprang his idea on Beth as they drove to the hacienda.

She wagged her finger at him. "You just want to have your way with me. If Uncle Gus knew, he'd horsewhip you. Does he even have a horsewhip?"

"Probably somewhere," Matt ventured. "And he likely knows how to use it. You did say you wanted to see the ranch, remember?"

"I do want to, but not at the expense of my virtue."

"So much for my brilliant idea," Matt grumbled.

"Wanting to spirit me away is very romantic." Beth moved closer. "Would you settle for a partial conquest?"

"Such as?" Matt put his hand on her leg.

"A weekend excursion to the ranch with you, me, Tía Consuelo, and Uncle Gus."

"How would that work?"

"I'm sure we can think of something if you'll remove your wandering hand from my leg and put your scheming, devious mind to work."

By the time they arrived at the hacienda, they'd polished their plan. Over dinner Matt explained that he would soon be taking Patches to the ranch and put forward the idea that the Mertons take a weekend jaunt and visit him there. Gus was less than enthusiastic, but Consuelo liked the idea of getting away from all the gloom and doom about the economy for a while. Beth pleaded with her uncle to accept the invitation, arguing with a pout that she'd seen virtually nothing of the state since her arrival. Matt proposed to meet them in Engle and guide them to the ranch to make sure they didn't lose their way.

"It's a far piece to the ranch," he added, "and you might want to stock up on extra cans of gas and water for the trip."

Gus raised an eyebrow. "Are we going on safari or to the Double K?"

Matt laughed. "It's the backlands, and folks have been known to get turned around every which way in the mountains and canyons. You'll have a separate casita all to yourselves, and there's beautiful scenery most folks never get to see."

"I'm all in favor," Consuelo said.

Gus glanced from his wife to his niece, who beamed a dazzling smile at him. "Very well, we'll go. I'll cancel next Friday's classes and we'll leave early for the Double K, which I'm told once harbored notorious outlaws. I hope they are long gone."

"Most of them are dead," Matt remarked with a delighted grin.

"That's reassuring. We must be home by Sunday night."

Beth clapped her hands, scooted to her uncle's side, and gave him a kiss. "Thank you, thank you."

Gus patted her cheek. "I'm putting you and your aunt in charge of packing provisions. I have no intention of eating overcooked beefsteak and pinto beans morning, noon, and night."

When the evening ended, Beth walked Matt to his car, pressed against him, and gave him a long, lingering smooch.

"How did you get Consuelo to go along with us?" he asked when the kiss ended.

Beth smiled slyly. "She's partial to you. All I had to do was ask."

"I hope I can get my pa to mind his manners and behave."

"That's up to you." She kissed him again and said, "Well, at least one of us will be spending the night in the hotel in Engle. Doesn't that mean you've made it to second base with me?"

"And I thought I was heading for home."

"Well, you are, in a way."

Matt laughed. "You're mean. It wasn't exactly what I had in mind."

She nibbled his ear and whispered, "Be patient."

* * *

Mr. Roybal's donkey, blind, barely able to stand, and perhaps the oldest living donkey on the planet, still announced each new morning to the neighborhood with its mournful bray. The honking sound woke Matt with a start, and he sat up in bed, stunned by the sudden realization he'd let his dumb, regrettable plan to seduce Beth spin out of control. What was he thinking inviting them all to the ranch? It was plain *loco.* He hadn't been to the Double K since Tía Teresa's funeral more than a year ago, and he had no idea what shape it was in. How would Pa react to his inviting guests to stay there without his say-so? He felt like a fool for behaving as though he was some sort of swell. Could he call the whole thing off without looking even more ridiculous? Would Beth think him a complete imbecile? Consuelo and Gus too?

No, by George, he would make it work. After all, they'd only be staying overnight. Besides, Ma had taught him everything about cleaning and putting a house in order. Hadn't he taken care of her when she was sick and mostly bedridden? If he got started to the ranch pronto and went right at what needed doing, full bore, he'd have the place fixed up and whistle clean before they arrived.

He slipped into his jeans and pulled on his boots. He had six days to get it done. He pocketed all his remaining money, drank yesterday's coffee for breakfast, bundled enough clothes to see him through a week, and wrote a note to Beth telling her he was on his way to the Double K with Patches and would meet her next Saturday morning in Engle.

At the depot, he bought a coach ticket, hurried Patches into a livestock car, dropped the note to Beth in the mailbox, and soon was on his way, the train whistle and the click-clack of the wheels drowning out the bells of St. Genevieve's Church summoning the faithful to morning Mass.

22

Matt was alone at the ranch for three days before Patrick appeared. He took one look at the spic-and-span house and asked Matt if he was moving back in. Half expecting a tongue-lashing, Matt explained what he was up to. Pa shook his head without saying another word, returned to his truck, and started unloading hay bales, tossing them one by one into the barn through the open door. When he finished, he stomped into the kitchen for a cup of coffee.

"The place ain't been this tidy in years," he said, pouring a cup. "I'd hire you on as my housekeeper, except I ain't got the money."

"Is that an insult or a compliment?" Matt demanded.

"Take it any way you want. Just don't expect me to lend a hand; I've got men's work to do."

Matt's temper flared. "Why do you always have to dig your spurs in my side? You're a sorry excuse for a father."

"I know it," Pa replied. "I always have been. Even when I tried to do better with CJ and you I made a mess of it. Best I can say is it ain't your fault. I'm just built this way and there's no changing it. Tell you what; I'll skedaddle up to the cabin before this gal and her relatives show up, so as not to embarrass you."

"That would be mighty civilized of you," Matt drawled.

Pa drained his coffee and guffawed. "Well, who has the sharp tongue now?"

"Runs in the family, I reckon."

"Reckon so." Pa put the coffee cup in the wash pan. "I'll be heading over to the Rocking J in the morning to help Al Jennings shoe some of his ponies."

"I'll surely miss your company."

Pa snorted and adjusted his upper plate of sparkling white false teeth with a thumb. "There goes that sassiness again. Remember, you got a job here if you want it. I won't offer it again."

"I'll keep it in mind."

"Is this gal you're trying to impress ornamental or useful?"

"Both."

"That's good." Pa gazed at the scrubbed-clean kitchen table, the polished windows, the scoured-spotless cookstove. "Because I figure you must have a powerful itch for her to go to all this trouble."

The truth of Pa's words made Matt stiffen. "I don't plan to embarrass myself."

Pa grunted. "Chase that notion out of your head. When it comes to womenfolk, we're always gonna make fools of ourselves now and then, no matter how hard we try not to."

"I guess you'd know something about that."

Pa paused at the kitchen door and looked Matt up and down. He'd filled out, gained an inch or two, and wasn't a kid anymore. "Hobble your lip and stop trying to rile me. I declare a truce between us right here and now. I bought fresh victuals in town and tonight I'm fixing Franco-American spaghetti with meatballs straight out of the can. Join me if you've a mind to."

"I'll see you at dinnertime."

* * *

For some reason, Pa had completely emptied the casita and stored all the furniture in Matt's old bedroom. Over the next two days, after getting rid of the black widows, mice, and centipedes that had taken up residence in the casita, Matt cleaned the corner fireplace and chimney, whitewashed the adobe walls, and scrubbed the oxblood dirt floors before moving the furniture back in. In the small front room he set up his old twin bed for Beth, figuring Gus and Consuelo would want her sleeping close by. He'd much rather have her sleeping with him, but since he'd be bunking on the living room couch, he figured that daydream was doomed.

In two of Ma's old chests he found bed linens, blankets, and towels, which he washed and dried on the clothesline. When he finally had the casita shipshape, he turned to the last and worst of his chores, cleaning the outhouse. Whitewash, bleach, elbow grease, and a bag of lime that he found in the barn made it tolerably clean and no longer stinky. Afterward he soaked and scrubbed in a tub of hot water to get the smell off.

In the kitchen Pa had sliced a canned ham and had spuds boiling on the stove. "You've done an ace-high job on this place," he said.

"Thanks. I thought you were fixing spaghetti."

"Changed my mind. The casita's yours to use whenever you want it."

"I'm obliged."

"Sit. Supper's about ready."

Pa poked a fork in the potatoes, declared them done, put the pot aside, quick-seared ham steaks in a hot fry pan, and served up supper along with fresh cups of Arbuckle's. Matt dug right in.

"I figured I owed you at least a decent meal for all the work you've done," Pa said as he sawed at his ham steak. "Your ma schooled you well. Are you sparking this young lady that's coming here?"

"I'm trying to, but she's making me wait until she gets better," Matt replied.

"What wrong with her?"

"Tuberculosis."

Pa stopped sawing. "She's a lunger?"

Matt nodded.

"Ain't life taught you nothing?"

"It's not the same as with Ma," Matt replied hotly. "Lots of folks with TB get cured. Beth is doing just fine with her treatments and all."

Pa chewed a bite. "Ain't none of my business. When do you go fetch her?"

"In the morning from Engle."

"Take the truck; you'll save some time."

"I'm obliged. The grub's good."

Pa smiled. "Glad you like it. There are store-bought cookies for dessert. You got dirty-dish duty 'cause I'm leaving for the cabin after we eat."

"Fair enough," Matt said between bites.

It was getting dark when Pa set off on Calabaza for the cabin. The pony had been up and down the mountain so many times, Pa could fall asleep in the saddle and still arrive there safely. After the dishes were done, Matt turned in early, hoping to get some shuteye, but he was too wound up and eager to leave for Engle and fetch Beth back to the ranch, especially now that it wasn't such a shoddy mess.

For a couple of hours he dozed on and off, with light dreams that flitted through his head and then evaporated each time he shook off the threat of real sleep. Finally he gave up and got out of bed. Fortified with hot, bitter leftover coffee, he started out for Engle in the truck, headlights cutting through the predawn darkness under a star-studded sky.

Dawn broke as he began the downslope out of Rhodes Canyon, daylight not yet cresting the San Andres and the Jornada slate gray and fading into a pitch-black western horizon. Only a light or two flickered in the slowly vanishing village of Engle, kept barely alive by the railroad, the hotel, the livery, and a few mercantile stores that catered to the surrounding ranchers. He pulled up in front of the hotel expecting to see Gus's car parked nearby, but it wasn't there. He circled the block and still didn't see it. Inside, there was no one on duty at the registration desk and the dining room had just opened. He asked a waitress who was wiping down tables if Professor Merton and his wife and niece were checked in. The woman shrugged and said she didn't know. At the desk he rang the bell until a sleepy-eyed old man emerged from a back room.

The man yawned and scratched his beard. "You need a room?"

"I'm here to meet Professor Merton, his wife, and niece."

"Are you Matthew Kerney?"

"I am." Matt held his breath.

"Hold on, there's a telegram for you." He thumbed through some papers and put it on the counter. Matt grabbed it. Dated Friday morning, it read:

MATTHEW KERNEY
C/O ENGLE HOTEL
ENGLE, NM
BETH RELAPSED YESTERDAY.
CONDITION UNKNOWN.
CONFINED TO SANATORIUM.

DOCTORS HOPEFUL.
TRIP REGRETTABLY CANCELED.
SEE US WHEN YOU ARRIVE BACK HOME.
GUS

Matt read it twice. "Dammit." He turned away from the room clerk before he choked up. Outside, he thought hard on what to do with Pa's truck. He damn sure wasn't going to drive all the way back to the Double K and lope Patches here to catch a train to Las Cruces. That would waste an entire day. At the livery, he paid Ken Mayers, the owner, to store the truck until Pa showed up, went back to the hotel and wrote a note to Pa to go in the mail explaining what had happened, and caught the first southbound train.

He didn't realize until he sat down in the almost empty coach car that he was sweating, his hands were shaking, and his heart was pounding in his chest.

23

A week passed before Matt saw Beth again. Propped up in bed, she smiled cheerfully at him as he joined Gus and Consuelo at her side.

"I'm fine," she said before Matt could question her about her condition.

Matt smiled broadly to hide the shock of seeing her so thin and pale. "You look great."

"Liar." She covered her mouth with a handkerchief and coughed. It sounded rough and thick. "Sorry."

Consuelo patted her hand. "Are you eating enough?"

Beth wrinkled her nose, but her eyes never left Matt as she said, "They're drowning me in milk. I hate milk."

"The doctor says it's of great benefit," Gus noted.

"What does he know? He doesn't have to drink it."

Gus laughed. "Your spunk hasn't diminished one bit."

"Then I must be on the mend," she replied, her gaze still fixed on Matt, who was paying attention only to her.

Consuelo glanced at them, looked at her husband, and pointedly said, "Don't we have a few questions for the doctor Beth's parents want answered?"

"Yes, of course." Gus planted a kiss on Beth's forehead. "We'll be right back." He followed Consuelo out the door.

"I'm a mess," Beth said apologetically, patting her hair.

Matt moved close and took her hand. "You're beautiful."

Beth laughed and started coughing again. She fought it off and said, "You're looking at me with your heart, not your eyes."

"Is that bad?"

"No, I love it. I'm sorry I ruined our weekend at the ranch."

"Don't you worry about that. There will be lots more weekends."

Beth's expression darkened. "I'm not so sure. Hasn't Uncle Gus told you? My daddy can't pay for me to stay here anymore."

Matt felt a pit open in his stomach. He grabbed her hand. "You can't leave."

"Would you have me remain in this horrid jail?"

"I didn't mean that."

She smiled and rubbed his hand against her cheek. "I know. If I have to go home to Cleveland, I'll just pack you in my trunk and take you with me."

"Why go at all? Stay here with me. I'll take care of you." What was he saying? He had no job, no money.

Beth touched a finger to her lips as Augustus and Consuelo returned looking very cheery. "Am I cured?" she asked them.

"Not quite yet," Augustus replied from the foot of Beth's bed. "Your father wanted us to find out when you could go home. Your doctor doesn't believe the weather in Cleveland would be conducive to your health."

"So you'll simply have to stay with us," Consuelo added gaily, noting the big grin spreading across Matt's face.

"I'll wire Darcy today," Augustus said. "I'm sure he'll agree."

Beth clapped her hands with glee. "Goody. How soon can you spring me from this place?"

"On Friday," Consuelo answered, turning to Matt. "Would you pick her up and bring her home?"

Matt wanted to whoop with delight when Consuelo said *home,* but he nodded instead. "I surely will."

Augustus wagged a finger at Beth. "Your doctor wants you to gain at least a pound before Friday."

"I will," Beth promised, beaming. "Bring me a quart of milk—two quarts."

"And you're to have no visitors until then," Consuelo added.

Beth pouted. "What a spoilsport he is."

"Just get better," Augustus ordered.

"What's the Spanish word for *better?*"

"*Mejorar,*" Augustus, Consuelo, and Matt said in unison, which left them all laughing.

Matt was last out the door. He turned to say good-bye one more time, and Beth threw him a kiss. Her dazzling smile lit him up, and in that instant he knew he would never love anyone more.

* * *

Beth was discharged from the sanatorium with doctor's orders to convalesce at home and avoid any unnecessary excitement for several weeks, which to Consuelo's way of thinking meant limiting Matt to short, supervised visits. Both Augustus and Consuelo took seriously their responsibilities to get Beth healthy and well, so Matt didn't mind being on his best behavior, although he yearned to have Beth all to himself, and soon. He was certain she was on the mend for good this time.

When he was with her, he avoided his worries of no job and bleak prospects. But he was truly almost broke, the food in his cupboard was running low, and the Studebaker's gas tank was on empty. With Sam Miller's permission, he'd parked the car on Main Street in front of the store with a FOR SALE sign on the windshield asking one hundred dollars, but there was no interest so far. With no cash for gas, he'd taken to walking to Mesilla to see Beth.

He found temporary work for a week unloading railroad freight cars at a warehouse from midnight to eight in the morning when an extra hand was needed. After his last shift, he walked home exhausted to a cold, dark house, but with the very good feeling of cash wages in his pocket and a grocery list in his head. Sadly, the warehouse boss had no more work for him the next week.

He turned onto Griggs Avenue to see smoke curling from the kitchen chimney of his house and lamplight shining in the window. He figured Boone Mitchell had returned to claim the suitcase he'd left behind. Since his visit, Matt had gotten several letters from Boone. In the last one, he wrote that several possible jobs hadn't panned out. Work was scarce and the competition fierce. He was on his way to San Francisco, where a ferry company owned by the railroad was hiring. If that fell through, he wasn't sure where he'd go next.

Just yesterday, Matt had received a note from Peggy wondering if Boone had been in touch. She hadn't heard from him for three weeks. Matt smiled. If Boone was still unemployed and back in Las Cruces, it wasn't all bad. At least Peggy could stop worrying about him.

Matt bounded up the front step, opened the door, called out, and got no response. Inside, the man at the kitchen table wasn't Boone. He was maybe thirty, thin, with an angular face, curly dark hair, a crooked mouth, and a long scar below his cheekbone.

The smile on Matt's face froze. "Who in the hell are you?" he demanded. On the table in front of the man were Matt's last can of sardines and a jar of pickled beets, both empty. In the man's hand was a cup of steaming-hot coffee from the pot boiling on the stove.

The man put the cup down, pushed back from the table, and stood, showing empty hands. "Easy there, fella. I'll pay you for the food I ate. Boone told me to come fetch his suitcase; that's all. But I got hungry waiting on you. You must be Matt. Fred Tyler's the name. I didn't mean to give you a fright."

"You startled me; that's all."

Tyler smiled. "Anybody would be troubled, finding a stranger in their home, unexpected and all. Coffee's hot and fresh. I'll pay you a nickel for my cup of Arbuckle's as well, as long as I get a re-fill. Mind if I sit back down?"

Matt shucked his coat. "Go ahead."

Tyler eased into his chair. "It's mighty kind of you not to kick me out."

"I haven't decided not to yet." Matt went to the stove, got cof-fee, and turned to find Tyler pointing a pistol at him. He froze, with both hands on the cup to keep from dropping it.

"Best you do as you're told; otherwise, I'll shoot you dead." Tyler didn't sound friendly anymore. "Walk on over here and empty your pockets."

Matt put the coffee cup down on the table and spilled his week's wages of nineteen dollars and fifty cents on the table in front of Tyler.

"Where's the rest of your money?"

Matt nodded at the empty coffee tin on top of the cupboard.

"Get it."

The barrel of Tyler's six-shooter followed Matt to the cupboard and back. Matt pushed the tin across the table, and when Tyler reached for it with his free hand, Matt threw his hot coffee in Tyler's face. Tyler yelled and dropped the pistol, both hands flying to his eyes. Matt picked up the fork Tyler had used to eat *his* sardines and stabbed him in the arm. Tyler yelped, dropped his hands, and blindly started searching for the pistol, but before he could snare it, Matt slammed Tyler's head against the table as hard as he could. Then he picked up a frying pan from the kitchen counter and hit Tyler again for good measure. Tyler went limp, his head on the table, blood squirting from his shattered nose.

Matt grabbed the pistol, threw open the front door, and yelled for Nestor to come and help. He arrived within a few minutes, took one look at Tyler unconscious and bleeding, and turned to Matt.

"What happened, Mateo?" he asked.

"He tried to rob and kill me," Matt explained, the pistol shaky in his hand.

"Get me some rope," Nestor said.

Matt fetched a lasso from his bedroom. Nestor hog-tied Tyler and dumped him on the floor. "He's not going anywhere."

"*Gracias.*"

"*De nada.*" Nestor took the pistol from Matt's hand and put it on the table. "I get the sheriff, okay?"

"*Sí.*" Matt went through the pockets of the winter coat Tyler had draped over a kitchen chair. It looked exactly like the one Boone had worn. In a pocket he found Boone's hip flask and an unsent letter to Peggy telling her that he had run out of luck and money and was returning to Las Cruces.

Matt searched Tyler's pockets. In his wallet he found Boone's union card from his job at the El Paso rail yards and a piece of paper in Boone's handwriting with Matt's name and address. There was also an expired Ohio driver's license issued to Byron

Boyd. The physical description on the license didn't match Fred Tyler at all.

Matt put the wallet and its contents on the kitchen table along with the pistol, whiskey flask, and Boone's letter to Peggy. He stared glumly at the evidence and thought that no matter who Fred Tyler really was, he'd mostly likely murdered Boone. The notion of telling Peggy turned his stomach. He couldn't do it unless he was absolutely sure.

*   *   *

The investigation of the crime on Griggs Avenue fell to Deputy Sheriff Máximo Castaneda, known to all as Moe. A slow-moving, thorough man, Moe stood five foot six, carried two hundred fifty pounds on his bearlike frame, and had been known to fell rowdy drunks with one thunderous punch to the solar plexus. Drunks were his specialty, not suspected felons, so Moe took extra care to get all the facts straight. An hour after careful questioning and evidence gathering, Moe concluded that Matthew Kerney had acted within his right to protect his life and property and hauled a whimpering Fred Tyler off to jail.

The next morning the local newspaper ran the following headline and story:

MAN FOILS ATTEMPTED ROBBERY

Early yesterday, Matthew Kerney of Griggs Ave. risked life and limb to protect himself from an armed intruder he found lurking in his home. With only a kitchen fork and a strong right arm Mr. Kerney severely wounded a transient named Mr. Fred Tyler who held the young man at gunpoint demanding money. Deputy Castaneda said to this reporter that the suspect, who is currently residing in jail awaiting his court appearance, should be grateful he wasn't killed by his intended victim. Inmate Tyler suffered several hard blows to his head, a stab wound to his arm, and burns to his face. Mr. Kerney sustained no injuries. His commendable bravery should be applauded by all law-abiding citizens who have occasion to greet him on the streets of our fair city.

That afternoon at the hacienda, Beth received him at the front door with a hug. "My brave hero."

Matt blushed. "Don't say that."

She pulled him inside and closed the door against the cold. "And why not? I'm about to send the newspaper clipping of your heroic act to Daddy, who has been recently advised by Uncle Gus that you are my beau. Daddy has written back demanding to know your pedigree. He can be such an old stick-in-the-mud sometimes. Even Uncle Gus agrees."

"Well, if your father knows I'm your beau, I guess that makes it official."

Beth kissed him. "*That* makes it official. Now, come with me to the library. Uncle Gus wants a full report. And so do I."

* * *

Matt's newfound reputation as an upstanding, commendable citizen brought him work. Tom Farnum, the warehouse foreman for Railway Express Agency who'd hired him temporarily, was so impressed by the newspaper account of Matt's heroics that he offered him a job as an on-call worker to fill in for absent or sick employees on any of the three shifts. Some weeks Matt worked sixty hours; some weeks he worked ten hours; some none at all. But over the course of a month, he averaged enough wages to pay his bills, keep gas in the Studebaker, and get the electricity and phone turned back on at the house. He also gained ten pounds of muscle from loading and unloading freight cars and carried a special deputy sheriff commission because of the valuables and cash that were transported by rail.

On the job, Matt got to know the railroad cops who worked the line from Texas to California. He told them what had happened with Fred Tyler and his suspicion that Boone had met with foul play. He gave them copies of Deputy Castaneda's official report and asked them to ask around about Boone when they had a chance. Because Boone was a union brother and a railroad man, the cops took Matt's request seriously.

While he waited, hoping the railroad bulls would learn something, Peggy sent him frantic notes every week asking of word from Boone. Matt always wrote back that he hadn't heard from him and telling her not to worry; Boone could take care of himself. It pained him to do it, but without proof his friend was dead, suspicion was one thing and fact another.

When he wasn't working or sleeping, he spent as much time as he could with Beth, who continued to improve with each passing day, so much so, she'd enrolled in a chemistry course at the college, a prerequisite for medical school. Her course work coupled with Matt's erratic work schedule meant that their time together was less spur-of-the-moment but still intensely passionate. It proved impossible for them to keep their hands off each other. They'd started talking about trying to find ways to complete their degrees in a world of crumbling expectations. The likelihood that they'd be unable to finish college anytime soon was depressing.

The day Fred Tyler appeared before Judge Horace Van Patten and pled guilty to breaking and entering and armed robbery, Matt was in the crowded courtroom. Before sentencing, Van Patten called Matt forward to describe the events that had occurred in his house. Matt used the opportunity to tell the judge that he believed Fred Tyler had killed Boone Mitchell. He submitted a copy of the missing person report he'd made to the police, which contained all the evidence found in Tyler's possession at Matt's house, including Boone's unsent letter to his wife and his union card, which Matt had found in Tyler's wallet. It wasn't enough to prove Tyler a murderer, but it got him the maximum consecutive sentence the judge could impose.

As he was led away, Tyler sneered at Matt and said, "I'll see you someday, pretty boy. Count on it."

The next day the newspaper ran the story of Tyler's sentencing and once again proclaimed Matt a fine example of the upstanding citizenry of the fair city of Las Cruces. Beth clipped the article and sent it to her parents as further evidence of Matt's bona fides. Two weeks later, she received a letter from her parents that they would be arriving with her sister for a visit in a month.

Matt was convinced that Beth's family was coming to take her away from him, and the news of their impending visit depressed him no end. His downheartedness deepened the next Monday night at work when Wilford Hawkings, one of the railroad cops looking into Boone's disappearance, stopped by to tell him Boone's remains had been found buried outside of a shantytown in Sacramento, California. He'd been identified by an expired railroad pass made out in his name and a letter from his wife found with the body. The local cops were treating it as homicide, and his family in Detroit had just been notified.

Though he'd suspected and feared Boone's death, the reality of it felt like a mule kick.

24

Beth Merton had come to New Mexico fearing she would be interminably bored. Instead, she now dreaded the possibility of leaving the still half-wild West she'd learned to love, an aunt and uncle she adored, and the young man who'd captured her heart. Her fears were not without cause; her father had lost his job with the Cleveland & Buffalo Transit Company. But his former boss, the president of the company, had recommended him to an old friend who was a partner in the Los Angeles Pacific Electric Railway Company. On the family visit to Las Cruces, Daddy would stop over for a few days before traveling on to Los Angeles to interview for a job. If he got hired, the family would of course move with him. Beth desperately hoped to avoid going with them. If she was fully recovered by then, she planned to beg Daddy to let her stay with Tía Consuelo and Uncle Gus and finish her baccalaureate degree at the New Mexico Agricultural and Mechanical Arts College. She would argue that it would be best for her health's sake to remain in New Mexico. Uncle Gus and Tía Consuelo were delighted with her scheme, which gave it a much better chance of success, but she'd said not a word about it to Matthew.

For months, she'd wanted to go to Mexico. How could she be so close to a foreign country and not visit it? She'd lived all her life in Cleveland, and Daddy had never once taken the family across Lake Erie on a steamship to Canada. What if she never returned to Cleveland and never, ever stepped into Canada in her entire life? She simply couldn't let such an unthinkable missed opportunity happen to her in New Mexico.

With wages coming in, Matt had kept the Studebaker, and Mexico was only fifty miles away by car. At a garage, Beth had picked up a road map that showed the highway to El Paso was rated first-class, which meant paved or oiled all the way, so getting there would be a breeze. Going alone with Matt to Mexico was the problem; Gus and Consuelo would never allow it. To get around them, she enlisted Matt in a deception. They would plan a picnic outing in the Organ Mountains, go to Juárez instead, and return late the same night using a flat tire as an excuse for their tardiness. Matt didn't need much convincing. The idea of getting her out of town alone was persuasive enough.

They left Las Cruces early one Saturday morning, traveling south on U.S. Highway 80, which paralleled the Rio Grande. Large farms dotted the riverside, creating swaths of green in sharp contrast to the brown upslope desert beyond. To the east, the Organ Mountains drifted down the valley into Texas before giving way to the Franklin Mountains, which overlooked El Paso.

Five miles outside of town, the radiator overheated. Matt pulled off the road, and they waited thirty minutes for it to cool down so he could add more water. They continued on, only to have it happen again just shy of the railroad yards in downtown El Paso.

Matt took a closer look at the radiator from the undercarriage and found a quarter-size hole in it, probably from a rock kicked up by a tire. Cussing in frustration, he gave Beth the bad news. "It will have to be taken out to be patched."

Beth peered at the engine. "How long will it take?"

Matt dusted off his hands. "A couple of hours at least, depending on when they can get to it. First we have to find a garage. I'll fill the radiator again when it cools and hope we can make it to a garage before the engine blows."

"Is our adventure ruined?"

Matt looked down the road at the nearby cluster of buildings that signaled downtown El Paso. "We'll probably have enough time to walk across the bridge to Juárez and back."

Beth pouted. "That's it?"

"This time, I reckon." Using a rag, Matt loosened the radiator cap and watched the steam hiss out. "How come when we first met, you told me you were Gus's only niece?"

"I fibbed because I didn't want you to find out about my sister, Emily."

"Find out what?"

"That she's prettier, smarter, and taller than I am. I hate her, of course."

Matt grinned. "I can't wait to meet her."

Beth punched his arm, hard. Matt pulled her to him and kissed her, hard.

With the radiator refilled and the engine off, Matt coasted the Studebaker down a street that sloped gently toward the river and rolled it to a stop at a garage just off the town plaza. While Beth waited, he talked to the garage owner. He soon returned, shaking his head and looking glum.

"He's here alone and can't get to it until first thing in the morning, but if I take it out myself, he'll weld a patch on it pronto."

Beth sternly shook her head. "Don't you dare do that. I'm going to at least set foot in Mexico today, and you're coming with me."

"We can't stay here overnight unless we sleep in the Studebaker. I don't have the money to fix the car and pay for a room."

Beth pointed to an ornate, ten-story brick hotel on the corner. Two wings with fancy gold parapets each sporting Old Glory on rooftop flagpoles were separated by a grand entrance under a huge domed ceiling. Ritzy new motorcars lined the street in front of the building.

"We'll stay there," she said.

Matt couldn't conceive what such a swanky place would charge for one night. "No can do."

"I have money." Clutching her small purse, Beth started toward the hotel, stopped, and looked back over her shoulder. "Shall we be Mr. and Mrs. Matthew Kerney for the night?"

Matt gulped and managed to say, "How do we get away with that? We don't even look married. You don't have a wedding ring." He stopped. Why was he putting up a fuss?

Beth looked at him like he was an idiot.

"It's okay by me," he added sheepishly.

She smiled approvingly. "Good. I'll explain to the desk clerk that our car broke down and you'll bring our luggage later. Meet me in the lobby when you're done."

"What luggage?"

She waved and turned to go. "Pretend we have some."

He watched her stroll to the hotel entrance dressed in walking boots, slacks with loose, floppy cuffs, a wide belt that accentuated her tiny waist, and a sleeveless sailor top. She was a knockout. His heart pounding in anticipation of the night ahead, Matt followed her with his eyes until she disappeared through the double doors of the hotel.

* * *

The desk clerk at the Hotel Paso del Norte assigned Mr. and Mrs. Kerney a small room with a double bed on a lower floor next to the elevator. A placard on the dresser informed guests that the hotel opened in 1912, the large glass dome in the lobby ceiling was made by Tiffany & Co., and during the Mexican Revolution folks gathered on the rooftop terrace to sip cocktails and watch skirmishes and firefights between federal troops and Pancho Villa's rebels across the river in Juárez.

Beth freshened up in the modern bathroom and returned to the lobby just as Matt came through the front door and stopped to look up at the two-story glass dome that diffused the sunlight into a rainbow of sparkling colors.

"Did they give you a room?" he whispered when Beth approached.

"Of course they did, Mr. Kerney." She pulled him outside by the sleeve.

"Where are we going?"

"We'll picnic on the town plaza and then walk to Mexico. The desk clerk said it's just a mile to the bridge."

They carried the picnic basket between them from the Studebaker to the plaza, spread a blanket under the shade of a big cottonwood, and ate their lunch of ham sandwiches, potato salad, and homemade lemonade. With liquor, beer, and spirits legal in Mexico, it seemed reasonable that El Paso wouldn't need speakeasies, but right across the street from where they picnicked stood what obviously had been a saloon in the old days. The door and picture windows had been painted black, and a carefully lettered sign above the door read:

EL PASO GENTLEMEN'S RIO GRANDE ROWING CLUB

MEMBERS ONLY

A row of cars filled the parking lane in front of the club, and there was steady traffic of men and women in and out the front door, which was guarded by a bouncer who sold memberships to potential patrons on the spot.

Beth sighed. "I'd love to see what a real speakeasy is like—dangerous gangsters, beautiful dames, shady proprietors, tough bulls."

"I'll take you."

Beth raised an eyebrow in surprise. "You have to buy a membership and you only have enough money get the car fixed."

"I've been watching the bouncer make change. A day's membership costs a buck."

"What about the car?"

"I told the garage owner I'd pull the radiator myself in the morning, and he agreed to weld it for me cheap."

"So you're not broke."

"Not yet."

Beth stood and smoothed the front of her slacks. "Let's go."

They repacked the picnic basket, left it under the tree, and crossed the street. Matt handed the bouncer a buck as he looked them up and down, giving Beth a careful once-over. He had a prizefighter's face, with a flattened nose broken too many times and heavy scar tissue above both eyes.

"Been here before?" he asked.

"No," Matt answered. "We're just down from Las Cruces."

"On our honeymoon," Beth added, smiling sweetly, her hands clasped behind her back.

"Honeymoon, eh?" He stood aside and opened the door. "Okay."

Beth batted her eyes. "Would you make sure no one takes the picnic basket we left under the tree?"

The bouncer grinned. "Sure, doll."

Inside, the air was blue with cigarette smoke, and well-dressed customers filled the tables. Waiters in white shirts and string ties passed through the throng, balancing trays of drinks and platters of food. Matt and Beth found a place at the long bar, which was populated mostly by older men without female companions who were intent on serious midday drinking.

"What are you going to have?" Beth whispered.

Matt eyed the drink price list on the wall behind the bar. "A glass of beer, I think. And you?"

"A cocktail," Beth announced emphatically. "A Manhattan cocktail."

After determining that Beth wanted rum in her cocktail, the bartender poured Matt's draft and put Beth's drink together right in front of her, mixing it up in a flash. He gave it a quick stir, added a cherry with a flourish, and pushed the glass carefully to her.

Beth beamed at the man in delight, clinked her glass with Matt's, took a sip, and said, "So this is demon rum. I like it."

She took another sip and glanced around the dimly lit room. There wasn't a sinister-looking man in sight, and all the women appeared reasonably respectable. On the far wall hung two crossed rowboat oars and an oversize red-and-white life buoy with EL PASO GENTLEMEN'S RIO GRANDE ROWING CLUB stenciled on it. A rowboat draped in semaphore flags was suspended from the ceiling. An upright piano, bass fiddle, and drum set occupied a small bandstand in a corner.

Everything about the place appealed to her. She wanted the musicians to appear and start playing so she could dance. She was happy the car had broken down, happy to be sitting in a speakeasy sipping a Manhattan, happy that Mexico was just a short walk away.

She felt grown-up and dangerously alive. She turned to Matthew and said, "The hotel desk clerk said the whiskey is better and cheaper in Juárez. He gave me the name of the best bar in the city, the White House. Let's go there and have another drink. We can hoof it."

Matt smiled, raised his beer glass, and drained it. "I'm ready when you are."

After stashing the picnic basket in the Studebaker at the garage, they joined a procession of pedestrians on the sidewalk of a street congested with cars, crossed the Rio Grande International Bridge, and stepped into the different world of Juárez, Mexico. Burros crowded the streets and slowed traffic. Men wearing straw sombreros, serapes, and huaraches surged around them carrying colorful baskets, hawking trinkets to tourists. Women in white peasant dresses with brightly colored shawls draped over their shoulders walked by crowned with huge baskets of flowers, offering bouquets for sale for a few pesos. *Braceros* on their way north to look for work hurried by. Horse-drawn wagons filled with produce and crates of squawking chickens and young pigs tied by the neck to wagon boards creaked down the cobblestones to the clip-clop of the ponies. Mariachi music poured from open bar doors. There were hunchback beggars, blind men singing, shoeshine boys snapping polishing rags, taxi drivers standing next to spotless cabs calling out for fares, and painted girls eyeing the unaccompanied men passing by. There were old men with chiseled Aztec faces, young women with high cheekbones and flashing Spanish eyes, men with the haughty look of grandees, and flocks of children following along behind mothers out shopping at the fresh-produce stalls.

Street-side merchants at rickety stands sold imported whiskey and liquor by the bottle and the case. The aromas from open-air food carts filled the air. Store windows displayed hand-tooled saddles, handmade guitars, native pottery from the interior mountains, hand-sewn festive skirts and blouses for ladies, carved and painted religious objects, fancy sombreros for men, and expensive cowboy boots with gleaming silver tips. The Depression had brought a halt to brisk commerce, and most of the stores were empty of customers, with forlorn merchants standing in shop doorways, desperately inviting passersby to come inside to buy their wares.

Doors and window frames were painted a rainbow of colors, including magenta, lime green, violet, and turquoise blue. The city was a riot of hues and sounds, with people unlike any Beth had ever seen. She was in love with the place, already scheming in her mind to travel the world and see every corner of it.

They passed a storefront wedding chapel, the façade painted pristine white. Matt stopped and said with a grin, "Want to get married?"

Beth twirled around and leaned against him. "To you?"

"Yep, to me."

"Yes, but not yet." She kissed him and pulled him away from the chapel down a side street that opened onto a large plaza. Across from a towering church with tall spires on the opposite side of the plaza, a long, high, whitewashed adobe wall hid all but the roof of a large hacienda shaded by two dozen ancient trees. A small sign above an almost unnoticeable courtyard gate in the thick adobe wall announced: CASA BLANCA.

She tugged at his sleeve. "There it is, the White House. Will you buy me another Manhattan?"

Matt nodded. "Then will you marry me?"

Beth shook her head teasingly. "I said not yet, but soon, maybe."

The gate opened onto a charming, serene courtyard filled with outdoor tables and chairs under the broad, leafy limbs of old trees. A series of rooms with large windows and heavy doors faced the courtyard, and from the far end of the hacienda, away from the street, came the sound of occasional laughter and soft, stringed music. It was a grand saloon with a high ceiling, furnished in rich, dark handmade tables and chairs. The bar had a mirror that ran the length of the back wall. In front of an open window a man with beautiful hands sat on a stool strumming a guitar. Because of the early hour, only a few tables were occupied, solely by couples. The young women, all of them petite and stunning, were in long dresses, the much older men in shirtsleeves, collars open at the neck.

At the bar, Matt and Beth dallied over their drinks, watching couples come and go. In the dining room, visible on the other side of a beamed hallway, waiters were polishing glassware and silver in preparation for the evening meal.

Once Matt figured out why all the couples leaving the saloon headed down the hall in the direction of the rooms that faced the lovely courtyard, he couldn't help but chuckle.

"What's so funny?" Beth asked.

"This place is more than just a fancy saloon and restaurant. You've brought me to a house of soiled doves."

"Soiled doves?"

"A high-class house of ill repute," Matt clarified.

Beth's hand flew to her open mouth. "A bordello? I'm speechless."

"That's a first," Matt said with a roguish grin.

Beth grabbed his hand. "Don't you dare leave my side."

"I have no urgent plans to wander off."

"That's not what I meant."

Intrigued by their newfound knowledge, they stayed a while longer watching the girls with their customers. Beth found the whole idea of prostitution distasteful, thought it degrading for the girls, and couldn't fathom how pleasure was to be found in the arms of strangers.

"Have you ever . . . ?" she asked, unwilling to finish her question.

Matt shook his head. "But I think my pa has."

"Does that bother you?"

Matt shrugged. "I don't care much what he does."

They detoured from the main drag on their way back to the border crossing, passing a group of old vaqueros smoking and talking on the porch of a small, run-down hotel, a ramshackle livery with a donkey hitched by a rope to its halter on a post outside, and rows of adobe casitas along a narrow lane that looked like Matt's Griggs Avenue neighborhood. They ventured through an area of small farms with fields watered by acequias before veering back to the noise and bustle near the International Bridge.

A lingering orange sunset greeted them as they crossed into El Paso and strolled hand in hand to the hotel.

"I don't want this day to end," Matt said.

Beth leaned against him. "Me either."

At the hotel, Matt tried hard to appear blasé about the grand lobby, the attentive doorman, the smiling desk clerk who handed him the room key, the elevator that whisked them to the third floor, the fancy room with pleated drapes covering the windows, the fresh, pressed bed linens, the authentic Mexican furniture, and the modern bathroom. He'd never stayed in such an elegant place before.

Beth slipped into the bathroom, and Matt eyed the double bed, wondering if he'd be sleeping in it or on the floor. He pulled his boots off and plopped down on the bed, propped a pillow under his head, and listened to the sound of running water from behind the closed bathroom door.

He pulled his remaining money from his pocket and counted

it. He had enough to buy them dinner at the taco place he'd spotted earlier on the plaza, pay for the welding job on the car radiator, and get enough gas to go home. Barely enough.

He glanced at the closed bathroom door. Beth was taking forever and he was starting to feel hungry. The door opened and she stood there wearing only her panties, her arms crossed over her breasts.

"Why are you still dressed?" she chided.

Words failed him. He tugged at his shirt, fumbled with his belt, yanked off his socks. When he turned to her, she was hidden under the covers with only her head showing, smiling timidly at him. She'd never looked more beautiful.

He slipped into bed and reached for her with a trembling hand. She turned and came eagerly into his arms. The touch of her naked body was an electric shock. They kissed, fondled, nibbled, stroked, looked at each other in amazement, and finally joined together with delighted gasps and contented sighs. Afterward they snuggled quietly, Beth's head on Matt's chest, their legs intertwined.

Finally, Beth whispered in his ear, "Can we do that again?"

Matt nodded.

She rolled on top of him, sat up, and put her hands on his shoulders. "Now?"

Matt grinned up at her. "Yes, ma'am, I am all yours."

25

Back home, Matt and Beth held firm to their story about the breakdown—which after all *was* true—fibbed about sleeping in the car, and left out all the rest. Augustus and Consuelo looked skeptical but didn't attempt an interrogation.

Beth was neither regretful nor ashamed of her night with Matthew at the Hotel Paso del Norte, and although she was fairly certain she'd timed her seduction of Matt to avoid getting pregnant, the thought she might have misjudged panicked her. During her weekly checkup at the sanatorium, she bravely confided to her physician, Dr. Bernard Stinson, that she was no longer a virgin and asked for advice about contraception. Stinson, who had served in France as an army doctor during the Great War, was well-informed on the subject, having treated and counseled many doughboys suffering from syphilis and gonorrhea. Additionally, he was quite liberal in his outlook about a woman's reproductive rights, due to the constant tutelage of his extremely modern, freethinking wife, Abigail.

After reminding Beth not to aggravate her tuberculosis with unnecessary physical exertion, Stinson explained how to use the rhythm method, discussed douching and the cervical cap, and strongly recommended her partner use condoms, which were just now becoming widely available in drugstores. As a precaution, he described the early symptoms of pregnancy and did an extra-thorough physical examination before sending her home with the good news that her remission had stabilized.

Beth continued to worry about being pregnant until her period arrived on time a week later. Greatly relieved, that evening she told Matt about her recent fear of being pregnant as they strolled around the Mesilla town plaza.

"From now on we need to use protection," she stipulated.

"I should have known better," Matt replied. "Boy, was I a sap."

Beth took his hand. "We were both in a hurry."

Matt grinned. "Yeah, we sure were." But the reality of what could have happened hit him like a sledgehammer. "I don't think we need to be making babies together yet."

"Not yet," Beth agreed. "But when the time is right, I want six babies."

"Six?" The number stunned him.

"Okay, five, if you think six is too much."

"You're bedeviling me."

"Only a little bit." Beth snuggled against him as they turned down the lane to the hacienda.

* * *

Beth's prediction that her parents and younger sister, Emily, would love Matt didn't quite pan out as she expected. Beth's mother, Clara, a sweetly disarming woman who seemed a bit flighty, took to Matt immediately. There was a touch of girlish enthusiasm about her that showed when she talked about the exciting possibility of living in Southern California. She had dreams of Emily becoming a movie star, Beth becoming a renowned medical doctor, and living on a beach in a climate where she could enjoy the sand and water no matter what the season and happily entertain the prospect of many grandchildren.

Emily, who was two years younger, but no prettier, no smarter, and no taller than Beth, was nonetheless a doll in her own right. She quickly took to shamelessly flirting with Matt and constantly teasing Beth about being in love, clutching her breast and sighing romantically with great dramatic effect whenever she found them together. Beth retaliated with good-natured teasing of her own, accusing Emily of a streak of petty cruelty that would surely turn her into an unmarriageable, miserable old maid. Their sisterly affection charmed Matt but also made him quietly lament the loss of CJ.

Beth's prediction that Matt would be embraced by all fell short with her father, Darcy Merton, an overweight bluenose of a man with a pinched face, a downturned mouth, and a self-important air; a man who dominated conversations and had opinions about everything, which he freely shared as though they were gospel truths. Darcy was so different in personality from Gus, if Matt hadn't known otherwise, he never would have guessed the two were brothers.

It wasn't that he spent a lot of time in his company. In fact, Matt was with him only twice before Mr. Merton departed for California, when the family arrived at the train station and the following night at the dinner hosted by Gus and Consuelo. In both encounters, Darcy Merton showed an eagerness to ignore Matt that included a reluctance to respond directly to anything Matt had to say.

Matt soon stopped trying to talk to him at all, but to be so quickly and unfairly dismissed dismayed him. He said nothing about it to Beth, but he found little to like about her father other than the fact that he delighted in his daughters and wife.

Soon after Mr. Merton left for California, Matt and Beth took a moonlight walk along a quiet Mesilla Valley lane near a sweetly gushing acequia watering a field of green chilies. As they walked hand in hand, Beth raised the subject of her father.

"Daddy's not really a prig; it's just that he's never comfortable with strangers. It was twice as bad with you because you're courting me and I told him we're in love. Mama promises to give him a good talking-to if he's rude to you again."

"I guess he doesn't want to lose his daughter to an uneducated no-account like me."

"Don't say that. He's not a snob. He just doesn't want me to get married too young and give up my dream to be a doctor."

"I don't want you to give up your dream either."

"Good." Beth pirouetted. "And will you be an engineer or a rancher? An army officer or a cowboy? A scholar or an auto mechanic?"

"Maybe all of those things," Matt teased.

"Oh, I like that," Beth replied, raising her face for a kiss. "A man of many talents."

* * *

Within two days of Darcy Merton's arrival in Los Angeles, he sent word by telegram that he'd been offered the position with the Pacific Electric Railway Company and had been asked to start work immediately. Clara and Emily were asked to return to Cleveland as soon as possible to supervise moving the family's possessions and then join him in California. He would rent until more permanent housing could be secured after they arrived. Beth would remain with Augustus and Consuelo until the family was completely reset-tled.

Beth thought the news was wonderful, but Matt wasn't so sure. Her father hadn't given her permission to stay and finish her degree at A&M.

Beth calmed his worries. "Daddy always needs to be pestered until we get our way, and Mama isn't opposed to me staying with Gus and Consuelo and going to college here as long as I go home on holidays and school vacations."

"Are you sure?" Matt inquired.

Beth nodded. "You just wait. Daddy will come around. I'm bursting to see California. I love the water. Lake Erie in the summertime was so much fun, swimming and boating and picnics on the shore. To be on the ocean will be magical—I just know it. Can't you imagine sunsets casting rainbow colors on the water? How beautiful it must be."

"I'd miss the mountains," Matt said.

"There are mountains near the ocean," Beth countered. "And miles of sandy beaches. We'll walk the beaches together and watch the waves break against the shore from the hillsides."

"You make it sound wonderful," Matt said.

Beth leaned against him. "It will be if you're with me."

"I don't want to miss out on that."

"You'll come with me on school vacations. We'll go swimming every day."

"Except for paddling around in a stock tank, I can't swim a lick," Matt confessed. The thought of being in an ocean of water with nothing firm underfoot or to grab onto made him shudder.

"I'll teach you," Beth promised. "And I won't let you drown."

"Promise?" Matt asked.

"Cross my heart," Beth replied as she skipped away.

She'd started coughing again. It was not a hard, troubling, long-lasting cough, and it would quickly subside. But it happened often enough to worry him. She said it was nothing, but Matt wasn't so sure. She was like Ma in that regard, always making light of what ailed her. When he pressed her about it, she gave him a chilly look to drop the subject. He did so reluctantly.

Three months after Darcy Merton relocated the family to Los Angeles, Beth received a letter from her mother.

My dearest Beth,

We are finally settled! Your father continues to be very happy in his new position and we have found a lovely cottage to purchase in the town of Santa Monica just outside Los Angeles. Our new house is in a modest but pleasant neighborhood with tree-lined streets and it is especially favored in occupying a bluff that overlooks the ocean. Although the cottage is smaller than our house in Cleveland, you and Emily have separate bedrooms that look out on a charming backyard with a large eucalyptus tree and a lovely flower garden. The ocean is but a short stroll down the hill. A nearby amusement pier attracts a lively crowd on weekends.

We are all becoming extremely spoiled by the weather. The climate is not unlike New Mexico, except the ocean breezes refresh and cool us and the sun is not so fiercely hot. I think when you come here you will find it just as salubrious as Las Cruces if not more so.

We've all decided you must visit your new home and soon, so I'm enclosing your train ticket and a money order your father purchased for expenses during the trip.

We will meet you at the station. We are all anxious to
have you with us. Emily sends her love and says she is eager
to take you exploring and have you meet her new friends.

Love,
Mother

Beth's excitement about the trip wasn't shared by Matt, who immediately wanted to know when she would return. She teased him about being a worrywart, which only made him mope and wonder if she'd vanish from his life. As the time for her departure drew near, her enthusiasm for the trip was so infectious, it made him more than slightly envious. He wanted to go with her except he hadn't been invited and didn't have the money anyway. Freight shipments on the railroad had dwindled to the point that there wasn't any work for him, so he was back to looking for a job, living on his coffee-can savings, and trying to sell the Studebaker again.

The day before Beth left, he gave her Ma's cherished fountain pen, which had been put away untouched since her death. He'd filled it with ink and wrapped it in some fancy paper from Ma's old stationery box.

"This was my ma's and now it's yours," he explained. "Write and tell me you miss me and when you'll be coming back."

Her eyes filled with tears. She hugged him tightly. "I already miss you and I promise to come back."

"I wish I had something nicer to give you."

"This is perfect."

The following morning he stood on the platform with Gus and Consuelo and watched Beth's train pull out of the station, already feeling lonely, already missing her.

26

B y the end of her first two weeks in Southern California, Beth thought it was the best possible place to live and wondered how she could convince Matt of that. The hope grew in her mind as she went about a daily routine that left her feeling better than she had since she was first diagnosed with tuberculosis.

In the mornings, she walked down to the beach with Emily for a swim. The gentle waves, the soft undertow, and the salt water were a tonic to her. Sometimes in the evenings before dinner, she went by herself for another swim. She couldn't get enough of the water.

Each day she swam a little farther; each day she felt a little stronger and had more endurance. As far as she could tell, her remission was complete: no coughing, headaches, chest pains, fever, or night sweats tormented her. She also had her figure back from the weight she'd regained.

On weekdays, she and Emily went motoring, sightseeing, and touring for hours, from the shoreline to the inland hills. They stopped whenever the fancy took them, for picnic lunches, hikes in the countryside, barefoot walks along the beaches, or window-shopping in downtown LA. On the days Mother accompanied them, they shopped in the local stores for fabrics and sewing patterns, admired new appliances Mother wanted for the house, and combed through the racks at dress shops. During one outing, Mother bought them new bathing suits in the latest style. The sleeveless suits fit snuggly around the waist, had scoop-neck tops, and were cut higher in the leg than the older styles. Emily couldn't wait to wear hers to the beach and show it off to Walter Armistead, a boy she was sweet on. As soon as they got home from the store, Beth and Emily changed into their swimsuits and took pictures of each other posing in the backyard in front of the eucalyptus tree. After the film was developed, Beth put a lipstick kiss on the back of her swimsuit photograph and sent it to Matthew along with a note never to forget her.

Beth found the weather sublime, the ocean constantly glorious, and the city fascinating. There were glamorous people in fancy cars whizzing by on wide boulevards; bell-clanging, crowded trolleys coursing up and down busy streets lined with palm trees; and streams of people filling downtown sidewalks to shop in the large department stores, which offered all the latest fashions and every new convenience for modern living.

She'd always considered Cleveland a big city, but it was a hamlet compared to Los Angeles and its surrounding metropolitan area of smaller towns and cities. There were valley farms and large ranches on rolling grassy hills. Along newly paved roads, spiderwebs of commercial growth sprang up almost by magic. To the east, remote barrier mountains were but a hazy blur unless gusty winds kicked up and cleared the sky.

Long stretches of empty, glistening beaches snaked up and down the coastline. Snuggled against the ocean just to the north of Los Angeles, Santa Monica drew people like a magnet to its beaches and nightlife. Gangsters and their molls hung out with movie stars in the village's ritzy speakeasies. Speedboats ferried customers back and forth to gambling ships three miles offshore. On weekend evenings, swing bands played on the pier for throngs of dancers who were up on all the latest steps, including the Lindy hop. The sound of the dance music would drift up the hill to the cottage, but despite their pleas, Beth and Emily were not allowed to go down to the pier at night unchaperoned, and their parents would not take them.

In spite of all the glitz and excitement, LA hadn't escaped the Depression. On Sunday afternoon family drives with Daddy, they frequently passed by unsavory places where vagrants lived in tent cities, hoboes clustered on street corners looking for handouts, and immigrant families had spilled into and filled some of the older, run-down neighborhoods. Food lines for the unemployed outside the churches stretched for blocks, and on cool nights the temporary shelters were quickly filled by the homeless. Big, beefy policemen patrolled in paddy wagons, rounding up tramps and beggars who were quickly replaced by new drifters.

Daddy made Beth and Emily promise to stay away from such places and threatened to take away their privileges if they didn't obey. Both girls swore to follow his wishes.

On weekday evenings after dinner, Daddy worked on business in his study while Beth, Emily, and Mother gathered in the front room to chat, listen to the radio, and write letters. Beth wrote regularly to Matt, describing where she'd gone, what she'd done, and what she'd seen in the most glowing terms possible, hoping he missed her so badly he'd be unable to resist coming to see her no matter what. In her attempts to sway him she'd repeatedly refilled the fountain pen he'd given her.

So far her appeal to his adventurous spirit had been trumped by his empty pockets, although in his most recent letter he said his boss at the Railway Express Agency might give him a free pass to ride the caboose on a freight train to Los Angeles. She was thrilled by the prospect. If she could get him here, he just might like it enough to want to stay.

She finished her latest letter to him, sealed it in an envelope, and settled into a chair on the front porch. Inside, Mother and Emily were listening to the *Amos 'n' Andy* show on the radio. Las Cruces had one radio station that played mostly instrumental music and went off the air at sundown. In the Los Angeles area, dozens of radio stations were on the air morning, noon, and night, many of them broadcasting national shows originating from Chicago, New York, and other cities. It was like listening in as the entire country talked, sang, joked, laughed, and danced. Mother was so fascinated by it she scheduled her evenings around her favorite shows.

The evening air was cool and pleasant and the neighborhood was quiet. All the houses on the street, which ran up a gentle hill behind the cliff that bordered the beach, were situated to give a view of the ocean. The cottage Daddy had bought sat on the crest of the hill, with a front lawn that sloped deeply down to the sidewalk. Although Mother had called the cottage small in her letter, it was the largest house on the street, with three bedrooms, a full bath, a study, a large kitchen, a walk-in pantry, a dining room, and a front parlor.

Beth had dreams about a house of her own with Matt, and someday a baby or two to love after he finished college. For now, there was no need to rush headlong into family life. She was sure that whatever Matt chose to do, he would succeed at it. He was confident, smart, and hardworking. For herself, she didn't want to be just a wife and mother. She'd dreamt of becoming a doctor since childhood and had no plans to abandon her goal. Now that she was better she needed to stop wasting time. She would visit the state university campus near Beverly Hills tomorrow and find out about the curriculum.

Suddenly impatient, she needed Matt sitting right next to her so the two of them could work everything out. Would it be Los Angeles or Las Cruces? College work here at the state university or at A&M? Matt's cute New Mexico casita or a darling cottage in LA? The mountains or the ocean?

In the gathering dusk, with the last bit of pink from the sun a thin ribbon draped along the far edge of the ocean, a convertible car with the top down pulled to the curb in front of the house. Walter Armistead, the fellow Emily secretly adored, hopped out and hurried up the pathway to the house. Beth had gone with Emily to a party Walter threw at his family's beach house and had met him there. His father, Harry Armistead, was a native Los Angeleno who owned farmland that enriched the family with revenue from the production of dozens of oil wells.

Walter was a college man at the state university. He was tan, handsome, charming, and wealthy. Beth had made it a point to advise Emily about the hazards of such a combination, but she wasn't sure her message had sunk in.

Walter reached the porch step and spotted Beth sitting in the shadows. "Hello, Beth," he said.

Beth rose and said, "How nice of you to remember me."

"I never forget a beautiful woman."

"Emily will be delighted to hear that."

Walter laughed. "Touché. Is she here?"

Beth opened the screen door. "Yes, come in."

Before Walter could take a step, Emily appeared at the door.

"Why, Walter, how nice it is to see you," she said sweetly, breaking into a big smile.

Instead of digging an elbow into Emily's side, Beth excused herself and joined Mother in the parlor. She made a conscientious effort not to eavesdrop by listening to Will Rogers cracking jokes about the Congress on the radio. After a few minutes she heard the sound of a car driving away.

Emily appeared in the parlor. "We've been asked to go sailing tomorrow," she said.

"Both of us?" Beth asked.

Emily nodded. "With Walter and another boy named Clarence. I didn't tell Walter you're madly in love with somebody else and he should forget about bringing Clarence."

"Are you trying to get me in trouble with Matt?" Beth asked, delighted at the prospect. She hadn't been sailing in ages. "What time?" she asked excitedly.

"Early in the afternoon," Emily answered.

"Perfect. In the morning we have to go to the university so I can find out what courses of study they offer."

"Are you sure you're ready to go back to school full-time?" Mother asked.

"I am. I must. Either here or back in Las Cruces."

Mother looked shocked. "You can't possibly be thinking of returning to New Mexico to continue your studies."

"The college there is very good," Beth answered, knowing her heart belonged to Matt first and foremost, no matter how lovely living in LA might be.

* * *

Beth returned from her morning visit to the university elated. Not only would all her college course work transfer if she decided to enroll, but she also qualified for resident tuition, which lowered the cost of attending considerably. She had also learned about the medical school at the University of Southern California.

Before leaving with Emily to meet Walter and his friend, she wrote to the school requesting information about admission requirements. With no such program in New Mexico, she would have to go elsewhere for her medical training, so why not LA when the time came two years hence?

They met Walter and his friend Clarence Whitmore at the Armistead family beach house, a large, two-story, pitched-roof cottage with rows of windows facing the beach, the ocean, and the nearby Santa Monica Pier. Clarence had a tan that matched Walter's, along with a very masculine physique, perfect teeth, and pale brown eyes. Beth reminded herself to warn Emily again to protect her virtue. But from her own experience with Matt, she doubted such a warning would have a lasting effect.

Although the marina was only a mile away, Walter drove them there in his Buick convertible. The cook at the beach house had packed a picnic basket and filled a wooden ice chest with bottles of wine, beer, and soft drinks. At dockside they loaded everything onto Walter's thirty-foot mahogany single-masted racing sloop, and soon they were cutting along smoothly on a quiet sea, the coastline receding quickly.

They sailed out to the casino ship, circled it twice, listening to the music and laughter coming from onboard, and then tacked southward for a time before furling the sail to drift while they picnicked. Beth sat aft with Clarence making small talk, barely listening to him as she nibbled a sandwich. The sky, the salty smell of the ocean, the sight of seagulls above, the gentle rocking of the sloop, the waves lapping at the keel—it was almost heaven.

She couldn't resist the water and slipped over the side. Emily soon joined her, followed by Walter and Clarence. They chased, dunked, and splashed each other for a time before setting sail for the marina. When they drew within less than a mile, Beth decided to swim the rest of the way. The water was warm, the waves gentle, and she'd been swimming longer distances with Emily in the mornings.

She put her bathing cap on and jumped back in the water. "You go on. Wait for me at the marina. I'll be fine."

"I'll come with you," Emily said reluctantly, leaning over the side.

Beth laughed and splashed her. "Go on or I'll beat you there." She pushed off from the sloop, kicked her feet, settled into a steady, easy rhythm, and turned her head in time to see the sloop cruise by, Emily smiling and waving madly.

She was almost halfway to the marina, where she could see the sloop tied up at the dock, when chest pains hit her. She stopped, floated, and waited for them to stop, but they only got worse. She started coughing and continued to tread water until the hacking stopped. When the chest pains lessened, she settled into a slow backstroke. She could feel the strength draining from her arms and legs. In her mind, she focused on reaching the dock and climbing out of the water, but every tortured muscle in her body ached. Her head pounded and the pain in her chest intensified into shock waves that traveled up and down her side.

She fought against the tide, but the marina came no closer. Finally exhausted, she could go no farther. She stopped, floated, and watched the shore recede as the tide took her out to sea.

* * *

When Sam Miller hired him for one day of work to clean and reorganize the storeroom, Matt thought he was just being generous as usual, but the storeroom was a mess. It took him a full day to get it shipshape. He was on the loading dock in the alley stacking the last of the empty crates and shipping cartons, eager to get home in the hope that a letter from Beth would be waiting, when Gus and Consuelo appeared in the doorway, both pale and teary eyed.

"What's wrong?" he asked.

27

After six months of getting by on occasional work and still flat broke, Matt moved back to the ranch with only his clothes, some personal possessions, and a few things he was unwilling to part with, including letters Ma had written for him to find after her death and CJ's letters he'd sent home during the Great War. He was glad to leave Las Cruces and escape everything that reminded him of Beth. He rented the house in town, furnished, to the new Railway Express agent and his family, and hired his old neighbors and friends, Nestor and Guadalupe Lucero, to keep an eye on the place and do any needed minor repairs for a few dollars a month. They were glad to earn the money.

Like most folks across the country, Matt had soured on banks. After a run on deposits, Edgar Worrell had closed his bank, leaving his customers out of luck. Because Matt had no more money to lose, the bank failure didn't hurt him in the pocketbook. But to avoid future financial catastrophes, he had his tenant pay the rent to the lawyer Alan Lipscomb, who took a small fee and mailed a monthly check directly to Matt at the ranch. Most of the money went for ranch expenses, primarily feed for the horses and such, but he socked away a little bit whenever he could and had twenty-two dollars reserved for his own use, which was now about two weeks' wages, if you were lucky enough to have a job.

The Studebaker had finally sold to a new instructor at the college who'd seen the notice at Sam Miller's store. He bought it the day before Matt moved to the Double K. Matt used the money to pay his delinquent property taxes and interest. It covered just what was owed.

In his free time at the ranch, Matt kept his distance from Pa by turning the casita into his private bailiwick. The small parlor became a library-study, with a handmade bookcase he built out of scrap lumber. Ma's sewing table became his desk, and a beat-up, mouse-chewed comfortable chair he found dusty and dirty in an unused barn stall was perfect for reading next to the corner fireplace. He'd brought only a few of his favorite books from home, but on each trip to town he picked up a couple more for a penny or two each.

The bedroom contained an ancient iron bed frame and mattress, a row of hooks he installed along one wall for his chaps, hats, jackets, and coats, a chest of drawers with a mirror he used for shaving, and a chamber pot. Tucked in the corner of the mirror was the photograph of Beth in her swimming suit, posing cutely for the camera. Although it broke his heart to see it every day, he couldn't put it away.

He'd done two mustang roundups with Pa since returning, and while they'd corralled more than fifty critters, only thirty wild, unbranded, sound-looking ponies were pastured at the ranch. The rest were too weak, lame, or sick and had to be turned loose. Most would become prey for coyotes and wolves, the resident mountain lion that roamed the ranch, or one of the few remaining black bears that still ranged the San Andres. Matt hated to see it done, but there was no other choice. With all their spirit, even the sick and lame wild ponies were a sight to warm any horseman's heart. Matt figured he'd never experience as much blood-pounding freedom as that of a wild mustang stallion running his mares to safety out on the flats.

Pa had signed up for a small monthly veteran's pension earned for both his Rough Rider service and the wounds he suffered in Cuba during the Spanish-American War. That went to buy staples, groceries, and necessities. Thanks to the pension and rent money coming in, the Double K was doing better than most outfits on the Tularosa.

Even with the luxury of cash money every month, the Double K suffered. Once the finest ranch on the western slope of the Tularosa, it was now sunblasted and in need of repair. Paint peeled off the barn siding, the ranch house roof was a patchwork of emergency fixes, the veranda sagged, the adobe courtyard wall was crumbling in places, the henhouse had collapsed, and drought had killed some of the big old cottonwoods in the windbreak and turned the pastureland brown. Most days brought blowing dust that cast a haze over the basin.

It was annoying to have so much go unattended because you either fed the ponies or fixed something, but not both. Still, the Double K was surviving while homesteads and smaller ranches across the basin were being abandoned. Some folks hung on without hope, living as squatters on outfits that had been sold out from under them for back taxes. It was a sad, mean situation.

The only time Matt spent with Pa was while they were working or at the meal table. They took turns with the cooking, but the fare was always pretty much the same: canned beans or vegetables, beef done up one way or the other but mostly fried, and bread with maybe some jam on it as a dessert. As far as Matt could tell, Pa wasn't drinking, and while he appreciated his staying sober, he didn't say anything about it. It was as though they lived worlds apart on the same speck of dirt under a blistering sky.

The nights were the worst for Matt, when everything was quiet except for the wind in the trees, the call of an owl, or an occasional coyote chorus. It was then that the pain of losing Beth was a torment. He'd kept all her letters, had all of them about memorized. They made him feel cheated out of being loved, just like Ma's death had cheated him. The notion that he was destined to lose every person he ever treasured or loved made him cynical and bitter.

When he was with Pa, not much talking got done. They could go sunup to sundown working ponies without a lot of chatter. Matt liked it that way just fine. By disposition Pa wasn't a talker, and since Beth's passing Matt had nothing much to say either, mostly for fear of breaking down like a weepy little kid. He'd had only one good cry since her drowning, and that had welled up the day he'd learned of her death.

One night at dinner, Pa showed Matt a letter from the U.S. Army at Fort Bliss soliciting contracts for cavalry horses to be delivered within three months, paid for upon the completion and passage of a fitness inspection. The army wanted geldings, fifteen to sixteen hands high, between five and nine years, sound in all particulars and saddle broken.

"We've got twelve, maybe fifteen, out in the pasture that will do," Pa said. "The army has bought from the Double K before with no complaints. I figure to sign us up. It means they'll send some officers out to see what we have before they give us a contract."

"Do you think the army is interested in mustangs as cavalry mounts?" Matt asked. "We've never sold those kinds of ponies to the army before."

"Don't see why not if they meet all the particulars. Besides, what other choice do we have?"

"Getting twelve or fifteen ponies ready in three months won't be easy."

"You got something better to do with your time?" Pa asked.

Matt shook his head.

Pa sent a letter off to Fort Bliss the next day, and while waiting for a response they worked the ponies hard, getting them gentled and saddle broke. Three weeks later, two remount officers from Fort Bliss arrived at the ranch in full regalia, including English riding boots, Sam Browne belts, and expensive hand-tooled riding crops. Out in the pasture, they looked at the mustangs in total disbelief, politely said they simply wouldn't do, thanked Pa for his interest in the remount program, and drove away in their army automobile. Matt leaned against the truck fender and waited on Pa's reaction.

"Dammit, they're just polo-playing sissies in army uniforms," Pa grumbled. "They think only Thoroughbred bloodstock makes for a good horse."

"Now what do we do?" Matt inquired.

"We keep at it with these ponies. I need to sell them by year end; otherwise, we're gonna be in a big mess."

"What kind of a big mess?"

"Losing the Double K. I'm past due on my taxes, and the little money I get from my monthly pension ain't gonna cover what's owed by a long shot."

"How past due are we?"

"A year come this November, when the next tax bill arrives that I also can't pay."

Pa's owing two years' taxes and saying nothing about it riled Matt. "Why didn't you mention this to me before?" he snapped.

"I didn't see a need to."

Matt shook his head in disgust. "I'm not your hired hand, old man, and I'm tired of you treating me like I've got no stake in this outfit."

"I've already told you the Double K is yours when I pass on. I've got it all written down on paper and put away in my desk."

"It's a proper signed and sealed will, right?"

Pa hesitated before shaking his head.

Matt laughed bitterly. "Now, why isn't that a big surprise? What in the hell did you do with all that money you took from my trust?"

Pa got hard-eyed. "You know damn well what I did with it. I put it into the Double K and then had to sell just about everything to pay the bank when those Wall Street idiots made folks like us dirt-scratching poor."

"You gambled some of it in stocks. You told me so yourself. How much did you lose?"

"Enough, dammit. Your trust would have lost it anyway when everything went to hell."

"It could've been used to pay taxes," Matt grumbled.

"Looking back, you can sure see how thickheaded I was," Pa snapped. "I did what I did and that's that. It was better to pay off the loan. We'd be squatters just like other folks if I hadn't. The county assessor can't just up and take the ranch. There's a whole legal rigmarole the government has to go through before a man's property can go on the auction block for back taxes. I bought some time."

"Well, I'll give you that." Matt eyed the mustangs. The remount officers were right to reject them. They were saddle broke and gentled to a point but much too high-spirited and aggressive to serve as cavalry mounts. Also, most were barely fifteen hands high, and Matt figured those spit-and-polish army boys liked to sit astride their horses as high up as they could for the whole world to see.

In a fit of unbridled optimism, they'd miscalculated. These mustangs weren't ranch breed stock with quarter horse bloodlines that could be easily worked into good ranch ponies. There was no way they could be put up for sale before tax time, if ever. They'd been sweating hard with these critters for long, weary weeks with their eyes closed to reality. Hell, the critters were so wild it took almost a month after each roundup before any of them acted interested in the hay trucked out to them. At first, they hadn't taken at all to drinking from the stock tank, and they sure didn't cotton to the high fences that had been put up to keep them penned.

Until now, Matt had never doubted Pa's savvy when it came to ranching and horses. But this scheme to turn mustangs into working cow ponies was plain wrongheaded. "This isn't gonna work," he said, expecting Pa to bluster and argue.

"You're right," Pa replied mildly, without hesitation. "It took those fancy army fellas for me to see it. We've been wasting our time. Don't look so shocked. Ain't you the one that's been telling me all these years I ain't perfect?"

Matt couldn't help but burst out laughing. "That's not quite the way I've put it. Now what do we do?"

Pa scanned the basin and the Sacramentos beyond as if he was searching for something or someone. "Pack it in, I guess. Let the tax man have it. I sure can't get any money from a bank with land that ain't producing and taxes owed to boot."

Hearing Pa talk of quitting flabbergasted Matt. "What else can we do *besides* that?"

Pa turned his gaze to the mustangs. They were amazingly fast ponies, and some of bigger ones had fleshed out to near sixteen hundred pounds. In smaller proportions, they had the same heads, necks, bodies, and rumps of workhorses. "They're strong and can learn to pull weight, I reckon," he speculated. "Not like a draft horse can, but buggies and the smaller wagons folks around here still use. We won't get near half what a good ranch pony can fetch, but it would be better than nothing."

"It's not near half the work either, I reckon," Matt added, wondering if that was just more wishful thinking on his part about the half-wild critters. "If we could sell them all, would that get us out of the hole with the county assessor?"

Pa climbed into the truck and fired it up. "Nope."

"Hold on," Matt said. "Let me think a minute."

Pa killed the engine. "About what?"

In the last two rent checks Lipscomb had sent, he'd included a note that the new Railway Express agent was interested in buying Matt's house. Both times, Matt had dismissed the idea of selling, but Pa's predicament now gave him pause, so he began to rethink it. "How much tax do you owe for this year and last?" Matt asked.

"Why do you need to know?"

"If I can pay off what's owed, would you sign the Double K over to me?"

"Make you the sole owner?"

"That's right."

"And I'd be what, the hired hand?"

Matt stared Pa squarely in the eyes and said, "I'll write out a paper that gives the outfit back to you should I die, and put it away handy in your desk in case you need it."

Pa's jaw muscles bulged in anger. "You're some piece of work."

Matt smiled, tight-lipped, in return. "That I am. Like father, like son, I reckon."

Muttering, Pa glared at him, cranked the engine, and drove away, the tires kicking up a cloud of dust in Matt's face. He waited until it settled before starting out afoot for home, wondering if Ma would approve of him selling the house she loved to bail out Pa and save the Double K. He decided she would. She'd loved the Double K and the Tularosa as much as anyone could.

* * *

Two weeks after Franklin Roosevelt won the election for president, not one mustang had sold. On a chilly, blustery November afternoon, Matt loped Patches to the mailbox, where he found two property tax bills from the county assessor, one stamped due and one stamped past due. He looked them over, rode home, and stuck them under Pa's nose as he came out of the barn.

"Shit," Pa said, eyeing the official government envelopes.

Matt waved the envelopes at him. "They raised the taxes for this year. I guess they figure every landowner has to pay more to help the government end the Depression."

"Let me see those." He snatched the letters and with his head bowed started reading as he walked slowly away.

On the way back from the mailbox, Matt had shot a large blacktailed jackrabbit. He dressed it for a stew for dinner, and it made a welcome break from beef. Matt ate dinner eagerly and in silence, and Pa matched him.

After sopping up the stew juice with a crust of bread, Pa pushed his empty plate aside. "I'm guessing that offer you made to pay the taxes means you would sell the house in town to do it," he said.

"That's right. And the offer still holds."

"How long would it take to sell it?"

"I've got a ready buyer. It could be done by the end of the year, I reckon."

"Would you see enough cash to get us even on the taxes?"

"And then some, I'm hoping."

"And you want sole ownership of the Double K in return?"

"Yep."

"I'd be working for you?"

"I don't see it that way. Except for borrowing money against the ranch or selling it, you'll still have a big say in running the spread. I don't plan to stay here forever. I still want to finish college. After that, I don't know what I'll do."

"I don't hanker on the idea of needing to come running to you to buy livestock, pay bills, or get credit at stores."

"Would it embarrass you to have folks know you've turned the Double K over to me?" Matt asked pointedly.

Pa swallowed hard. "I guess it ain't fair of me to think of it that way. If you're willing to save the only place I've ever called home, I'll be proud to tell folks you're the ramrod and owner of the Double K."

Pa's words stunned Matt into silence. He offered his hand across the table and Pa shook it. "We have a deal, with one minor condition," he said.

"What's that?"

"If Juan Ignacio ever wants to be part of the Double K, you'll welcome him back as your son and treat him as a partner."

Pa bit his lip and fell silent.

"It's right and you know it."

Pa nodded in agreement. "You have my word on it."

They shook hands again.

By the middle of December the deal was done. The house on Griggs Avenue sold for two-thirds of what it was worth before the crash but still produced enough money to pay all the taxes, leave enough to cover two more years, and have some extra for operating expenses.

As they completed all the paperwork with Lawyer Lipscomb, Patrick remembered back to the day Emma had forced him—in the very same office—to acknowledge Matt as his son. On that day, he'd been raging mad at her, never imagining that child would grow up to save his old bones and the Double K.

He signed the special warranty deed giving Matthew title and sole possession of the ranch, shook his son's hand, took him to dinner to celebrate the event, and raised a glass to toast him as the new owner of the Double K. In a way he'd never imagined, it felt like a burden lifted.

Wondering what had gotten into the old man to make him so amicable under the circumstances, Matt was flabbergasted once again.

28

With taxes paid and a little extra in the kitty, Matt and Patrick doubled their efforts with the mustangs, only to meet with continued failure. Unless each pony was ridden daily, they reverted to blowing snot, pitching, bucking, and twisting as soon as Matt or Patrick stepped into the saddle. They were thrown so often, it soon became clear no amount of hard work or horse savvy would tame the critters enough to make them useful.

In late winter they turned the mustangs loose and watched them gallop onto the flats, tails high and whinnying gleefully as they thundered through the mesquite and crossed the wide arroyo. Matt was happy to set them free.

After dinner that night, they held a council. If they hunkered down, bought a few steers to fatten on the high-country pastures and slaughter for their own use, sold the truck, and bought harness ponies for the wagon, they could get through the year without much hardship. Patrick would take care of the ranch and use his pension money for feed, victuals, and whatever repairs they could afford while Matt looked for work. They put pencil to paper and figured if Matt found work at forty dollars a month, they might be able to survive until the drought ended, the economy improved, and on-the-hoof beef prices rose. Then they'd restock, Matt would get back to ranching full-time, and maybe they'd eke out a small profit. It was the best they could hope for.

To get started, Patrick would sell the truck and buy the livestock while Matt made the rounds of the big outfits, looking for work. If nothing panned out, he'd scout for town jobs in Las Cruces, Alamogordo, Capitan, or Carrizozo. They'd part company in the morning, Matt heading east to the Three Rivers outfit to start searching for work, and Patrick west to Hot Springs to sell the truck, scout for harness ponies, and buy a couple of steers. Matt would send a note if he landed a job. If not, he'd be back at the Double K in two weeks.

In the morning Matt left on horseback, packing all his cowboy gear, trying to imagine what the old-time Texas stockmen must have thought seeing the belly-high grasses of the Tularosa for the first time. They probably figured to have discovered paradise, not knowing that drought and overgrazing would turn it into a desert landscape in less than a generation.

Patches set a steady pace and Matt's thoughts roamed to Gene Rhodes's story of Ma making a hand. Would he have made a hand in her eyes? He sure hoped so.

Thoughts of Ma and the old days didn't keep him from worrying if trying to save the Double K would cost him his dream of finishing college. If the Depression hadn't struck the country like a tornado, he'd be an upperclassman now, with money in the bank, a steady income from the trust, a house free and clear, and prospects for a good life. The memory of Beth popped into his mind, and he shook off the what-ifs. It did no good to dwell on them.

In Tularosa he stopped at the general store and was surprised

and happy to learn that Porter Knox, Evangelina, and Juan Ignacio had returned and were temporarily staying with Evangelina's
parents until they could find a place to rent. Matt hadn't seen
them since Tía Teresa's funeral, so he hurried over to Flaviano and
Cristina's casa to say hello. When he knocked on the door, Evangelina opened it, squealed in delight, and wrapped him in a bear
hug.

"Look at you," she said after releasing him. "You are so grown-
up and handsome."

Matt blushed as she pulled him by the hand into the warm,
empty kitchen. It was late in the day but there was nothing cooking for dinner but a big pot of frijoles. The Depression and the
drought had hit the Hispanic villages extra-hard.

"None of that talk, now," Matt joshed. "Where are my brother
and your husband?"

"Sit first and have some coffee."

As Evangelina scooted to the fireplace for the coffeepot, Matt
noticed a big hole in the toe of one of her shoes and the thread-
bare shawl that covered her shoulders. She'd lost weight and her
hair was streaked prematurely gray. She brought him a full cup
and sat with him at the table. The black brew tasted more like
chicory than coffee, but it was hot and Matt drank it gratefully.

Evangelina said, "Porter and Juan Ignacio are in the fields with
my father preparing for spring planting—God willing we get some
rain. They should be back soon." She forced a smile. "You'll stay
for dinner."

"That's mighty kind," Matt said, thinking he needed to contrib-
ute something to the supper pot, like a dressed chicken from the
butcher shop. "I never expected you would leave Albuquerque,"
he added. "I heard at the general store that you've moved back. Is
it for good?"

Evangelina shrugged, the bright smile frozen on her face. "*Tal vez*. Time will tell. Porter lost his job and we had to give up the house." She paused to keep her composure. "He'll find work; I know he will." She patted his hand and changed the subject. "Are you still living in Las Cruces?"

"I'm back at the Double K."

Evangelina's expression clouded and she bit her lip to keep silent.

Matt smiled reassuringly. "It's okay. You don't have to worry about me; I own the brand now."

Her eyes widened. "The ranch is yours? Patrick is dead?"

"Not dead; he's just not the boss anymore."

Evangelina laughed in pleased amazement. "I must hear how you did it. Emma always said you were going to be one smart hombre."

"I got my smarts from her. Do you think Juan Ignacio will remember me?"

"*Sí*, he remembers you. I never let him forget who he is and where he comes from. He'll be so happy to see you."

Evangelina's mother, Cristina, entered the kitchen with a pretty little girl in her arms, whom she introduced as her granddaughter, María Teresa Armijo Knox. Released from Cristina's arms, María smiled shyly, ran straight for her mother's lap, and settled in. As Evangelina stroked her daughter's hair, she told Matt with great pride all the wonderful things her María could do—so many he lost count.

Cristina also insisted that Matt should stay for supper, adding that he must spend the night before traveling on to the Three Rivers Ranch. She'd aged some and grown wide around the waist, but her eyes still sparkled as she talked about how happy she was to have Evangelina and her family home and not so far away in

Albuquerque. Evangelina said nothing to contradict her mother, but her expression was resigned and much less enthusiastic.

Flaviano, Porter, and Juan Ignacio arrived from the field, chilled by a dry, cold wind that had swept into the basin from the north. After warm greetings and handshakes all around, Matt sat with Juan Ignacio outside in the sunny courtyard, protected from a breeze that whistled through the trees.

At ten, he was tall for his age, all arms and legs under a frayed sweater and blue jeans that stopped at his ankles.

"You're gonna be taller than me, I bet," Matt predicted.

"That's what Madre says. She says we look alike *también*."

Matt studied Juan's face carefully. "Maybe so—a little bit anyway. What do you think?"

Juan stared at him for a moment and said, "Kind of, I guess."

"Is that all right with you?"

"Well, at least you aren't *mucho* ugly," Juan said with a grin.

"Ouch, that hurts," Matt said. He punched him lightly on the arm and asked if he was happy to be back in Tularosa.

Juan's smile faded and his expression turned bitter. He spat out, "No." Complaints tumbled out of him. All his friends were in Albuquerque, his school was better there, his teachers nicer, and until they moved they had their own house with a garden and a yard, electricity and a bathroom. He missed swimming and playing along the Rio Grande with his pals. Porter had sold his bicycle to a neighbor, and the radio too. There was no radio or even electricity in his *abuelo*'s house, and no money to go the movies or even buy a penny candy.

His new school was boring and he hated it. The kids called him a coyote because he was only half-Spanish and teased him, saying he was a *güero* because of his lighter-colored hair. They laughed at the way he spoke Spanish in the northern style and said he was a *maricón* because he knew all the answers in class. He'd been getting into fights and never wanted to go back to school again. He just wanted Porter to move the family back to Albuquerque.

Juan's misery brought back memories of the anguish Matt had felt as a child, especially over CJ's dying in France and Ma's long sickness and eventual death. He knew sympathy wouldn't soften Juan's distress. He stood up and said, "I'm going to the grocer's. Want to come?"

Juan wiped his nose with a sleeve to hide his sniffles, shrugged, and nodded. "Okay."

Matt walked down the lane, with Juan silent and moody at his side. "Do you like chocolate?" he asked.

"Yeah."

"What's your favorite candy bar?"

Juan brightened a smidgen. "Baby Ruth."

"Let's go get you one."

At the store, Matt bought two Baby Ruth candy bars for Juan, a big homemade apple pie baked by the grocer's wife, a gallon of milk, and a bag of Arbuckle's coffee. Next door at the butcher shop he picked out two fat, dressed chickens. He paid for everything with some of the money he'd saved from the rent payments he'd received on the Griggs Avenue house.

"What's all that for?" Juan asked, his mouth full of candy bar as they stepped outside into the cold wind of a gathering dusk.

"I think we should have a fiesta to celebrate our family reunion," Matt replied.

Too busy chewing to talk, but obviously in an improved mood, Juan nodded in complete agreement.

"Does your *abuelo* keep any beer or liquor in the casa?"

Juan swallowed. "*Sí,* beer he makes himself."

"Good, that will make it a real party." He watched Juan rip the cover off his second candy bar and take another big bite. "Let's get cracking, kid brother; I'm cold and getting hungry."

"Me too," Juan Ignacio Kerney Knox replied.

* * *

With dinner over, the roasted chickens picked clean, and several gallons of potent homebrew consumed, Matt and all the extended family members Flaviano and Cristina invited to dine with them were in a festive mood. Calling for silence, Flaviano raised a half-drunken toast to Matt. He thanked Matt for the fiesta and announced that he had decided Matt should marry into the family. To facilitate such a union, he offered the last of his unmarried nieces, thirteen-year-old Bennia, as Matt's bride-to-be.

Wide-eyed in shock and blushing in embarrassment, Bennia stared at her uncle in disbelief before rushing from the room, hand to mouth to stifle either sobs or giggles. Matt couldn't tell which. All the Armijo men, including Bennia's father, Tobias, laughed and pounded the table, demanding her return, but it was to no avail.

Over coffee and apple pie, Porter—who was more than tipsy—asked Matt if he'd heard about an emergency work program President Roosevelt had proposed to Congress. All Porter knew was that it had something to do with conservation—planting trees and so on. It would put young men to work, as well as tradesmen with certain skills. Matt liked the idea that the government was finally going to do something about unemployment. "I hope it's true," he said.

As the evening ended, Flaviano and Tobias cornered Matt. In a conspiratorial whisper, Flaviano said, "You can do no better than Bennia as your bride."

Rocking on unsteady legs, Tobias agreed. "She is beautiful, no? And she is young and strong."

"You honor me with your offer," Matt replied. "I'll sure think on it some."

As he rolled into the bed Cristina had prepared for him, he wondered if he was truly the most favored prospective suitor for young Bennia. Or were the Armijos simply looking for a way to feed one less mouth in hard times?

Early the next day, Matt said good-bye to his hosts, ruffled Juan Ignacio's hair and gave him a hug, and rode out of the village, groggy from too much beer and too little sleep. Over the next ten days he rode a wide loop, visiting the big outfits at Three Rivers, the Hondo Valley, and Lincoln, Capitan, and Carrizozo. Everyone was sympathetic but not hiring. In the tradition of ranching hospitality, Matt was always offered a meal, conversation, and a bunk for the night, which he gratefully accepted.

In the towns, once thriving businesses were shuttered, banks had gone under, and some of the swanky houses on the main streets stood empty. Warning signs posted on the outskirts advised hoboes, transients, and vagrants to move on or face arrest.

On the Carrizozo Road he passed two families out of West Texas traveling in horse-drawn wagons, hoping to homestead some land in New Mexico. They questioned him with interest about the Tularosa. He told them about the drought, and their keenness turned sour.

In Carrizozo, he stabled Patches in the livery, fed him a bag of oats as a well-deserved treat, and gave him a good brushing before bedding down for the night in a fifty-cent hotel room. At dawn, ten cents bought him breakfast at a diner across the street from the railway station. After a second cup of coffee, he set out astride Patches with the sun at his back, taking it slow and easy on the old trail that crossed the edge of the malpais. Stray off the path and the thin volcanic crust would give way under a horse and rider and drop them into a deep crevice, never to be seen again. Over the years, many unwary travelers and lost pilgrims had disappeared forever that way.

He arrived back at the Double K expecting Pa to be home, but the corral and pasture held no new ponies and the house was dark and empty. He turned Patches out in the pasture. Calabaza came over to greet him, and the two ponies trotted away for a private conversation. In the house, Matt lit a fire in the cookstove to warm up the kitchen and fixed a meal of canned vegetable soup and stale salt crackers. Through the window he watched dusk quickly turn to night. The ranch felt like an outpost empty of people and cut off from civilization. He resolved to look harder for work, not just for the money but for the human contact it would bring.

He tried reading, but Pa's absence distracted him. While Matt was gone, Pa had had plenty of time to sell the truck, buy some livestock, and get back to the ranch. Where was that old man?

Matt went to bed restless, lonely, and wanting company. It was a miserable feeling that kept him awake and staring at the ceiling.

29

Matt struck out from the Double K in the morning to find Pa. Hoping he might have sent a note explaining his delay, Matt checked the mailbox. In it was a short letter from Augustus Merton asking Matt to visit the next time he came to town, as he had a matter to discuss. Matt wondered what Gus had on his mind, but the tone of his message didn't sound urgent.

He stuffed the letter in his pocket and started Patches toward Rhodes Canyon, his thoughts returning to Pa. There was no good reason for him to be gone for so long. After he'd sold the truck, he'd planned to visit Johnny Dines at the old Bar Cross horse camp to buy two ponies and move on to the Jennings ranch to purchase two steers. He'd taken his saddle along to ride one of the ponies home and trail the steers over the mountain from the Rocking J. Even with the time Pa could have spent loitering to jawbone with Johnny and Al, he was long overdue.

He was a punctual man by nature, so Matt reckoned that either something unforeseen had happened to slow him down—such as not being able to quickly sell the truck—or he'd taken up the bottle again. Matt hoped it wasn't liquor. If it was, he'd want nothing more to do with the man.

The east face of the San Andres was far more rugged and treacherous than the gently sloping western descent. The same was true of the road that the state had taken over but not yet improved through the pass. In places it had been crudely cut into the mountainside, barely wide enough for a horse and wagon or a motorcar to navigate. Wheels and tires ran perilously close to the edge and often showered stones and small rocks into the jumbled ravines below. On three sharp, blind curves, drivers sometimes had to back up to let oncoming vehicles through.

As Matt rounded the final curve, a burst of reflected sunlight winked brightly from the narrow ravine below the road. He slid off Patches for a closer look. The severed head of a four-point mule deer, eyes picked out by vultures, tongue and lips eaten by other critters, rested in a large, dried blanket of blood on a narrow ledge ten feet below the roadway. Clearly, someone had field dressed the carcass and packed home a bonanza of fresh meat. Farther down, Pa's truck was wedged between two boulders. Everything suggested that Pa had come around the blind corner, saw the buck in the middle of the road, tried to avoid it, and crashed into it anyway. Both went over the edge.

Heart pounding, Matt scrambled down to the truck. It was empty, the passenger door sprung open. There was blood on the cracked windshield and patches of deerskin, hair, and blood on the front fender. Pa's saddle and gear were missing from the truck bed.

Around the truck Matt found a jumble of footprints: three— no, four—different sets. The bushes on the side of the ravine leading to the road above had been flattened by what might have been a board used as a litter to get Pa out of the ravine, alive or dead.

They would know in Engle. Matt clambered up to Patches and urged him into a fast lope to town. For the longest time he'd known Ma was gonna die, yet when she passed he wasn't prepared for it at all. With Pa it was different. He'd never thought about him dying, although there were times he'd wished him dead. He'd figured him to always be around, ornery and indestructible. If Pa was truly dead, Matt wasn't sure if he'd be sad or sorrowful. He doubted he'd grieve much.

* * *

In Engle, Matt learned from Elliot Barker, the stationmaster at the train depot, that Pa had been rescued from his truck, unconscious, with a cracked skull and a badly broken leg, and taken by ambulance to a doctor in Hot Springs.

"But there ain't no need for you to go there," Elliot added, handing Matt a telegram. "This here has been waiting on you for a week. I was starting to wonder if you'd ever show up. The doc in Hot Springs patched your pa up as best he could and sent him down to Doc Stinson in Las Cruces."

Dr. Bernard Stinson had been Beth's doctor at the sanatorium. "Why was he sent there?" Matt asked.

"The doc in Hot Springs told the boys Stinson had been an army sawbones in the war and if anybody could save your pa's leg it was him. When they brought your pa down from the canyon, his left leg was an awful sight. Bone sticking out, his knee smashed and swollen, his ankle twisted. There was blood caked to his face like he'd fallen headfirst into a bucket of it. The old boys who rescued him said he was lucky to be alive."

"Was he conscious when they brought him here?"

Elliot shook his head. "Nope, not even when they got him to

the doc's office in Hot Springs. He was still out cold, the boys said."

"I better get down to Cruces." Matt counted out the cash for a ticket to Las Cruces.

"Put that away," Elliot said gently. "The boys who found your pa pooled money for you and your pony to get to Las Cruces. They all know your pa and wanted to make sure you didn't have any hardship getting there to look after him."

The unexpected act of kindness caught Matt by surprise. "That's mighty kind. Who are they? I need to thank them."

Elliot handed Matt a card. "I wrote down their names for you."

"Thanks." Matt recognized the names: two cowboys from the Diamond A, the Engle dry goods store clerk, and Ken Mayers, the owner of the livery.

"Ken over at the livery has your pa's saddle and gear safely stored. He wants to know if he can salvage the truck. He says the engine block is cracked and ruined. He'll split fifty-fifty whatever he gets for the parts he sells."

"Tell him sure," Matt said. "Have you heard anything more about my pa since he got to Las Cruces?"

"Not a word. Southbound train is due in ten minutes. Best get your pony ready to board at the ramp."

"Thanks."

Elliot patted Matt on the shoulder. "Give your pa my best."

"I will, and thanks."

Matt waited for the train with Patches at the livestock-car boarding ramp, hating the idea of visiting Pa at the sanatorium. He recalled the day Beth had pressed a note into his hand asking him to rendezvous with her at night under the cottonwood tree. How she'd snuck out of her room that night to meet him and convinced him to take her for an illicit drive. How she'd told him he was her beau. He recalled their other nights together, spooning in his car or at his casita on Griggs Avenue, and that wonderful weekend when they snuck away to El Paso and Juárez. They were all painful memories.

The locomotive chugged past him, brakes squealing to a stop. He got Patches settled in an empty livestock car and boarded with him, settling down on the floor with the door wide-open to watch the countryside roll past. *Why in blazes didn't the doc in Hot Springs send Pa to a sawbones in Albuquerque or El Paso, where they had hospitals? Why did it have to be Dr. Stinson Pa got sent to?* He shook his head to ward off any more questions from rattling around in his brain.

* * *

The head nurse at the sanatorium wouldn't let Matt see Pa until he talked to Dr. Stinson. Within a few minutes, Dr. Stinson came into his office and nodded at Matt. "Ah, it is you," he said cordially. "Professor Merton assured me Mr. Kerney was your father, but I wasn't sure who from the family would show up to claim him."

"I'm all the family he's got," Matt replied. "How did Gus find out my Pa was here?"

"I called Augustus wondering if he knew if Mr. Kerney was related to you."

"Can I see him now?"

"In a minute. I first want to tell you about his present condition. He is in a leg cast from his toes to his hip. He'll wear it for the next two to three months. It cannot be removed no matter how hard he begs. The fracture was severe."

"Why would he beg to have it taken off?"

"His leg will start to itch, sometimes unbearably. It will drive him to distraction and cause many sleepless nights. For example, he'll need to sleep on his back in one position without turning over. He may find it unnatural and frustrating. But the cast is all that is holding the broken bone in his leg together, so it cannot be damaged or jolted in any way. To heal, the bone needs to fuse, and that takes time."

"Will he be able to walk again?"

"Yes, but perhaps not as naturally as before," Stinson replied.

He explained that the ankle break had been minor, but Pa's cracked knee might never heal properly if the torn ligaments were too severely damaged. Stinson wouldn't know until the cast came off. He went on to say that Pa would need constant care until the leg completely healed. "He'll be on crutches well after the cast is removed, until he regains strength in the leg," Stinson added. "Even then, I'll need to see him at least once a month to check his progress."

"I understand," Matt replied.

"Then there's the matter of his head wound," Stinson noted.

Matt froze. "What's wrong with his head?"

"He suffers from some confusion and headaches, plus his vision is slightly blurry in his left eye. I'm hopeful it will clear up. Time will tell."

"How bad is it?"

"He's coherent and logical most of the time. But you must realize, the brain recovers more slowly than other organs. For example, he'll sleep more than usual. That's the brain's way of healing itself. Also, he may get testy every now and again. With that said, he does have a lovely scar over his eye to go with the story of how lucky he was to survive that crash."

"Will he go *loco* on me?"

"I can't answer that," Stinson replied. "But keep him away from liquor. Any kind of alcohol would only exacerbate any symptoms he develops. Who will look after him?"

"I will," Matt answered, unhappy with the prospect. It was hard enough to take care of someone you loved. With Pa it would be twice as hard.

"Will you be able to manage?" Stinson asked pointedly, reading Matt's worry.

"Of course I can," Matt retorted. "Just tell me what I need to do."

"I'll have written instructions for you to follow once he's released. He told me he served with the Rough Riders under Teddy Roosevelt at San Juan Hill. A brave bunch, that lot."

"Yes, they were." Matt hesitated. "I have no money to pay you right now."

Stinson smiled. "Not to worry. Your father made it clear you're not to be held responsible for his medical care. He'll make a monthly payment from his veteran's pension."

Matt nodded, thinking now they were about to be worse than broke.

"Professor Merton wants to see you in his office at the college as soon as you've finished your visit. I'm to call him when you're on your way."

"Do you know why he wants to see me?"

Stinson shrugged. "No, I don't. You can see your father now."

"What room is he in?" Matt asked cautiously.

Stinson ushered him out of the office and down the hall. "We have a two-room ward for noncontagious patients. Your father is there." He paused before opening the door to the ward. "We all were so sorry about Beth's passing. She loved you very much."

"Yeah, I know," was all Matt could muster. Inside the ward he looked at Pa through the open door to his room. He was asleep on the bed with his head thrown back on the pillow, mouth open, snoring.

For some reason Matt felt like crying. "How long does he need to stay here?" he asked.

"You can take him home the day after tomorrow," Dr. Stinson said as he turned to go. "I'll see you then."

Matt made his way slowly to Pa's side. There was a dent in his forehead and a beauty of a scar all stitched up and starting to scab over. He counted thirty five stitches. Pa's broken leg was in a cast suspended on a sling held up by a pulley. It looked damn uncomfortable. Matt pulled a chair next to the bed and waited for Pa to wake, his mind churning over the fix he was in. He hoped Pa still had the money for the ponies and steers he was going to buy. If not, all they had was the sixteen dollars in Matt's pocket.

"Did you bring Calabaza?" Pa asked groggily. "I want to go home right now."

"You're not going anywhere until the doctor says so, and you sure ain't going anywhere on horseback for a time."

"Says who?" Pa snapped. "Don't go giving me orders, boy."

"You still got the money for the critters you were supposed to buy?" Matt shot back.

"I gave it to the doc for my care."

"Then we ain't got a dime."

"I made a mess of it, didn't I? Did you find work?"

"Nope."

Pa lifted his head off the pillow. "Then we're sure in a fix."

"I know it."

"Who got me out of the truck?"

"Carlos Graham, Billy Baily from the store, Harvey Ralston, and Ken Mayers from the livery."

"I owe them my life; that's for certain. Now what do we do?"

"Get you better and all fixed up," Matt proposed, trying to sound positive.

"And starve in the process," Pa snapped.

"I'll get work."

"Even if you find a job, how are you gonna look after me until I get back on my feet? It's not likely you can do that working else-where. Hell, just carry me up to the cabin and leave me there to die. You'd be doing me a favor."

"Doc Stinson said you might be a little muddleheaded."

"I'm talking straight, dammit!"

"Not as far as I can tell."

"Do yourself a favor and do as I say."

Matt headed for the door. "That might be something you could do if someone asked, but it's not my nature. Stop talking *loco*."

"Where are you going?"

"I have someone to see." Matt paused in the doorway. "I'll be back to carry you home day after tomorrow."

Without waiting for a reply, he hurried down the hallway, in a pure rush to find out why Gus Merton wanted to see him.

* * *

Through the open door Matt saw Augustus Merton sitting at his desk, head bowed over some papers. When Matt knocked to an-nounce himself, Gus looked up, smiled broadly, and came across the room to greet him.

"My boy, it's good to see you," he said, ushering Matt to a chair next to a small office table.

"Likewise," Matt replied with a smile.

Gus patted his shoulder as he sat. "I was sorry to hear about your father's accident. I trust he will recover."

"Dr. Stinson says I can take him home soon, but he'll need care for some time."

Augustus searched Matt's face. "That's good news for him, but what about you?"

"He's my pa," Matt replied tonelessly. "There's not much I can do about it but look after him."

"Yes, of course, a son's duty. That's very admirable, but not what I have in mind for you. The government is starting a new national program to put young men to work on a massive scale, and the college has been given the responsibility to help organize the effort in southern New Mexico. I've been asked by the college president to oversee the project and I am in need of several capable assistants. You are my first choice."

The offer dazed Matt. Here was a job he needed, working for a man he respected. A job he couldn't accept. "I truly appreciate your offer, but I can't say yes, at least not right now."

Gus smiled sympathetically. "Will you at least hear me out before you say no? In the next several months a quarter of a million young men will be put to work in the Civilian Conservation Corps, a new federal program that will build roads in the wilderness, plant trees in forests, rid rangelands of pests, create new parks, restore grasslands, and do a host of other worthy projects."

He paused to let Matt digest the information. "Here in New Mexico, we'll have dozens of camps spread across the state. Young men will be selected from impoverished families, employed for six months, and given food, shelter, training, and supervision. They'll be paid thirty dollars a month, with twenty-five dollars of their pay sent home to their parents. The army is to build and operate one thousand three hundred and thirty camps across the nation by July. New Mexico must have no less than two hundred young men enrolled within the month and in camps as soon as possible."

"That sounds like a mighty big job."

"It is. I've been asked to coordinate the establishment of a dozen CCC camps in southern New Mexico within the next thirty days, and I need your help right now."

Matt shook his head. "I just can't do it."

Gus dismissed Matt's rejection with a wave of his hand. "I'm aware of your situation. So I propose to give you two weeks' advance salary and a week's time to arrange for suitable care for your father at the ranch. You'll be headquartered here at the college. But be prepared to travel, as your first assignment will be to scout suitable locations for the camps."

"I have a week's grace?" Matt asked, stunned by the offer of the best job he could ever hope to have since the day the stock market crashed. All he had to do was get Pa home and in good hands.

Gus nodded. "Yes, one week's grace. You'll be paid sixty-five dollars a month. Starting out you'll live on campus in the men's dormitory, rent-free. Once the camps are up and running, we'll discuss what other assignments to give you. Are we agreed?"

"Yes, sir," Matt said. "I'm deeply obliged to you for this."

Gus smiled and handed Matt an envelope with two weeks' pay inside. "No need for that. You're doing me an important service. Be back in a week."

Matt smiled. "You can count on it."

After Matt departed, Augustus returned to his desk. Neither of them had said a word about Beth. He wondered if it would ever be possible to talk about her with Matt. Knowing how much Matt had loved her, he guessed it could take years.

30

Matt paused in front of his old house on Griggs Avenue. It looked pretty much the same, except the new owners hadn't watered the old cottonwood in the front yard and the drought had taken a big toll on it. The top was bare of new leaves, and several of the thick lower branches were dead, half broken off and dangling awkwardly to the ground. Still, the place didn't look better or worse than the rest of the houses in the neighborhood. The vibrant painted wood trims that adorned most of the homes were faded, once carefully tended front yards were full of weeds and litter, and the inviting shady porches where folks had passed hours in friendly conversation appeared neglected and unused.

Next door at Nestor and Guadalupe Lucero's house a public notice tacked to the front door announced that the property was to be sold at auction at the courthouse for back taxes. Matt had hoped to save the cost of a hotel room by asking Nestor and Guadalupe if he could bunk on the parlor floor, but there was no answer to his knock. He peered through the window at the empty front room. Through the kitchen window he saw only bare walls, empty counters, and the chipped porcelain sink.

Matt walked Patches two blocks away to the house where Nestor and Guadalupe's oldest son, Roberto, and his family lived. Parked outside was Nestor's horse and wagon, with a hand-painted sign on the side boards written in Spanish and English that read FOR HIRE 50 CENTS A DAY.

He found Nestor and Guadalupe inside, jammed together with their youngest son, Felipe, his wife, and their two children, as well as Roberto and his wife and three children. Three generations—eleven people—living in a casita with space barely adequate for five.

Warmly welcomed, Matt sat squeezed between Roberto and Felipe on a worn davenport, their wives on wooden stools, Nestor and Guadalupe in straight-back chairs, young grandchildren at their feet, the older kids with knees at their chins sitting on straw mattresses. He quickly learned that Felipe had lost his house to foreclosure, both he and Nestor were unemployed, none of the women had work, and Roberto was supporting everyone on wages of sixteen cents an hour as a laborer on a road crew. With their food pantry now empty, they ate one meal a day at the train station soup kitchen.

Although their pride hadn't been completely drained, the hardship had wiped away all optimism. They were skinny and gaunt, listless and humorless, but they did their best to keep up appearances.

As they made small talk about neighbors who'd died, gotten married, had children, or moved away, an idea came to Matt that made him smile. He turned to Nestor and asked, "Would you and Guadalupe be willing to move to the Double K ranch and take care of my pa until he recovers from an accident?"

He explained what had happened to Pa, told them about his job at the college starting in a week, and offered to hire them right away.

"You'll have a private casita, free board, and a salary of thirty dollars a month, first month paid in advance," Matt proposed. "If you agree, we'll leave the day after tomorrow to take Pa home by horse and wagon."

A long moment of amazed silence settled over the room. Nestor's eyes widened in astonished appreciation of the offer, and Guadalupe's smile alone dispelled a lingering gloom that had permeated the room. The pinched worry etched on Roberto's and Felipe's faces softened and their wives sighed with audible relief.

"We will gladly work for you again," Nestor said. "*Muchas gracias, Mateo.*"

"*Maravilloso.*" Matt gave him thirty dollars. "I need to hire your horse and wagon for the journey to the ranch. How much more do you want?"

Unbelievingly, Nestor stared at the money. "This is enough."

"*Bueno,*" Matt said as he rose to his feet. "There will be provisions for you to pick up at Sam Miller's store tomorrow afternoon. We'll leave here early the next morning. Pack what you need for a long stay."

Nestor closed his hand over the bills. "We'll be ready at first light, *jefe.*"

Guadalupe stood and hugged Matt. "You are a saint."

Matt shook his head. "No, it is you and Nestor who are doing me a great favor."

He left knowing Guadalupe and her daughters-in-law would be at the grocer's buying the fixings for dinner as soon as he was out of sight.

* * *

The day before leaving for the ranch, Matt met with Dr. Stinson at Pa's bedside and went over a list of instructions, which were to be followed exactly. Stinson showed Matt how to help Pa use a bedpan, the proper way to assist him when getting in and out of bed, and how to elevate his leg when he was prone. He gave Matt written instructions on how to bathe Pa and showed Pa how to use his crutches.

"I want you up and moving around on those crutches every day," Doc Stinson said. "Understood?"

Pa nodded. "I ain't one to lay about."

"Don't you fall on that leg before it's completely healed," Stinson cautioned. He turned to Matt and suggested purchasing a wheelchair.

"I'll get one before we head home," Matt promised.

Stinson turned back to Pa. "I'll want to see you in a month."

Pa snorted. "I'll be fit as a fiddle by then."

"No, you won't," Stinson countered. "And if you don't do as I've instructed, that leg won't heal and I'll have to break it and reset it, which will keep you flat on your back and in that cast twice as long, with only a fifty-fifty chance you'll ever walk on it again."

Pa shut up but continued to scowl.

After Doc Stinson left, Matt told Pa he was starting a job soon and he'd hired Nestor and Guadalupe to look after him and the ranch.

"I don't want nobody but you looking after me," Pa groused.

"If that's your druthers, I'll fire Nestor and Guadalupe and put the Double K up for sale today," Matt replied. "That way, you'll be sitting in that wheelchair all by yourself until the sheriff comes to auction the place for taxes."

Pa grimaced at such an unpleasant prospect. "What's this job you've got that pays enough to hire two Mexicans?"

"Don't you go calling them Mexicans," Matt snapped. "They've got names; use them."

He gave Pa a nutshell version of his new job and left to find an inexpensive wheelchair. On his way, he wondered if he'd done Nestor and Guadalupe a disservice by unleashing Pa on them.

* * *

They left the next morning and traveled toward a rising sun cresting the mountains. Pa was stretched out in the wagon amid supplies, the used wheelchair Matt had bought cheap at a junk shop, and several bundles of Nestor and Guadalupe's clothing and personal possessions. Up front, Nestor held the reins, with Guadalupe sitting beside him. Matt led the way on Patches. Near the long-abandoned ruins of Fort Selden, now nothing more than bleeding adobe remnants of buildings melting back into the earth, they left the highway and followed the ruts of the old El Camino Real, forged long ago by Spanish settlers traveling deep into the uncharted territory of Nuevo Mexico.

The road, mostly forgotten and used primarily by the large ranches swallowing up hundreds of square miles, cut through the heart of the Jornada del Muerto—the Journey of Death—a vast, tilted tableland straddled by shimmering mountains, ribbon-cut by arroyos, dominated by flat-top mesas, and studded by mesquite now dry and dusty in the drought.

In places, the road paralleled the tracks of the Santa Fe Railway. Each time a train sped noisily by, the land soon engulfed it. The locomotive and cars vanished into the distance, the sound of the clacking wheels fading to silence.

Matt kept the little caravan going until dusk and stopped overnight at a windmill and water tank south of Engle. The next day, they rolled into town well before noon and rested in the shade of the livery, Pa fast asleep in the wagon. Doc Stinson had been right about the knock on Pa's noggin making him sleep a lot, which suited Matt just fine on the journey home.

He gathered Pa's saddle and gear from the livery owner, Ken Mayers, thanked him for rescuing Pa, and asked if the truck had been salvaged. Ken told him he'd sold the truck to a fella in Hot Springs for fifty dollars cash money and figured that with the time and effort getting the wreck out of the ravine and towed to town, he owed Matt no more than twenty of that fifty.

Matt readily agreed with Ken's accounting and gratefully took the twenty dollars. He bought oats for Patches and Nestor's horse and took Ken to the hotel for a beer, stopping first at the general store to invite Billy Baily to join them.

Outside the hotel, Pa was propped up in the wagon. Matt, Nestor, and Guadalupe watched as Billy and Ken stepped onto the hotel porch, raised their glasses to Patrick, and wished him a speedy recovery.

"Thank you for saving my hide," Pa said. "I'd surely like to toast you in return, but the sawbones says I can't drink."

"That's a shame," Billy said.

"What's a busted leg got to do with drinking?" Ken asked.

"I think not drinking is a fine idea," Matt countered, stopping further discussion of the subject as he threw a leg over Patches. "It's time to get moving."

He started the little caravan eastward at a smart clip, eager to deposit Pa at the Double K and get on with his new job in Las Cruces.

* * *

Patrick sat in the wheelchair on the veranda with his left leg stuck straight out, watching Matt and Nestor finish building a ramp on the steps to roll him up and down. He'd been sleeping a lot since arriving back at the Double K, dozing mostly. It was welcome relief from the numbness and dull ache in his head that didn't want to go away. For the last several years, he'd known that he was getting old, but now he *felt* old, and he didn't cotton to it one bit.

He'd quit bellyaching about being looked after by Nestor and Guadalupe. In fact, he didn't intend to gripe about it again. In just one day and part of another, they'd moved themselves into the casita, arranged the furniture so he could easily navigate around the ranch house in his wheelchair, fixed meals, done the critter chores, put things in order, got him in and out of bed, and cleaned him up as needed without so much as a frown or complaint. Matt had been smart to hire them on.

Hands clasped tightly in his lap to keep from digging his fingers into the cast to scratch the incessant itching of his leg, he watched Matt nail the last board for the wheelchair ramp in place.

In the back of the wagon on the trip home, he'd been awake when they passed by the Fort Selden ruins. Years ago, his father, John Kerney, had found him there living with an army doctor and his wife who'd taken him in. As hard as he tried, he couldn't even remember their names, couldn't even remember why he'd been so scared when John Kerney came to fetch him to the Double K.

He wondered if Matt would be interested in hearing the story of how John Kerney found him. Maybe not—which might be the best, since he wasn't very good at telling yarns.

Before the day ended, Patrick would offer Matt his hand and tell him he was a helluva lot smarter than his old man and a far better son than he deserved.

He nodded off, head on his chest. When he awoke hours later, Matt had already left.

31

Matt's first month on the job turned into a nonstop rush to identify a dozen potential U.S. Forest Service conservation campsites in Arizona and New Mexico and help get them up and running. The Department of Agriculture, which included the Forest Service, had set up shop on the New Mexico Aggie campus to plan for an onslaught of Civilian Conservation Corps enrollees, soon to arrive after two weeks of physical conditioning at Fort Bliss in El Paso. Starting out, the men were to live in tent camps the army established close to towns and villages so they would be easy to equip and supply.

Regional foresters in New Mexico and Arizona had proposed a number of remote camp locations, and Washington had granted the Forest Service additional time to get started. Field inspections of the proposed camp locations were ordered to ensure that all sites could be accessed by motorized vehicles and that sufficient reliable water sources were available.

The task of certifying that Forest Service CCC campsites were suitable for occupation fell to the U.S. Army. The officer assigned to oversee the Forest Service campsite selection, First Lieutenant

John Cunningham, a cavalry officer and graduate of the Virginia Military Institute, wheeled onto the New Mexico A&M campus in a shiny new army staff car, ready to take charge. He was a spit-and-polish officer in a starched uniform with gleaming brass and a contemptuous glint in his eye. He had absolute veto power over any of the potential campsites that Hubert Roddy, the tall, lanky tobacco-chewing, easygoing Forest Service supervisor, had in mind.

At six foot four, Roddy towered over Cunningham's five-ten frame. Roddy's work wardrobe consisted of a pair of scuffed lace-up hiking boots, sturdy blue jeans, wrinkled long-sleeve shirts open at the collar, and an old Marine Corps campaign hat. His casual nature, unkempt appearance, and dislike for anything officious only served to fuel Lieutenant Cunningham's by-the-book rigidity. The two men were like oil and water right from the get-go.

In spite of Roddy and Cunningham's endless squabbling, Matt loved his job. He was driver, wrangler, mechanic, camp cook, Spanish translator, bellhop, and recording secretary on a month-long trek that took them deep into the forests of Arizona and New Mexico by truck, on foot, and on horseback. From Sitting Bull Falls in the rugged Guadalupe Mountains, to the Gila Wilderness backlands, to the Coronado and Apache National Forests in Arizona, Matt saw a wide, beautiful slice of the country.

With Roddy guiding, Matt drove the expedition across magnificent untrammeled mountain ranges, through vast stands of virgin forests, over brown, thirsty, grassy hills outside of Bisbee, across a harsh, windswept saguaro landscape near Tucson. They hiked trails up barren mountains, rode horseback into hidden canyons, and climbed to the tops of mesas filled with ancient pueblo ruins.

Matt saw Santa Fe on a two-day stopover. It sat in a shallow river

valley pressed against mountain foothills, quaint and foreign looking, with narrow, crooked streets and low-slung adobe buildings.
At Taos Pueblo, while Roddy and Cunningham met with tribal
elders, Matt wandered around the two- and three-story mud-
plastered adobe buildings, stark against an azure sky, wondering
what the place had been like before the first European trappers
stumbled over the mountains.

By the end of the month, Roddy and Cunningham had haggled, argued, debated, and finally compromised on where to es-
tablish the New Mexico and Arizona CCC campsites.

As Matt saw it, there had been little need to butt heads. Every
place they'd scouted needed a helping hand. Land had been overgrazed, creeks and streams polluted and degraded by overuse,
stands of trees killed by bark beetles, soil ruined by forest fires, and
mountainsides eroded by clear-cut logging. There were stock
tanks to build, fences to put up, meadows to reseed, seedling trees
to plant, check dams to build, and much more.

Roddy wanted trails, fire lanes, and truck roads built, fire lookout towers thrown up, and electricity and telephone lines installed.
In some locations he proposed permanent tourist campgrounds,
ranger stations with a headquarters building and staff housing,
district maintenance and mechanic sheds, and corrals and stables
for saddle and packhorses. It all made sense to Matt.

Roddy outgunned Cunningham in the brain department. He
hung tough with the lieutenant, who wanted only what was easiest
and most convenient for army logistics. As a result, Roddy got
most of what he wanted.

When they returned to Las Cruces and said adios to Cunningham, Matt was genuinely relieved to see him go. Cunningham
seemed equally pleased to get away. Hubert Roddy grinned happily as Cunningham sped away in the army staff car.

"That man's a piece of work," Roddy allowed, clamping a friendly hand on Matt's shoulder. "Are you willing to help me with reports that have to go out pronto to the higher muckety-mucks?"

"Yes, sir."

"Good. I need to set out exactly what each camp is supposed to accomplish. My bosses are gonna be real persnickety about the details. We're gonna need maps, drawings, estimates on man-hours for each project, specific goals, camp location coordinates, side camp cost estimates—that sort of thing."

Matt beamed. "What's a side camp?"

Roddy chuckled. "That's where we're gonna put temporary work crews of forty to sixty men for a week or two in some of those places the lieutenant refused to certify because he didn't want to get his boots dirty."

Matt grinned. "That's downright crafty."

Roddy nodded. "I agree, but it ain't my idea to claim. We've been planning from the start to spread out as far as we can reach with what the CCC gives us. There's just too much to be done. Lord knows how long the politicians in Washington will fund the program before they pull the plug. Let's get started."

"I'm your man," Matt replied, excited by the possibilities.

* * *

Eight more weeks of work and long hours kept Matt away from the Double K right up to the day he was let go from the job. From the start he knew it was only a temporary position, but he'd hoped by diligence and hard work to turn it into something more permanent. Instead, he got replaced by the nephew of an Arizona congressman who was friends with the bigwigs running the whole shebang out of an office at Fort Sam Houston in Texas. Matt was given a termination notice by an office clerk and told to pack up and move out of the men's dorm pronto.

An embarrassed Hubert Roddy caught up with Matt as he was leaving the campus. "This wasn't my doing," he said. "If they'd foisted that dolt on me a month ago, I could have found a place for you here. But now all the jobs are filled. Best I can do is sign you up as an enrollee."

Matt shook his head. "I appreciate the offer, but I got things that need doing at the ranch, and now's a good time to head on home."

"I've got some friends in the Park Service. Let me ask around."

"I'd be obliged."

"Stay in touch."

"I surely will."

Matt cashed his check, bought a ticket to Engle, and waited at the station for the next northbound train. He refused to be too disappointed about his sudden reversal. Jobs had come and gone for him during the tough times, but at least he'd found work, while others went without. Maybe Hubert Roddy would find him something; maybe not. Gus Merton couldn't help him. He was now working in Washington, on loan from the college, drafting legislation to get public funding to build courthouses, schools, and other community facilities nationwide. Matt had been lucky to have Gus's helping hand in the past, but he couldn't count on such good fortune in the future.

He decided it was best to get back to the Double K for a spell. He hadn't seen Pa since the day Nestor and Guadalupe had brought him to town to have his leg cast removed. With the cast off, Pa's leg was a sight to behold. The skin was pasty white from a lack of sun and skinny from a lack of use. When Doc Stinson let the leg go, it dropped like rag-doll leg on the examination table, scaring the bejesus out of Matt and Pa. By now Pa should be up and walking. Matt hadn't heard from him and had no idea how things were going. Okay, he hoped.

He counted his money. There was enough to keep Nestor and Guadalupe on the payroll for two months, with some left over for essentials. After that, if he didn't find work, he'd be forced to let Nestor and Guadalupe go. Then it would be just him and Pa trying to scratch out a living at the Double K. Suddenly he felt downright morose about being unemployed again.

To save money, he slept on a bed of straw in the Engle livery and in the morning hitched a ride with the mailman, who dropped him at the Double K ranch road. He hoofed it home under a relentless late-summer sun with his gear in a bundle slung over his shoulder. In his back pocket he'd crammed a bunch of letters he'd found stuffed in the chock-full mailbox. One letter contained the paycheck Lawyer Lipscomb had mailed to Nestor and Guadalupe more than a week ago. It caused Matt some worry. Surely they would have gone to fetch it as soon as it was due to arrive.

At the crest of the last rise in the pasture Matt paused to take in the ranch headquarters. All was quiet, and no one was in sight. Pa's wagon stood next to the barn, but Nestor's rig was missing. Stony, Patches, and Calabaza were in the corral, but Nestor's pony was nowhere to be seen. Maybe they were all off to town for groceries and supplies.

He stopped at the corral, and all three ponies came over to him, snorting their displeasure. They looked scrawny and uncared-for. In the corral, the horse apples hadn't been raked up and the water trough was empty. He gave them water, hay, and a promise to return as soon as he got settled. He climbed the stairs to the veranda next to the ramp he'd built for Pa's wheelchair and called out at the closed kitchen door before entering. He found

Pa in the dark, quiet living room, asleep in his wheelchair. He had a week-old beard, his false teeth were missing, his clothes were dirty, and he smelled bad.

Matt shook him awake. "Where are Nestor and Guadalupe?"

"They're gone."

"Did you fire them?"

Pa shook his head. "They just up and left when their two boys came to fetch them."

"When was that?"

Pa shrugged. "A week ago. The whole damn family was pulling up stakes and moving over to Silver City. Their boys had found jobs on some government project. They were sorry to go and would've stayed until I hired new help, but I told them I'd be all right."

"Have you been in the wheelchair ever since?"

Pa nodded. "Mostly."

"Were you walking before they left?"

"Some," Pa replied.

Matt glared at Pa. "Stand up!"

"What for? The leg don't work and it ain't gonna."

"Stand up, dammit."

Looking cross, Patrick pulled himself upright on wobbly legs.

Matt yanked the wheelchair away, rolled it onto the veranda, smashed it into pieces against a post, and threw the debris over the railing. He turned to find Pa dragging his way to the open kitchen door.

"Why in the hell did you do that?" Pa snapped.

"I don't have time for some old man to carry on like a cripple on my ranch," Matt answered. "I'll help you just this once get cleaned up, shaved, in fresh duds, and on your crutches. After that, you stay on your own two feet and help out with the chores. You savvy?"

Patrick lowered his head and nodded.

"Good. You wait there while I get the cookstove fired up and water boiling for your bath."

"Just stay standing here?"

"Yeah," Matt said as he brushed by Pa. "Put some weight on that leg while you're waiting. It'll do it some good."

* * *

As the day passed, it was hard for Matt to keep from grumbling. But he kept his trap shut as he got Pa looking human again, gave the ponies a good brushing, put them in clean stalls, and shoveled the horse apples out of the corral. He took a long soak in the stock tank before fixing a dinner of canned beef stew with some peeled potatoes mixed in and a fresh pot of coffee. He served it up at the table and devoured his first meal since breakfast without saying a word to Pa.

Bent over his plate of stew, Pa didn't talk either, which helped Matt keep his resentment in check. After dinner, he made Pa help with the dishes, which didn't sit well with him. Matt had no sympathy for Pa as he hobbled back and forth from the table to the washtub, using a crutch for his bad leg. Keeping Pa upright and moving was the best medicine Matt could think of.

Matt couldn't figure what had made Pa give up and become a crippled old man. He'd never seen quit in him before. Why now? He couldn't imagine that Guadalupe and Nestor had coddled him. That wasn't who they were.

He'd known Nestor and Guadalupe for years, and they didn't have any quit in them either. They never would have left if Pa had asked them to stay until he found a replacement. He wondered if Pa was lying to him. Did he drive them away? Matt vowed to find out the truth.

The night was deep and Matt was wide-awake. He settled behind the desk in the living room, glad to be off his feet and have Pa quiet in his bedroom. The top desk drawer was stuffed with more unopened mail. He started sorting through it, looking first at what he'd carried home from the mailbox. There was a letter to Pa from Al Jennings asking to lease the Double K high pasture to run fifty cows. Al had written that he'd taken a careful look at the pasture and found enough browse and water for more than fifty head, but he had no more to run. He'd pay for the lease from the profits he made come fall selling beef to a butcher in Hot Springs who had a contract to supply the CCC camp at Elephant Butte.

Matt appreciated Al's smart strategy. If he had any Double K cattle and the grass and water were there to be used, he'd do the same thing.

The army quartermaster at Fort Bliss had a list of merchants, grocers, butchers, and farmers who could supply CCC camps in southern New Mexico and Arizona with perishable food supplies such as milk, fresh vegetables, beef, pork, chicken, eggs, and fresh fruit, along with any other items the army couldn't transport and supply in bulk because of spoilage. It was a program to put government money into the local economy and create some jobs.

While working for the Forest Service, Matt had seen a new pamphlet from the quartermaster corps for use in the CCC camps. It listed more than five hundred required food items, set minimum daily meal portions for each enrollee, and outlined menus and recipes for camp cooks to use. The pamphlet called for a lot of beef to be served to those hundreds of hungry CCC boys just about every day.

Matt put Al's letter aside. Tomorrow he'd ride up to the high pastures and take a look at the land. Although it was frustrating not to have Double K cattle grazing in the high country, if he agreed with Al's assessment, he'd mosey over to the Rocking J and make the deal. He'd take Patches and trail Calabaza. Both ponies needed the exercise.

He pawed through the rest of the mail and unearthed a letter from a Texas rancher that got his full attention. Mr. Kenneth Killebrew, owner of the Double K Ranch outside of San Angelo, had recently bought a second spread in the Cimarron to use for spring and summer grazing. Killebrew wanted to know if the Double K stock brand registered in New Mexico was for sale. If it was, he offered five hundred dollars.

Matt crumpled up the offer to throw it away but stopped. Five hundred dollars was a huge windfall. It was enough to put some cattle back on the land, pay for feed, hire a hand, and get the critters fattened up in time to sell after fall works. With new CCC camps scheduled to open in Mayhill, Capitan, Carrizozo, Corona, and a dozen more spots near the basin, the market for beef would grow. Now was the time to restock and sign delivery contracts with the butchers who'd be supplying the beef to the camps. Producers were looking to unload their herds and were selling cheap. Maybe Al Jennings would be interested in throwing in with Matt on a larger scale.

Pa wouldn't like giving up the brand, but he didn't have a say in it. Either sell the brand or lose the ranch. Matt pulled the brand book out of a bottom desk drawer and thumbed through it, looking for a brand to replace the Double K. As far as he could tell, the 7-Bar-K brand was available. If so, it would do nicely. Seven was a lucky number, and seven Kerneys had lived on the ranch since John Kerney staked his first claim to it.

It was time to make a fresh start with a new brand. With five hundred dollars of Kenneth Killebrew's money, he just might be able to whip the god-awful Depression and the lingering drought, or at the least fight them to a draw.

32

Patrick Kerney reached down, carefully guided the foot of his bad leg into the stirrup, and told his new pony, Ribbon, to walk on. It was an hour past sunup, and out in the pasture Calabaza nuzzled Stony, ignoring Patrick completely. He turned up the trail that led to the high country, where Shorty Gibson, the cowboy Matt had hired two years ago for room, board, and twenty dollars a month, was encamped at the cabin for the summer.

Calabaza and Stony were old ponies now and well past their prime, as was Patrick. Assuming he had the year of his birth right, he was sixty. At his age, he had no quarrel with putting those two ancient ponies out to pasture in spite of what it cost to feed them. It brightened his day to get up every morning and see those two old friends lazing and loitering together.

At the top of the hill he paused at the family cemetery, where John, Emma, and Molly were buried along with Cal Doran, John Kerney's partner, and George Rose, a top hand and old friend. Patrick had once told Emma that CJ belonged buried among his comrades in a military cemetery in France, but he'd changed his mind. CJ should be resting here with his family on Kerney land, with the wide, forever views of the Tularosa.

Ribbon snorted in impatience and Patrick gave him rein. He was a sturdy eight-year-old gray gelding with a thin stripe that curled like a black ribbon on his right haunch, thus his moniker. He wasn't the fastest pony, or the smartest, but he suited Patrick just fine. He had a nice, steady gait, an abundance of endurance, and a calm personality.

It was an unusually cool July morning by way of a cloudy sky. Although the drought hadn't ended and the monsoons hadn't arrived, a series of light rains over the past month had somewhat refreshed the high meadows and pasturelands. Up-country, eighty head of cattle grazed on the only good patch of grass on the entire eastern slope of the San Andres. The rest of the range was dust covered and sandblasted.

Matthew had asked Patrick to spell Shorty for a long overdue promised weekend off. Patrick was glad to do it. In fact, he liked the fact that Matt ran the show, and although he'd never say so, it eased his mind considerably to have him in charge. Modern ranching required men with more smarts and education than he had, and Matt had plenty of both to spare, plus damn good horse sense.

Matt had shamed him into getting back on his feet, forced him back to work, and saved the ranch. It was the Double K no longer. Matt had sold the brand to a Texas oilman who masqueraded as a rancher. Now it was the 7-Bar-K Ranch. Although Patrick still had a hard time getting his mind around the change, he harbored no resentment. In fact, not much aggrieved him anymore.

Matt had used the oilman's money to buy a small herd of cows and throw in with Al Jennings to sell beef to butchers in Silver City,

Roswell, Las Cruces, Socorro, and smaller towns that supplied CCC camps across the southern part of the state. They were resting the high pastures every winter to allow the grass to recover, supplementing with feed when they restocked in the spring, and, so far, selling every animal after fall works.

Each of the last two years, both outfits had made enough money to stay debt-free and pay taxes, which put them way ahead of most other family-run outfits that were still in business. But Matt wasn't satisfied with getting by in hard times. He'd also taken on all the temporary work the Forest Service sent his way, and he poured his paychecks into a small herd of ponies he was training with Patrick's help to be topflight cutting horses. Once they were finished and ready for sale, Matt planned to put out an auction notice to regional stockmen's associations and the six-year-old Rodeo Association of America. If he could attract the interest of rodeo cowboys and the big ranchers who promoted the sport, training cutting horses might become a steady, lucrative enterprise.

Patrick had grown up thinking of rodeoing as nothing more than a cowboy pastime done for fun and bragging rights. It had taken Matt's savvy to recognize that it was now a business that needed quality horseflesh in order to operate.

Matt was away from the ranch for several weeks, ramrodding a Forest Service roundup of livestock from a grazing allotment in the Lincoln National Forest. In his absence, Patrick worked the ponies. Although his gimpy leg limited how much he could do in the saddle, he made progress with each of the twenty-five.

Patrick made good time to the cabin. Happy Jack, Shorty's horse, was saddled and waiting in the corral next to the cabin when he arrived. He dismounted and called out a hello that brought Shorty to the open door, spurs jingling. He was stocky and short, with wide shoulders and legs about as bowed as could be.

"You look ready to skedaddle," Patrick said.

"I'm a man hungering for some female companionship," Shorty allowed, fixing his hat firmly on his head. "I moved the herd to the tank pasture this morning. They've got water and grass. No need to trouble yourself with them until I get back, unless you're just hankering to ride up and take a look-see."

"Maybe come morning." Patrick handed Shorty his pay envelope. "Where you headed?"

Shorty grinned. "First to Engle, then on to El Paso by train. I'll get me a room at the Hotel Paso del Norte and look up a little lady friend of mine name of Millie, if she's still in town. I'll be back in three days."

"Does that give you enough time to kick up your heels?"

Shorty laughed as he stepped to the corral. "It will have to do. She'll have my pockets emptied by then anyway. Adios."

Patrick waved good-bye as Shorty loped his pony down the trail. Not sure if he wanted to loll around the cabin until morning, he tied Ribbon to a corral post, went inside, stoked the coals in the woodstove, warmed up the half-full coffeepot, poured a cup, and wandered back out the front door. From the looks of things, Shorty's anticipation of a weekend with Millie had distracted him from work. He should've been cutting winter firewood for the cabin. Instead, he'd let the woodpile get way too low. And the corral gate hung lopsided from a sloppy piece of work where he'd reattached a hinge to the post.

Back inside the cabin, Patrick noticed that all Shorty's gear and clothing were gone, cleaned out like he wasn't coming back. That struck Patrick as odd, as the old boy had just rode out with only his saddlebags and the clothes on his back.

He climbed aboard Ribbon, trying to decide which direction to take, north or south. If Shorty had moved the herd north to the tank pasture, he'd done it a month early. What cause did he have to do that? And if a body was in a big hurry to get south to El Paso, why use the trail that led to the state road? Making horse tracks over the mountain and down the gentle western slopes of the San Andres would save a lot of time.

If Shorty had moved the herd like he said, Patrick would cut trail after an hour of fast riding. Should he spend his time checking on the herd or follow Shorty? Since hiring on, that old boy hadn't done anything untrustworthy. Still, logic told him it was best to keep an eye on the cowboy, not the cattle.

He urged Ribbon down the trail, careful to stay far back and out of sight. Horse tracks showed that Shorty had set a fast clip. Patrick wondered if his uneasiness was misplaced. Could be the cowboy was simply in a hurry and riding to town on the trail he liked best. He mulled turning back until he caught sight of Shorty cutting across the open teardrop canyon where they gathered cattle for shipment. There were at least forty cows in the stock pen and two empty livestock trucks idling nearby.

Shorty was selling more than half the herd to cattle thieves. Patrick marveled at the idea of stealing cows by the truckload and figured it to be a first, because he'd never heard of such a thing before.

He backed up behind the ridgeline and made a slow descent out of sight, contemplating the situation. By the time he got below, slow and easy so as not to be spotted, the cattle would be loaded. If they were ahorseback, he could shoot the two drivers out of their saddles. But once they were under way in the trucks, he'd have a hell of a time stopping them. Counting Shorty, the odds were three to one against him.

Patrick considered his options. The stock pen was a mile in from the state road on a dirt track that squeezed through the canyon with passage for one vehicle at a time. If he wanted to stop them, he'd have to hurry. He eased Ribbon down the rocky back side of the canyon to a narrow arroyo and spurred the pony on. Blowing hard and lathered, Ribbon got him there just as the sound of the approaching trucks drew near. He dismounted, pulled his long gun from the scabbard, shooed Ribbon away out of danger, dropped to one knee, chambered a bullet, and waited. The nose of the first truck appeared around the bend. He put a bullet in the radiator and another in the windshield next to the driver's head. He got to his feet and hobbled as fast as he could for cover, expecting to hear gunfire and feel the jolt of a bullet in his back. All he heard was cursing.

On the back side of the canyon, he crawled to the summit, dragging his bad leg, with loose stones clattering underfoot. No gunfire yet, so he hadn't been spotted. But where the hell was Shorty with his Winchester?

Out of breath and sweating like a pig, he took a quick peek down at the trucks. There was no one in sight. He put two bullets through the hood of the lead truck to disable the engine, and two into the second truck.

"You son of a bitch," a man called out.

"Turn my cattle loose," Patrick yelled back.

"If we do, then what?"

"Where's Shorty?"

"He turned tail."

"I don't believe you."

"I swear to it, mister."

"Let me see you and your partner with no pistols showing."

"You ain't gonna kill us?"

"I should. The last man that tried to steal from me is dead. Come out where I can see you, let my cattle go, and you'll live."

Only one man was doing the talking, and that troubled Patrick. He squirmed a few yards away and turned on his back to keep an eye out for a sneak attack from behind.

"What about the law?" the man called.

"I reckon by the time I get my cows back to the stock pen and go to town for the sheriff, you boys will be long gone."

"What about our trucks?"

"While I don't cotton to the notion of cattle thieves going scot-free, the trucks stay where they are and you leave by shank's mare."

"We gotta think on that."

"Take your time." Patrick glanced over the edge. There was no sign of either driver. He turned back, caught sight of a figure sneaking to the cover of a boulder twenty feet down the canyon wall, and shot him in the shoulder. The man—more a boy than not—yipped like a puppy in pain, his eyes wide. Patrick slid down and disarmed him.

"Did you kill him?" the man below bellowed, worry in his voice. "Is he dead?"

"Not unless I shoot him again."

"No need for that," the man replied, his voice quavering. "I'll free your cattle now. Just bring the boy to me."

"He's your kin?"

"He's my son."

"I winged him; he'll survive. Tell me again where Shorty is."

"He's long gone with our money, I swear."

"Put your pistol and any other weapons on the hood of the truck and I'll bring him to you once my cows are loose."

"Yes, sir."

Patrick kept his eye on the man until he shucked his pistol and released the first truckload of cattle. Then he turned his attention to the boy, a kid no more than sixteen, who was shaking in shock and fear.

"Have you done any thieving like this before?" Patrick asked, wrapping his bandana tight against the boy's wound.

The boy shook his head. "No, sir. Am I bleeding to death?"

"Nope," Patrick said as he helped the boy to his feet. "You'll live. Let's go. Slide down backward facing me."

When they reached the dirt track, he poked the barrel of his rifle in the boy's back and told the man to show himself. He hurried into view, and there was no doubting the family resemblance. Both had the same long noses, big ears that stuck out, and yellow hair. Neither looked like the hardened criminals Patrick had known in the Yuma Prison, but that didn't soften his attitude. When the second cattle truck was empty, he pointed his rifle in the direction of the state road and said, "Git, and don't ever come back."

The man nodded as he led the boy away. "I swear we won't."

Patrick whistled for Ribbon to come. When the pony trotted to him, he mounted quickly and followed behind the would-be rustlers to the state road.

The man stopped in the middle of the road. "My boy needs a doctor," he pleaded.

"Then its best that you get a move on," Patrick replied with a wave of his long gun. He was not in a charitable mood.

He watched them disappear from sight before turning to gather the cattle and push them along to the stock pen, where he'd rest them for the night. It had been a helluva good day, one of his best in years.

⟩THREE⟨

Anna Lynn Crawford

33

Matt drove the small Forest Service remuda west out of the national forest, through the village of Cloudcroft, and on to the tiny settlement of Mountain Park. Nestled against a mountainside in a narrow valley with stunning views of the Tularosa Basin and San Andres Mountains beyond, Mountain Park was a farming settlement known for producing tasty apples and sweet cider. It was a sparkling clear day and Matt could just make out the faint dip above the flats north of Rhodes Canyon that defined the boundary to the 7-Bar-K Ranch.

The roundup in the Lincoln National Forest was Matt's fourth in a year, each prompted by the need to get half-wild cattle off the land so CCC crews could start building fences and catchment dams on overused, eroded grazing allotments. Hubert Roddy, his old boss, now working out of Fort Bliss as the head honcho for all Forest Service CCC projects in the two-state region, had hired Matt as the boss for the roundups. The money meant the difference between barely scratching by and getting back into the business of raising quality beef and training the finest cutting ponies in the state. If the drought continued to ease and the economy kept improving, Matt had hopes for a brighter future.

Mountain Park wasn't much more than a bend in the road, but it was pretty, with a small white church in a stand of cedar trees sprinkled with benches and tables for summer picnics, and a substantial fieldstone grade school on a level spit of land tucked into a hillside. Neat rows of apple trees spilled into the valley, interrupted by farmsteads on a long ribbon of tillable bottomland. Towering above the village was the massive wooden railroad trellis, which snaked up to the cool pines in Cloudcroft. Below the settlement, a canyon cut into the flank of the foothills. The Forest Service ponies were bound for a pasture leased from a small farm belonging to Anna Lynn Crawford. A single woman in her mid-thirties who lived alone, Anna Lynn raised bees in hives behind her tidy cottage and sold the honey to grocers in the towns up and down the basin.

Matt always looked forward to returning the remuda to Anna Lynn Crawford's farm. He enjoyed her company and the chance to spend a pleasant hour with her over a cup of coffee in her kitchen. Although she was tall, always dressed in jeans and work shirts, wore little makeup, and was tanned from the sun, Anna Lynn was pure female. She intrigued him. In conversation, she could quickly fall into silence and look at him as though he was a complete stranger. If he asked what she was thinking, she'd answer with either a slight smile or a shake of her head and change the subject.

He was watering Patches at the trough in the pasture when she called out to him from the cottage porch to stay for coffee. He waved in reply, left Patches to graze, and joined her in the kitchen.

"Have you seen the newspaper recently?" she asked as he settled in at the table.

"Not for some time," he answered.

"I thought not." She handed him the front page from the *Alamogordo News*. The headline read:

RANCHER FOILS CATTLE THIEVES!

Last Tuesday, Patrick Kerney of the 7-Bar-K Ranch in the San Andres stopped rustlers in their tracks as they tried to make off with two truckloads of his cattle. According to Sierra County Deputy Sheriff Bob Singleton, a 7-Bar-K hand named Shorty Gibson threw in with the thieves to steal cattle from Kerney by trailing them to a shipping pen close to State Road 52 near Rhodes Pass, where he was to meet his criminal cohorts.

Suspecting something was amiss, Kerney, a former member of Teddy Roosevelt's Rough Riders, tailed Gibson to the rendezvous, winged one of the bandits, and disabled the trucks the thieves were using to transport the cows, thus foiling the theft.

Two men, Steve Havell and his son John, who was wounded by Kerney, were later apprehended by officers in Alamogordo at the train station after hitching a ride from an unsuspecting motorist. The abandoned cattle trucks were later determined to have been stolen from an El Paso livestock hauler, who was pleased to get his property back but dismayed that rancher Kerney had shot up the trucks, causing considerable damage.

When interviewed at the 7-Bar-K Ranch by this reporter, Patrick Kerney made no comment other than to say he was glad not to have lost his cattle to the thieves. He hoped the livestock hauler didn't try to sue him for damaging his trucks.

Kerney's son, Matthew, who manages the 7-Bar-K Ranch, was on a job with the Forest Service removing cattle from a Lincoln National Forest grazing allotment and unavailable for comment. Shorty Gibson remains a fugitive, and local authorities believe he may have left the state.

"Well, I'll be. Shorty a crook and Pa a hero," Matt said, skimming the story again. "Doesn't that take the cake?"

Anna Lynn refilled his coffee cup. "I suppose you need to hurry back to the ranch."

"Not necessarily," Matt replied. "It appears the old boy has things well in hand."

Anna Lynn smiled. "Will you stay for an early supper? I've a pork roast in the oven."

Matt nodded. "With pleasure. I've been trying not to drool at the aroma."

Anna Lynn rose from her chair. "Good. I'll get you a towel and you can wash up at the sink."

As Matt dried his hands at the sink, a boy's voice called out from the porch, "Miss Anne, I've got those drawings you ordered."

He turned to see a scrawny kid with a big head standing in the doorway with a sketch pad in his hand.

"Come in, Billy." Anna Lynn retreated from the cookstove and wiped her hands on her apron. "Let's see what you've done."

"Yes, ma'am," Billy said, staring at Matt as he crossed to the table. "Is that saddled pony in the pasture yours?"

"It is." Matt extended his hand. "I'm Matt Kerney. That pony is Patches."

The boy's eyes lit up as he shook Matt's hand. "Billy Mauldin. Your pa stopped the rustlers. It was in the papers."

"So I've just learned. What have you got there?"

"Drawings Miss Anna Lynn asked for." He opened the sketch pad and placed three drawings on the table: a nicely rendered sketch of Anna Lynn's cottage, a drawing showing Anna Lynn in her beekeeper hood standing next to the row of hives, and a scene of the Forest Service ponies in the pasture.

"These are wonderful," Anna Lynn gushed as she examined each carefully.

"Thank you, ma'am," Billy said, looking pleased.

"How much do I owe you?" Anna Lynn asked.

"Seventy-five cents apiece," Billy replied. "That's two dollars and twenty-five cents."

"I'll get my coin purse." She stepped into the bedroom.

Billy looked out the open front door at Patches loitering in the pasture. "I'll do a drawing of your pony for a dollar," he proposed.

"Right now, on the spot?" Matt asked.

Billy nodded. "I'll do a quick one now for fifty cents. But for a dollar, I can do a nicer one. That's a fine-looking pony you have."

"And you're quite a salesman," Matt replied, putting a dollar in the boy's hand. "When you've got it done, leave it here and I'll pick it up the next time I ride through."

Billy grinned and pocketed the dollar. "Thanks, mister."

"Call me Matt."

"Okay, Matt."

Anna Lynn returned with her coin purse and tumbled some coins into Billy's outstretched hand. "Have you found another customer?"

"Yes, ma'am, I'm doing a portrait of Matt's pony."

"Would you do a portrait of Matt for me?"

"You bet I will," Billy said with a smile. "And because you're a repeat customer, it's gonna cost only seventy-five cents."

"I'll pay you now." More coins fell from Anna Lynn's to Billy Mauldin's hands.

Billy pocketed his earnings and had Matt sit on the porch step while he did some rough sketches. While Billy worked on his sketches, Matt asked how he'd learned to draw. Billy told him he was paying for a mail-order illustration course with the money he earned painting window signs, poster signs, and advertising banners for businesses up and down the roadway.

"I'll have this ready in a few days," he said after releasing Matt from his pose. He stuck his sketch pad under his arm and said, "Adios."

"Adios," Matt replied as Billy hurried off on rickety legs to the pasture gate. He squatted on his haunches and started sketching Patches, who seemed to know what was up and stood stock-still as Billy worked.

Matt turned to Anna Lynn. "Why would you want a portrait of me?"

Anna Lynn smiled. "To keep, of course. Come inside and I'll serve up our dinner."

Over dinner, Matt learned that Anna Lynn had been raised by a strict Lutheran farmer in Illinois who'd lost his wife at a young age. When he died, his five daughters sold the farm and went their separate ways, Anna Lynn coming west to New Mexico.

"On your own?" he asked.

"Yes."

"To farm?" Matt asked.

"I wasn't sure what I wanted to do until I saw this land."

"You've done all this by yourself?"

"Yes."

Matt grinned. "My ma would have liked you."

"Tell me about her."

He told her about Emma, including her time on the ranch and the short story Gene Rhodes had written about her. He was drying dinner dishes standing next to her at the sink, their shoulders touching every so often, when he ran out of words. For a wonderful moment he felt contented and aroused. After the last dish was dried, he praised her cooking, thanked her for her hospitality, and stepped outside into the gathering dusk. Had that much time passed?

She was right beside him on the porch, their shoulders touching. "If you don't kiss me right now, I'll scream," she whispered.

He pulled her to him, lifted her head, and kissed her, long and deep. "I could stay a while longer," he said, his heart pounding.

Anna Lynn rested her head against his chest. "I'd like that." She reached her hand deep into a front pocket of his jeans. "Come to my bedroom."

"As you wish," he mumbled.

She lit the bedside lamp and undressed before him, unselfconsciously, slowly, revealing her long, slender legs, her narrow waist, her firm breasts. He stumbled out of his clothes and into her arms. They made wonderful love. As soon as they finished, they did it again.

"Can I spend the night?" he asked, not yet fully spent.

"Oh, please do," Anna Lynn replied, nibbling his ear. "It's been a very long time since I've had a man in my bed all night long."

He searched her face, beautiful in the lamplight, thought to ask when that might have been, but instead turned and pulled her warm body close. He felt her melding into him and decided it didn't really matter.

34

Every time Matt visited Anna Lynn in Mountain Park, Billy Mauldin made an appearance with more sketches to sell, always at a discount for his best customers. Matt went home after each visit with one or two of Billy's drawings. He tacked them to the walls of the casita, where he bunked.

Young Billy had talent, especially as a cartoonist. But Matt's favorite piece was the drawing Billy had done of Patches loafing in Anna Lynn's pasture. He kept it in a special frame on the table in the sitting room next to the chair he used for reading.

On one of Matt's overnight stays in Anna Lynn's bed, she asked him if he thought she was wicked and immoral.

"I haven't thought about it or considered it," he replied, taken aback. "Why do you ask?"

"I am not a whore, Matt," she said seriously.

Her tone made Matt sit up in the bed. "Have I done something to make you think I don't respect you?"

Anna Lynn shook her head. "No, I just want you to understand that I'm virtuous in my own way."

"And what way is that?"

"I'm faithful to all of my lovers."

Matt raised an eyebrow. "All of your lovers? How can that be?"

She sat up next to him. "I only have one lover at a time. As long as he shares my bed, no other man can have me." Her expression left no doubt that she meant what she said.

Matt carefully weighed his response. "You're giving me fair warning, right?"

Anna Lynn's eyes lit up. "Thank you for understanding without making a fuss about it. I'd hoped you would."

"Why is that?"

"Not once have you tried to lay claim to me."

"That's an interesting way to put it," Matt said. "Perhaps I've just been biding my time."

Anna Lynn shook her head. "I don't think so. But I want you to know that I have no wish to marry, ever."

Matt wondered why she was opposed to marriage but thought it best not to ask. "If you're planning to replace me, should I start having hurt feelings now, or wait until I'm dumped?"

Anna Lynn laughed wickedly, threw the covers back, rolled over, and straddled him. "I'm not through with you yet, cowboy. Not by a long shot."

Over the course of a year, deep into the summer of 1936, Matt saw Anna Lynn whenever he could. It was always satisfying, but there was never enough time together for either of them. In fact, her only complaint was that his visits were too infrequent. Matt felt the same, but work came first.

On a late July afternoon in Mountain Park, Billy Mauldin arrived on Anna Lynn's porch with news that his parents had split up and he was striking out with his older brother, Sid, for Arizona.

They'd lived there once before and they knew a lady who ran a boardinghouse who had agreed to take them in on credit until they got jobs.

"Since my brother fixed the engine on the Model T, I've gotta pay for the gas and oil on the trip," Billy said. "So I'm selling the last of my sketches to raise the money."

He spread the drawings from his sketchbook on the porch and waited patiently while Matt and Anna Lynn selected ten each at the discounted price of fifty cents apiece.

Anna Lynn gave Billy a worried look along with a five-dollar bill. "Are you and Sid going to be all right in Phoenix on your own?"

Billy's grin was cocky and self-assured. "We'll get along okay. You can bet on it." He pocketed Matt's money and shook his hand. "You keep those doodlings of mine, because someday I'm gonna be a famous cartoonist."

"I sure will," Matt promised.

With a good-bye wave and a lopsided smile Billy sauntered up the canyon to the highway.

"He's a pistol," Matt said. "I'm betting he'll do just fine."

"Speaking of barrels," Anna Lynn said, her hand reaching inside his shirt. "I'm in desperate need of some attention inside."

"With pleasure, ma'am," Matt said with a grin.

* * *

Forest Service work had kept Matt busy to the point of forcing him to turn over the joint cattle operation to Al Jennings of the Rocking J and his son, Al Jr. Al had agreed to manage the herd, get the beef to the butchers in the fall, and split the profits equally with Matt, since the 7-Bar-K high-country pastures continued to have the only decent grazing land on either spread. That freed up

Matt to spend his ranch time with the ponies and saved the cost of hiring a man to replace Shorty Gibson, who, according to rumors, was somewhere in Louisiana hiding from the law and living under an alias.

Patrick carried his load around the ranch without complaint. He kept the operation organized, well stocked, repaired, and in working order. He helped out with the horse training as much as his bad leg would allow and always had good advice on ways to school a reluctant pony.

He rarely went to town and had stopped drinking completely. Whatever fueled Patrick's suspicious and antagonistic nature had simmered down into an old man's occasional crankiness. For Matt, that change in Patrick was cause for great relief. He'd stopped worrying about his going off half-cocked into one of his rants and rages.

In spite of Matt's attempt to interest rodeo cowboys in his ponies, he'd sold only a few to some calf-roping and steer-wrestling cowboys who were just starting out on the circuit. But word was getting out that the 7-Bar-K sold quality horseflesh at a fair price. If those rodeo cowboys who'd bought from him started winning buckles and prize money, Matt was sure business would pick up.

In the fall, Matt planned to auction three of his top cutting horses and a half dozen of his best roping ponies. With the proceeds, he'd restart a program to raise ponies for breeding stock just like they'd done before the Depression.

In August, a letter came from Hubert Roddy asking Matt to visit with him within the next two weeks at Fort Bliss about a special job he had for him. Intrigued by the notion of taking a break from the ranch and the ponies, Matt wrote back setting a date when he'd come by and visit. Then he rode over to Anna Lynn's place and asked her to take a long-weekend getaway with him to El Paso.

She got excited about his invitation right away. After a long siesta in her bed, they agreed to rendezvous at the Hotel Paso del Norte after his meeting with Hubert Roddy. On Matt's way home, he called the hotel from a gas station in Tularosa and made the room reservation.

He loped Patches homeward thinking about his night in El Paso with Beth. They'd been so young and innocent in so many ways. It was a sweet memory etched into his mind forever. Matt wondered how different his life would have been if Beth was alive and with him now. He still loved her and maybe always would. But it wouldn't stop him from loving again.

* * *

On the day of his meeting with Hubert Roddy, Matt traveled to El Paso on an early train so he could get business out of the way and start his weekend getaway with Anna Lynn. Roddy's office was in a cramped room in an old converted barracks that housed the Forest Service CCC administration unit on the sprawling, dusty Fort Bliss army base just outside the city. He greeted Matt with a warm handshake, poured him a cup of coffee, plopped his boots on top of a knee-high pile of official-looking bound documents stacked on the floor next to his desk, and got right down to business.

"I need your help, Matt. One of my staff who did camp inspections took a promotion to California two months ago, and I haven't been authorized a replacement. I've got two men hurt and on limited duty, and my bosses are nipping at my heels about overdue reports. I need you to conduct six inspections in the next four weeks."

"What exactly would I be inspecting?" Matt asked.

"Everything," Roddy replied. "Don't worry, we've got all the forms and instructions you'll need, plus you'll be trained. The six camps are spread from hell-and-gone across Arizona and New Mexico, so I've arranged for the army to lend us an airplane and pilot to fly you around. Hell, I'd go myself if I had time, just to rubberneck from the wild blue yonder. Are you game?"

"I am, but I can't start until midweek."

Roddy grunted in displeasure. "That'll have to do, I guess, since you're doing me a big favor. Be back here next Wednesday. I'm doubling your pay for this."

Matt grinned. "That's good news."

"You'll earn it. Camp inspectors aren't very popular, especially with the crooks who like to steal from Uncle Sam. Don't let on you speak Spanish; it may give you an edge."

"Do I get a badge and gun?"

Roddy laughed. "I wish. The most I'm allowed to do is fire the miscreants. Washington doesn't want even a hint of scandal to surface about President Roosevelt's pet project. Pack light and don't worry about where you'll bunk here. We'll have a VIP room reserved for you at the Bachelor Officers' Quarters."

"A VIP room," Matt remarked, raising an eyebrow. "You bureaucrats sure live high off the hog."

Roddy chuckled, swung his feet to the floor, and stood. "Ain't that the truth."

* * *

Matt walked into the lobby of the Hotel Paso del Norte, thinking he had an hour or two to kill before Anna Lynn arrived, only to find her curled up in an easy chair with reading glasses perched on her nose, engrossed in a book. He bent down and got her at-

tention with a kiss on her cheek that brought her out of the chair
and into his arms. He'd never seen her look lovelier. She wore a
pleated skirt, full at the hemline just below the knees, and a flow-
ered blouse with padded shoulders and billowy sleeves.

"You're beautiful," he said.

"Careful, or I may begin to think you're courting me," she cautioned, her eyes twinkling,

"Never, my lady. May I carry your valise to our room?"

"I'll permit you to do that, as long as you behave properly when
we're alone," she answered regally.

They checked in, went to their room, and made love before
venturing outside to stroll around the old plaza. The El Paso
Gentlemen's Rio Grande Rowing Club, the classy speakeasy Matt
had visited with Beth, had gone the way of Prohibition, replaced
by a seedy, stale-smelling bar filled with loud, foulmouthed drunks.
After wandering in and out of shops, they returned to the hotel
and had drinks in the fancy bar before Matt hired a taxi to take
them to the Casa Blanca in Juárez for dinner. It was still a high-
class bordello with the best restaurant in the city, filled with
beautiful señoritas and wealthy clients from both sides of the
border.

They left hours later, contented, satiated with fine food and
wine, and pleasantly entertained by a cellist playing Mozart in the
grand dining room. As they walked to their cab, Anna Lynn
squeezed Matt's arm and said Casa Blanca was now and forever
her favorite nightspot for secret rendezvous, lascivious liaisons,
and decadent, scrumptious dining.

"It arouses all your senses," she said. "Can we dine there again
tomorrow night?"

"You bet," Matt replied, feeling flush with the money he was
about to earn on the Forest Service job.

"How did you come to know of this place?" she asked as she slipped into the taxi.

"I can't tell you," Matt said mysteriously as he slid next to her. "It's a secret."

She laughed and pressed against him. "Oh, I do like you, cowboy. Tell the driver to hurry to the hotel."

When they kissed and parted at the train station on Sunday evening, they had exhausted each other in all the best possible ways.

* * *

Captain Cornelius Franklin, U.S. Army Air Corps, flew over the 7-Bar-K ranch house, dipped a wing of his Curtiss Falcon biplane, landed on the nearby hardpan alkali flats, and quickly decided the expanse of desert that stretched between the two mountain ranges was much more interesting from the air. He shut down the engine, climbed out of the open cockpit, lit a cigarette, and waited for his passenger to arrive. Within a few minutes two riders approached from the ranch, Matthew Kerney, whom he'd met at Fort Bliss, and an older fellow introduced as his father, who wanted a close look at the flying machine.

Accustomed to such requests, Cornelius walked the old gent around the plane, answered his questions, let him peer into the cockpit and the forward observation deck, and explained that the aircraft was used to provide commanders in the field with information on enemy armaments, positions, supplies, and troop strength. The old-timer shook his head in wonder and announced it was a shame such a contraption didn't exist when he was charging up San Juan Hill with Teddy Roosevelt.

A West Point graduate and avid student of military history, with sixteen years of stateside service, Franklin shook Patrick Kerney's hand and congratulated him on such a splendid accomplishment before getting Matt and his gear loaded onboard. He cranked the engine, gave a thumbs-up to the old Rough Rider, and went airborne, turning the Curtiss west toward the Gila Wilderness as they quickly gained altitude.

Spellbound, Matt craned his neck from side to side, trying to see as much as he could of the land rocketing by hundreds of feet below, the 7-Bar-K Ranch exposed in high relief with all its contours, ripples, peaks, and valleys spread out against an endless horizon.

All thoughts of his assignment, the endless forms he'd studied, the check sheets he was to use, the minutiae he had to scrutinize for each camp inspection, flew out of his head. Never had he seen anything so marvelous as the earth from the sky. The plane skipped over the green and muddy brown ribbon of the Rio Grande, rose over wrinkled, juniper-studded foothills, and fought headwinds as it climbed above the roadless, forested Black Range wilderness.

Suddenly, Franklin banked, slowed, and brought the biplane to a bumpy landing on a dirt airstrip that ran on top of a pencil-thin mesa. Landing gave them a telescopic view of a grassy plain encased in a wide, enormous basin. Franklin throttled back the engine, pointed at the ground, and shouted, "This is your stop. I'll see you in two days."

Matt threw his bag to the ground and climbed out of his seat. "Where's the camp?"

Franklin pointed at the back side of the mountains. "Up there, where I can't land. They'll send someone down to get you after I fly overhead and wiggle my wings at them to let them know you're here."

"How long will that take?"

"Not long." Franklin threw a half salute, turned his plane around, taxied, and took off.

Matt sat on a rock on the edge of the airstrip and watched as the plane became a speck in the sky, the sound of the engine fading to a distant buzz. Telltale cigarette butts ground into the dirt attested to the fact that he was not the first passenger to be kept waiting for transportation. But he wasn't a bit impatient. Instead, he used the time reliving his plane ride, trying to remember all that he'd seen from the sky. He'd be flying in Captain Franklin's Curtiss Falcon a whole lot more in the coming weeks, and the prospect pleased him. What a way to see the world.

An hour passed before a horseman trailing a saddled pony came into view. Matt grabbed his gear and walked briskly to meet his guide, who turned out to be none other than Nestor Lucero.

"Mateo, is that you?" Nestor asked.

"My old friend." Smiling, Matt took the reins to the saddle pony from Nestor's hand. "Where have you been hiding?"

Nestor shrugged. "Working, not hiding, amigo. Come, we must hurry for supper."

On the ride to the camp, Matt learned that Guadalupe had died two winters ago and that Nestor and his two boys, Roberto and Felipe, all had jobs with the Forest Service at different CCC camps. Both sons were now supervisors of roads and trail crews.

"This is my third camp," Nestor said proudly. "I teach how to cut wood, log trees, build fences, and I make all the repairs for the camp. Most of the boys here are from faraway cities, some from Texas. Only a few are from here."

"Well, they've got a good boss in you," Matt said.

Nestor smiled. "I even teach some of them to speak a little Spanish."

Matt fished out thirty dollars and handed it to Nestor. "I owe you this. How come you left the ranch in such a hurry?"

Nestor rubbed the bills between his fingers before pocketing the windfall. "Your father, he didn't want us to go, but Guadalupe was not happy there away from her grandchildren."

"My Pa didn't drive you away?"

Nestor shook his head. "No, he said he'd get help, but I didn't think he would. He liked to be alone, I think. He was very sure he would always be a cripple. Is he still alive?"

"*Sí*, and doing better. I'd always thought he'd bullied the two of you into leaving."

"No, it was Guadalupe's wish that we leave. She was too lonely for her family and the grandchildren." Nestor shrugged. "Sometimes I think she knew she would not have a lot of time to be with them. Much like your *madre* knew."

Matt nodded in agreement.

"I left a message with the lawyer Lipscomb to tell you we were leaving the ranch," Nestor added. "Did you get it?"

"You spoke to Lipscomb personally?" Matt asked.

"No, I told a boy in his office. He said he would write it down and give it to Lipscomb."

"I never got the message, but no harm done," Matt said.

Nestor smiled with relief. "*Bueno.* Have you come to inspect the camp?"

"*Sí.*"

"You will find all is good here."

"I hope so," Matt replied, eager to see Forest Service Camp FS-34, also known as Beaverhead.

* * *

Hubert Roddy had given Matt a mound of paperwork to study in preparation for his temporary position as a camp inspector. As a result, Matt learned that much had changed since the early days of the tent camps. Now there were wooden barracks that could be dismantled and moved as needed when camps closed and new ones opened. No longer were the cooks and supervisors soldiers. Only the officers who ran the show were military; the rest were local craftsmen, tradesmen, and supervisors. Most of the cooks were ex-military or had been trained by the army. Doctors and dentists rode the circuit from camp to camp to keep the boys healthy and treat the sick. Clergymen held services and preached moral values, and the teachers taught reading, writing, and arithmetic to students eager to improve themselves.

In some camps furniture making, carpentry, and cabinetmaking were taught by local craftsmen. Other camps offered typing classes, surveying courses, animal husbandry skills, and blacksmithing, depending on the skills of the staff.

All the camps were laid out in a precise military order, with all the buildings arranged according to a prescribed plan. The placement of the barracks, the mess hall, the recreation center, the hospital, the administration building, and the classrooms and supervisors' quarters never varied from camp to camp.

From a distance Matt could tell that Beaverhead Camp had prepared in advance for his inspection. All the pathways were lined with rocks freshly painted white. Not a piece of litter or junk was in sight. In the middle of the assembly field, Old Glory fluttered at the top of a flagpole. Having read the last inspection report, Matt knew that a nearby field was to have been cleared and made into a baseball diamond. Now finished, the field boasted sturdy bleachers behind home plate, a scoreboard in center field, and dugouts for visiting and home teams.

Nestor led him past a long line of unusually quiet enrollees waiting outside the mess hall for the supper bell to ring and drew rein at the administration building. All the camp trucks were parked out front in a neat row. Behind the building, a dirt road ran through a lovely grove of pruned old-growth pine trees and down a series of switchbacks to the canyon below.

Nestor stopped in front of the camp commander's door just as it opened to reveal First Lieutenant Marcel Gustav Dobak, a middle-aged reserve ordnance officer from Pittsburgh, Pennsylvania, on his third tour with the CCC.

"You'll see, Mateo," Nestor predicted as Matt dismounted. "Good camp, no problems, I promise."

35

M att's inspection of the Beaverhead Camp proved Nestor Lucero right. Everything was in order except for a few misfiled
documents, some missing automotive parts and supplies, and
shortages in clothing for new enrollees due to a delay in shipping.
Matt flew away in Captain Cornelius Franklin's biplane wondering
if he'd really done a good job of the inspection or been bamboozled for being the greenhorn he was. Either way, it had certainly
been exhausting.

Back at the Fort Bliss Forest Service offices, he briefed Hubert
Roddy, who skimmed Matt's paperwork, pronounced it satisfac-
tory, and gave him hints on language to use in the narrative report. Through his open office door, he pointed at a vacant desk
and told Matt to get to work on it pronto. Late that afternoon,
Matt dropped his report on Roddy's desk; Roddy shooed him
out and read it behind closed doors while Matt dawdled and
waited.

Roddy finally emerged hat in hand, in a hurry to get somewhere, and said, "Now write a summary and leave it on my desk."

"Was it okay?" Matt asked.

"You did a good job," Roddy answered. "But I gave you an easy one. Tomorrow morning you'll fly out to inspect a new camp near Mimbres. Captain Franklin will pick you up at the BOQ. This next one won't be so easy."

He was gone before Matt could ask any questions.

* * *

When Matt and Cornelius Franklin flew over the Mimbres Camp, two hundred enrollees were lined up on both sides of the airstrip waiting to greet them. On landing, they were met by a young marine officer, Lieutenant Morrison, who said he'd delayed sending the work details out because most of the boys had never seen an airplane up close. He figured it would be a big boost for morale since many of them were from back east and already homesick.

Matt thought it was a smart thing to do. He watched as Franklin talked about his aircraft to the wide-eyed boys clustered around the Curtiss Falcon. When all their questions were answered, they were ordered onto waiting trucks and rode off to their work assignments laughing and joking.

Because it was a new camp and had been operating for less than six weeks, Matt's visit was an initial inspection, and as such it had been announced to the staff in advance. He'd expected to find everything still in disarray. Instead, the camp appeared shipshape. Four barracks, a bathhouse, latrine, mess hall, infirmary, recreation hall, supply building, and several garages comprised the core camp buildings. There was a general assembly area in front of the administrative headquarters, which also contained two private rooms for guests. After settling in, Matt and Captain Franklin, who was spending the night, toured the buildings and grounds with Morrison. The lieutenant was on his first CCC camp posting and eager to do a good job of it. Over coffee in the mess hall, Matt gave him a thick folder of materials Roddy had prepared on side camps he wanted set up and operating as soon as possible. Cornelius Franklin consulted a map, located the sites, and offered to take the lieutenant up in the Curtiss Falcon and fly him over the sites. Morrison grinned in delight at the offer, and Matt was soon abandoned in the mess hall, listening to the sound of the biplane taking off from the airstrip.

The camp cook, an older man with a chipped front tooth, cauliflower ears, and a pair of boxing gloves tattooed on his right forearm, refilled his coffee cup.

He put the pot down and sat. "I ain't seen you inspecting before."

"I'm filling in," Matt replied. "Have you worked at other Forest Service camps?"

The cook nodded. "I was at the Mayhill camp over by Cloudcroft for two years. Name's Vic Suter. The army taught me how to cook. I boxed some in the service, won the regimental title twice. I teach the boys the sport that wants to learn."

"I bet they enjoy that. Why did you leave Mayhill?"

Suter hesitated, then shrugged. "It was time to move on. Here I get to do things my way in the kitchen."

"Isn't that the way it's supposed to be at all the camps?"

"Supposed to be is right," Suter allowed.

"But not at Mayhill," Matt ventured.

Suter pushed back his chair and stood. "Forget I said anything. I ain't there anymore, so it's none of my business."

"If you've got a complaint, I'd like to hear it," Matt prompted.

Suter waved the coffeepot at Matt's empty cup. "Nah, I ain't no rat. You want more java?"

"No, thanks. Are you sure you don't have something to tell me?"

"I got work to do in the kitchen. Steaks are on the dinner menu, special for you tonight. The boys sure do pack away the beef."

"Sounds great," Matt replied, wondering if he'd be eating 7-Bar-K beef at mealtime.

Vic scooped up Matt's coffee cup and returned to his kitchen, where the boys on KP were busy clanking pots and pans and razzing each other in loud voices. Vic had something on his mind about the Mayhill camp, that was for certain, but prying it out of him wouldn't be easy. Matt decided to make another attempt to get the cook to open up before he finished his inspection.

After Lieutenant Morrison returned from his aerial survey of side camp locations, Matt discovered why Roddy had told him the inspection wouldn't be easy. The problems at the camp had nothing to do with infractions and everything to do with getting a new camp with a novice commander fully operational. For two days, Matt was closeted with Morrison. They went over hiring practices for local tradesmen, wage and salary rates for employees, requisitions for bedsheets, blankets, and towels that had yet to arrive.

Morrison wanted to know why telephone service to the camp had been delayed. When would the three trucks he was short arrive? Did Matt know when he'd get a teacher assigned to the camp? Where was the medical equipment Morrison needed for the dispensary?

Matt left Mimbres with a huge list to pass on to Roddy. On a stopover in Tucson to refuel the plane, Matt telephoned Roddy and told him of Morrison's most pressing needs.

"I'll get on it," Roddy said. "Anything else?"

"You were right about it being tougher," Matt said. "But I wouldn't worry about Morrison. He'll do a good job."

"I figured as much."

Back in the air, Matt gawked at sprawling mountain ranges that seemed to stretch forever before tumbling into the desert. He did a final inspection to close one camp, which was a paperwork nightmare of endless forms, certifications, inventories, and shipping documents, including a camp disposition report that detailed every item to be salvaged. It took two extra days to finish, and the demolition crews were dismantling the buildings around Matt's head the day he left.

By the start of his fourth inspection, at a remote camp he reached on horseback, Matt was feeling almost like an old hand. Deep in the mountains east of Phoenix, the camp sat at the head of a serpentine canyon. Most of the staff and enrollees had been there for more than a year working on a dam and flood-control project designed to protect downstream settlements. It was a major undertaking, and the men and boys doing it were rightly proud of their work.

When he finished, he took the train from Phoenix to El Paso, and it was almost as much fun as soaring in an army biplane. He worked on his reports as he traveled, pausing frequently to rubberneck at the vast stretches of open range, the colorful desert landscapes, and the small railroad towns they passed through. Determined to have his paperwork finished before the journey ended, Matt continued to work at night in his sleeping compartment. He reached Fort Bliss well after dark and, bleary-eyed, checked into a room at the BOQ.

After breakfast the next morning, he walked to the Forest Service office only to discover that Roddy was at a CCC meeting in Albuquerque and out for the day. Matt dropped his reports on Roddy's desk, hitched a ride into town, and went shopping for a new pair of boots and a present for Anna Lynn. At a shop that sold handmade boots, he bought a sturdy pair that fit just right at a fair price. In a nearby Indian jewelry store, he picked out a silver-and-turquoise bracelet for Anna Lynn and had the clerk gift wrap it. Then he stopped at a Mexican cantina within sight of the Hotel Paso del Norte and had enchiladas smothered in green chili and a cold beer. As he pushed back from the table, he decided he needed to entice Anna Lynn to go on another getaway with him, maybe to Albuquerque this time.

He woke from a nap at the BOQ and went for a drink at the Officers' Club. It was after duty hours and Cornelius Franklin was at the bar.

He waved Matt over and asked, "When's our next trip?"

"There isn't one. I head home tomorrow."

"Pity, I've enjoyed your company. Ever think about joining up? The army could use a man like you." He waved the bartender over and ordered a beer for Matt.

"Do they offer commissions to cattlemen?" Matt asked.

Cornelius laughed. "No, but maybe we should. It might improve the quality of meals in our mess halls. However, we do make officers out of veterinarians. The one here on post even outranks me. I think he's about a hundred years old."

The door opened and Roddy stepped over to the bar. "I've been looking for you." He eyed Matt's full beer glass. "I didn't know you drank."

"I started when I went to work for you," Matt replied, lifting the glass to his lips.

Roddy shook his head in dismay at the wisecrack, plunked money on the bar, and ordered a round. "What's this note you left me about Mayhill?"

"The cook at Mimbres wanted to tell me that something fishy was going on at the Mayhill Camp but just couldn't bring himself to do it. He gave some powerful hints, though."

"About what?"

Matt shrugged. "The conversation didn't get that far."

"Who's the cook?"

"Vic Suter. He used to be at Mayhill."

Roddy nodded. "I know Vic; he's a good man. I pulled the Mayhill inspection reports and there's nothing in the file indicating anything unusual going on there that warrants an investigation."

"So everything is copacetic," Matt ventured before draining his glass.

Roddy looked doubtful. "Vic was happy at Mayhill. He once said he planned to stay there for as long as they'd have him. So I think something might be up. A surprise inspection is in order. Will you do it?"

"Of course he will," Cornelius said.

Roddy raised an eyebrow at Matt. "Well?"

"Okay."

"Good. I had my clerk deliver the prior inspection reports to your room. Go through them tonight. In the morning we'll meet and put a plan together. Figure on three days at the camp and a day back here to debrief."

"If I uncover a wrongdoer, what do you want me to do?"

"Fire his ass and kick him out of the camp."

Cornelius drained his glass and stood. "Shall we say oh eight thirty hours at the airfield?"

"He'll be there," Roddy said.

"Excuse me, but when did you guys decide to start talking for me?" Matt inquired. It got a guffaw from both men.

* * *

From the material Roddy supplied, Matt knew in advance of his arrival that Juan Ignacio's stepfather, Porter Knox, was the supervisor of the Mayhill Camp woodworking shop. Enrollees in Porter's classes made furniture and cabinets for WPA public building projects throughout the state. It was a highly touted CCC enterprise that had earned national recognition from Washington as a model for teaching young men a skilled vocational craft.

Past inspectors had given the camp the highest marks possible for the condition of the buildings and grounds, and Matt understood why as soon as he saw it. The camp was nestled in a slender valley of the Sacramento Mountains surrounded by an old-growth pine forest. A wide, welcoming porch with sturdy chairs had been added along the front of the otherwise plain, rectangular administration building. His rooms in the nearby separate guest quarters contained finely crafted pine furnishings with hand-chiseled motifs. On the wall were attractive landscape paintings done by enrollees. Throughout the grounds, hand-carved signs on posts identified each building. Across a grassy field stood a huge barn, with a large corral and sturdy hay shed out back. Closer to the barracks but set apart was Porter Knox's woodworking shop and an adjacent lumberyard filled with sorted and stacked milled and rough lumber.

Max Simmons, the supervisor who greeted Matt and showed him to his quarters, was a little nonplussed about the surprise visit. It was the first Saturday after payday and the camp was mostly empty of staff and enrollees. Except for the cook, Simmons was the lone employee on duty.

"This is the first time anyone has flown in here," Simmons said nervously as he walked at Matt's side around the compound. "That army plane sure had me looking skyward. Our camp commander, Lieutenant Gossing, and the other supervisors are gone for the weekend. We've got a telephone. I can call and get them back."

Matt smiled reassuringly. "There's no need for that. I reckon the two of us can get through today without any problems at all. Tell me what you do."

"I'm the garage and vehicle foreman. I keep the vehicles running and supervise transportation to the work sites and side camps."

"Let's start in the mess hall first. I understand you've got a new cook."

Simmons pointed at the gravel path to the mess hall. "Yeah, our old one left to go to a new camp."

On the baseball field, several guys were in the outfield snagging fly balls hit by a burly fellow at home plate. They were yelling back and forth to each other in thick East Coast accents. Through the open door and windows of the recreation building Matt could hear the sound of a pool game, the chatter of some men playing cards, and the strumming of a guitar. In the mess hall kitchen, Simmons introduced Matt to Eddie Nelson, the new cook, a skinny man with a pointed chin and acne scars on his cheeks.

"Jeez, am I in trouble?" Nelson asked. "I ain't been inspected before."

Matt laughed. "Relax. Tell me how you found the kitchen when you took over."

"Everything was as it should be, the dining room and kitchen were spic-and-span, and all the foodstuffs were accounted for. The old cook left things in good shape."

"Let's take a look," Matt said.

The kitchen, mess hall, and food locker were in good order. Inventories and requisition orders were up-to-date. Camp cooks reimbursed their local suppliers with cash upon delivery through a special mess account. "Let me see your mess cash account," Matt said.

Nelson shook his head. "I don't have one. Everything gets paid by administration."

Matt turned to Simmons. "How long has that been going on?"

"Since we lost our second-in-command six months ago. He used to supervise all the cash accounts for local vendors and suppliers. A replacement has been held up because Washington wants to have a civilian appointed and the army wants to keep it military. So for now, all cash disbursements go through administration."

"All of them?" Matt asked.

Simmons nodded. "Including vehicle parts and supplies for my shop."

"Let's visit your shop next," Matt said. On the way to the garage he asked Simmons about Vic Suter.

"He was a friend of mine," Simmons said as he swung open a garage bay door. "I never figured him to leave." He stood aside to let Matt enter. "You're gonna see a mess in here. But I keep our trucks running and teach the lads a thing or two about being good mechanics."

Matt's eyes adjusted to the dimness. Simmons was right: The garage was a mess. Tools were scattered on the workbenches, truck tires were stacked in a haphazard pile against the wall, grease-stained coveralls were draped over truck fenders, a trunk engine sat on top of a grungy wood worktable, and a partially disassembled rear axle rested on a tarp on the floor. The smell of gasoline and oil hung in the air.

"Why did Vic leave?" Matt asked.

"Vic got crossways with another supervisor."

"Who was that?"

"Porter Knox. He's king of the roost around here right now. The lieutenant's number one favorite and his acting second-in-command. In Gossing's eyes, Porter can do no wrong. I understand it. Knox has earned a lot of praise, what with the success of his woodworking and furniture-making program."

"How did Vic get crossways with Knox?"

"I don't know; Vic wouldn't talk about it. But it happened soon after Knox took over as acting executive officer."

"Let's visit the woodworking shop."

"Knox keeps it locked when he's not around."

"Has he always done that?"

"No, he used to let the fellows use it after hours and on weekends until he got made acting XO."

"Is there a locked key box in the administration building?"

"There is," Simmons said.

In the camp commander's office, Matt pried open the locked key box and found a spare key to the woodworking shop. With a worried Max Simmons trailing behind, Matt hurried to the shop, opened the door, and stepped inside to the smell of freshly sawed wood. Knowing Porter, Matt wasn't surprised to find the place orderly. All the hand tools hung on wall pegs, and the concrete floor was swept clean of sawdust, wood shavings, and litter. Furniture in various stages of construction filled a large work space. Off in a corner was a separate room used for staining and painting. A desk, two chairs, and a file cabinet were positioned at the back of the shop, away from the large table saws. Both the desk and file cabinet were locked.

Matt sat at Porter's desk wondering what the rift between Porter and Vic Suter had been about. What had Knox done to make Vic leave a job he obviously liked and enjoyed?

"Porter handles the cash payments to local suppliers now?" Matt asked.

"Yeah, like I said," Simmons replied. "He's acting XO. He pays them right here."

That meant Porter handled five cash accounts. Matt knew the maximum amount of money allowed in any one cash account was two hundred dollars. There could be a thousand dollars locked in Porter's desk.

"Can you open the desk?"

Simmons shook his head. "I don't have a key."

The desk looked identical to the one in the garage. "Does your desk have a key?" Matt asked, wondering if the locks were universal.

"It does, but I never lock it."

"Please go get the key." Matt stared at Porter's desk. He hated the notion that Porter might be a thief. Maybe Vic Suter's gripe with Porter was simply personal.

Simmons's key opened the desk. One cash box was empty except for two dollars in change and receipts totaling fifty-seven dollars, which meant about one hundred forty-one dollars was missing. He opened the four other boxes and tallied the receipts and cash on hand. All were short in lesser amounts. He locked all the cash boxes, pocketed the keys, and left the boxes on top of the desk.

"Can you unlock the file cabinet?" Matt asked.

"It don't need a key," Simmons said. "It's just like all the rest of them we got from the army. Give the top drawer a good yank. That'll spring the lock."

Matt yanked and the lock sprung. He flipped through the labeled files, pulled the ones marked as accounts paid, and laid them out in order on a long workbench.

"What are you doing?" Simmons asked uneasily.

"Just looking," Matt replied. "How long would it take Lieutenant Gossing to get here?"

"Two hours at the most."

"Call him, and only him." Matt looked up from the folder in his hand. "Tell him I'm here on a surprise inspection. Don't say anything more than that. Clear?"

Simmons nodded. "I got it."

It took Matt until lunchtime to finish his review of the contents of Porter's file cabinet. He left most of the files out on the workbench, carried the petty cash boxes to his quarters, and locked the door. He ate a noontime meal in the mess hall with a group of talkative enrollees who answered his questions about their work projects, their experiences at the side camps, how they liked the food, and how they were treated by staff. Their gripes consisted of being worked too hard, being fed too much of the same old grub, and being too far from any place with girls.

He was about to leave the mess hall when the camp commander, Lieutenant Erik Gossing, burst through the door. Of medium build, with a blocky jaw and small ears that lay tight against his head, he came straight at Matt.

Matt stood and met Gossing with a smile. "Hello, Lieutenant."

Gossing returned a forced smile. "I'm sorry I wasn't here to greet you. How can I be of assistance?"

Matt scraped his plate at the dirty-dish station. "Let's talk in the woodworking shop," he suggested, out of range of his tablemates.

The shop door was open, the electric lights were on, and Porter Knox was at his desk, a worried frown plastered across his brow.

He managed a shaky smile. "Matt, what's this all about, for chrissake?"

"Yes, indeed," Gossing snapped. "What is going on here?"

Matt stared at Gossing. "Nothing I'm happy about, Lieutenant.

Porter has been stealing petty cash from the camp for some time now. He's forged receipts, padded bills of sale from local suppliers, and created phony inventories of some of the milled lumber. There may be more, but that's what I've uncovered so far."

"That's a lie," Porter blustered.

Matt stayed focused on Gossing. "Your old cook, Vic Suter, was onto him. But I'm guessing he couldn't prove it. Maybe out of loyalty to you or the camp, he chose to leave rather than report his suspicions."

"You have proof?" Gossing demanded.

Matt patted a thick file he'd carried with him from the mess hall. "I do."

Gossing held out his hand. "Let me see it."

"Not yet." Matt turned his attention to Porter, who stared at the desktop, hands tightly clenched. "If I've got it figured right, you have a hundred and forty-one dollars that belongs in one of the petty cash boxes. You didn't even bother to leave a receipt for the money. That wasn't very smart."

"I took that money and bought hardware supplies needed for a furniture order," Knox puffed. "It will be delivered on Monday. The bill of sale is at home."

Matt pulled a receipt from the file and waved it at Knox. "Are you talking about *this* receipt for hardware dated today from an Alamogordo store that I found in your cabinet?"

Porter dropped his head.

Matt looked at Gossing. "Four other cash accounts are short as well. A full audit will be required to produce an exact accounting."

Matt put his hands on the desk and stared at Porter. "Were you hoping to return the money to petty cash?"

Defeated, Porter nodded. "You don't understand . . ."

Matt held up a hand to stop him. "How much did you bring?"

"Two hundred and sixteen dollars."

"Hand it over."

Matt took the money and turned to Gossing. "Because Porter Knox is my kid brother's stepfather, Mr. Roddy will be here shortly to relieve me. He's flying up from El Paso. Until he arrives, take Knox to one of the guest quarters and stay with him. Is that understood?"

Gossing nodded grimly. "Of course. What's going to happen to him?"

"Nothing good," Matt predicted, thinking Gossing was probably in for some rough sledding as well. He watched Gossing march a trembling Porter Knox out the door. What Knox had done would have a terrible impact on Evangelina, Juan Ignacio, and Juan's little sister. Matt wanted to grab Porter and give him a good thrashing. Instead, he counted the money Knox had given him, put it in his folder, and went to wait for Hubert Roddy.

36

Hubert Roddy made sure Porter Knox's dismissal caused no scandal, and a small ripple of local gossip occurred but quickly faded away. Officially, nothing was said about the two thousand dollars in total Porter had embezzled from the camp. He simply lost his job due to insubordination and was barred from future U.S. government employment. The punishment was far less than the prison sentence Porter richly deserved, but it prevented an embarrassing blemish from marring the sterling reputation of the Civilian Conservation Corps. That kept the Washington bosses happy.

Faced with Roddy's strong recommendation that he step down, Lieutenant Gossing applied for a transfer. His request was quickly approved and he was sent off to be a regimental supply officer at a National Guard fort in Wisconsin. To replace Gossing, Roddy brought in an experienced CCC commanding officer from another camp, hired a Hispanic cabinetmaker from Santa Fe to fill Porter's position, and appointed one of his foresters who held a reserve commission in the army to serve as the acting executive officer. His swift and decisive action earned him some well-deserved recognition from his immediate boss and a temporary posting to the Rocky Mountain Region with orders to clean up a number of disasters brewing in the Wyoming camps. As a result of his absence, offers for Matt to take on additional temporary Forest Service assignments dried up completely.

The lull in temporary work couldn't have come at a better time. Matt's campaign to drum up interest in his ponies had started to pay off. Fifteen ranchers and eight rodeo cowboys had sent notice they planned to attend a fall auction at the 7-Bar-K. Encouraged, Matt buckled down to finish the ponies and get them in tip-top shape before the sale.

He was as nervous as a cat on auction day, both hopeful and scared. Pa had enlisted Al Jennings, his wife, Dolly, and Al Jr. to come over and lend a hand. They set up a long picnic table full of eats for guests to munch on, filled tubs of cool water with beer and soda pop, and spruced up the grounds, barn, and corral.

The Hightowers also came early and pitched in. Addie made a sweep through the house and gave it a lick and a promise while Earl helped Matt and Pa curry and brush the ponies until their coats glistened like fancy show horses'. Earl made an offer for a calico gelding he favored and Matt pulled the pony from the auction and sold it to him on the spot with a handshake.

Matt had hired Merlin Lane, the best auctioneer on the basin, to run the sale, and with luck, he'd wisecrack, joke, cajole, and browbeat the crowd into a buying frenzy. With his comedian's flair and rapid-fire bid calling, he'd put on an entertaining show. Dolly Jennings had volunteered to be Merlin's bid spotter, Pa would record the winning bids, and Al and Al Jr. would saddle and bring the ponies one by one to the corral.

Matt had decided on a scheme to put each pony through its paces so potential buyers could see what they were getting. He was nervous the ponies would do a better job of it than he could.

Fifteen minutes after the auctioneer arrived, a long line of cars and trucks came down the ranch road, throwing up dust. When the glad-handing and jawboning ended, the horseflesh had been looked over, the trays of food devoured, and the tubs of beer and soda pop emptied, it was time to start. More than fifty people congregated at the corral, where Merlin Lane, dressed in his pressed white shirt, string tie, and white cowboy hat, waited to start the proceedings.

Al Jr. brought out the first pony, and Matt's nervousness dissolved as he threw a leg over the saddle. He forgot about the rodeo cowboys with their fifty-dollar hats pushed back, the ranch managers and owners in their hand-tooled hundred-dollar boots, and everyone else who'd come just for the socializing and entertainment. All that mattered was the horse under him and what they would do together.

One by one he worked the ponies, showing off their speed and quick reactions, how they stopped, turned, and responded to commands. When the final gavel fell, he'd sold all but two, all for higher than hoped-for prices.

Hot, sweaty, and tired, Matt grinned from ear to ear as folks congratulated him and thanked him for his hospitality and such a fine horse show.

That night after everyone left, he sat with Pa and went over the proceeds. Combined with the 7-Bar-K share of profits from beef sold to area butchers and Matt's past earnings from his Forest Service work, the net gain from the auction put the ranch in the black, with a decent reserve.

"I'm gonna buy some breeding ponies and enlarge our cowherd," Matt announced.

"Ponies first, I reckon," Pa said.

"That's right," Matt said.

"You've done a helluva job," Pa said.

Matt put the paperwork aside. "If we can shake off a bit more of this drought, the outlook for next year might be just rosy."

"I wouldn't count on Mother Nature to oblige us," Pa said.

"We'll keep the belt cinched tight."

Pa nodded his approval.

"But not too tight," Matt added. "I'm hankering to do a little celebrating in town. Want to come along?"

Pa shook his head. "I'll stay put. I've got nowhere I need to go and no one I need to see. Besides, I'm at my best when I'm not around people all that much."

Matt laughed.

"What's funny?"

"I think you're finally getting a handle on yourself, old-timer," Matt replied.

Pa grumbled and stood. "I'm going to bed."

"Before you go, answer me one thing: Who is Pat Floyd?"

Pa glared at Matt before settling back down in his chair. "Damn, you're persistent; I'll give you that." He pressed his lips together before continuing. "I'm Pat Floyd."

"I figured as much. You don't have to say more, if you don't want to."

"What else do you want to know?"

"What happened to Vernon Clagett?"

"He was in Yuma Prison with me. The night of your ma's fiesta, he broke into my footlocker, found the pardon, and hid it. When I braced him about it, he tried to shoot me. I killed him dead with a ball-peen hammer and buried his body miles from here."

For a long minute Matt was speechless. "I'll be," he finally managed.

Pa got to his feet. "I told Jake Owen all about it and we went

together to the district attorney, who cleared me. Called it justi-
fied. Except for them two hombres and Tom Sullivan, you're the
only other person who knows. You got any more questions?"

"Why did Ma divorce you?"

Pa took a deep breath and paused before answering. "I didn't
figure you to ask that. It's none of your business. But it shames me
each time I think about it. Now I'm going to bed."

Thunderstruck, Matt stayed up late into the night, long-ago
memories whirling through his head.

* * *

A week before the auction, Matt had hired a man to smooth out
the ranch road with a grader and spread gravel where needed to
accommodate the folks traveling to the sale in their automobiles
and trucks. When the fellow came for his money, Matt was busy
with the ponies and sent Pa out to look the job over before paying.
Pa returned and reported that the road was much improved, so
Matt paid the man and thought no more about it. Riding Patches
over the road on his way to town, he was surprised by how much
better it was. It was in such good shape he thought maybe it was
time to get a truck. If he could find a good used one in Alamogordo
at the right price—maybe one that needed some work done to
it—he'd stay over in town for a day or two to fix it up and drive it
back to the ranch.

He decided to stable Patches at a livery in Tularosa and hitch a
ride to Alamogordo. If he wound up buying something, he'd hire
a stable boy to bring Patches back to the ranch.

As he loped Patches along, his thoughts turned to Porter Knox.
While they were currying the ponies before the auction, Earl
Hightower told him he'd heard Porter had abandoned his family

and left Tularosa. Evangelina and the children were back living with her parents. Word was that Knox had stolen the money from the camp to wager on cockfights held at an arena on a small farm near Three Rivers.

Matt wondered if he knocked on Flaviano and Cristina's door, would he be welcomed or turned away? Would they blame him for not turning a blind eye to Porter's wrongdoing? Would it matter if they knew how much it grieved him to bring ruin down on Evangelina, his own younger brother, and little María Teresa?

Matt hadn't seen anyone from the family since the day Knox had confessed to his crime at the Mayhill Camp. Surely they knew the part Matt had played in Porter's downfall. He decided not to visit the Armijos. He didn't owe them an explanation for what had happened. There was no way to explain doing your duty instead of not doing it.

The coming of dusk brought heavy clouds that darkened the sky early, but a short string of brand-new streetlights on Main Street, courtesy of a new federal program to bring electricity to rural places, cast a bright white glare that bounced off store windows and illuminated empty sidewalks. He settled Patches in at the livery and walked down Main Street to the filling station on the south side of town, which stayed open late to serve stray travelers passing through. He hunkered down on a stool by the soda pop cooler, hoping for a motorist to stop for gas so he could thumb a ride.

He got thinking it might be fun to show up at Anna Lynn's in a new truck and take her out to dinner in Alamogordo. Maybe surprise her with some chocolates as well. After dinner, they'd drive to White Sands National Monument and watch the moonrise over the dunes.

The sound of voices on the street drew Matt's attention. Four boys appeared, laughing and joking with each other in Spanish as they made a beeline for the soda pop cooler. One of them was Juan Ignacio, who stopped in his tracks as he drew near and glared at Matt. He was fifteen now and not a skinny kid anymore. He'd filled out in the chest some and towered over his companions.

Matt got to his feet as Juan approached. "Hello, *hermano.*"

"I ain't your brother," Juan said as he balled his fists and barreled into Matt, flailing wildly at him.

Slammed against the filling station wall, Matt wrapped Juan in a bear hug. "Jesus, calm down, little brother."

"Don't you call me that," Juan hissed. "You ruined everything."

Matt tightened his hold, eyeing Juan's three companions, who stood motionless, watching. "Porter did that, not me."

Juan struggled in Matt's grip. "We've got nothing now because of you."

"It wasn't me that did it," Matt reiterated. "If I let you go, can we talk?"

After a long minute Juan nodded.

Matt released his hold. Juan punched him in the eye and danced back out of reach, his face flushed with anger.

"Hit him again," one of Juan's buddies encouraged. His two companions hooted their approval.

"Don't try," Matt cautioned. The commotion brought the filling station attendant to the open bay door holding a large wrench in his hand.

Juan hesitated before dropping his fists to his sides. "I spit on you. Stay away from me and my family." He turned to his companions. "Let's go."

Quietly and in unison the boys backed away.

"Are you all right, mister?" the attendant asked.

Matt's watery eye started to swell. "Yeah, thanks."

Excited chatter and boisterous laugher from Juan and his buddies cut through the night air. Juan Ignacio paused and looked back at Matt one last time before disappearing into the darkness.

* * *

In the morning, Matt awoke in his Alamogordo hotel room with a beauty of a shiner and the sad memory of his encounter with Juan Ignacio. After breakfast, he did his banking and went looking for a truck from one end of town to the other, stopping at every garage and automobile dealership along the way. His black eye got a lot of attention, but no mention was made of it. A cowboy with a shiner was no rare sight.

He was halfway into his search when a helpful garage owner named Billy told Matt about some folks he knew who were trying to sell a truck he'd serviced for them since it was new. Billy vouched that the vehicle was in good shape.

He paid the owner a visit and struck a good deal for his 1934 Chevy half-ton pickup in need of a tune-up and a new starter. He drove it to Billy's garage and spent the remainder of the morning installing new spark plugs and a rebuilt starter and changing the oil and filter. He fired it up and let Billy take a look under the hood.

"You want a job?" Billy asked.

Matt laughed. "Nope, but thanks for the compliment." He paid his bill for the parts and the oil and drove the Chevy out of the garage.

On New York Avenue, he stopped and bought a box of fancy chocolates at a drugstore. At a nearby barbershop he got a shave and a haircut before heading out to Anna Lynn's farm.

He'd kept his hotel room for another night, hoping to entice

Anna Lynn back after dinner and a romantic moonlight stroll through the White Sands dunes. He glanced at his face in the truck's rearview mirror and had to laugh. There sure wasn't anything appealing about his battered mug. He hoped the idea of a night out would trump his bruised and beaten appearance.

He drove with the windows down and the wind blowing through the cab. The Chevy felt solid on the road. The engine hummed, with no worrisome rattles or shakes of the chassis. He turned off the pavement onto the gravel road that snaked up the foothills through High Rolls and Mountain Park, before the steep climb to Cloudcroft.

He was feeling good and his head had almost completely stopped aching. He couldn't think of a better way to celebrate his successful horse auction than in his new truck on a night out with his sweetheart.

At Anna Lynn's, Matt brought the truck to a stop and tooted the horn. He hopped out with the box of chocolates in hand, grinning in anticipation. She met him on the porch before he got halfway up the path, and she wasn't smiling.

"You can't come in," she said without emotion.

Matt's rush of good feelings evaporated. "Why not?"

Her face was a mask. "I'm seeing someone else now."

"Is he here with you?"

Anna Lynn shook her head. "No."

"Who is he?"

"You don't need to know."

"Tell me anyway."

"So you can go do something stupid?"

"That's not why I asked."

"What happened to your eye?"

"An angry kid punched me because his pa did something stupid."

"What did he do?"

"You don't need to know."

"You're angry."

"Hurt."

"I told you from the start who I am."

"Yeah, but it doesn't make it hurt less. Don't worry, I won't be a pest."

Anna Lynn's expression softened just a bit. "I wish you'd had more time for me, Matt."

"I didn't choose to be neglectful."

"I know that." She shrugged. "I wasn't criticizing."

Matt turned to leave.

"We can be friends," Anna Lynn offered.

Matt swiveled back to face her and placed the box of chocolates at her feet. "Adios, friend."

She stood rooted on the porch with her arms folded and didn't say another word.

He drove away thinking there are good times and there are bad times, and he'd just had both come tumbling down one after the other. He had nobody left now except Pa, who wasn't a damn bit good at being a paterfamilias. It took Matt most of the way back home to shake off feeling sorry for himself.

On his next trip to Alamogordo he learned that Anna Lynn's new lover was the High Rolls CCC camp commander, who could get to work in a jiffy whenever he stayed over. According to those citizens most interested in Anna Lynn's personal affairs, he was an overnight guest more often than not.

Matt worked hard at trying to be angry at her, but the fact that he missed her got in the way.

37

Matt returned from town with a Chevy pickup, a black eye, and a sour mood that hung around for a long time. He wouldn't talk to Patrick about what happened and he stayed close to home, going to town only once in two months for necessary business. All of his time and efforts went into the ranch, the ponies, and the cattle grazing in the high pastures. He seemed to want no company other than the companionship of the animals. Patrick let Matt alone. Sometimes silence was the best gift you could give a body who was hurting inside.

When it came time to restock groceries, supplies, and feed for the critters, Matt sent Patrick to town on the errand. In Tularosa, he learned about Matt's scuffle with Juan Ignacio, who'd accused Matt of getting Porter Knox fired from his job. In Alamogordo he ran into a fella from Mountain Park who told him that Matt's lady friend had thrown him over for another man, some army guy from a local CCC camp.

Patrick knew Matt had lost people close to him, especially Emma and that gal Beth he'd been sweet on. But what had happened to him in Tularosa and Mountain Park steamed Patrick. To be undone by some fickle, heartless floozy and assaulted by Juan Ignacio for something not Matt's fault was unfair. He had cause to sulk some, but Patrick didn't want him turning hard, mean, and suspicious. That had caused his own downfall with Emma and all his children. Matt deserved better.

As the end of the 1930s drew near, both the weather and the economy had improved a mite. Not enough to cause unbridled optimism—no rancher ever felt that secure about the future—but enough to hold out some hope for a few more profitable years. In the spring of 1939, Matt held another successful pony auction. In the summer he sold six geldings to the army boys from Fort Bliss who unexpectedly showed up and liked what they saw. At the end of fall works, they realized a nice increase in beef prices. As a result, the ranch was on the way to the best year since the stock market crash of '29.

Patrick was proud of what his son had accomplished and told him so, but Matt quickly brushed the compliment aside. Matt had stopped being sulky and sour in favor of acting brusque and fretful. It showed in the permanent furrow etched across his forehead and the downturn in his mouth caused by the lack of a smile.

The ranch still had no electricity or telephone or even a promise from public officials that those utilities would come to the Tularosa Basin anytime soon. But when regular air delivery of the Albuquerque newspaper to El Paso, Las Cruces, and a few other towns started, Matt paid the pilot to drop a copy of the Sunday edition in a paper bag when he flew over the ranch headquarters. Much to their dismay, the paper sometimes wound up in the water trough, unreadable. But it quickly became a Sunday ritual for the two men to settle down after chores and read the paper together over a fresh pot of coffee.

The headline for September 3, 1939, read:

BRITAIN, FRANCE DECLARE
WAR ON GERMANY!

The lead story described Germany's massive invasion of Poland early on a Friday morning and the stunning retreat of the Polish Army across wide stretches of the country.

"We'll be in it for sure," Patrick predicted, his bad leg elevated by a cushion on top of a crate in front of the couch, his coffee cup within handy reach on a side table.

"Roosevelt says we're staying neutral and out of it," Matt countered from behind the desk.

"That's not gonna happen. We'll be in the thick of it soon enough. When the drums start beating, stay out of it if you can."

"I'll serve if called," Matt replied, thinking of CJ.

"You'll be called up, bet on it. But you don't have to prove anything to me. I'm not partial to the idea of you getting shot or worse."

"You served in Cuba and CJ was in the last war."

"Yep, and I got wounded and CJ got dead. That ought to tell you something about how god-awful war is."

"You'd worry about me if I went?" Matt asked, somewhat surprised.

"And then some," Patrick replied. "Besides, who'd look after the ranch and the ponies? I'm too old and crippled to handle it all by myself."

"Well, it's nothing we have to worry about right away."

"Still, you think on it. The army's gonna need beef, and a lot of it, once our part in the shooting war starts. A cattleman who helps feed an army is just as important as a soldier in the trenches."

"I never figured you to be a pacifist."

Patrick guffawed. "I ain't. But sane men don't start wars; politicians and dictators do. And it's always because they want something that doesn't belong to them, no matter how many big words they use to pretty it up."

"I take it back; you're unpatriotic."

Patrick grinned, showing his set of perfect false teeth. "That's a helluva thing to say to an old war veteran."

* * *

Over the course of the next year, the welcome arrival of more moisture and the gathering promise of war improved the price of beef enough to allow Matt to put more cattle on the high pastures. The 7-Bar-K finished up fall works in the black once again. On September 7, 1940, when the Nazis started bombing London, Matt figured it was only a matter of time before America entered the war. Nine days later, Congress passed the Selective Service Act, requiring all men between the ages of twenty-one and thirty-five to register for the draft, and he was sure of it.

In spite of Pa's advice to stay out of the fighting if he could, Matt decided to serve when his time came. He registered and was given a II-C deferment by his draft board because of his occupation as an agriculture producer. With the country still at peace, he decided to take the deferment until he could find a way to keep the ranch operating and Pa looked after while he was in uniform.

In November, he took off for the high-country pasture trailing a packhorse loaded with cabin supplies, with plans to stay up-country to fix fences, cut cordwood for the cabin, do maintenance on the dirt tanks, and patch the cabin roof. He told Pa he'd be gone two, maybe three weeks but didn't say he first planned to slip

over to the Rocking J to propose a scheme to Al Jennings and his
family.

He made good time to the cabin and got the supplies put away
and the ponies fed and bedded down in the corral. He patched the
roof, lit the stove, and fixed supper. After a good night's sleep, he
saddled Patches and started a leisurely ride in the chill of a crisp,
clear autumn morning over the mountain to the Jennings spread.

He always enjoyed visiting the Rocking J, sheltered as it was in
a pretty forest meadow with a view through the pines of the Jornada, vast and seemingly empty. The squat wooden windmill next
to the water tank greeted him with a slow creak in a light breeze.
The small stone and mud-plastered adobe ranch house, surrounded by a fence to keep out grazing ponies and their droppings, looked as though it had been fixed to the land forever.
Smoke lazed up from the chimney. Under the shade of the porch
Matt could see Al Jennings in his favorite chair, watching his approach.

"Light," Al said. "Now that morning chores are done, Dolly has
brewed up a fresh pot."

Matt slid down and Patches trotted away for a drink from the
water tank. "I'm obliged."

"What brings you visiting so early in the day?"

"I've got an idea in my head that needs explaining to you, Dolly,
Al Jr., and his new bride, if you'll kindly hear me out."

Grinning, Al rose from his chair. "We're always interested in
what the Kerney menfolk are scheming. Come on inside and we'll
make a powwow."

The front of the ranch house consisted of the kitchen and a
small parlor with a fireplace. There was just enough room for six
people to squeeze around the kitchen table for a meal, and the
small parlor could accommodate the same number if two stayed

standing. To the rear were two tiny bedrooms, barely large enough to turn around in. The house had sufficed for Al, Dolly, and Al Jr., but with the arrival of Brenda Jennings, formerly Brenda Cowen of Hot Springs, the place was downright crowded.

Matt had danced with Brenda at her wedding reception in Hot Springs after drinking a whiskey to celebrate with Al Jr. outside the church reception hall. She was a calm, hefty gal with broad features and a warm smile who always brought the word *comfortable* to Matt's mind.

Al jokingly assembled his family at the kitchen table by announcing that Matt had asked to waste everyone's time to talk about some harebrained scheme. Dolly brought cups and the coffeepot to the table and they made small talk for a sip or two until Al Sr. ordered Matt to get on with it.

He smiled and took another sip. Nine months ago, Al Jr., who was a year younger than Matt, had severed his left thumb and forefinger in a roping contest with a half-wild stray bull. As a consequence, he'd been classified as physically unfit for military service by the draft board. Making no mention of those facts, Matt quickly proposed to hire Al Jr. as the 7-Bar-K ranch manager, effective the first of the year. He explained that he needed to give his full attention to the ponies and wanted to increase the herd in their cattle-raising partnership. With the grasses coming back, both spreads could put more land into use. That meant more time would be needed to throw cows onto fresh pastures. Also, he needed someone to take over most of Pa's chores now that he was slowing down on a bad leg that would never get any better.

"I want Al Jr. as my ranch manager above anyone else," Matt said. "He knows horses, cattle, and how to run a spread. And I'll pay a fair wage and provide housing."

He turned to Brenda. "The casita will be yours." She'd swooned over it during a visit to the 7-Bar-K. "And you'll earn housekeeper wages for looking after Patrick. He's not that much of a bother."

Brenda beamed at Matt, grabbed Al Jr.'s hand, and squeezed it.

"Do I get to manage the ranch as I see fit?" Al Jr. asked.

"We'll do it together when I'm there," Matt replied. "When I'm away, you'll have full authority over all ranch business."

Matt glanced at Al Sr. and Dolly. "Think of it as another partnership between our two families. Al Jr. can help out at the Rocking J as much as needed. We can share costs and cut our expenses. When necessary, we'll hire hands to work both spreads during spring and fall works. If we do this together, we'll be more efficient."

"And we'd be right next door," Al Jr. said, looking directly at his ma. "One spread over."

"I know," Dolly said with a sad, accepting smile.

"Are you planning to go marching off to war when we get pulled into it?" Al Sr. asked Matt.

"No, sir, at least not right away," Matt replied solemnly. "But if I do, I know things will be taken care of and looked after."

"I'd go if I could," Al Jr. said softly.

"Thank God you don't have to," Brenda said.

"Yes, thank God," Dolly whispered.

"Do we have an agreement?" Matt asked, directing the question to Al Sr.

Al Sr. nodded his consent.

"I'm obliged," Matt said. "Let's get started by the first of the year."

"That's perfect," Dolly said as she poured another round of coffee.

* * *

Matt spent the next three weeks at the cabin, riding fence lines, tending to the dirt tanks, cutting firewood, and repairing the two windmills that supplied reliable water for livestock in the spring and summer and wildlife in the winter. He saw plenty of deer and coyote tracks and a few wolf prints, but no sign of bear. Some San Andres ranchers were of a mind to believe that all the black bears in the mountains had been wiped out. Al Jennings had heard the last bear had been taken by a hunter two years back. Matt had seen no fresh sign for more than a year and didn't doubt it. But if the black bears were gone, it was a sad prospect.

He left the cabin feeling peaceful, content, and eager for the future. Although he wasn't sure how it had happened, his broken spirit had been mended.

Back at the ranch, he sat Patrick down and told him what he'd done and why.

"Now's the time to throw more cattle on the land," Patrick agreed. "Last Sunday's newspaper had a story about rising cattle prices because of shortages and rationing in England. The same thing happened in the Great War."

"Al Jr. and Brenda will move over here the first of the year," Matt said.

"Are you gonna be bullheaded and join up?" Patrick asked, scowling.

Matt shrugged. "I'm not sure."

"When are you gonna do it?" Patrick prodded.

"I don't know," Matt replied pointedly.

"I hate to think the day might come when there's no Kerney living on the ranch."

"That day will come one way or another, I reckon," Matt rebutted.

"Not in my lifetime, I hope."

"Nor mine, if I can help it," Matt added. "Al Jr. and Brenda will do right by us."

Pa nodded. "We couldn't do better." He handed Matt a letter from the side table. "This came while you were gone."

It was a letter from Anna Lynn asking him to visit her on his next trip to town.

"From that woman?" Pa asked harshly.

Matt nodded. "She wants me to stop by and see her."

"What for?"

"She doesn't say."

"Are you gonna do it?"

Matt tapped the letter against his lips. In one way he was over her; in another way, not. When he thought about her now, it was more a vague, pleasant memory. "I just might," he mused.

"A smart critter doesn't put his paw in the same trap twice," Pa philosophized.

"That wasn't quite what I was thinking," Matt replied.

* * *

Matt debated hard if it would be wise to visit Anna Lynn. He kept putting off a decision. Two weeks before Christmas, on his way to Alamogordo, he impulsively turned onto the Cloudcroft Road and pulled to a stop in front of Anna Lynn's Mountain Park farmhouse. It was shirtsleeve weather, with a bright sun and calm winds. On the front porch a little girl no more than two looked at him from the back of a small wooden rocking horse and called out for her ma. Anna Lynn appeared, stepped off the porch, and greeted him with a smile.

"I didn't think you'd come to see me." She'd aged some, but she was still mighty handsome, and the spark in her eye looked as fiery as ever.

"I almost didn't." Matt studied the little girl from the cab of his truck, unsure if he should stay or drive away. "What's her name?"

"Virginia, but I call her Ginny," Anna Lynn said as she stepped to the open truck window. "She's just now eighteen months old."

He killed the engine. "Are you married?"

Anna Lynn laughed and leaned against the truck door. "Heavens no."

"Where's her father?"

"He's a lieutenant in the army on active duty now."

"Is he the guy who ran the High Rolls Camp?"

Anna Lynn nodded.

"He didn't want to marry you?"

"He was already married. Does that shock you?"

"Nope."

"Come in for coffee."

"I'd like that."

Anna Lynn's kitchen looked the same, everything clean and tidy, without a lot of frill. A shelf over the counter was crammed with bottles and canisters of spices and herbs from her garden. The shelf above held her home-harvested honey in quart jars.

Little Ginny was a charmer. Before the coffee was served, she'd crawled onto Matt's lap clutching paper and crayons, asking him to draw a picture for her. He did a stick-figure cowboy twirling a lasso and sitting on a silly-looking pony. It met with her approval, although she added a sun with rays shooting out of it for a finishing touch. She had the same inquisitive, intelligent look about her as her ma, right down to tilting her head the same way when she asked a question.

Coffee segued into a tasty supper of chicken potpie topped with enjoyable conversation. Afterward, with the dirty dishes stacked in the sink, he had a pleasant time helping Anna Lynn get Ginny ready for bed. When she was all tucked in, they returned to the kitchen and sat quietly in soft lamplight, Matt remembering other nights after dinner with Anna Lynn that had begun the same way.

"You'd make a fine father," Anna Lynn announced.

"Are you looking to recruit one?"

She smiled sweetly. "No, thank you."

"I didn't think so. Do you like being a mother?"

Anna Lynn sighed contentedly. "Oh, yes, I was made for it. I should have found my calling sooner and had six more."

"Ah, so it's potential sires you're looking for," Matt proposed.

Anna Lynn shook her head. "No, at my age you need have no fear of that. I was lucky to have had my beautiful little girl."

Matt pushed back from the table. "I best be on my way."

Anna Lynn reached for his hand. "Stay the night."

"Doesn't that violate your one-lover-at-a-time rule?"

"I'll never break that rule. Will you stay?"

"Only on one condition."

"Which is?"

"I want you to promise to give me more notice the next time you plan to throw me over for someone else."

"Hm," Anna Lynn said, her hand caressing his chest. "I agree to your terms, but I may not ever want to do that again."

It wasn't until late afternoon the next day that Matthew Kerney left Anna Lynn's house, with a promise to return the next weekend. Never had he felt better, leastways not in a very long time. It was as though cobwebs had been dusted from his head. He decided making love to a beautiful woman who truly enjoyed it was about the best experience a man could ever have. And it sure had a positive effect on one's outlook.

The Bill Mauldin sketch of Matt still hung in Anna Lynn's bedroom; she'd never taken it down. He drove the highway with a smile on his face, vowing to simply enjoy Anna Lynn's company for however long it lasted.

38

The following Sunday morning, Matt looked out the window of Anna Lynn's bedroom and saw a brilliant sunrise. It looked like they were in for a mild, sunny day. He turned back over in bed toward Anna Lynn, who regarded him with a thoughtful smile.

Matt smiled back at her and said, "How about we have an early breakfast and take Ginny for a picnic at White Sands?"

"That's a wonderful idea," Anna Lynn said. "But let's not rush ourselves." She reached over, cupped her hand behind Matt's neck, and pulled him to her for a kiss.

After what was still an early breakfast, all things considered, they packed a light lunch, got in Matt's truck, Ginny sitting on Anna Lynn's lap, and headed down to the basin.

For many years the old wagon road between Tularosa and Las Cruces skirted the untouched gypsum sand dunes that stretched deep into the basin. Now a modern highway ran from Alamogordo past the dunes all the way to the Arizona state line. Where once there had been nothing more than a sign announcing that motorists were entering White Sands National Monument, now there was a modern pueblo-style National Park Service headquarters building at the entrance.

After they'd toured the small museum in the building, Matt drove the loop road into the heart of the monument. Huge, crescent-shaped dunes, some forty feet high, drifted slowly northeast, pushed along by prevailing winds.

As soon as he stopped the truck, Ginny was out in a flash, running up the nearest dune, with Matt and Anna Lynn on her heels. Halfway to the top, her little legs churning in the soft sand, Ginny lifted her arms in a signal to be carried. Matt hoisted her on his shoulders and waded to the crest. They looked out on a sea of sand rolling to a distant ridgeline of serrated dunes that edged against the Alkali Flats.

"Isn't this marvelous?" Anna Lynn said. "How beautiful."

"Put me down," Ginny commanded, unimpressed with the view. As soon as her feet touched the sand, she plopped on her tummy and rolled down the back side of the dune, giggling all the way.

Matt pointed at the San Andres Mountains, which dominated the western horizon, bleak and foreboding to the naked eye. "You can almost see the 7-Bar-K from here."

"I would love to see it up close," Anna Lynn replied.

"You would?" It had never entered Matt's mind that she would want to visit the ranch.

"Yes, I would, very much."

"Well, sure you can," he said, pleased by the notion, wondering why it hadn't occurred to him.

"When?" Anna Lynn asked.

"Whenever you want."

Ginny crawled back up the dune to where they stood, her face a mask of powdery, glistening sand. Anna Lynn knelt to brush the gypsum from her face and hands. "You're a mess, young lady."

"Am not." Ginny pushed Anna Lynn's hand away and rolled down the dune again.

"Today," Anna Lynn said, rising.

"What?"

"I'd like to visit your ranch today."

"It's a far piece to travel, and I haven't laid in any supplies for company."

"Can we go? Yes or no?" Anna Lynn asked.

"Can you be gone from your place overnight?" Matt countered.

Anna Lynn nodded. "The Forest Service has moved their ponies to Deming for the winter, my hives are dormant, and my garden is fallow. Yes or no?"

"Yes."

Anna Lynn clapped her hands. "Goody. We'll buy groceries in town, pack what Ginny and I need at home, and be on our way," she said in a rush. "How long can we stay?"

"As long as you like."

"Don't tempt me," Anna Lynn said jokingly. She jumped feet-first off the crest of the dune and rolled to where Ginny waited, half buried, pouring sand through her fingers into her hair. She pulled Ginny onto her lap and blew Matt a kiss. "This is so much fun. Let's eat and go for a short hike. There are some plants in the dunes I've never seen before."

"Yes, ma'am," Matt said, marveling at how she seemed to have shed twenty years.

* * *

The few ranches Anna Lynn had seen on the Tularosa were bitter, lonely places, tenuous and grim at best. On their drive to the 7-Bar-K, she questioned Matt about the ranch. He spoke of it proudly but without much detail, saying it sat on a nice slice of land with some pretty high-country pastures and views. His comments made her worry about what to expect. Perhaps the whole idea of visiting the ranch had been a big mistake. The fact that Matt was different—in some ways sweeter, in some ways smarter—from any other man she'd allowed into her life didn't necessarily mean he gave a thought to how he lived. Not many bachelors did. She hoped she wouldn't take one look at the ranch and immediately want to be driven home.

Upon their arrival, she almost sighed aloud in relief. Matt's description didn't do the ranch justice. Anna Lynn marveled at how the ranch house was perched on a ledge, perfectly positioned with the broad shoulders of guardian foothills as a backdrop, looking out on a landlocked expanse of desert. The view was splashed in snowy white, ebony black, and gunmetal gray under wispy tendril clouds floating in an azure sky. The land was veined by wide arroyos ringed by massive island mountains springing up to the heavens. Anna Lynn doubted a lovelier, more picture-perfect location existed on the Tularosa.

She spun around slowly to take it all in. The ranch house with its wide veranda, the casita with its thick adobe walls, the sturdy, weathered barn, the windmill and stock tank, were all in scale and harmonious. The large corral with the pasture beyond where a herd of pretty horses idled looked idyllic. She wondered how many men's and women's hands had shaped the 7-Bar-K over the years.

"It's heavenly," she said, her arms cradling Ginny, who wiggled to get down.

Matt unloaded her bags from the bed of the Chevy. "You've hardly seen the place yet."

"Ponies," Ginny screeched, pointing.

Anna Lynn released her and she raced to the fence for a closer look at the faraway ponies. "I should have known it would be this lovely."

"Why do you say that?"

She rested her head on his chest. "Because of who you are."

Matt wrapped an arm around her. "I've never heard you gush like this before."

Anna Lynn laughed. "True, you've caught me fair and square. Unhand me and show me to our quarters."

She ran to Ginny, caught her up, and followed Matt to the casita. She laughed with delight when he opened the door and sunlight cascaded on a parlor wall filled with Billy Mauldin's sketches.

"You've kept them all," she said, delighted.

"I thought you knew I was a connoisseur of fine art," Matt said as he put the luggage on the floor. "Make yourself at home while I unload the victuals. Tonight, I'm doing the cooking. Over supper, I'll tell you the story of Ignacio Chávez from the village of Tularosa, a wounded veteran of the Apache Wars, who built this casita for his bride-to-be with only one good arm."

"It's a love story?"

Matt grinned. "*Sí*, of the very best kind."

"I can't wait to hear it." Anna Lynn looked through the open bedroom door. "Where will you be sleeping?"

"Here, with you. I'll fashion a bed for Ginny in the parlor and we'll leave the bedroom door open."

Anna Lynn smiled. "Oh, you do know how to please a lady."

Ginny tugged hard at her mother's hand. "Ponies," she cooed. "Let's go see the ponies."

"Give me a minute and I'll get old Stony from the barn and we'll give you a ride on him."

Ginny stomped her feet in glee.

* * *

Anna Lynn and Ginny stayed at the 7-Bar-K Ranch for five glorious days. Every day, either by truck or on horseback, Matt showed them his ranch and the rugged San Andres Mountains. They traveled hidden canyons, high pasturelands, wide mesas, and forested mountaintops. He took them to the malpais, into the secluded Oscura Mountains, to the secret springs in Hembrillo Canyon, where the Apache chief Victorio and his braves gave a big shellacking to the horse soldiers during the Indian Wars. They spent two nights in the remote cabin on the 7-Bar-K high pasture, snug and warm on their last night after a surprise snowstorm draped a pristine white blanket over the highest peaks.

Matt's warning to Anna Lynn that his father would probably be grumpy and reclusive didn't hold true. For some unknown and unexplainable reason, little Ginny took to Patrick Kerney the instant they met. She pestered him endlessly while in his company, wanting to sit on his lap, asking him to pick her up, following him around the ranch house and the barn, and begging him over and over to let her ride Stony.

Much to Matt's amazement, Patrick willingly obliged the little girl. Patrick further confounded Matt by showing uncharacteristically good humor in Anna Lynn's company, telling her stories about the ranch and the old days. One afternoon, Patrick took Anna Lynn and Ginny to the family cemetery on the hill, where he told them about the people buried there and CJ lying with his fallen comrades in France. Anna Lynn impulsively hugged him when he finished, and Patrick didn't even flinch.

On the drive home to Mountain Park, Anna Lynn thought how perfect it would be if she and Matt could visit back and forth at the ranch or the farm whenever they wished. As she watched Matt drive away, the memory of their lovemaking every night at the ranch gave her a little shiver. More of that was certainly in order.

Matt returned from carrying Anna Lynn and Ginny home to find Pa outside the barn waiting for him.

"That woman and her little girl are real good medicine for you," Patrick said.

"But not for you?" Matt asked with a laugh.

"Both of us, I reckon," Patrick admitted. "She reminds me of Emma in a way."

"You think so?"

"I do. A touch more tame, I reckon. Or less tame; I'm not sure which."

Matt waited for more elaboration, but Pa fell silent and clomped into the barn, pitchfork in hand.

* * *

Anna Lynn and Ginny returned to the 7-Bar-K four more times in the spring and summer of 1941. Matt made an equal number of visits to Anna Lynn's farm, staying over on long weekends.

The addition of Al Jr. and Brenda to the ranch didn't cause a problem. Matt just moved Anna Lynn into his old bedroom in the ranch house and set up Ginny's bed in the living room right outside the bedroom door.

If Al Jr. and Brenda thought Matt and Anna Lynn's affair was scandalous, they didn't say a word about it or show any disapproval. Brenda clearly enjoyed Anna Lynn's company, and Al Jr. treated her like a lady. Ginny never wanted to leave the ranch or Patrick, who spoiled her like she was his granddaughter. He was teaching her to ride on Stony with her very own saddle, which he'd given her as a present.

After fall works and another successful pony auction, Matt and Anna Lynn had more time together. They trekked to the high-country cabin or burrowed in at the farm, where they spent blissful days forgetting half the world was at war.

On Sunday, December 7, they were at the farm listening to music on the radio when an announcer interrupted to report that the Japanese had attacked Pearl Harbor in Hawaii. The news sucked the breath right out of them.

"You're going to war; I just know it," she said, clutching his hand across the kitchen table.

Matt nodded grimly as he turned off the radio.

"When?" Anna Lynn asked.

"I don't know. But I'm not all that eager to get shot at."

"Why go at all if you don't have to?"

"I'm not quite clear about it in my own mind," Matt said. "It has to do with not embarrassing myself and standing up for my country. I've never been wildly patriotic, but I wouldn't want to live anywhere else."

Anna Lynn shook her head. "Men."

Matt smiled. "When I do go, you've got to promise not to wait for me."

Anna Lynn's eyes widened. "Why did you say that?" she demanded.

"Because I don't want to get a Dear John letter while I'm gone."

Anna Lynn slipped out of her chair and into his lap. "I've always favored a man in uniform," she said gaily. "I may not throw you over."

"It's your nature; you told me so."

Anna Lynn shook her head. "We don't have to talk about something that hasn't happened—might *never* happen—do we?"

Matt smiled and squeezed her close. "It's okay by me to change the subject. Let's be happy while we can."

"I like that idea," Anna Lynn said, wondering how long happiness could last for anybody with the world at war.

* * *

Nineteen forty-two began with bad news from the war on the front page of every Sunday edition of the Albuquerque newspaper. The Allies fighting Field Marshal Rommel in North Africa were getting mauled. Singapore fell, and the British forces there surrendered to the Japanese. In the North Atlantic, German U-boats were torpedoing massive amounts of shipping bound for Great Britain. Washington imposed mandatory nighttime blackouts along portions of the Eastern Seaboard. In the Mediterranean, a British fleet got stung by the German Nazis and Italian Fascists. After Singapore, the Japs took Burma, Mandalay, and Rangoon, rolling up tens of thousands of Allied soldiers as prisoners of war, massacring countless civilians, and leveling cities, towns, and villages along the way.

The hardest blow to bear in New Mexico was the surrender of Bataan and Corregidor in the Philippines in April and May. The 200th Coast Artillery Regiment, which counted hundreds of New Mexico boys in its ranks, had trained at Fort Bliss and shipped overseas less than three months before Pearl Harbor. Many were reported killed, missing in action, or taken prisoner.

Soon after, the Albuquerque paper published a list of the men killed in action; it included Lieutenant James Hurley, Ginny's father, who had been awarded the Purple Heart posthumously. A photograph showed Hurley's grieving widow and his three children receiving the decoration from an army officer. The accompanying article reported that Mrs. Hurley would receive a widow's pension and monthly benefits for her children totaling eighty-five dollars, as well as the monthly proceeds from a ten-thousand-dollar life insurance policy.

Ginny, born out of wedlock, unrecognized by both her father and the government, got nothing. Matt thought it unfair, but Anna Lynn was unperturbed. She'd always expected to raise Ginny on her own, without help from anybody.

Good news from the front came in June with a decisive American naval victory over the Japanese at the Battle of Midway. But it wasn't enough to lift a persistent gloom created by a war now encircling the globe.

Through all this the 7-Bar-K thrived. The War Department bought cattle, and the army wanted replacement ponies. Rains had come in record amounts, greening up the pasturelands. Matt bought cattle to fatten for market and sold all the ponies except his breeding stock. He took a close look at his land after fall works. With good browse for another year, he immediately started replenishing his stock. Agricultural commodities were exempted under the new price-stabilization law, and when shortages and rationing began, the price of beef would go even higher.

In October 1942, Matt sat down and wrote out a plan for the 7-Bar-K of what he hoped to accomplish over the next few years. Indoor plumbing, a bathroom, and electricity were at the top of the list. He wanted several ranch roads built to handle truck traffic and two good work trucks to get around on the spread more quickly. If the money was there, a garage with automotive tools and spare parts and a gasoline storage tank to fuel his trucks would give him greater independence. Last on his list was the luxury of a new hay barn.

Not knowing exactly what the next few years would bring, he wasn't sure that much of his wish list was realistic. He sat down with Patrick and Al Jr. for a confab and went over the plan with them. Al Jr. suggested replacing some old stock tanks and Pa argued that some new fencing was needed.

Matt added the items, handed the list to Al Jr., and said, "That's a hefty list. See what you can get done."

Al Jr. looked sharply at Matt. "You're gonna enlist, aren't you?"

"Yep, after the holidays."

"Damn fool," Patrick grumbled. "Does Anna Lynn know?"

"She will this weekend. I'm going to ask her and Ginny to spend Christmas and New Year's at the ranch. We'll get a Christmas tree up, put a roast in the oven, have some presents under the tree, and make the old homestead look festive. In fact, I'd like to have a real shindig and invite our neighbors over to celebrate the New Year."

"Sounds like you're throwing a good-bye party for yourself," Patrick groused.

"And why not?" Matt countered with a smile.

Patrick grinned. "I ain't opposed to it, really."

"Brenda will love it!" Al Jr. said, pushing back from the table.

Matt stood. "If there's no other business, the meeting is adjourned."

* * *

On Saturday night at the farmhouse, after Ginny was tucked in and asleep, Matt told Anna Lynn of his decision to enlist in the New Year. She fell silent and got busy tidying up the kitchen. When she finished and returned to the parlor, she sat quietly in her favorite chair and began reading, her spectacles perched on her nose.

"Aren't you going to say anything?" Matt asked in frustration from the davenport.

Anna Lynn looked over the rims of her glasses at him. "What for? Your mind is made up, isn't it? What branch of the service have you chosen?"

"The army. I'm not much of a swimmer. I've been thinking you should marry me."

She took off her glasses and stared at him. "If I didn't care so much about you, I'd ask you to leave my house right now."

"Hear me out. I figure we get married and I claim Ginny as my own. If I don't come back, you get a pension and a little bit of extra money for her."

Anna Lynn's stare turned into a glare. "Absolutely not. I will not profit from your death. I'd feel responsible if something happened to you. It's a terrible idea."

"It wouldn't be your fault."

She shook her head. "I know what you offered comes from the heart, but I never want to discuss this with you again."

Defeated, Matt rubbed his chin and looked away. Finally he said, "Okay, how about spending Christmas and New Year's at the ranch? We'll do the whole shebang: a Christmas tree, presents, a big roast in the oven, and a holiday shindig with friends and neighbors. We can celebrate the good fortune and good times we've had together."

Anna Lynn's glare melted. She rose and joined him on the davenport. "That's a wonderful idea. How can a man as sweet as you want to go to war?"

Matt shrugged. "I've tried to talk myself out of enlisting. So has Pa, who got shot pretty bad in Cuba."

Anna Lynn sighed. "I suppose there is no easy answer." She reached for his hand. "Take me for a moonlight walk. We'll bundle up, look at the stars, and pretend the world is at peace."

They strolled past the corral and up the canyon. On the basin below, the lights of Alamogordo, a short distance away, winked in the night. To the west of the town, they could see the lights of the new Alamogordo army air field, soon to become operational, with aprons, runways, taxiways, and hangars already built.

Although they didn't speak of it, both knew that when the army planes started flying, the reality of the war, no matter how far away it was for now, would change the Tularosa forever.

39

In January 1943, Matt enlisted and was promptly sent for basic training at Camp Hood, a new army base in central Texas, outside of Killeen and south of Waco. At thirty, he was the oldest member of his basic training company. Soon everyone started calling him Pops, and the moniker stuck.

There were tens of thousands of soldiers in basic training at the camp, but it wasn't much different from the CCC camps, just put together on a much grander scale. His training unit was one of dozens with barracks, a company HQ, rec halls, and mess halls arranged in the same layout as the Forest Service camps he'd inspected for Hubert Roddy.

At first, he worried he might not hold his own with all the young bucks. But by his second week it was clear that many of the guys were having trouble keeping up with him. Used to getting up before dawn and working long past sunset, he was in better shape than most of the eighteen- and nineteen-year-olds. In physical training he lagged only in the runs, although he managed to stay in the middle of the pack. As the days passed, he picked up speed and stamina and started closing in on the front-runners.

At the start of third week of basic, Matt was ordered to report to the first sergeant. His platoon leader had recommended him to be an acting squad leader. He was given an armband with two stripes to wear to show his acting rank. As soon as he got back to the barracks, he got razzed for being an apple-polisher.

It was winter in Texas, but it felt more like a hot, steamy spring, with temperatures hitting the low eighties. The days were mostly humid, and Matt didn't enjoy the mugginess. It sucked the energy out of him.

While it was greener than home, with more trees in the lowlands, the absence of mountains seemed unnatural to his eye. The creek bottoms were pretty and the grass more lush, but the land didn't grab Matt's attention like the Tularosa did.

The camp had a newspaper, *The Hood Panther,* and one issue featured a story about how the camp of more than two hundred thousand acres had been created almost overnight by moving more than three hundred families off their land and demolishing the small towns of Clear Creek, Elijah, and Antelope. Although the article trumpeted the willing war sacrifices made by the displaced farm and ranch families, Matt figured there had to be another side to the story. He didn't think folks whose families had been on the land since the days of the Texas Republic were overjoyed to give up all they'd worked for over the years. He wondered if any of them had dug in their heels and tried to stay put. Knowing country folk, he didn't doubt it.

On the rifle range, Matt qualified as expert with the M1 rifle, the carbine, and the .45 semiautomatic. A few other country boys who'd grown up squirrel hunting did the same, but all together they formed a small, elite group of five men in the entire company. Even with the temporary rank of acting squad leader, Matt wasn't immune to KP, a duty universally hated by all, but he pulled it without complaint, as he did guard and latrine duty.

Three days before graduation and a day after the company completed a twenty-mile forced march with a full pack, weapons, and gear, Matt was ordered to the company HQ. He dragged his weary, sore feet into the XO's office, snapped to attention, and saluted.

Lieutenant Fultz consulted the papers on his desk. "Private Kerney, you have one year of college and speak fluent Spanish. Is that correct?"

"Yes, sir."

"You've been selected for admission to the Army Specialized Training Program."

"I never heard of it, sir," Matt said.

"Now you have. You get to go to school courtesy of the army," Lieutenant Fultz said with a slight sneer. "I've been told it's easy duty, Private."

"What kind of school is it, sir?" Matt asked.

The lieutenant paged through the paperwork in front of him. "You're going to learn Italian at a college in Massachusetts, Amherst."

"Why Italian, sir?"

Fultz stared at Matthew. "Because that's what the army wants you to do, Private. Your orders come with a priority flag, which means somebody somewhere thinks this is important. Because you're already fluent in Spanish, you'll be in an advanced, accelerated class. There's a booklet in your orders that describes the program."

"Can I turn these orders down, sir?" Matt asked. "I'd like to stay with the outfit."

"No, you cannot." Fultz handed Matt the paperwork. "You are ordered to report to your new detachment immediately. Your travel orders are inside. You don't get any leave to go home. But buck up. I've been told if you finish the program, you'll be in line for a commission. You just might get to sit out the war at some stateside desk job."

"I didn't enlist for this, sir," Matt said.

"I don't like it myself," Fultz replied. "You've the makings of a good noncom."

Matt scanned his travel orders. "Excuse me, sir, these orders show my rank as private first class."

Fultz grinned. "You've been promoted by the CO for finishing basic at the top of your class." He shook Matt's hand. "Congratulations, Pops. Get those stripes sewn on your uniform before you clear the post."

"Yes, sir," Matt said, executing a perfect hand salute.

Matt took his promotion orders to the PX, bought stripes for his uniforms, returned to the empty barracks, and started sewing. By the time the platoon returned from a tactical field exercise on the obstacle course, Matt was packed, in uniform, and ready to go. His squad gathered around and cheered him out the door, while across the quadrangle, the company commander; the XO, Lieutenant Fultz; and the first sergeant stood outside the company HQ watching. Matt stopped, saluted, and moved out smartly to the camp personnel hut, wondering what he would find at Amherst College in Amherst, Massachusetts.

* * *

Matt sat in his college dormitory room at the small study desk beneath a window that looked out on a campus covered in a thick blanket of snow. Located on a hill, the college was postcard pretty. From his room he could see Pratt Quad, with a view of the statue of one of the college's founders, Noah Webster. It was a blustery late afternoon, with only a few students crossing the quad in a hurry to get out of the cold.

After the barracks at Camp Hood, Matt's dorm room was pure luxury. He shared it with one roommate, and it was warm and cozy as opposed to cold and drafty. And the showers down the hall had both hot and cold water.

He was three weeks into the program, grinding away twelve hours a day with classes and homework, his head filled with a jumble of Italian conjugations, pronouns, adjectives, and common phrases. The work was so demanding, three students had already failed to make the cut and been sent off for advanced infantry training.

He closed his book, rubbed his eyes, and reached for paper and pen. He'd written Anna Lynn only once since leaving home, a short letter from Camp Hood telling her where he was and that he was all right. She'd not written back. He wondered if she might have already moved on to someone else.

He stared at the blank piece of paper, decided to write again, and began:

Amherst College
Amherst, Massachusetts

Dear Anna Lynn,

I hope this letter finds you and Ginny in good health. I'd planned to come home on leave after basic training, but at the last minute I received orders to travel to Amherst College

*to attend a language training school and had to report
immediately. I tried to get out of it but couldn't, so here I am
learning Italian at this all-male college in New England
with no gals around to distract me.*

*It's a pretty campus right next to the town, which is very
quaint. Everything about the place seems so settled and
permanent, with lots of stately brick buildings, huge old trees
lining the streets and campus walkways, and rows of
Victorian houses with carefully tended lawns. I now
understand why our part of the country seems so wild and
untamed to easterners.*

*I didn't realize until I arrived at Amherst that I would
have been disqualified for the program because of my age, if
hadn't known how to speak Spanish. How about that? The
army considers me old. The boys in my unit here have taken
to calling me "Pops," just like the guys in my company did at
Camp Hood.*

*Most of the soldiers here are eight to ten years younger
than me, with more college under their belts, but I'm holding
my own in the advanced class. Why they have me learning
Italian, since Spanish is also taught here, is beyond me.
Sometimes "the army way" doesn't make much sense.*

*The first day of class, our instructor walked in and said,
"Today we are studying the Italian language." That has
been the last thing he said in English. He's a retired professor
who speaks five languages fluently. We're learning both the
northern and southern dialects. Except for history and
geography, all my other classes are also in Italian.*

*The work is intense. We were supposed to get to go on
leave after the first twelve-week period, but instead we're to
start the second term immediately. The only guys who aren't*

*bitching are the few married men who live off campus with
their wives. Why the big hurry, no one knows.*

*The program is officially known as the Army Specialized
Training Program, and we even have our own patch: a lamp
of learning with an upright sword thrust through the middle
of it. Except for wearing a uniform and an occasional head-
count formation, it's like being a civilian.*

*I got promoted to PFC before I left Camp Hood, and
there's a possibility that I might be commissioned a 2nd
Lieutenant if I successfully complete the training. Even if I
don't get bars for my collar, the course work will put another
year of college under my belt. That should count for
something.*

*New Mexico seems so far away, and I'm missing you a
lot. Write if you want; it'll boost my spirits considerably. Give
a hug and kiss to Ginny.*

Love,
Matt

Matt read through the letter and sealed it. He wrote a short
note to Pa and a slightly longer one to Al Jr., letting them know
how he was doing and asking how things were going at the ranch.
He bundled up against the cold and headed outside to the mail-
room. When he got back, his roommate, Dominic Amato, a five-
foot-five Sicilian from New York City who loved opera, had
returned from the library. A naturalized citizen, Dominic spoke
both Sicilian and Italian. Matt did language drills with him every
night after chow, and it was paying off richly in his classes.

"Are you ready to practice speaking the possessive adjectives?"
Dominic asked him in Italian. "Your accent is still too American."

Matt groaned and began.

* * *

Three weeks into the second term, Matt and Dominic received special orders to report immediately to the Forty-Fifth Infantry Division at Camp Pickett, Virginia. With the orders came promotions for both of them to the rank of technical corporal.

A quick check of a world atlas at the library showed that the camp was located fairly close to the shipping port of Newport News.

"We're going to invade Italy," Dominic crowed. "I hope we go to Sicily first. I've got relatives there."

"Maybe it's a big mistake, and we're being sent to invade Norway, where nobody speaks Italian," Matt replied, studying his promotion orders. "I thought we were supposed to become lieutenants."

"What'sa matter, you don't like being a corporal, Pops?" Dominic countered. "Besides, we didn't finish, did we? You only get to be an officer if you finish."

"I'm not complaining," Matt replied. "*Corporal* has a nice ring to it. Napoleon was a corporal."

"Yeah, and so was Hitler," Dominic added.

"Ouch," Matt replied. "What do you know about the Forty-Fifth?"

"Nothing. You?"

"Nothing, except it's infantry. I would have preferred the cavalry." Matt hoisted his duffel and looked around their dorm room.

"You'd think the army would get a horse just for you, Pops. A man your age and a real-live cowboy after all." Dominic emptied his sock drawer into his duffel bag.

"Call me *corporal,* not Pops," Matt corrected. "Say good-bye to the good times and easy duty."

"*Addio*," Dominic said, throwing his duffel over a shoulder.

"*Arrivederci*," Matt added, following Dominic out the door.

* * *

Camp Pickett was in a frenzied state of mobilization when Matt and Dominic arrived. They reported to the S-1 personnel officer, a major with dark circles under his eyes and a disapproving look on his face. He read their orders twice.

Outside his office, clerks were frantically typing while others were handing out paperwork to soldiers in a line that stretched outside the building.

"Jesus H. Christ, Italian interpreters," the major finally said. He sized up Matt and Dominic as they stood at attention in front of his desk. "Just the two of you?"

"As far as we know, sir," Matt volunteered.

"You're probably supposed to go to Intelligence," the major remarked. "But S-2 has already left the post. We decamp for Newport News in two days. Without orders you'll be left dockside."

The major bit his lip, pondered, and then started writing. When he finished, he handed one paper to Matt and one to Dominic.

"Give those to my clerk, the PFC just outside my office. He'll cut temporary orders assigning you to a company that's short a couple of men. That'll make you official until S-2 can be advised. Get over to post commissary and get your rank and division patches for your uniforms. Then come back here for your orders."

"Yes, sir," Dominic said.

"Welcome to the Forty-Fifth," the major said without much enthusiasm. He looked the two soldiers up and down one last time. At least they weren't going to be his problem anymore. "When you're finished here, report to the quartermaster and draw your gear and weapons. You may have to do more than speak Italian to help win the war."

"Yes, sir, thank you, sir," Matt said, saluting and turning on his heel in unison with Dominic.

It took several hours of running around, waiting, and filling out forms before Matt and Dominic, loaded down with combat gear, M1 rifles, uniforms, and duffel bags, reported to the first sergeant of Company K, Second Battalion. He was a lanky Oklahoman named Roscoe Beal who silently mouthed the words he read as he went through their orders.

When he finished, he looked up from his desk and said, "Well, at least you're both qualified with the M1; that's something, I guess. As for your rank, as far as I'm concerned you don't have any while you're in my outfit. Get them stripes sewn on, but don't think about ordering anybody around."

He looked Dominic up and down. "You're Amato?"

"Yes, First Sergeant."

"You go to the Heavy Weapons Platoon; see Lieutenant Church."

"Yes, First Sergeant," Dominic said.

"Kerney, you see Lieutenant Daugherty at Third Platoon."

Matt nodded.

"One more thing," Master Sergeant Roscoe Beal said. "I don't care if you two college boys can speak Italian like natives. You're mine until the brass says otherwise, got it?"

"Understood," Dominic said.

"Get going and don't cause me any trouble."

Outside on the packed earth of the company assembly area, Dominic smiled and said, "Well, at least we fell into this can of worms together. Think we'll get out of it before the shooting starts?"

Matt shrugged. "Don't hold your breath."

* * *

After one day with Second Squad, Third Platoon, K Company, all the men, including the squad leader, a fresh-faced twenty-year-old buck sergeant, started calling Matt Pops. On the second day, his moniker had spread to the entire platoon, including Lieutenant Daugherty, who was seven years Matt's junior. A wise-guy gambler in the First Platoon heard about the old tech corporal who'd rotated in and started a betting pool as to who was the oldest dogface in the company. Was it Matt? The CO, Captain Marshall? First Sergeant Beal? The XO, Lieutenant Nelson? Or Corporal Dutton, who had six years in uniform?

A five-spot to a clerk in personnel answered the question. Matt was the oldest man in the company by six months over Roscoe Beal. Dominic had bet heavy and won a hundred dollars.

The Forty-Fifth was a National Guard outfit made up of men from Oklahoma, Arizona, Colorado, and New Mexico. But K Company was almost a hundred percent Okie. When he could, Matt tried to find other New Mexicans in the division. But the rush to mobilize provided little time for it, and he soon stopped trying.

Ten days were spent at Newport News loading the invasion fleet, bound first for Oran, Algeria. Each day Matt and Dominic looked for fresh orders reassigning them to S-2. Each day, their hopes diminished. They worked long hours with the other men of K Company, unloading trucks filled with crates and boxes of equipment, supplies, and clothing for transfer to the cargo vessels.

From the moment Matt boarded the troopship at Newport News with his platoon and was led down to a hold below the waterline, he was miserable. Canvas bunks fifteen inches apart and twelve inches above each soldier's nose hung from floor to ceiling. Hundreds of them filled the windowless hold, lit only by dim bulbs that created a permanent artificial dusk. Every sound, every voice, every fart, reverberated off the steel-plated bulkhead, creating an interminable noise that made him wince.

He'd never felt claustrophobia before, but it quickly settled over him like a panic. His hands shook as he stowed his gear. His bunk, up against the port-side hull, would be a perfect spot for a U-boat captain to aim a torpedo. The idea of it gave him shivers. He rolled into his bunk, closed his eyes, folded his arms across his chest, and lay perfectly still until the urge to get up and run to the deck and jump overboard subsided. He forced himself to think of home, the vast Tularosa Basin with its endless sky and magnificent mountains.

By the end of the first day at sea, the hold reeked of vomit, sweat, and the stink of men. It only got worse as time passed. It was impossible to read and almost impossible to move about the cramped quarters, and the only form of diversion consisted of standing in line for chow three times a day, and occasional excursions topside to gaze at the gray North Atlantic Ocean and the vast convoy guarded by a dozen destroyers stretching off into the distance. It was the most depressing time of his life.

The two-week passage ended with a predawn disembarkation off the Algerian coast by amphibious landing craft, with whole regiments put ashore miles from their destinations. It was such a major snafu, the brass had them doing amphibious landing drills almost to the day of their departure for Sicily.

Matt, who had enlisted in the army to stay away from the water, half drowned each time he stepped out of the landing craft into five feet of water, loaded down with fifty pounds of equipment, clothing, weapons, and ammunition as he slogged his way to shore. As he dried out after the final practice run, the company orderly brought him three letters: two from Anna Lynn sent to Amherst

College and one from Augustus Merton that Pa had forwarded from the ranch. Matt read Augustus's letter first. He was working as a civilian for the War Department in Washington, supervising the inspection of munitions plants across the country, and wanted Matt to go to work for him. The job would keep him out of the draft for the duration, Gus noted. Matt smiled at the thought of working someplace with his feet on solid ground and little chance of getting shot at. He set it aside for a quick reply later.

In Anna Lynn's first letter she wrote that Patrick had been visited at the ranch by MPs who'd warned him to stop shooting at the warplanes practicing bombing and strafing tactics over the basin. Pa said he'd stop once the pilots quit shooting the livestock and scaring the ponies. According to what Al Jr. told Anna Lynn, Patrick escorted the MPs off the ranch by shotgun and warned them not to return. That prompted the arrival the next day of an apologetic officer from the airfield, who wanted Patrick to fill out official forms so the government could reimburse him for the dead cattle. A month later, no check had arrived, and Patrick was still grumbling about it. She sent her love and said Ginny missed him.

Anna Lynn's second letter, written a week later, contained sobering news about her youngest sister, Danette, who was eight months pregnant and living alone in a small Idaho town. Her husband, David Shirley, a crew member in an Air Corps bomber, had died in a training accident in Florida. Anna Lynn was leaving to fetch Danette back to live with her in Mountain Park until the baby came and other arrangements could be made. She closed by saying how glad she was he was safe and sound in college at Amherst.

From the postmark on the letter, Matt figured Anna Lynn was back from her trip to fetch her sister and most likely an aunt by now.

He was writing his regrets to Gus and explaining that the government had found other work for him, when Dominic rushed up waving papers.

"Did yours come?" he asked.

"What are you talking about?"

"Orders to report to G-2, ASAP." He was grinning from ear to ear. "I'm assigned to division."

Matt plucked the orders out of Dominic's hand and scanned them. "Well, I'll be damned. Congratulations."

Dominic's grin evaporated. "You didn't get orders, did you?"

"I sure didn't," Matt replied.

"That sucks. Look, I'm to pack up and make my way to G-2 right now. As soon as I get there, I'll find out what the snafu is and get it straightened out."

"Don't screw anything up for yourself on my account," Matt cautioned.

"Come on," Dominic replied, "it's probably nothing more than a paperwork glitch."

Matt smiled and squeezed his pal's shoulder. "Yeah, come get me when it's all straightened out."

"Wilco," Dominic replied.

Half hoping Dominic was right, Matt waited throughout the heat of the day, fighting off a growing feeling that he wasn't going to be leaving K Company before the invasion of Sicily. He broke down his M1 and gave it a thorough cleaning. He borrowed some saddle soap from a squad member and worked it into his leather combat boots to help waterproof them, and he wrote farewell letters to Pa, Anna Lynn, Al Jr., Gus Merton, and even a little note to Ginny, just in case he didn't make it.

Surrounding him, tens of thousands of men waited to go to war, most, like him, for the very first time. The nervous chatter of anxious, scared boys, their forced laughs, their rough horseplay, their loudmouth ribbing of one another, was like an eerie, discordant Greek chorus.

Behind the huge encampment that snaked along the coastline, the ancient town of Oran, liberated a mere seven months before, looked down on the latest army to come this way after the Romans and Carthaginians, the Spanish, the Ottomans, the French, the Germans, and now the Allies.

Matt's mouth was dry. He drank half a canteen of water, but it didn't seem to help. Tomorrow, he'd board another troopship for another almost unendurable sea voyage. Operation Husky, the invasion of Sicily, was about to begin.

40

Matt stood crammed together with hundreds of scared, sweating men in the upper hold of a transport ship, listening to a thunderous naval bombardment of coastal defenses on the western shores of Sicily. The last day of sailing had been the worst. A storm and rough seas had made every soldier on board sick, and the hold stank of vomit. Matt had lost everything in his stomach twice, if that was possible. Once topside, he shuffled along the deck, the soldier in front of him inches from the tip of his helmet, craning to see some of the vessels in the vast armada. More than twenty-six hundred ships were going to deposit a hundred and eighty thousand men on Sicilian beaches, along with hundreds of tanks, thousands of vehicles, countless artillery pieces, and millions of tons of ammunition and supplies. Overhead, Allied fighter planes and bombers roared inland to strafe and bomb, adding to the deafening roar. Shot down by big guns from a destroyer, a German plane exploded in midair and fell in pieces into the sea.

Matt went over the side, down the cargo net, and tumbled into the landing craft looking for a familiar face. He found his young squad leader, Sergeant Tom Kesling, crouched next to him, his face pasty white from seasickness, the M1 shaking in his trembling hands.

"You okay, Pops?" Kesling asked, barely getting the words out before he threw up at Matt's feet.

Matt nodded as the landing craft pitched forward in choppy waters, drenching the men as it dipped and rose over the waves. Most of the men in the boat were part of Matt's platoon. In the prow, his platoon leader, Lieutenant Daugherty, was praying the rosary, his head bent over the beads in his hand.

"You'll be all right," Kesling consoled, looking around at no one in particular, his eyes glazed with fear.

Matt nodded again, but he didn't expect to survive. The Germans and Italians had at least a two-to-one advantage, and all the officers and noncoms in Company K had forecast heavy resistance.

Closer to shore, they passed swamped and capsized landing craft, half-submerged trucks and howitzers, and blown-up landing craft surrounded by bodies floating in the water. The navy coxswain slowed the boat and lowered the bow ramp, and at the urging of the lieutenant, the men plowed into the chest-high water, weapons held above their heads, mortar and artillery shells exploding all around them. Matt reached the beach untouched and made it to cover under sporadic small-arms fire to Lieutenant Daugherty's position at a sheltered dune.

"Where's Kesling?" Daugherty asked, scanning the surf. Two dozen men huddled around him with not another corporal or three-striper in sight.

"I don't know," Matt replied, following Daugherty's gaze. There were bodies of men sprawled in the lapping surf. Officers ran around ordering men to dig foxholes. Medics tended to the wounded and dying. Down the beach, a small group of Italian soldiers marched with their hands up toward an engineer company offloading equipment. A mile out to sea, smoke billowed from a burning merchant ship. Behind him, machine-gun fire from higher ground tore into a soldier trying to drag a buddy to cover. Matt flinched at the sight.

"Where's Kesling?" Daugherty demanded again, looking undone.

"I don't know, sir; he was right beside me."

"The squad is yours until he shows," Daugherty said. "Take ten men up that draw and clear any enemy resistance you encounter. I'll go left and we'll meet at the top. Got that?"

Matt nodded, gathered his men, and moved out. That was the last he saw of Lieutenant Daugherty and a dozen other men from Third Platoon. Halfway up the draw Matt looked back in time to see enemy artillery rounds blow them to shreds as soon as they broke cover.

Above the beach, Matt and his squad got close enough to clear a machine-gun nest of Italian soldiers with hand grenades without taking casualties. Thinking they probably weren't facing German soldiers, Matt had the squad hunker down and started talking Italian to enemy troops lodged behind a fortified, dug-in position twenty-five yards ahead.

In between the mortar bursts and automatic-weapons fire the Italians poured at the squad, Matt cupped his hands and told them they were doomed if they didn't surrender immediately.

"You will all be killed," he warned in Italian. "I will radio your position to our destroyers and they will blow you up with their heavy guns."

The firing didn't stop.

"What are you saying to them, Pops?" a young soldier named Barry Peters asked.

Matt translated.

"The radio got blown up with the lieutenant and those other boys," Barry noted.

"I know that," Matt hissed. He cupped his hands again, waited for a lull in the shooting, and shouted in Italian, "Save yourselves. Retreat with honor or you will all be slaughtered."

Firing from the Italians slackened.

"Do not hesitate, brave Italian soldiers," Matt yelled as loud as he could. "You have fought for far too long. Leave your position now before I give your coordinates to our navy. Live to return with pride to your wives and mothers. You have two minutes to decide."

The firing ceased. Up ahead, Matt could hear snatches of Italian, but he couldn't make out what was being said. On either side of him, skirmishes and firefights raged along a ragged front, with some platoons stalled and others pushing slowly inland.

When the whispering stopped, it got quiet. He waited three minutes before wiggling out of the machine-gun nest and slowly crawling toward the enemy position. Either his ruse had worked or he was about to become dead. He didn't start breathing again until he reached the abandoned fortification, cleared the area, and called the squad forward.

Barry grinned as he plopped down next to Matt. "Jeez, that was something, you sounding like a real Italian and all. I'm stickin' with you, Pops."

"It was just dumb luck," Matt replied. "We'll hold here until the CO or some other officer arrives," he added after the last man tumbled safely into the trench.

The enemy defenses had been breached, a little bit at least. He sent one man back to the machine-gun nest to direct the foot traffic of soldiers now pouring up the draw, and had the rest of the squad take up covering positions facing inland. When Captain Marshall arrived and learned what had happened, he shook his head in amazement and promoted Matt to buck sergeant on the spot. He assembled what was left of the company plus a few stragglers and led them forward.

They met pockets of heavy resistance from German troops that controlled fields of fire from wooded thickets. The company suffered several casualties, and Matt lost a squad member to a mortar round. That night, the regiment regrouped and Matt's squad was folded into First Platoon and placed on sentry duty at a forward position.

The men dug foxholes, ate cold K rations, and smoked cigarettes. Enemy mortar rounds exploded around them all night long. Nobody slept. In the morning, the regiment moved out, only to get strafed by the Luftwaffe, which scattered whole companies into olive groves for cover while the German planes destroyed trucks on the roadway, bombed tanks, and blew up jeeps.

Over the next several days, they engaged a stubborn element of the elite Hermann Göring Division from dawn to dusk, secured an airfield, and liberated two small villages to the wild cheering of the townspeople. Ordered to stand down for the night, the men commandeered churches and public buildings for billets and secured perimeters with sentries.

Much to the dismay of an ancient priest and his equally decrepit housekeeper, Matt and his squad took up quarters in a church rectory. Early in the morning, word came down from division that they would move out at ten hundred hours. After a K ration breakfast and a cup of coffee, Matt used the precious extra time to shave, wash his feet, and put on a pair of clean socks.

He stepped outside the rectory just as a jeep with two soldiers pulled to a stop in front of the church.

The driver jumped out and hurried to him. "Are you with Company K, Second Battalion?"

"Yep," Matt replied.

"I'm Don Robinson with the *45th Division News*. I'm looking for the guy who talked a bunch of Italian soldiers into surrendering on the beachhead."

"They didn't surrender; they retreated," Matt corrected.

"You were there?" Robinson gestured to his buddy in the jeep.

"I was."

"We want to do a story about what happened for the newspaper. That guy helped get a couple hundred GIs safely off the beach and out of harm's way. You know where I can find him?"

Matt nodded.

Robinson yanked a notepad from his shirt pocket as his buddy, a short, skinny sergeant with big ears, came up, gave Matt a careful once-over, and said, "What's your name, Corporal?"

"It's sergeant, and the name's Matt Kerney."

The skinny sergeant broke into a grin. "I'll be damned. Matt Kerney from the Tularosa? I'm Bill Mauldin."

Matt's jaw dropped as he took a closer look. "By God, it *is* you, Billy."

"Sure as shooting," Bill Mauldin replied, thumping Matt on the back. "It's been a long time."

"Yes, it has," Matt said, grinning.

"Okay, it's real sweet that you two guys know each other from back home," Robinson said impatiently. "But enough of the lovey-dovey stuff. Where can we find this Italian-speaking dogface?"

"You're looking at him," Matt replied with a laugh.

"Seriously?" Robinson asked.

"Seriously," Matt confirmed.

Robinson licked his pencil point and said he wanted all the details, and Matt told him what had happened. Robinson asked a few more questions before hurrying off to interview the squad members who were lounging in the graveyard next to the rectory. That gave Matt a chance to catch up with Billy, who told him he had joined the National Guard in Arizona in 1940 and had been cartooning for the *45th Division News* ever since, trying to turn it into a full-time job.

Billy asked about Anna Lynn just as Lieutenant Church drove up in a jeep and called Matt over. Billy tagged along.

"You're wanted at regiment," Church said.

"What for, L.T.?"

"Seems the colonel is awarding you the Bronze Star," Church answered, looking none too happy. "Why anyone would get decorated for scaring away the enemy by speaking Italian is beyond me."

"Maybe my Italian is so bad, they couldn't stand listening to it anymore," Matt replied, straight-faced.

Church's dour expression didn't change.

"Now, that's even a better story," Bill Mauldin hooted, turning on his heel to locate Robinson and scurrying away.

"Who was that?" Church asked sternly.

Matt shrugged. "I don't know his name, Lieutenant, some reporter from the division's newspaper."

Church groaned and put the jeep in gear. "You're due at regimental HQ in fifteen minutes. Bring your squad."

Matt saluted. "Yes, sir."

* * *

After a hastily called regimental formation, where Matt and a dozen other soldiers were decorated by the colonel, Company K formed up and moved out, pushing deeper inland. A day of light resistance turned into heavy fighting the following morning when a paratroop drop to seize and hold key objectives got so screwed

up that troops were scattered miles behind enemy lines. Entrenched enemy positions that should have been overrun and in
friendly hands by the time ground forces arrived were offering
heavy resistance. By nightfall, the regiment had retreated, with
many casualties.

When the division finally broke through, Matt and his squad
wound their way slowly through bare, brown coastal mountains
where the enemy continued to have the high ground. He lost another squad member on a company assault of a ridgetop bunker.
In the same action Lieutenant Church went down with a serious
wound that put him out of action. Roscoe Beal, the first sergeant,
took over the platoon. By the end of the week he'd won a battlefield commission.

Matt was damn glad to have Beal helming the platoon. He was
cautious when necessary and decisive when it counted, worked
hard to keep morale up, and went easy on the terrified new re-
placements sent up from the rear.

Matt, on the other hand, didn't have a reservoir of goodwill for
anybody except the men in his squad. Combat dulled his sensibil-
ities, although he tried not to let his men see it. He no longer paid
much attention to the villages, which were dingy and dull to begin
with, or the smiling Sicilian people, who cursed the Fascists as the
company marched by. The rows of olive groves and the few hillside
houses weren't scenery, only places where the enemy could hide.
And the rugged mountains, denuded of trees, held the hidden
dangers of booby traps and antipersonnel mines.

He had no enthusiasm for war, yet it was all he thought about:
enemy minefields, machine-gun nests, sniper positions, camou-
flaged panzer tanks, heavy-artillery pieces zeroed in on his position. Everything out there was designed for the sole purpose of
killing him and every other member of his squad. He thought

death was inevitable and he didn't like the idea of having no future.

Night patrols were the worst. Every sound, even the single chirp or flutter of a disturbed bird, signaled potential death and destruction. The only benefit of the darkness was that his men couldn't see his hands shaking.

He often thought of Tom Kesling, the young sergeant who threw up at his feet in the landing craft, as sick as a dog and trying hard to lead in spite of it. Word had come down that his body had washed up on the shore, drowned, not shot. Would his parents ever learn how brave their young Tom had been in the face of death on a hostile, embattled shore?

Matt lost track of the days of the week. He couldn't even remember how long he'd been in Sicily. All that mattered were the hours, minutes, and seconds he spent waiting to move out, waiting for the mortar barrages to begin, waiting for the artillery shelling to commence and for the next order to advance.

His uniform was crusted with sweat, and he stank. He dreamt of a hot shower and clean clothes. He thought about food a lot, especially ice cream. For some reason he really hungered for ice cream.

One evening as he boiled water for coffee, too tired to think, Roscoe Beal came by to tell him the Italian dictator, Mussolini, Il Duce, had been thrown out of office and arrested.

"That's good news, I guess."

"G-2 is saying the Italian Army is abandoning their positions in droves and surrendering in growing numbers."

"Wouldn't that be nice."

Beal handed Matt a folded paper.

"What's this?"

"Open it."

It was the *45th Division News* and on the front page was Don Robinson's story of how Matt had cleared an enemy beachhead position by urging the Italians in their native tongue to retreat, and got the Bronze Star for doing it. Next to it was a Bill Mauldin cartoon of a smug-looking buck sergeant with a medal pinned to his chest explaining to an admiring dogface: "I got it for scaring the enemy away by speaking Eye-talin to them."

Matt laughed.

"I'd save that if I were you," Roscoe said with a smile. "I kept a copy for myself."

Matt folded the paper and put it inside his shirt. "Thanks, Roscoe."

"Get some sleep," Beal advised as he left.

* * *

The collapse of the Italian Army made for easier going, except for the pockets of fanatical Fascist units and battle-hardened German troops encountered along the way to Palermo. Overwhelming Allied forces quickly destroyed them. A day before Lieutenant General George Patton entered the city, Matt and his squad were far to the east, on point for the regiment and approaching the front line two miles distant. In an open field, they came upon a large herd of cavalry horses and pack mules left behind by the retreating Italians. Some of the ponies were saddled.

The sight of the ponies lifted Matt's spirits. He turned to his boys and said with a grin, "How many of you know how to ride?"

Three hands went up.

"What are you waiting for?" Matt said. He removed his helmet and handed his M1 to Barry Peters, who'd just made corporal. "Cover us, just in case."

He walked into the herd, gently touching each horse as he

made his way to a saddled chestnut gelding with four stocking feet. It nodded in greeting as Matt approached. He talked to the pony as he adjusted the stirrups and eased into the saddle. The familiar feel of the animal under him made the war go far away, as if he'd entered a time warp.

He started the chestnut at a trot, then urged him to a fast lope and finally a full gallop, flying back and forth across the pasture. The three men on horseback chased after him, whooping with glee. For a moment Matt was back on the Tularosa at the 7-Bar-K. He wheeled the pony toward Barry Peters, who had decided to give horseback riding a try. He was bareback on a pony, trotting it around in circles, holding on to its mane, bouncing wildly up and down. He got bucked off when the pony skidded to a sudden stop, and landed in soft grass. The squad laughed as he bounded to his feet, grinning sheepishly.

Matt charged the chestnut straight at the men, and they scattered before him. He drew rein and sat in the saddle, grinning like a kid who'd been given his first pony.

He looked down at Barry, shook his head, and said, "From what I saw, its best you stay afoot."

Barry's sunburned face turned a darker red. "Wilco."

"I'm going to reconnoiter the next hill."

"Think you should?" Barry asked.

Matt nodded and pointed at the three soldiers on horseback. "If I'm not back in ten minutes, send the posse."

He spurred the chestnut up the hill, jumped him over a low rock wall, and followed a winding mountain stream before crossing to a meadow. He drew rein to take in the view of the regiment trudging along the road below, just shy of where he'd left his squad.

He galloped back to find Roscoe Beal and Captain Marshall

waiting for him with a chewed-out, glum Barry Peters standing nearby.

"I should have your stripes for this," Marshall snapped as Matt slid out of the saddle.

"Take them, Captain," Matt replied. At that moment, he didn't have a care in the world.

Marshall scowled.

Roscoe Beal said with measured caution, "It seems to me, Captain, that Sergeant Kerney has captured a fine herd of animals we could put to good use packing our equipment through these hills."

Marshall huffed, gave Matt a sour look, and said, "You've got a point, Roscoe. Okay, Kerney, get your men started jury-rigging packs for some of these animals. I'll put another squad on point."

"Yes, sir," Matt said.

When Marshall walked away, Roscoe whispered under his breath, "Don't expect another Bronze Star for this, Kerney."

"I don't see why not," Matt replied in feigned disappointment.

* * *

Ordered to take the coastal town of Santo Stefano, the Forty-Fifth came up against German forces waging a slow, deliberate retreat to Messina across the rugged terrain. The Germans were fighting to gain time to cross to Italy before the Allies overran them and forced their surrender.

Captain Marshall got regimental permission to assemble a special mounted unit using some of the captured Italian Army horses and mules to pack ammunition, weapons, and supplies across the rough mountainous terrain, and he put Matt in charge of it. As a result, the regiment outflanked and destroyed a number of hastily thrown-up German defensive positions. It allowed the regiment to reach the outskirts of Santo Stefano ahead of schedule, while the rest of the division mopped up from behind.

The small town climbed a steep seaside cliff, vulnerable and exposed by land. The main road from Palermo to Messina ran through it. Captain Marshall blocked the road west of the village and deployed two platoons on either side to stop any straggling German troops from escaping. He gave permission for Matt and his men to rest the animals.

When word came down that the division would be late in arriving and Santo Stefano would not be liberated until the next day, Matt sent his squad out to scavenge feed from a nearby farm and requisition a regimental water truck. In a field ringed by a low stone fence, Matt spent the afternoon with the ponies, making sure all were watered and fed. He got them bedded down for the night just as the first of the advance mechanized troops came roaring down the road. If there were still Germans troops in the village, they knew the division would soon be knocking at their door.

He was boiling water for coffee when a soldier passed by handing out the latest issue of the *45th Division News*. The headline read:

COMPANY K CAPTURES ENEMY HORSES!

Next to the story was a Bill Mauldin cartoon showing a grizzled infantry sergeant pointing a finger at a sorrowful-looking horse with its head bowed and saying, "As a POW, do you promise to abide by the rules of the Geneva Convention?"

Roscoe Beal plopped down beside Matt, newspaper in hand. "Ain't that something?"

"It's pretty funny," Matt allowed.

"I've got something that will top it," Beal drawled. "You, me, and the captain are gonna receive the Army Commendation Medal for coming up with the scheme to put those ponies to good use in our rapid advance to Santo Stefano."

Matt could hardly stop laughing. "Well, at least it isn't another Bronze Star," he finally said.

When Roscoe went on his way, Matt read the rest of the newspaper over a cup of coffee. An editorial complained about stateside newspapers and magazines trumpeting the Sicily campaign as a cakewalk for Allied troops. Back home, the writer noted, only the families of the fallen and wounded knew how hard fought the battle had been. The writer wondered if the day would come when Operation Husky was nothing more than a footnote in World War II history.

Matt didn't doubt it.

* * *

Next morning, the Germans chose to put up a fight at Santo Stefano, and the whole division was thrown into a battle outside the town on a ridgeline. The shooting stopped when darkness fell and the Germans retreated, leaving rearguard units to slow the advance. Division casualties were high, and not just from the fighting. Intense heat had settled over the island, and increased cases of malaria had thinned the ranks.

To ready it for the Italian invasion, General Patton pulled the Forty-Fifth out of combat for some well-deserved R & R and replaced it with the Third Division. There were hot showers, clean uniforms, hot chow and plenty of it, and as much rack time as Matt needed. It was almost heaven. Mail call brought letters from home—nothing from Anna Lynn, but a note each from Patrick and Al Jr. telling him how good the ranch was faring, what with the summer monsoon moisture and strong cattle sales.

The last letter he opened was from Evangelina, postmarked Lubbock, Texas. Lance Corporal Juan Ignacio Kerney Knox had been killed in action while serving with the Fourth Marine Raider Battalion on New Georgia in the Pacific.

Matt stared blindly at the note, his breath caught in his throat. He remembered how angry Juan Ignacio had been at him the last time they met. He wondered if Evangelina had told Patrick about Juan Ignacio's death. With all the misery that had passed between them, he doubted it. He wrote to Pa, sealed Evangelina's note in the letter without comment, and mailed it.

He'd decided to take a walk through town down to the shore to clear his head when a sergeant from the heavy-weapons platoon hurried up.

"You'd better check on your animals," he said. "Some of the boys have turned them loose and are spooking them."

"Dammit." Matt wheeled and headed for the field where the ponies and mules had been contained behind a rope corral to keep them from scattering. The rope corral was down and the soldiers were chasing horses, some throwing stones at them. Others were trying to ride bareback. The agitated animals were snorting, throwing snot, showing teeth, and prancing. To escape the harassment, Matt's chestnut had cleared a low rock fence at the far end of the field. It had its ears lowered and was shaking its head in frustration.

Matt grabbed a soldier off a mule and threw him to the ground. "Get up and tell your buddies to stop," he growled, not waiting for a response.

He strong-armed another GI about to stone a horse. Behind him, men from his squad poured onto the field to help clear the troops. When the GIs were removed and all the animals except the chestnut had been corralled, Matt went to coax him back over the rock fence.

He climbed over and tried to calm the pony, but it was still spooked and shied away. He took a step forward. The chestnut stepped back. He offered it sugar in the palm of his hand. The chestnut hesitated, shook its head, snorted, and stepped back again. Then the horse blew up in a shower of hide, horsehair, intestines, and blood that slammed into Matt with a stabbing pain in his head that hammered him unconscious.

41

Matt regained consciousness, tried to open his eyes, and felt a shock of pain in his head so severe it made him scream. It felt like an ax had split open the left side of his face. He tried to touch his head, but his hands were tied at his sides.

He struggled to get up, but hands pressed against his chest, holding him down. He howled at the pain that consumed him, the sound of his voice faraway and strange.

"Relax, soldier," a calm voice said. "I'm going to put you back to sleep."

He started to ask where he was, what had happened, but couldn't get the words out before he fell into a black, dreamless sleep. When he awoke, the pain had lessened to razor-sharp, needlelike pulses that made him dizzy.

"Welcome back," a voice said.

"Am I dying?" Matt asked. A hand patted his shoulder.

"No, you're in a field hospital. You've had a serious shrapnel injury to your left eye. I got most of it out, but you'll need more surgery. We're going to move you to a hospital ship tomorrow."

"Am I blind?"

"Not by a long shot, soldier. You're going home."

He felt a needle in his arm and went back to sleep. In the morning, a medic removed the bandage covering Matt's right eye.

"Can you see with that eye?" the medic asked.

"Yeah," Matt said with a big sigh of relief, looking at the kid, who was barely out of his teens.

"Are you right-handed?" the medic asked.

"Yeah. Why?"

"Because it means your right eye is dominant, and that's gonna be good for your recovery. I'm gonna bandage that because we don't want you using it for a while. You want more morphine before we transport you?"

Matt shook his head. It hurt like hell and made him change his mind. "Maybe a little," he said. "But don't knock me out."

An hour later he was transported by ambulance to the Palermo docks, where a landing craft ferried him and other wounded GIs to a U.S. Army hospital ship. Hoisted aboard by block and tackle, he was carried into an operating room for a second round of surgery to remove several tiny metal fragments embedded in his cornea.

When he came to, his left eye was patched but the bandage covering his right eye had been removed. A doctor hovered over him. He patted Matt's hand and said he was going to be just fine.

"Does that mean you've saved my eye?" Matt asked.

"We won't know that until the patch comes off in a couple of days," the doc replied.

The look on the doctor's face wasn't encouraging.

Two days later the patch came off. Serious damage to the retina had caused permanent blindness. The doc joked that with an eye patch Matt would look like swashbuckling movie star Errol Flynn. Matt laughed, although he didn't think it was funny.

It took twelve days to cross to the States, and during that time Matt found plenty of reasons to stop feeling sorry for himself. There were guys blind in both eyes; guys missing feet, hands, arms, and legs; and guys who were badly burned. Late one night, Darrell Lawrence, a boy in a bed next to Matt who had lost both legs, took a sudden turn for the worse. He died holding Matt's hand before help arrived.

After the orderlies took Darrell away, Matt tried to blot out the young soldier's death, only to have Jimmy Potter's fall from the cottonwood tree flood into his mind, followed by the faces of the men in his platoon who'd been killed in action, never to go home. It took willpower to keep from crying in the silence of the night. The people he'd lost over the years—especially Ma, Beth, and Boone—were way too many.

The ship put in at Charleston, South Carolina, and the ambulatory patients disembarked first. The sight of hundreds of empty stretchers with fresh bedsheets and pillows, lined up on the dock in front of the open doors of dozens of ambulances, unsettled Matt. GI litter bearers in fatigues and helmet liners stood by to carry the seriously wounded soldiers off the ship. It was a sad, bleak reminder of the human wreckage of war.

Matt was taken by ambulance to Stark General Hospital, located on an army cantonment outside of town. It was brand-new and army-style, with rows of wooden barracks that served as wards and an assortment of other low-slung, pitched-roof buildings used for administration, personnel, supply, recreation, and medical purposes.

He waited for a week for an eye specialist, a light colonel from Atlanta, to come and evaluate him for transfer to an army hospital outside Santa Fe or discharge from the service. He gave Matt a careful checkup, confirmed that the blindness in the left eye could

not be reversed, rated him as fifty percent disabled, and cleared
him for separation from the service. Quartermaster supply issued
him new uniforms, finance gave him his back pay, and personnel
typed out a form so he could purchase his ribbons and stripes at
the PX. He had the option of either taking leave right away or
traveling by train to Fort Bliss to be discharged.

He thought about visiting places like Washington, D.C., and
New York City, but the pull of home was too strong. He hadn't
written Anna Lynn, Patrick, or Al Jr. because he had nothing to
say other than he was blind in one eye and coming home. He
wondered how they'd react when they saw him with his eye
patch.

When Matt took it off, he hated what he saw. The eye was dead,
empty, and awful. Maybe someday he'd get used to it, but not yet.

In uniform, with his stripes, unit patch, and ribbons, and with
travel papers in hand, he caught a ride to the train station and
waited to begin the long journey home.

* * *

It was a relief to reach El Paso and escape all the fresh-faced, raw
recruits on leave from basic training. Their unsure, worried questions about combat seemed to tumble out of their mouths as soon
as they spotted Matt's eye patch and ribbons. He tried to reassure
them, but it was malarkey and they knew it.

Halfway through the trip he took to feigning sleep whenever a
nervous young soldier approached. Only twice was he questioned
by gung ho MPs looking for AWOL soldiers and deserters at train
stations.

Although much had changed, Fort Bliss was a homecoming for
Matt. The familiar, starkly beautiful Franklin Mountains still

loomed over the fort, which looked down on El Paso, the sluggish Rio Grande, and the city of Juárez across the river. There were new buildings everywhere, and the post bustled with activity. Lines of brand-new trucks, jeeps, and antiaircraft artillery pieces were parked on acres of land adjacent to the headquarters compound. The days of the horse soldier were gone forever.

The building that once housed Hubert Roddy and the Forest Service during the CCC era still stood. It was now a supply warehouse containing hundreds of mattresses stacked to the ceiling.

He checked in at personnel. A clerk scanned his service jacket and told him to report to the William Beaumont Army Hospital for his discharge medical examination. No longer contained within the confines of a lovely Spanish colonial brick and stucco building, Beaumont had been transformed into a larger version of the army hospital in South Carolina, with rows and rows of barracks converted to hospital wards.

Matt found his way to the correct office, got an appointment for the following afternoon, and settled in at a billet before heading out to the NCO club. So close to home, he was suddenly anxious to be done with war. He wanted to forget the army and put 1943 behind him.

It was early and the club was empty except for a bartender and an old master sergeant drinking coffee, smoking a cigarette, and reading a newspaper at the end of the bar. Matt ordered a draft beer, raised his glass in memory of Lance Corporal Juan Ignacio Kerney Knox, U.S. Marine Corps, and drained it. He walked back to his billet with the afternoon sun still blazing in the western sky and a hot desert breeze kissing his face.

The personnel clerk had told him that in three days he'd wake up a civilian again. He could hardly wait to board the train for Engle.

* * *

The train pulled into the Engle station, where not a soul waited on the platform to board. From the coach window Matt could tell the slowly dying village hadn't profited one lick from the wartime boom. There were no cars or wagons parked outside the general store, the hotel had a FOR SALE sign nailed to the porch railing, and the old barbershop had been torn down. Ken Mayers still hung on at the livery. Matt found him out back tending to some horses in the corral and asked if he could borrow a pony to ride home. Ken thumped him on the back, said, "Hell no," and offered to drive him to the ranch in his truck.

Along the way, Matt learned that Al Jr.'s pa had died from a sudden stroke a month ago. Al Jr. and his wife, Brenda, had returned to the Rocking J to take over the ranch and look after the widowed Dolly. Ken didn't know if Patrick had hired any help.

Ken wasn't much of a talker and didn't ask about the war, which suited Matt just fine. It gave him the quiet he needed to get reacquainted with home. He drank in the view of the basin, silently grateful that he still had a good eye left to see it again.

At the ranch, the sound of Ken's truck brought Patrick to the veranda. He grabbed Matt in a bear hug as soon as he could hobble down to meet him. Ken waved good-bye and drove off.

"Dammit, you're alive," he said after releasing him.

"And only half blind," Matt joked.

Pa studied Matt's face. "Some officer wrote us from Sicily that you'd been wounded but he didn't know how bad. Did you lose an eye?"

"It's there, but just for show," Matt replied. Patrick had shrunk some, and there were more wrinkles in his weathered face, but he looked sober and fit.

"Has the army let you go?"

"Yep, now I'm a veteran with a pension, just like you." Matt picked up his duffel bag and paused to look at the ponies in the pasture. "The ponies look healthy."

"They are, but nobody's buying. The army bought some to give to the coast guard to use to patrol shorelines, but that's it. And the cow pony market has dried up. Ranchers are using trucks more and wanting fewer horses."

"Now that Al Jr. and Brenda have pulled up stakes to take care of his ma, is he still looking after the cattle on the high pastures as agreed?" Matt asked.

Pa nodded. "He is. I figured Ken told you about Al. Damn shame."

"Yes, it is." From the veranda, Matt looked out on the Tularosa with Sierra Blanca looming in the distance beyond the malpais and White Sands sparkling to the south. "Have you hired any help?"

"Didn't need to yet," Pa replied. "We can talk about all that later. You get settled in, I'll brew us a fresh pot, and then you have to get going, if you're feeling up to it."

"Get going where?" Matt asked.

"Over to Mountain Park. Ever since I went and told Anna Lynn you'd been wounded in action, she drives here twice a week to learn if there's any word from you. She came by yesterday with a pot of chili to help ease my troubled mind about you maybe being dead."

"Is that the truth?"

Patrick smiled and raised his hand. "I swear on it. I reckon you're in for a tongue-lashing for not writing to her."

Matt smiled. "I'll take that over the silent treatment."

"There ain't nothing worse than that from a woman," Patrick said. "I'm glad you're home, Matt."

"Me too," Matt replied.

* * *

It was evening, with a full moon cresting the Sacramentos, when Matt stopped the truck in front of Anna Lynn's farmhouse. Little Ginny appeared in the doorway, squealed in delight, and ran into his outstretched arms. Anna Lynn stood in the doorway with a bag of flour in her hand. When he put Ginny down, Anna Lynn hit him in the chest with the flour, white powder billowing into his face, his hair, her face, her hair.

"You son of a bitch, why didn't you write?" she demanded, tears in her eyes. Then she kissed him.

Author's Note

Writing historical fiction requires paying a great deal of attention to an accurate recounting of the myriad aspects of the world the characters inhabit in a story. For information about the Civilian Conservation Corps, a groundbreaking federal program that put hundreds of thousands of boys and young men to work during the Great Depression, I turned to Richard Melzer's *Coming of Age in the Great Depression: The Civilian Conservation Corps Experience in New Mexico, 1933–1942*; John C. Paige's *The Civilian Conservation Corps and the National Park Service, 1933–1942: An Administrative History*; Alison T. Otis et al., *The Forest Service and the Civilian Conservation Corps: 1933–42;* and Major John A. Porter, Q.M.C., "The Enchanted Forest: Army Quartermaster Support to the Civilian Conservation Corps During the Great Depression," *The Quartermaster Review* (March–April 1934).

Over lunch, my friend Bryan J. "Chip" Chippeaux provided me with valuable information about his great-great-grandfather John W. "Jake" Owen, a former Lincoln County sheriff at the turn of the twentieth century, and gave me permission to use Jake as a private detective in *Backlands* investigating the mysterious disappearance of a man from the Double K Ranch on the Tularosa. Bill Martin and Molly Radford Martin's book, *Bill Martin, American,* was a surprisingly helpful resource in my understanding of New Mexico law enforcement practices in the early years of the twentieth century, as was Chuck Hornung's *New Mexico's Rangers: The Mounted Police.*

A charming self-published memoir by Gretchen Heitzler, *Meanwhile, Back at the Ranch,* provided me with a wealth of information about the Tularosa Basin, the surrounding area, and ranch life during World War II.

Information about the World War II Army Specialized Training Program came from a 1948 publication by Robert R. Palmer et al., *The Army Ground Forces: The Procurement and Training of Ground Combat Troops,* and Louis E. Keefer's book, *Scholars in Foxholes: The Story of the Army Specialized Training Program in World War II.* My understanding of Operation Husky, the World War II Allied invasion of Sicily, was greatly enhanced by *Brave Men,* written by the famous American war correspondent Ernie Pyle, who was killed in action in the South Pacific near the end of the war.

Bill Mauldin, a New Mexico native son, two-time Pulitzer Prize–winning cartoonist, and creator of the famous World War II cartoons featuring Willie and Joe, two combat foot soldiers, wound up in *Backlands* because of a dinner I had with Bill's son Andy. For me, it was a lot of fun to put Mauldin on the page and learn about his life. Revered by his comrades in arms, he died in early 2003, and millions of veterans mourned.

Todd DePastino's biography, *Bill Mauldin: A Life Up Front,* gave me a handle on the Forty-Fifth Infantry's landing on Sicily and Mauldin's experiences there. Two of Mauldin's memoirs, *The Brass*

Ring: A Sort of Memoir and *A Sort of a Saga,* helped me understand his boyhood years on the Tularosa and his later life.

Finally, over the course of fifteen years and ten books, Brian Tart, the publisher and president of Dutton, has done much to make me a better writer. For that I say with heartfelt gratitude and deep appreciation, *muchas gracias, jefe.*

In the pale moonlight that floated through her bedroom window, Anna Lynn Crawford studied Matthew Kerney's face. Fortunately for both of them, tonight he slept quietly. When he stayed the night over at her house, he often woke with a start from bad dreams that left him shaking, and she would find him sitting silently alone on the front porch at first light. When he was restless, Anna Lynn took to curling up on the floor with a pillow and a comforter in the hope her absence would have a calming effect on him. Sometimes his breathing eased and the night passed peacefully. But most mornings, she found him on the porch in her rocking chair, unmoving, his hands clutching the armrests, his face moist with sweat.

Six months ago, Matt had returned home from the war with a patch covering his left eye, which had been destroyed in a land mine explosion during the Allied invasion of Sicily. He removed it only at night. As he lay quietly sleeping, Anna Lynn snuggled close to examine the wound Matt insisted made him ugly.

His upper left eyelid was missing completely, shredded during the explosion, and there were tiny, jagged shrapnel scars around the socket of the eye, which was covered in a murky film. There was a slight puffiness under the eye she hadn't seen before. She wondered if it was causing him pain.

You're still a handsome man, you fool, she thought to herself. *You still look like you.*

She'd told him that if he stopped wearing the patch folks would soon pay the injury no mind. But Matt immediately dismissed the suggestion the two times she'd made it, the second time so vehemently that she hadn't mentioned it since. She had to try again to persuade him to listen to reason, but dreaded his reaction. He was, and he wasn't, the man she had known before he went into the army.

What she knew about Matt's war experience came mostly from an army press release printed in every New Mexico newspaper the week after his discharge from Fort Bliss, the army post outside of El Paso. He'd been decorated for bravery under fire for clearing a fortified enemy position above a beachhead where troops had been pinned down and were taking heavy casualties. His actions had allowed a battalion of men to move inland without suffering further serious losses. He'd been promoted to platoon sergeant on the spot and was later awarded another medal for using captured enemy horses to carry equipment through rugged, mountainous terrain, which aided the Allied advance against a large retreating enemy force. He'd lost his eye in the final push to liberate the island and had been evacuated to a hospital ship, where he'd received the Purple Heart from a general after his surgery.

She snuggled closer and gazed at Matt's face, remembering the only time he'd talked about those experiences. After making love early one morning, they had sat quietly together on the veranda of his ranch house overlooking the wide expanse of the Tularosa Basin, her daughter, Ginny, sound asleep in bed and Matt's father, Patrick, away in town. She'd broken the silence by asking Matthew to finally tell her what had happened to him in Sicily. It earned her a sad-faced grin and a loud chuckle.

"What's so funny?"

"It was all a big frigging joke," he answered without rancor.

"How so?" Anna Lynn asked.

Still smiling, Matt rose from his chair. "Wait here and I'll show you."

He returned and gave her two cartoons from the pages of an army newspaper. One showed a sergeant with a shiny medal pinned to his uniform explaining to a ragtag private that he'd been decorated for scaring the enemy away by speaking "Eye-talian" at them. The second cartoon displayed a grizzled sergeant pointing a finger at a sorrowful-looking horse, demanding to know if, as a POW, the animal would abide by the Geneva Convention.

Anna Lynn looked up from the cartoons. "I don't see what's so funny."

Matt smiled at the only two memories of Sicily that brought him any pleasure to recall. "What makes them funny is they show exactly what happened to get me decorated like some kind of hero. On the beachhead, all I did was talk some Italian soldiers into not shooting at us anymore. They withdrew from their position and we were able to move inland. There was nothing heroic about that. Later on, when we were in the mountains, my platoon stumbled on a herd of abandoned enemy ponies that we commandeered for the regiment to use as pack animals in the high country. Because it helped force the Germans into a hurried retreat, I got another medal, and it wasn't even my idea in the first place. That's the sum total of my so-called bravery."

Anna Lynn gazed at his face and his eye patch. "That may well be, but it doesn't make you less of a hero. You were smart and saved lives, and besides you were gravely wounded."

Matt's mood shifted as he thought about the men in his platoon he'd lost. His expression turned somber. "I didn't save enough lives. And I lost an eye for being stupid and not paying attention to what I was doing."

The image of Private Joey Cohen taking a bullet in his head, twirling around and dropping dead at Matt's feet, replayed though his head, as it did at least once a day. He shook it off and pointed at the signature on the bottom left corner of each cartoon. "I thought you would have noticed by now who drew these," Matt said, trying to sound lighthearted. "They're both signed, 'Bill Mauldin—Sicily.'"

"Bill Mauldin!" Anna Lynn squealed in surprise. "Our very own little Billy Mauldin?"

Matt smiled and nodded. "Yep, the one and the same scrawny kid who peddled his drawings and cartoons to folks up and down the west slope of the Sacramento Mountains. I still have a stack of them put away somewhere. He sends you his regards."

"Oh, that sweet, lovely boy," Anna Lynn said, blinking away a tear. "Is he a war correspondent?"

"Nope, he's a soldier in the Forty-Fifth Infantry Division, if he isn't already among the dead from all the casualties we took in Italy."

Anna Lynn's face clouded at the mere thought of it. "Oh, please don't let that be true."

"I sure hope he survived," Matt agreed. "I figure he's gonna become rich and famous if he comes through the war alive and intact. The troops already love him." Matt took the cartoons from Anna Lynn's hands. "That's all the talking I want to do about my time in the army. I'm home now and that's the end of it. Understand?"

Anna Lynn nodded. "If that's what you want."

"It is."

Matt countenanced no more talk about the war after that morning, although he diligently followed the battlefront newspaper and radio reports, especially the ones from Europe, which often threw him into a funk. As time passed, his interest waned in anything or anybody other than the war, Anna Lynn's five-and-a-half-year-old daughter, Ginny, and the ponies on his ranch. He withdrew, turned inward and silent. His visits to her farm became less frequent; their conversations, once so engaging, became awkward; their lovemaking, always passionate, turned perfunctory at best.

The changes between them chilled Anna Lynn. Here, close to him in her bed, his warm breath against her cheek, she wondered if she'd lost Matt completely because of the terrible war. If so, it would have been far less of a heartbreak to have lost him to another woman.

Tomorrow, he was to travel to William Beaumont Army Hospital at Fort Bliss for a follow-up physical disability examination. If he failed to keep the appointment, his monthly pension benefits might be suspended, and Anna Lynn knew he could little afford the loss of that income. She wanted to go with him, but he wouldn't hear of it. She fell asleep, hoping the army doctor might have in his pocket a miracle to restore Matt's eyesight. If he were made whole again, at least in some psychological way, perhaps her constant fear of trying to endure an unhappy future with a man who'd once filled her heart with so much happiness and joy would vanish.

* * *

In the morning, Anna Lynn fixed steak and eggs for Matt and pancakes for Ginny, who sat next to Matt with syrup dripping down her chin as she chewed a bite and stared at Matt's eyepatch. She reached up with sticky fingers to touch it and he yanked her hand away.

"Don't touch," he snapped.

"Why not?" Ginny demanded, shocked at Matt's scolding.

Matt took a deep breath to calm his anger and forced a smile. "Because I look like the boogeyman without it and that would scare the dickens out of you."

"It would not," Ginny replied bravely, not completely sure of herself or of Matt's warning.

"Well, it sure would scare the hell out of me," Matt said, tousling Ginny's hair. "Now, eat, and don't be such a pest."

Reassured, Ginny put another big bite of a pancake into her mouth, closed her left eye, put her hand over it, and looked around the room. She saw Mom's jars of honey she got from the bees lined up neatly on the shelves above the kitchen cabinet and sink, Mom's reading chair next to the table with the lamp and radio, the box under the window with her toys and books, which had to be put away neatly every night before bed, and the open front door with the screen gently flapping in the cooling morning breeze.

"I can see okeydokey with one eye," she announced matter-of-factly.

"But it's better with two eyes," Matt countered, forking the last of his steak. "Don't you think?" he asked after his last bite.

"Yeah," Ginny agreed with a grin.

"We'd like to keep you company today," Anna Lynn said casually as she cleared Matt's plate.

"Can we?" Ginny pleaded, clapping her hands. She loved trips to town.

Matt shook his head and wiped his mouth with a napkin. "There's no need," he replied, ignoring Ginny's pout. "I'll stop by on my way home to the ranch tonight and tell you what the army doc had to say."

Anna Lynn dipped Matt's plate into the soapy dishpan at the sink. "You'd better," she cautioned.

She turned her head from the sink to look at him and he grinned at her in agreement. A forced grin, she thought, trying her best to smile in return. The left side of his face twitched involuntarily. She was sure he was in some pain. She was also sure he knew that he couldn't hide it completely from her.

"Stop worrying about me," Matt ordered gruffly.

"I just want you to be okay."

"I am okay." Matt pushed back from the plank-board kitchen table. "And I'm trying my damnedest to stay that way."

He exchanged hugs with Ginny, which left her sticky syrup fingerprints on his shirtsleeve, kissed Anna Lynn quickly good-bye, and headed out the door. Below the small village of Mountain Park, the Tularosa Basin sat under a cloudless, brilliant blue sky with blinding sunlight, which swept clean all color except for the snowy gypsum dunes at White Sands National Monument and the foreboding dark uplift of the San Andres Mountains forty miles westward.

War had brought serious gasoline rationing to civilians, and most country folks had parked their cars and gone back to traveling by horse. In his pickup during the short drive to Alamogordo, Matt passed a dozen or so people in buggies or a-horseback clip-clopping along the highway heading to town. Only two passenger cars, an army truck, and a delivery van breezed by him, traveling northbound on the two-lane concrete road, which gave way to gravel shy of Three Rivers. It was as though time had reversed to the early 1920s, when horses and wagons had still dominated the mostly rutted, hard-packed dirt roads of rural New Mexico, which became mud pits after a heavy rain.

At the Alamogordo train station he bought a ticket to El Paso and waited on a bench in the shade of the covered platform, watching war planes rise up from the army airfield outside of town, grouping into formations high above to practice bombing runs at the north end of the basin.

Just about every rancher on the Tularosa had filed claims with the government to get reimbursed for livestock that had been killed by trigger-happy turret gunners eager to shoot anything that moved on the ground. Matt was still waiting on payment for two old ponies he'd found riddled with bullets and half eaten by coyotes in a high country pasture on his San Andres ranch.

After boarding the train for the ninety-mile trip to El Paso, he fished a lapel button out of his pocket. Given to him as an afterthought by a personnel clerk at Fort Bliss the day he'd mustered out of the army, it was a small button made of brass depicting an American eagle with wings spread beyond the confines of an encircling wreath. It identified the wearer as having been honorably discharged from the armed services, and was jokingly known as "the ruptured duck."

Matt attached it to the top buttonhole of his long-sleeve work shirt. Soon after the train left the station, two MPs on the train looking for AWOL soldiers entered his coach compartment. They scrutinized his eye patch and ruptured duck and gave him a nod and a smile of acknowledgment as they passed by.

In downtown El Paso, the ruptured duck and his medical appointment letter to see Dr. S. Beckmann at William Beaumont General Hospital got him a free ride on an army bus to the fort. Matt rubbernecked on the ride up the hill with the Franklin Mountains towering close by. Not long ago, El Paso had nestled quietly along the Rio Grande across from the Mexican town of Juarez. Now the city was spreading north along newly paved streets lined with bars, diners, pawn shops, and motels that catered to the soldier boys stationed at Fort Bliss. The war economy had brought new life to the once-dusty, somewhat dismal town. Matt guessed that the bars, nightclubs, and whorehouses in Juarez were also likely thriving during these boom times.

The bus driver dropped him off outside the old Spanish Colonial brick-and-stucco hospital building now used for offices, where a clerk directed him back outside to one of the army-style barrack buildings that served as hospital wards, rehabilitation clinics, surgical theaters, and medical specialty centers. Considered temporary construction, each building was a long rectangle, two stories high, with a gable roof, horizontal wood siding, double-hung windows, and an external staircase to the second floor. Dozens of the buildings, marked with numbers and signs, stretched out in long, neat rows with the barren brown Franklin Mountains as a backdrop. After presenting his appointment letter to a receptionist in the Ophthalmology Clinic, Matt was led to an examination room, where he was greeted by an attractive older woman with eyeglasses perched on her nose and captain's bars on her uniform shirt. She had curly blond hair cut short, warm brown eyes, and a small raspberry red birthmark above her right cheek.

"Take a seat, Sergeant Kerney," she said, smiling and motioning to a stool as she looked up from a medical chart. The nameplate on her desk read CAPT. SUSAN BECKMANN, M.D.

"I'm Dr. Beckmann and I'm new to this man's army," she said, with a hint of humor in her voice. "And I've been told by my commanding officer, who is still instructing me in matters of military etiquette, that you must call me ma'am, Doctor, or Captain."

Matt nodded as he sat on the gray metal stool. "I didn't expect to be seeing a lady doctor for my exam, Captain."

Beckmann's smile froze as she paused to study her patient. He was tall, in his early thirties with square shoulders, a darkly tanned face, and intelligent features. "We're a rare commodity, I'll grant you. Do you have a problem with that, Sergeant?"

Matt touched the ruptured duck lapel button on his shirt and shook his head. "No, ma'am, and since I'm a bona fide, one hundred percent honorably discharged civilian, you can drop the sergeant moniker. Please call me Matt, Dr. Beckmann."

Beckmann's smile warmed. "Fair enough, Matt." She left her desk, sat on a stool, scooted it close to him, and said, "Now, let's take a look at that eye."

As she lifted his eye patch, her smile faded. There was no doubt the loss of sight in the eye was permanent, but the surgery to remove the shrapnel had been neatly done. The worrisome thing now was redness and swelling around the orbital cavity, which suggested the possibility of infection.

"See, Doc, it just doesn't work right," Matt joked lamely.

"Does it cause you any discomfort?" Beckmann asked as she slipped her hand into a sterile glove and probed gently with a finger above and below the eye.

Matt shrugged. "Not much."

Dr. Beckmann paused and gave him a quizzical gaze. "Really?"

Matt's jaw tightened. "I do okay."

"You aren't a very good straight-faced liar," Beckmann scolded with a sigh. "I've never understood why some men have a hard time being honest with doctors. You didn't strike me as that type."

"What type is that?"

"The stupid type," Beckmann explained, softening her criticism with a smile. "Let's start over. Do you experience any pain?"

Chagrined, Matt nodded.

"Describe it to me."

"Sometimes when I move my eye, it feels like I've been stabbed in the eyeball and it hurts like hell."

Susan Beckmann nodded and continued questioning Matt. He sometimes had severe headaches, which laid him low for an hour or more. Occasionally his head tingled as if insects were crawling on his scalp, or he sensed a slight trembling of his head, almost like a palsy that was hard to control. The bad eye just ached dully much of the time, but the pain often intensified and spread to the entire left side of his face. It got worse if he had a beer or some whiskey. Taking aspirin frequently helped but it usually took a long time for the pain to lessen.

"How much do you drink?" Beckmann asked.

"Not much," Matt allowed. "Maybe twice a week I'll have a beer or a whiskey before supper."

"How's your memory?"

"I don't have trouble remembering things."

"Not even little things?"

Matt shook his head. "Nope. What are you getting at here, Doc?"

"The orbital cavity around your eye is inflamed and possibly infected. And I'm thinking the optic nerve behind the eye may be involved, which is partially causing your pain."

"Partially?"

"Yes. You received excellent surgical care for the eye injury, but you also suffered trauma to your brain when the shrapnel penetrated your eyeball. That could be causing some of your symptoms as well."

"Can you fix it?"

Susan Beckmann paused before responding. "Yes, by removing the eyeball and fitting you with a prosthetic eye." She didn't mention that some patients who'd suffered the traumatic loss of sight in one eye eventually lost vision in their sighted eye. It could happen within months or take years, and there was no way of predicting who went totally blind or when. For now, she wanted Matt focused solely on the immediate need for surgery and not the unknown future.

"A glass eye?" he asked.

"Yes, but you could always continue to wear the patch if you like. At this point, doing nothing is not an option. If there is an infection, I don't want it to spread to your brain. It could kill you. If I find only inflammation, surgery is still our best option and I can treat it immediately. It should significantly reduce your episodes of pain and discomfort."

Tired of the pain and the headaches, Matt didn't hesitate. "When can you do it?"

Susan Beckmann returned to her desk and consulted her calendar. "Early tomorrow morning. You'll be first up in the operating room," she said. "I'll arrange for you to be admitted to our presurgical ward this afternoon. Be back here at four o'clock. Eat a good lunch because it will be the last food you'll have before I operate." She waved a finger at him. "And absolutely no alcohol."

Matt nodded and stood. "How long will I be stuck here after you saw my bones, Doc?"

Beckmann smiled. "Two to three days, depending on what I find."

"See you at four, Captain."

Matt shook her hand and headed out the door for the NCO club, stopping first at the Post Exchange, where he bought postcards and stamps and scrawled notes to Pa at the ranch and Anna Lynn in Mountain Park, writing that his doctor had ordered some tests that would hold him over for a few more days but it was just routine and there was no need to worry.

He doubted the postcards would be delivered much before he returned home, but since neither Pa nor Anna Lynn had telephones, it was the best he could do.

At the NCO club he ordered a hot turkey sandwich, mashed potatoes, green beans, and apple pie. As he sipped coffee and waited for his meal to arrive, Matt wondered why Dr. Beckmann had hesitated when he'd asked her if she could fix him. Had she given him the whole scoop or was she holding something back? He had reason to be a little wary about medicos. He'd seen too many army doctors and medics tell dying men they were going to be all right.

* * *

Groggy from the general anesthetic, Matt Kerney woke up to find a cute young brunette in a crisp white nurse's uniform with gold second lieutenant bars on her collar taking his pulse. Her name tag read LT. R. HARTMAN.

"Hi, Matt," Nurse Hartman said brightly. "You'll be just fine. Your surgery went perfectly. The doctor will be here in a jiffy to give you the once-over. And your wife and daughter are waiting to see you."

"My wife and daughter?" Matt asked, still scatterbrained from the heavy dose of painkillers used to knock him out.

Hartman looked up from her wristwatch. "Yep, Anna Lynn and Ginny. What a cutie that little girl is. I want one just like her some-day."

"You shouldn't have any trouble finding willing suitors ready to volunteer," Matt predicted.

Lieutenant Hartman almost giggled. "I sure hope not." She patted Matt on the shoulder. "You just rest and stay put now. We'll get you moved to the post-op ward in a little while, as soon as Dr. Beckmann gives the okay."

The nurse's perky, friendly manner made Matt smile. "What's your first name?"

"Raine," she answered. "Bet you didn't expect a handle like that."

"Nope, I didn't," Matt allowed as he watched Raine Hartman swish out of the room. He wondered how in the blazes the post-card he'd sent yesterday could have arrived in Anna Lynn's mail-box the same day. That was impossible. He was still only half awake when Captain Beckmann breezed into the room, smiling broadly.

She took a quick look at his chart before speaking. "Good news, no infection. You'll be out of here in no time. How are you feel-ing?"

"Dopey," Matt replied.

Beckmann nodded. "I'll check on you again later in the day." She told him how long the bandages needed to stay on, how he was to care of his face until his next outpatient appointment in a week, and when he would be scheduled to return to be fitted with his new eye. "I'll go over all of this with you again," she added.

"Is all this what you weren't telling me yesterday?"

Beckmann looked surprised. "Why, yes," she lied. "I didn't want to overwhelm you with too much information."

Matt laughed. Beckmann might be new to the army, but she already had the right stuff when it came to keeping the troops in the dark.

"Why is that funny?" Beckmann asked.

"No reason, Doc," Matt replied, figuring only another dogface would see the humor. He wondered what kind of cartoon Bill Maul-din might have dreamt up about it. Matt couldn't come up with anything, but Mauldin with his mile-wide funny streak would have thought of something hilarious.

Beckmann shook her head in puzzlement and left.

As the fog from the anesthetic dissipated, Matt's mood con-tinue to improve, and when the orderlies wheeled him to the post-op ward, he got to thinking that maybe Doc Beckmann had not only fixed the problem of his awful pain and headaches, but had also rid him of his sulky temperament. More likely he was just giddy from the heavy dose of drugs.

No other patients had come out of surgery so far that morning, and all the other beds were empty. One of the orderlies, an older private with a pronounced limp, gave Matt a sharp look as he helped move him off the gurney onto the hospital bed. Before he left, he took another close look at Matt, paused momentarily to glance at the chart, and seemed about to say something. Instead he retreated silently down the corridor as Anna Lynn and Ginny came hurrying to his bedside.

Matt didn't recognize the man at all, but he looked vaguely familiar. He gave up trying to put a name to his face and turned his attention to his visitors, smiling broadly. Tongue-in-cheek he said, "Well, if it isn't my own little family come to visit."

Anna Lynn wrinkled her nose at his wisecrack and kissed him on the lips. "Your doctor wouldn't have let us near you if I hadn't lied and said we were married. So I'm your wife, but only until we can take you home."

"I've got no complaints with that," Matt replied, grinning. He asked her how she'd found out about his surgery.

Anna Lynn smiled. "You're the most reliable man I've ever known, and when you didn't return as you promised, I knew there had to be a problem. So we drove to Alamogordo and I called the hospital from the train station and learned you were scheduled for surgery this morning. We drove right down."

"We slept in the truck, and we're going to stay over in the city until we take you home," Ginny said excitedly, as if it were a grand adventure, looking at Matt from his bedside. "But you still have only one eye," she announced with great disappointment.

"My doc says I'm gonna get a new one soon," Matt said.

Ginny smiled at the prospect. "Then will you stop wearing that patch? Mamma hates it."

"Maybe," Matt replied.

Footsteps down the corridor announced the impending arrival of Lieutenant Raine Hartman.

"I think we're about to be shooed away." Anna Lynn gave Matt another smooch. "We'll leave you in the hands of your pretty young nurse. Don't flirt with her too much."

"Why not?" he asked, feigning innocence.

The lighthearted tone in Matthew's voice, missing for so many months, brought a warm smile to Anna Lynn's face. She kissed him again. "On second thought, go ahead. A little flirtation might be good for you."

* * *

With the realization that Doc Beckmann's first surgery patient of the day was quite possibly none other than Matthew Kerney, his Matthew Kerney, Private Fredrick Robertson Tyler forgot about keeping his nose clean and getting out of the army with an honorable discharge. Known as Fred to his buddies on the base, Tyler stood outside the Ophthalmology Ward, lit a cigarette, and mulled over his discovery. First off, he needed to make damn sure that he wasn't mistaken about the man he'd helped wheel from surgery to post-op. If it was Kerney, it would be stupid to reveal himself to the woman and little girl who were visiting him at his bedside. A closer look at Kerney's medical chart should do the trick, and if Tyler needed more proof about the patient's identity, a pal in personnel could let him have a look-see at his service jacket.

Tyler took a long drag on his smoke, hoping the woman and

little girl would come out of the building before his cigarette break was up. He wanted a closer look at Kerney's happy little family for future reference.

When the war started, Fred figured he was too old, too lame, and too undesirable to be drafted into the army. But at the age of forty-four, with an armed robbery conviction on his sheet and a smashed foot courtesy of a fellow inmate at the New Mexico State Penitentiary in Santa Fe, his local draft board classified him as acceptable for limited military service. A month later he had been inducted into the army, put through an abbreviated Basic Training course for men unfit for combat unit assignments, and sent to Fort Bliss along with a few other semicripples, misfits, and miscreants to serve as medical orderlies.

Years of living in prison surrounded by dangerous men made the army a cakewalk for Fred Tyler. He figured he'd remain safe and sound stateside at Fort Bliss, frequent the Juarez whorehouses when he had money and some leave, maybe earn a stripe or two, and get out with everyone else who'd been drafted for the duration plus six months. Then he'd return to the business of robbery.

But if he was correct about the man in post-op, he had to change that plan some. Years ago, he'd been expecting to rob a kid named Matthew Kerney living alone in a house his mother had left him, only to have the kid scald him with boiling-hot coffee, stab him in the arm, knock him unconscious with a frying pan, and get him arrested by the cops. Later, in open court, Kerney had accused Tyler of killing his friend Boone Mitchell, which Tyler had done, though it couldn't be proved, because no body had been found at the time.

Kerney's accusation caused the presiding judge to hang two consecutive sentences on Tyler, doubling his prison time. For that alone he needed to settle accounts. Moreover, it gnawed at him that a punk kid barely out of high school had gotten the best of him. Now, miraculously, here was an opportunity for a reckoning. Tyler figured something much more painful than a bone-breaking beating or a slow, painful death for Matt Kerney was in order.

The price Kerney paid needed to be steep. As Kerney's wife and daughter stepped out into the hot early-morning sun, Tyler got the idea that maybe Kerney losing his family might just be the ticket. As they approached him, that notion became even more appealing.

He field-stripped the cigarette butt, smiled, touched a finger to his fatigue cap, and said as the woman and child drew near, "Don't you worry none about your man, ma'am. We'll take good care of him and get him back home to you in a jiffy."

The woman took a half step back, gave him a studied look, smiled through thin lips, and thanked him rather stiffly as if he was some low-life crud looking for a handout.

The tight-assed bitch's reaction pleased Tyler. He watched her hurry to the visitor parking lot, clutching the little girl tightly by the hand. This just might be a lot of fun, he thought.

* * *

Anna Lynn drove through downtown El Paso past the ritzy ten-story Hotel Paso Del Norte, which soared over the nearby plaza. Several years ago, she'd stayed there with Matt on an unforgettable romantic weekend that still brought a smile to her lips every time she thought about it. But with money tight, she couldn't afford such luxury. Instead, she stopped at a motor coach inn on the street to the Rio Grande where the international border separated El Paso from the Mexican city of Juarez. She rented one of the brick bungalows with attached garages shaded by a grove of trees and sheltered behind an adobe wall. Each bungalow came with a double bed, radio, telephone, hot plate, coffeepot, and icebox.

At a nearby market run by a Mexican couple, Anna Lynn stocked up on some groceries. Back in the bungalow, she gave Ginny a bottle of cold soda pop along with several children's picture books she was using to teach her to read that she'd hurriedly packed in her suitcase before leaving Mountain Park, and then brewed a pot of coffee.

Ginny sat at a small table under the window that looked out at the walled courtyard, happy with her soda and books, reading aloud the words that she'd already learned as she turned the pages. Recently, she'd started reading the Sunday funny papers all by herself. Propped up on the squeaky bed, Anna Lynn sipped her coffee and thought about the soldier who had greeted her outside the hospital ward. The man's leer masquerading as a smile, the belligerent look in his eye, and his aggressive tone had disturbed her. Had he been deliberately waiting for them? For what reason? To stop them solely to reassure them about Matt's care made no sense.

He'd given her the willies. Her instincts warned her that he was dangerous. Did it have something to do with Matt, or was he one of those monsters who raped and murdered women or kidnapped and molested young girls like Ginny? She could think of no other reasons why a complete stranger would behave in such a threatening way.

Anna Lynn decided not to bother Matt about it. But she'd keep a watchful eye out for the soldier with the angular, mean-looking face and long scar below his cheekbone. She turned on the radio just in time for the hourly news broadcast and joined Ginny at the table. After lunch and a nap, they'd go back to see Matt again and visit with his doctor. She wanted to know exactly how to care for Matt after his return home.

Photo by Sean McGarrity

Michael McGarrity is the *New York Times* bestselling author of *Hard Country*, the Anthony Award–nominated *Tularosa*, and eleven other bestselling Kevin Kerney crime novels. A former deputy sheriff for Santa Fe County, he also served as an instructor at the New Mexico Law Enforcement Academy and as an investigator for the New Mexico public defender's office. He lives in Santa Fe with his wife, Emily Beth.

CONNECT ONLINE

michaelmcgarrity.com